PRAISE FOR
BY FORCE OF ARMS
THE REVOLUTION AT SEA
TRILOGY:
BOOK ONE

"Nelson's seagoing experience is evident in his clear, convincing description. . . . The characters are strong and realistic, the plot and action believable and brisk . . . a fine adventure series."

—*Publishers Weekly*

"Jim Nelson's *By Force of Arms* strikes a blow toward establishing an American counterpart to Patrick O'Brian's brilliance. With square-rigger experience in his wake and far horizons before Nelson, we can expect him to achieve one victory after another in the spirit of his British namesake."

—David Brink, S.A.I.L., Inc.

"Set sail with Jim Nelson into a world where he will lead you with the same command presence that he led his shipmates as third officer aboard the very real twentieth-century sail training ship H.M.S. *Rose*. Plant your feet firmly on Nelson's decks and you will smile as Patrick O'Brian has at Jim Nelson's grace, wit, and humor."

—Captain Richard Bailey, Sail Training Ship H.M.S. *Rose*

"A lively and highly readable account. Exploring the lives of seamen, merchant captains, and Royal naval officers, *By Force of Arms* offers a realistic and minutely detailed account of shipboard life during the period."

—John G. Kolp, assistant professor, Department of History, U.S. Naval Academy

Also by James L. Nelson

By Force of Arms

Published by POCKET BOOKS

THE MADDEST IDEA

REVOLUTION AT SEA TRILOGY

BOOK TWO

JAMES L. NELSON

To Brad Read,
Best Wishes

42° 21. 24.' N
71° 03. 25' W

POCKET BOOKS
New York London Toronto Sydney Tokyo Singapore

This book is a work of fiction. Names, characters, places and incidents are products of the author's imagination or are used fictitiously. Any resemblance to actual events or locales or persons, living or dead, is entirely coincidental.

An *Original* Publication of POCKET BOOKS

POCKET BOOKS, a division of Simon & Schuster Inc.
1230 Avenue of the Americas, New York, NY 10020

Nelson, James L.
    The maddest idea / James L. Nelson.
        p.   cm.
    ISBN 0-671-51925-5 (pbk.)
    1. United States—History—Revolution, 1775–1783—Naval
operations—Fiction.   2. United States—History, Naval—18th
century—Fiction.   I. Title.
813'.54—dc20   96-42484
                                                        CIP

First Pocket Books trade paperback printing February 1997

10 9 8 7 6 5 4 3 2 1

POCKET and colophon are registered trademarks of
Simon & Schuster Inc.

Cover design by Matt Galemmo
Cover art by Dennis Lyall

Printed in the U.S.A.

For Lisa and Elizabeth,
whom I love

It is the maddest idea in the world to think of building an American fleet. Its latitude is wonderful. We should mortgage the whole Continent.

—Samuel Chase,
Maryland delegate to the
Second Continental Congress,
October 3, 1775

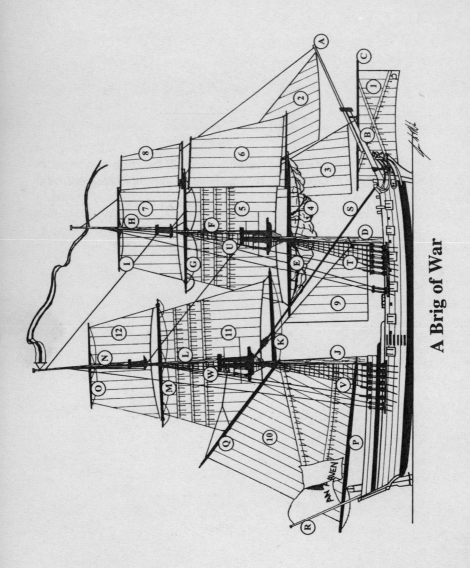

A Brig of War

Sails
1. Spritsail
2. Jib
3. Fore Topmast Staysail
4. Foresail (clewed up)
5. Fore Topsail
6. Fore Topmast Studdingsail (removable)
7. Fore Topgallant Sail
8. Fore Topgallant Studdingsail (removable)
9. Main Staysail
10. Mainsail
11. Main Topsail
12. Main Topgallant Sail

Spars and Rigging
A. Jibboom
B. Bowsprit
C. Spritsail Yard
D. Foremast
E. Foreyard
F. Fore Topmast
G. Fore Topsail Yard
H. Fore Topgallant Mast
I. Fore Topgallant Yard
J. Mainmast
K. Mainyard
L. Main Topmast
M. Main Topsail Yard
N. Main Topgallant Mast
O. Main Topgallant Yard
P. Boom
Q. Gaff
R. Ensign Staff (removable)
S. Mainstay
T. Fore Shrouds and Ratlines
U. Fore Topmast Shrouds and Ratlines
V. Main Shrouds and Ratlines
W. Main Topmast Shrouds and Ratlines

*For other terminology and usage see Glossary at the end of the book

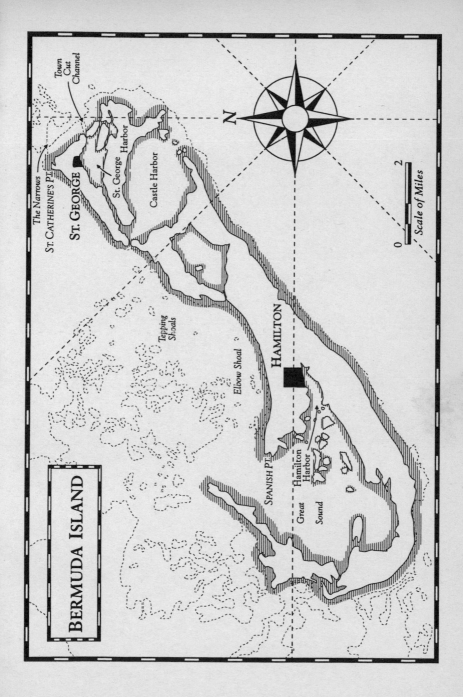

BERMUDA ISLAND

ST. GEORGE

Town Cut Channel

The Narrows

St. Catherine's Pt.

St. George Harbor

Castle Harbor

N

Scale of Miles

0   2

Tepping Shoals

Elbow Shoal

HAMILTON

Spanish Pt.

Great Sound

Hamilton Harbor

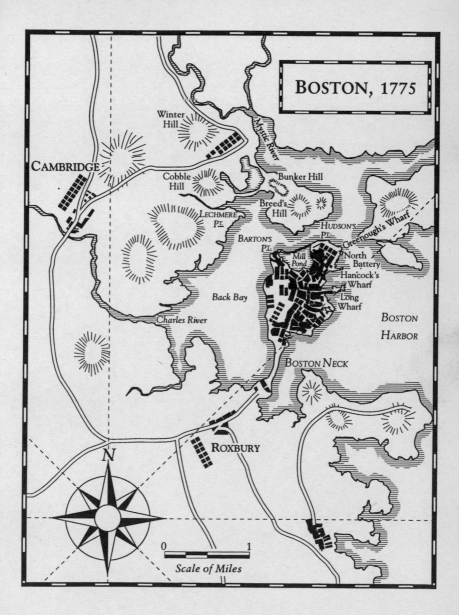

BOSTON, 1775

Winter Hill

CAMBRIDGE

Mystic River

Cobble Hill

Bunker Hill

LECHMERE Pᵀ.

Breed's Hill

Hudson's Pᵀ.

Greenough's Wharf

BARTON'S Pᵀ.

North Battery

Mill Pond

Hancock's Wharf

Back Bay

Long Wharf

Charles River

BOSTON HARBOR

BOSTON NECK

ROXBURY

N

0   1

Scale of Miles

CHAPTER
1

Charlemagne

CAPT. ISAAC BIDDLECOMB STEADIED HIS TELESCOPE AGAINST THE backstay of the armed brig *Charlemagne* and fixed the distant topsails in the lens. The ship he was watching was just visible at the southern end of Narragansett Bay, and he imagined that she had just cleared out of Newport. He considered for a moment the clarity of the air that allowed him to see that far, even with a glass. He would expect such fine visibility in Rhode Island during the winter; for mid-July it was exceptional.

Through the lens he watched the topsails turn and flutter as the vessel came about on a new tack. He had seen those topsails in the daylight only once before; still, he was in no doubt as to which ship they belonged. She was, on that particular summer day in 1775, the most powerful ship within one hundred miles. She was a British frigate, the *Rose* of twenty guns, Capt. James Wallace commanding. She was the enemy.

Isaac Biddlecomb was a few months into his twenty-ninth year, having spent the past sixteen of those years as a merchant seaman. Of those sixteen years at sea he had served as a ship's captain for the last five, a successful merchant captain with a reputation for fiscal cunning. Still, he was not a man who stood out in a crowd; his height was an unremarkable five foot ten inches, not fat though certainly not thin, dark brown hair tied in a queue and hanging down just past his shoulders.

It was only on the quarterdeck, on the captain's stage, the weather side, that he became more than just another sailor. He stood there now, hands clasping a telescope behind his back, a well-worn cocked hat pushed down over his head. In grudging deference to his current attachment to the fledgling Rhode Island naval force, he wore a long blue coat over a passably new waistcoat and white breeches; not a uniform by any stretch but clothing more formal than he would have worn on the quarterdeck of a merchant ship under his command. He hooked a finger under his neck cloth and tugged at it with mounting irritation.

Around and about him the crew of the *Charlemagne* were engaged in the chaos of setting sail and clearing for action. The smell of fresh paint, tar, new running rigging, and canvas overpowered any scent from the brackish water or the shore. This was hardly surprising; the *Charlemagne* was a brand-new vessel. Only yesterday they had crossed the last of the new man-of-war-style yards with the sails, cut navy fashion, bent on. This morning was the first time that she had ever been under way.

"Sheet home the fore topgallant sail! Haul away your halyard!" Biddlecomb heard Rumstick's booming voice over the din of rushing feet and the running in and out of the brig's guns. Ezra Rumstick was acting first officer, a big man, over six feet tall and two hundred and fifty pounds and had a voice to match. "Avast haul—!" Rumstick's shouted order was cut short by the sound of tearing and flogging canvas. "God damn that bloody sailmaker to hell!" he cursed, firing off a string of obscene invectives aimed at the craftsman who had built the *Charlemagne*'s new suit of sails.

Biddlecomb looked aloft. The fore topgallant sail was torn clean in two from foot to head, the canvas blowing forward and flapping like a tattered ensign.

"Hands aloft!" Rumstick called. "I want the number two topgallant sail bent! Let's go!" Four men leapt into the rigging and scrambled aloft as if driven by the force of his voice. Four more ran down the forward hatch to wrestle the number two fore topgallant sail topside. Rumstick leapt up the short ladder to the quarterdeck and stepped over to the larboard side. He swept off his hat and held it out from his side in a smart salute.

"Ezra, must you salute every time you come aft to speak with me?" Biddlecomb asked as he grudgingly swept off his own hat. "It's a great nuisance. You're as bad as Whipple," he added, nodding his head over the starboard rail. Directly abeam of the *Charlemagne*, and one hundred yards away, sailed the sloop *Katy*, her big gaff mainsail winged out in the following breeze, three of her six four-pound guns run out and men stationed at her numerous swivels.

"Whipple ain't such a bad commodore," Rumstick said, replacing his hat. On the *Katy*'s high quarterdeck the portly figure of Captain, now Commodore, Abraham Whipple could be plainly seen, standing alone at the larboard rail.

"He's a first-rate merchant captain, and I've no doubt he's a first-rate naval captain. I just wish he wouldn't take this navy thing so damned seriously."

"We're at war, Isaac. I think it's customary to take it seriously."

"I believe you were coming aft to tell me about a fore topgallant sail?" Biddlecomb changed the subject. Rumstick never missed the chance to expound on his extreme political convictions, like some fire-and-brimstone preacher, and it annoyed Isaac greatly. The fighting at Concord and Lexington, and just recently at Bunker Hill, had only served to whip Rumstick into a greater frenzy.

The two men stepped up to the break of the quarterdeck where they could see past the main topsail to the men on the fore topgallant yard. The torn sail had been lashed into a canvas sausage, and a gang on deck was lowering it down on a gantline.

"Goddamned sailmaker left a panel out. We tore it clean in two sheeting it home. Bolt rope parted, must have been rotten," Rumstick explained.

"That sailmaker's either a thief or an idiot. Both, I'll warrant." Biddlecomb watched the men aloft shuffling out onto

3

the yard. They were taking the *Charlemagne* into a fight before they had had a chance to put her through her paces, to find and correct the little defects such as the poorly made topgallant sail that they had just discovered. It was not what he considered a good idea.

Biddlecomb did not think of himself as the captain of a naval vessel. He knew little about it, and when he stood on the quarterdeck and looked down the line of guns, he felt entirely at a loss, like an actor who is thrust out onstage without benefit of a script or director. Despite Rumstick's assurance that Isaac was born for such work, he felt like a fraud, and it was a feeling that he loathed. He found the traditions and trappings of the military to be irritating in the extreme.

That attitude notwithstanding, he was already famous in the colony for inciting a mutiny aboard a British brig of war, the *Icarus*, onto which he and Rumstick had been pressed. Together, and with the men of the *Icarus*, they had fought their way back into Narragansett Bay. They had made it halfway to Providence before the *Rose*, the same *Rose* now on the far horizon, had beaten the ship into kindling. Any thoughts that he had entertained of himself leading men into battle died that night, along with more than half of the *Icarus*'s company.

And then his employer and mentor, William Stanton, got the notion of privateering. Stanton was a prominent radical in Rhode Island, as well as one of the colony's most wealthy merchants, and like many of his ilk he saw privateering as a way of helping the cause and greatly enriching himself all at once. He had built the *Charlemagne* and asked his favorite captain, more an adopted son than an employee, to take command. Biddlecomb could not bring himself to refuse.

But a privateer was one thing; as a privateer one assiduously avoided fighting, avoided risking men's lives, and he had had enough of leading men to the slaughter. One night of that was enough. One night of slaughter, and then seemingly endless nightmares, dream images of dead men waving to him from the shattered wreck of the *Icarus*, barely visible through the dark water. The thought of sleep terrified him now. He would not be a naval captain. But a privateer was different.

Then a week before the privateer brig *Charlemagne* was to get under way, Capt. James Wallace, patrolling Narragansett Bay in the frigate *Rose*, captured two American packets, the *Abigail* and the *Diana*. As if their capture were not outrage enough, he then fitted them out as armed vessels to use against their former owners. The Rhode Island General Assembly purchased the *Katy* and appointed Captain Whipple to command her, and Stanton loaned to that fledgling navy his new privateer and her captain. And now, together, they were going to take the packets back.

"Number two fore topgallant sail's bent, sir." Nathanial Sprout, the *Charlemagne*'s acting boatswain, addressed the officers from the waist. Sprout was no taller than Biddlecomb, but he outweighed the captain by a good eighty pounds. His girth was not composed of the fat of lethargy, but the solid mass of physical power. Nathanial Sprout was every inch a boatswain.

"I'll get that set, sir, if the panels're all there," Rumstick said, saluting again.

"Very good, Mr. Rumstick," said Biddlecomb, scowling as he returned the salute.

He let his eyes wander over the *Katy*, the flagship of their tiny fleet. She was a lovely example of the craftsmanship of the New England shipwrights, fast and weatherly. Her armament seemed pathetic, even in comparison to the little *Charlemagne*. But Whipple took pride in her and cheerfully drove her into battle as if she were a first-rate ship of the line.

Two small bundles rose up a flag halyard to the *Katy*'s yardarm. They reached the yard and broke out into bright-colored signal flags.

"Oh, for God's sake."

"Signal from the flag!" David Weatherspoon piped up brightly. Weatherspoon was fourteen and serving in the capacity of midshipman. He dug through the signal book that Whipple had created for his little fleet. "Enemy in sight," he announced at last.

Biddlecomb put his glass to his eye and swept the lower reaches of Narragansett Bay. Whipple couldn't be referring to the *Rose;* she had been in sight for the past twenty minutes. He fixed the frigate in his lens. She was closer now, much closer, making for the Rhode Island fleet, beating straight into a light breeze from the north. But it would take Wallace some time to come up with the Americans, no matter how weatherly his ship or how well he sailed her.

Biddlecomb stepped down off the quarterdeck and made his way forward. To larboard and starboard the men were just running out the guns, buckets of water and smoldering match beside each. Rumstick stepped over and walked forward with him.

"Cleared for action, sir," the first officer reported.

"In a mere forty-five minutes."

"This ain't a man-of-war's crew, Isaac, this is the first time most of them have cleared a ship for action. Most of them ain't even sailors." He was hurt by the implied criticism, and Biddlecomb was immediately sorry for his words.

"You're right, Ezra, of course. I'm sorry. I've a great deal on my mind."

"I can well imagine. But remember, you've been captain of a proper man-of-war, so its natural this crew seems slow to you. They don't have your experience in these matters."

" 'Captain of a proper . . .'? Well, I suppose that's one way of looking at it. God help us all." In the brief time that he had commanded the *Icarus,* Biddlecomb had learned as best he could the art of commanding a man-of-war as he battled the vessel back to America. It had been a perfunctory and brutal training. "God help us all," he said again.

The two men arrived at the bow. Biddlecomb stood on the heel of the bowsprit and swept the horizon with his telescope. Off the northern end of Gould Island he saw the sloop, the former packet *Diana,* the ship for which he had come.

She was as familiar a sight as the islands beyond or the wooded shores of Rhode Island to larboard. The little sloop was well-known on the Bay, like an acquaintance often seen strolling the neighborhood. She was on a larboard tack, and with her sails drawn in she looked lean and fast, plunging north against the wind, an occasional flash of white water boiling around her cutwater and streaming aft along her oiled sides, even in the light air. She was lying as close to the wind as she could, and that was very close.

The *Diana* was no longer a benign packet. Biddlecomb could see flying from her masthead the white ensign with the red cross, the Union Jack in the upper left corner. There were carriage guns on her deck, six in all, run out from gunports pierced through the sloop's bulwarks. The upper deck was crowded; at least thirty men were aboard her. When sailing as a merchant packet her crew had never numbered above ten.

That was all that he needed to see. "I'm laying aft, Mr. Rumstick," he said. "See that the men are at quarters and ready to jump."

The brig was just drawing abeam of the southern end of Prudence Island when the *Charlemagne*'s captain took his place alone at the quarterdeck's weather rail. He looked over the taffrail at Dyer Island in their wake.

It was there, just past Dyer Island, that the *Rose*, lying hove to, had opened up with her murderous broadsides. The memory of the lightning and thunder of gunfire, the screams of the wounded men, the dark blood on the *Icarus*'s deck, were as vivid now as they had been on the night of that one-sided battle over three months before.

He forced himself to remember those who had survived: Israel Barrett, Appleby, Dugan, and the rest. They were safe now and better off than they had ever been, given a sizable bounty by William Stanton and hurried off to western Pennsylvania, beyond the reach of the British navy.

But that was less than half the crew. The bones of the rest, the bones of his friends, the men who had trusted him, lay among the wreckage of the *Icarus* in the deep, cold water of the bay. They had followed him because he had tricked them into thinking that his was a good idea, and now they were dead. Images of the slaughterhouse that was the *Icarus*'s deck floated before his eyes.

He had come as close to dying as any of them, of course, but that thought did not bother him, indeed it rarely occurred to him. He had led other men to their deaths; he himself might as well have fired the shots that tore them apart and spilled their blood on the white planking. The memory haunted him, tortured him when he could no longer resist the urge to think about it.

Will all great Neptune's ocean wash this blood clean from my hand? Biddlecomb was afraid that he would be sick. He squeezed the quarterdeck rail tight, felt the sweat under his palm, slick on the oiled wood. He swallowed hard. He could not allow himself to be sick in front of the men. The Icaruses had been butchered by their own navy, he told himself, not for the first time. But he had led them to it. He had led them to it.

"*Diana*'s coming about, sir," Rumstick said in a low voice.

Biddlecomb startled and looked up. He had not even heard Rumstick approach. He looked over the big man's shoulder. The former packet was on the starboard tack now and heading more directly toward the two Americans. "Thank you."

Rumstick followed his gaze out toward Dyer Island. "Men die in war, Isaac," he said after a pause. "They was men-of-war's men, and they made a choice."

"I know, Ezra. Thank you." Biddlecomb looked forward again. The *Diana* was almost a mile away, but on their converging courses the three ships were closing fast. The *Rose* was now clearly visible even without the telescope. She was on a starboard tack, clawing north as fast as she could, which was not nearly as fast as her fore-and-aft-rigged consort.

"We best think of how we'll engage," Biddlecomb said. His stomach knotted and he was again afraid he would be sick. Damn it, damn it to hell, he thought. He was tired of fighting this demon. He looked aloft at the spread of canvas; foresail, topsails, and topgallants as well as the huge gaff-headed fore-and-aft mainsail, winged out to starboard.

"Let's clew up the foresail," he began, starting to work out solutions to potential crises. The knot in his stomach eased. "Then set the jib. Take the best seamen you have and station them at the braces. The gunners'll have to fend for themselves."

"Aye, sir." Rumstick hurried forward. So glad was Biddlecomb to have this to occupy his mind that he returned Rumstick's salute without a thought.

The foresail rose like a curtain, revealing behind it the *Diana* less than a quarter mile away. Biddlecomb was startled by how quickly the distance was closing, but the *Diana* had always been fast, and the *Charlemagne* and *Katy* were swift sailors as well. The *Diana* was still on starboard tack. If she held that course she would pass down the *Katy*'s starboard side, and the *Katy* would shield her from the *Charlemagne*'s guns and possibly prevent the *Charlemagne* from getting into the fight.

Commodore Whipple stood on the *Katy*'s quarterdeck, his arms raised as a servant buckled his sword belt around his waist. He looked for all the world as if he were surrendering, and Biddlecomb smiled at the sight. Then he wondered if he should have brought a sword. He did not in fact own a sword, save for his fencing foils, the one sport for which he had a passion, but they would be useless in a real brawl. In any event it was too late. If it came to hand-to-hand combat, he would find something with which to fight.

The *Diana* was less than five hundred yards away, still on a starboard tack. Then suddenly she turned up into the wind and her small square sail braced around and came aback. Her speed dropped until she lay hove to, as if she were fixed to the bottom.

"What ship is that?" the *Diana*'s officer called through a speaking trumpet.

Commodore Whipple answered immediately, "Rhode Island ships *Katy* and *Charlemagne*. Strike. Strike or we will sink you immediately!"

The two colonial ships were silent, all eyes on the sloop. Biddlecomb wondered if she would turn and run for the protection of the *Rose*'s guns. Then her square sail braced around and filled and the big mainsail was sheeted in and the *Diana* resumed her previous course, heading as directly as she could for the Americans.

"Give that rascal a shot!" Whipple called, and instantly a swivel gun fired from the *Katy*'s bow.

A puff of smoke belched out from the *Diana*'s side, and a jet of water shot up between the two colonial ships.

"Signal from the flag," Weatherspoon piped, and a moment later said, "Engage the enemy."

"Acknowledge, Mr. Weatherspoon," said Biddlecomb, only half-listening to the midshipman. Isaac could see the men crowded onto the packet's deck, the blue-coated officer aft. What will he do? Biddlecomb tried to plumb the stranger's mind. As thorough as his understanding was of the ways of man, an understanding honed to a fine edge through hundreds of hours bartering for cargos all over the Atlantic, he was only now beginning to understand the machinations of a mind that wanted him dead.

The former packet, now less than two hundred yards away, flew up into the wind, her big jib flogging as she turned. She tacked smartly, settling on her new course, now heading for the *Charlemagne*. He would come up the *Charlemagne*'s larboard side, Biddlecomb realized, run the *Diana* into the brig, and his large and disciplined crew would pour over the rail in a rush of boarders, overwhelming the *Charlemagne*'s crew. Or so he intended.

"Mr. Rumstick! I believe they're hoping to grapple, larboard side!" There was little time; the *Diana* was no more than one hundred yards away. "We'll spin on our heel right in front of them! Stand ready at your braces! Starboard guns will fire, then all hands to the larboard guns! Let's go! Starboard your helm!" This last order he called over his shoulder to the men at the tiller.

If the Charlemagnes had not been able to grasp those hurried orders, there was nothing for it. Rumstick at least would understand. From the corner of his eye Biddlecomb saw the helmsman pushing the tiller to starboard. The *Charlemagne* heeled slightly as she came broadside to the wind, and overhead the yards braced around to Rumstick's direction. Forward the captain of number one gun peered over the barrel and out the gunport.

"Fire as you bear!" he shouted. The captain of number one gun stepped back and brought the match down to the touchhole. The gun roared out and slammed back on its breeching, and the crew abandoned it as they ran to the larboard side. Pieces of bulwark were torn from the *Diana's* larboard bow. The boarders who had gathered there now jumped back and ducked below the rail.

The *Charlemagne* continued to turn, presenting more and more of her broadside to the oncoming sloop. One by one the six-pounders roared out, blasting dark holes in the *Diana's* sails and knocking pieces of her hull into the air. If their range had been farther than the twenty yards that it was, Biddlecomb knew, the *Charlemagne's* neophyte gunners would not have scored so many hits.

Number seven fired, the aftermost gun on the starboard side, and the last of the gun crews raced over to man the larboard battery. The *Charlemagne* was still turning, showing her stern to the *Diana* as the sloop continued her pursuit. The headsails began to flog as the brig came up into the wind. It was time to tack.

"Helm's alee!" Biddlecomb shouted to the helmsmen. "Let fly the headsails! Mr. Weatherspoon, cast off that leeward mainsail sheet."

The bowsprit was pointing north and Biddlecomb felt the changing angle of the wind on his face. The bow swung up into the wind, up and up. "Mainsail, haul!" he shouted, but the words were lost in an explosion of gunfire. The deck jarred under his feet, and with the bellow of the guns came the sound of shattering wood and breaking glass.

The *Diana* had turned to bring her broadside to bear on the *Charlemagne's* exposed stern. Small-arms fire crackled and Biddlecomb could see the muzzle flashes through the smoke of the broadside. Musket balls thudded in the rail and plowed thin furrows across the deck at his feet.

No time for this, he thought as he turned his back to the *Diana*. He looked aloft. The mainsails were braced around and starting to fill. It was time to order the foresails braced around as well.

The *Diana* fired again, her small cannon sounding inordinately loud over the short span of water. He could hear the sound of round shot crushing wood, could feel the impact in the deck beneath his feet, and knew that his great cabin below was reduced to wreckage.

"Let go and haul!" he shouted, and the foreyards squealed around. They were through the wind now, and Biddlecomb turned to concentrate on the enemy.

"Larboard side, fire as you bear!" he ordered, and the aftermost gun went off.

The *Katy* was fifty yards away, trying to get into the fight, firing as best she could into the *Diana*. Whipple was standing on the quarterdeck, his sword in his hand, his face frozen in a broad grin as he drove her into the fight. He seemed to be genuinely enjoying himself. The forwardmost of *Katy*'s four-pounders and half a dozen swivel guns fired at once, their report sounding more like big muskets than cannon.

The *Diana* tacked just as the *Charlemagne* had, the British officer still hoping to grapple and board the American. Broadside to broadside, separated by no more then thirty feet of water, the two vessels pounded away. Thick white smoke hung between them, like the densest fog, and was whisked away in patches by quirks of wind, giving Biddlecomb sundry glimpses of his adversary.

"Mr. Rumstick, we'll have that foresail, if you please!" he called forward, and seconds later the big sail was again set and drawing.

With the extra canvas the *Charlemagne* drew ahead of the *Diana* but could not shake her. Whipple had managed to bring the *Katy* in closer, and now both Americans were pouring fire into the British sloop. The activity on the *Diana*'s deck was furious, the muskets firing as fast as they could, firing over their larboard and starboard sides, the gun crew working frantically at their weapons. A section of the *Charlemagne*'s bulwark crumpled, and Biddlecomb saw one of his men fall, eyes wide, clutching his thigh.

He felt the *Charlemagne* heel, ever so slightly, in a cat's paw of wind. The breeze lifted the smoke like a blanket and carried it away. He put his telescope to his eye, and at that short range he was able to see every detail of the activity on the *Diana*'s deck. A gun captain was pointing at him, and the gun crew trained the cannon around until it was aimed straight at the *Charlemagne*'s quarterdeck.

It's not polite to point, Biddlecomb thought ridiculously. The man straightened, a linstock with smoldering match in his hand. Biddlecomb tensed for the blast of the gun. He hoped desperately that it would not be canister shot. He wondered if in the next instant he would be dead. And then, before he could fire the gun, a musket ball shattered the gunner's left arm.

The man grabbed the broken limb, tossing the burning match aside. Confusion seemed to sweep across the *Diana*'s deck like grapeshot. Biddlecomb saw some men freeze as if turned to stone in various attitudes of surprise and horror. Others dropped their weapons and fled fore and aft. And then the *Diana* exploded.

CHAPTER
2

Diana

BIDDLECOMB DROPPED THE TELESCOPE TO THE DECK. HE HEARD THE
sound of shattering glass as he doubled over and pressed his
hand against his eye. He could feel the tears streaming through
his fingers. His telescope had been aimed directly at the explosion, and the flash, much magnified in the lens, had all but
blinded him in that eye.

The gunfire had stopped. He straightened and tried to open
both eyes, but his right eye could see only dark and light
patches. The tears came with renewed vigor. He closed it and
held his hand over it and with his left eye he surveyed the
scene.

A tower of black smoke rose from the *Diana*. She looked like
a whaler trying out blubber. Men swarmed around her decks,
and the clanking of the pumps was loud even over the running
and shouting. Two seamen manning the deck-wash hose directed a stream of water at the base of the column of smoke.

"Are you all right, Isaac?" Rumstick asked, rushing up the
quarterdeck ladder. "Was it a splinter? Were you hit?"

"No, I was just looking straight into the damn explosion.
Can't see out of my right eye. Here"—he pulled his handkerchief from his pocket—"tie this over it, will you?"

Rumstick took the handkerchief and tied it around Biddlecomb's head, covering his injured eye. "That whoreson

Wallace keeps saying we're nothing but pirates. At least now you look the part."

"Ah, better. What in the hell happened?"

"Looks like a powder chest blew up. Don't seem to have done any damage, except to throw 'em into full-on confusion."

Biddlecomb looked over to the *Diana* again. She was in a perfect position to rake the *Charlemagne*'s stern, but the men on her deck were too involved in the aftermath of the explosion to even notice their advantage.

"It'd be a famous help if all the British navy would blow itself up," he observed. "Let's get hands to the braces, see if we can cut off their escape."

"Aye," said Rumstick, saluting and hurrying forward.

Biddlecomb's good eye caught a distant flash. He looked south past Gould Island, and as he did, a spout of water shot up less then one hundred feet from the *Charlemagne*, a ranging shot from the *Rose*'s bow chasers. The frigate was coming up with them, driving hard with studdingsails aloft and alow. She was still three-quarters of a mile away but coming up fast, much faster than he had thought she would. The tide was flooding now, and carrying the frigate north. They did not have much time.

"Hands to the braces, Mr. Rumstick," he shouted, realizing with annoyance that he had already given that order and that the men were already there. "Put your helm to larboard, steer to cross the *Diana*'s bow," he said to the helmsmen. The brig began her turn and the yards came around in accompaniment.

The *Diana* was just off their starboard bow and fifty yards away. The fire from the exploding powder chest was nearly under control, but the fight was out of the *Diana*'s crew. The *Katy* was peppering her decks with shot from the swivel guns. Those not fighting the blaze were loitering in the bows, as far from the *Katy*'s fire as they could get, and hunkering down behind anything solid. No one seemed to take an interest in defense of any description.

The British officer was pacing the *Diana*'s quarterdeck, seemingly oblivious to the hail of shot that the *Katy* was pouring into the packet. He glanced alternately between the *Katy*, the *Charlemagne*, and the rocky shore of Conanicut Island, with which he was closing rapidly.

The fire from the *Katy* stopped, and in its place came Whipple's voice. "Do you strike?" he called. The British officer paused in his pacing to stare briefly at the American sloop, then resumed without a word.

Fifty yards away a plume of water shot up, and a second later the rumble of the cannon fire rolled down on them. Biddlecomb felt his stomach tighten. He looked south. The *Rose* had covered another quarter of a mile.

He turned his attention back to the *Diana*. It was clear now that her commander intended to drive the sloop ashore rather than suffer the ignominy of striking. He was less than a cable length from the steep-to shore of Conanicut Island, and there was nothing the Americans could do to stop him. Biddlecomb smiled as he considered the irony; he had escaped from the *Rose* once by doing just this thing.

"Mr. Rumstick, we'll heave to." He knew that the water was deep right up to the bank, but still he was as close to the rocky ledge as he cared to be. "Main braces, let go and haul! Strike the jib, if you please."

The main sails braced around again and the *Charlemagne* stopped dead in the water and hung there, balanced between the opposing pressures on her canvas. Whipple had hove to as well, and Isaac could see the *Katy*'s crew readying to launch their whaleboat.

The *Diana* closed with the island, her jibboom spearing the thick vegetation on the shore and driving on through, presenting Biddlecomb with the odd sight of a vessel's headrig disappearing into the woods.

And then her forefoot struck the rocks. Her mast swayed forward with a loud groan and the vessel shuddered, but the shrouds and backstays held and the mast remained intact, snapping back to its original angle. In the gentle late-afternoon breeze her speed was not above four knots, and Biddlecomb doubted that the impact would result in much damage.

The *Diana* had not even come to rest before the British crew began to abandon her. They swarmed forward over the bow and along the bowsprit, then one by one fell to the ground and disappeared from sight under the sloop's jibboom. Last of all, the officer made his way forward, walking rather than running. He looked over his little command one last time, then he too went over the bow and disappeared into the woods.

The *Rose* fired again, the shot sounding much louder than before. A spout of water shot up between the *Charlemagne* and the *Katy*. In twenty minutes they would be under the frigate's broadside.

The *Katy*'s whaleboat came off her deck and soared outboard at the end of the yard tackles. It hit the water and twenty armed seamen, eight more than the boat could safely hold, clambered over the side and took their places on the thwarts. Whipple took up his speaking trumpet and pointed it at the *Charlemagne*.

"I'm sending a landing party to hunt those rascals down!" Whipple called over the twenty yards of water that separated the two vessels. "Can you spare some men?"

Biddlecomb looked at the stranded *Diana* and then at the *Rose*, quickly closing the distance between them, and made a decision. "I'm going to pull the *Diana* off," he called back. If they left the sloop for the British to retake, then they would have to go through this nightmare all over again. There was not much time, but if there was any possibility of taking the *Diana* back, then it was worth a try. It was the only way, he knew, that he would be released from his service to the Rhode Island navy and allowed to go privateering. It was the only way he could avoid having to order these men to their deaths.

"Very well, Captain!" Whipple shouted. "Advise how I may assist!"

Biddlecomb waved and then turned to the problem at hand. The *Katy*'s whaleboat was nudging ashore and the men piling out. He was amazed that the boat had not swamped with the eight inches of freeboard remaining.

"Mr. Rumstick, we'll need a cable run aft. We better run it

through whatever's left of the great cabin." Isaac gave orders rapidly as he worked through solutions to the problem of pulling the sloop off the shore. It would not be easy. In fact he was not certain it could be done at all in the time allowed, but unlike with military considerations he was comfortable and expert in matters of seamanship. "The light hawser, the eight inch, will serve. I'll leave it to you to run the hawser over to the *Diana*."

Rumstick nodded and began issuing his own orders. The *Charlemagne*'s whaleboat lifted off the booms and was soon floating beside the brig. "Boat's crew away," Biddlecomb ordered, and the boat's crew clambered over the side and took up their oars. "Mr. Rumstick, give me a shout when the hawser's fast. I want you to take command of the sloop when she's off."

"Aye, sir."

"We'll have to set the kedge anchor and pull her off with the capstan. I'll do that while you get the hawser aboard the *Diana*."

Rumstick nodded and swung himself over the side of the brig, disappearing below the level of the deck. "Give way," he called out, and the order was followed by the creaking of the oars in the tholes.

The *Rose* fired and a black hole appeared in the *Charlemagne*'s fore topsail.

"Son of a bitch!" The frigate was less than half a mile away and clearly getting the range on her bow chasers. And they still had to get the hawser aboard the *Diana*, get the *Charlemagne* under way and set the kedge anchor, then tow the *Diana* off the ledge. It would be close, if it happened at all. And if it did not, then Rumstick and his men would be trapped.

"Beg your pardon, sir, but there's a boat from *Katy* alongside," Weatherspoon said, pointing over the leeward rail. Biddlecomb looked over the side. Riding there was the *Katy*'s gig with five seamen aboard.

"Commodore Whipple's compliments, sir, and he reckoned

as you only got one boat, will you have us set your kedge, sir?" asked the seaman at the tiller.

Biddlecomb looked skeptically at the little boat. "Will the gig bear the weight?"

"I reckon. The commodore had us lash up some water butts under the stern here." Biddlecomb followed the man's pointing finger. Just below the surface of the water he could see the empty barrels lending their buoyancy to the after end of the boat. For all his irritating qualities Whipple was a seaman through and through.

"Woodberry," Biddlecomb called out, rethinking his orders as he did. "We'll sway the kedge anchor aboard the gig. You"—he turned to the man beside Woodberry—"get the anchor runner and tackle aloft. Do you know what that is, at all?" he asked, prompted by the confusion on the man's face.

"No, sir," the man said sheepishly.

"Does anyone here know what the runner and tackle is?"

Several men looked down at the deck.

"Please, sir, I do!" Weatherspoon called out.

"Very good, Mr. Weatherspoon, see that it's set up and we'll get the kedge anchor over the side." The *Rose* fired again, the shot landing less than ten yards from the *Charlemagne*'s side, the spray falling across the brig's deck. "I need not tell you to hurry."

Rumstick and his crew were aboard the *Diana*, and a thin messenger line stretched from the packet across the water to the *Charlemagne* and disappeared into the great cabin below Biddlecomb's feet. Rumstick waved in reply to some unseen signal from Gardiner in the great cabin, and the men aboard the *Diana* began hauling the messenger in. A few seconds later the hawser, eight inches around, emerged from the *Charlemagne*'s great cabin and began snaking across the stretch of open water.

Biddlecomb heard the crushing sound of iron on wood as a shot from the *Rose*'s bow chaser struck the *Katy*. The frigate was well within range now, and if Wallace decided to turn and bring his broadside to bear, rather than continue to close the distance, then the Americans would be helpless under his devastating fire.

"Have we time for this, Biddlecomb?" Whipple called across the water. His voice betrayed no concern; his tone was the same as he might have used to ask his fellow captain aboard for dinner.

Biddlecomb paused before answering. "Mr. Weatherspoon, the other end of the tackle goes aloft. Yes, that end." He then called across to Whipple, "I think we can have the sloop off in five minutes. Any more than that and we'll have to leave her."

"Five minutes is it," Whipple replied, "you have not a second more than that!"

"Haul away!" Weatherspoon shouted, his voice too high-pitched to give the proper weight to the order. Still, the men pulled with a will and the kedge anchor lifted from its resting place on the fore channel and was eased into the waiting gig.

On the *Diana*'s foredeck Rumstick had run the hawser up to the sloop's windlass and Biddlecomb could clearly hear the pawl falling in place as the men hove the slack out of the line. A splash forward told him that the kedge anchor had been dropped. Gardiner was standing at the break of the quarter-deck, hat in hand, saluting, a habit he had picked up, to Biddlecomb's annoyance, from Rumstick. "Hawser's aboard the sloop and made fast at both ends, sir."

"Very good." They were almost done. Now they had only to haul the sloop off. "Rig the capstan, please, and heave away."

As Gardiner began pushing the men into position, Biddlecomb turned back to the *Diana*. "We're going to heave away now!" he called through the speaking trumpet. Rumstick waved in acknowledgment. "Heave round!" Biddlecomb shouted forward, and the men at the capstan stamped around in a circle, their pace growing slower and slower as they strained to pull both the *Charlemagne* and the *Diana* toward the set anchor.

Suddenly the air was filled with the scream and rush of round shot and chain, passing close. Two black holes appeared in the *Charlemagne*'s mainsail, and the *Katy*'s topsail yard sagged like a broken wing, the slings shattered. Just over a quarter mile away, now all but invisible in her own gunsmoke, the *Rose* had hove to, presenting her full battery to the American ships. The men at the capstan ceased heaving and stared stupidly at the frigate as the muted sound of the gunfire followed after the shot.

"Oh, damn me to hell," Biddlecomb muttered. He felt the first wave of panic rush over him. "Heave, God damn your eyes!" he shouted to the men at the capstan. With the sound of the broadside came the living memory of the horror that the *Rose* had visited on him before. His breath was coming fast and shallow. "Do you want to leave this place?" he added, and with that the men fell to heaving again with a will.

Again the *Rose* fired. Wood shattered forward, torn canvas flapped overhead, but the steady rhythm of the capstan continued, and with an audible groan the *Diana* pulled away from the shore. The sharp report of a small cannon burst out nearby, then another and another. Whipple was impudently firing back with his four-pound guns.

Armed men poured out of the woods under the *Diana*'s bow. Biddlecomb's heart leapt and he felt suddenly sick to his stomach. If the *Diana*'s British crew tried to retake the vessel, they would overwhelm the small American force, and Rumstick would be taken. Worse, he realized, Rumstick would fight to the death.

He raised his speaking trumpet to shout a warning, and in that instant he realized that the men in the woods were the *Katy*'s landing party returning from the hunt.

"Anchor's at short peak!" Gardiner sang out, indicating that they had hove in as much anchor cable as they could. And still the *Diana* remained fixed to the shore.

The *Rose* was under way again, leaving a cloud of gunsmoke in her wake. Wallace had paused long enough for two broadsides, and now he was again closing the distance. She was a quarter mile away, less than a quarter mile, coming fast. Her next broadside would be at point-blank range.

The hawser connecting the *Charlemagne* to the *Diana* was like an iron rod, straight and ridged, the pressure squeezing the water out of the fibers of the rope, but still the sloop did not move. Something was holding it fast.

Then he saw it. A small tree had passed between the mast and the fore topmast stay, and as they hauled the sloop off, the two had become completely entangled. The mast was bending under the great force exerted on it, holding the sloop fast, and Rumstick did not see it.

"Rumstick! The fore topmast stay!" Biddlecomb shouted. He saw Rumstick looking at him, saw him put a hand to his ear. "The stay! The goddamned fore topmast stay!" The *Rose* was three hundred yards away, swinging around, bringing her great guns to bear.

Rumstick spun around, and when he did, he saw what was hanging them up. He snatched up a cutlass and charged toward the bow. He leapt over the windlass and raced out along the bowsprit, chopping wildly at the tree.

"No! Not the tree! Cut the stay!" Biddlecomb yelled, not knowing if Ezra could hear him. It was not in Rumstick's nature to cut a perfectly good stay, but this was absurd, this time the rigging had to go.

"Rumstick—," he shouted again, and the *Rose* fired, so close that the blast of the guns was mixed with the shattering of wood and falling gear into one prolonged nightmare sound, and Biddlecomb was once again on the deck of the *Icarus*, watching his men being torn apart. The *Charlemagne*'s spritsail yard was shattered and the *Katy*'s jibboom snapped like a twig. He held his breath, waiting for the screams of wounded men, but none came.

"Rumstick, God damn it!" he shouted, but the first officer now saw what had to be done. He stepped back, wound up, and severed the fore topmast stay with one stroke.

The *Diana* came instantly alive. She surged away from the shore as the hawser between the vessels went limp. The men on board, the men from the *Charlemagne* and the *Katy*, leapt to get the sloop under way. The hawser was slipped and slid into the water; below in the *Charlemagne*'s great cabin eager hands hauled it aboard the brig.

The *Rose* was close enough now that Biddlecomb could hear the sound of heavy gun carriages rumbling across wooden decks as the great guns were loaded and run out.

"Shall we haul up the anchor, sir?" Gardiner called from the bow.

"No, damn the anchor, cut it away! Hands to braces!"

Gardiner's ax fell on the taut anchor cable, parting the stiff line. "Anchor's gone, sir!" The *Charlemagne* was free of the bottom and starting to drift.

"Signal from the flag," Weatherspoon piped.

"Just a minute, Mr. Weatherspoon." Whatever Whipple had to say was secondary to getting the *Charlemagne* up the bay to safety. He looked over at the *Diana*. She was gathering way already, close hauled with Rumstick at the helm.

"Brace up, sharp larboard tack!" The yards on the *Charlemagne*'s main mast swung around and the sails rippled and filled and the brig gathered way. "Full and bye," Biddlecomb said to the helmsman.

The *Rose* did not fire. Wallace was getting her under way, opting to chase rather than try to cripple the Americans. It was a good choice, good, at least, for the Rhode Island navy. The heavy frigate would not catch the smaller vessels in that light air. Once around Conanicut Island they would be shielded from the frigate's guns and would soon be in water too shallow for the *Rose* to follow.

Biddlecomb looked over the starboard side. *Katy* was under way as well, gathering speed, quickly moving beyond the reach of Wallace's guns. His eye was brought back to the bright flag streaming aft on the *Katy*'s yardarm.

"Very well, Mr. Weatherspoon, what's the commodore signaling?" He suspected that he already knew the answer.

"All vessels disengage the enemy, sir," Weatherspoon said brightly.

The commodore did not disappoint.

CHAPTER
3

Cambridge

IT WAS THREE HOURS BEFORE THE TIME HE WOULD NORMALLY HAVE risen had he been back at his father's estate in Virginia when Maj. Edward Fitzgerald felt the servant's hand on his shoulder, shaking him from his sleep.

"Hour to sunrise," the servant said softly.

Fitzgerald swung his feet out of the bed and onto the smooth wood floor and sat for a moment in that position, orienting himself. A candle stood on the nightstand, placed there by the servant, the flame dancing in the drafts. "Thank you," he muttered, and the man disappeared as silently as he had entered.

Fitzgerald let out a low moan. It was already warm, and already humid. July was miserable in Virginia, but he was quickly discovering that it was worse in Massachusetts. He had left home with a vague idea that it was always cold that far north.

Fitzgerald looked around the room, as far as he could see in the light of the single candle. The white plaster walls glowed yellow in that light. Lurking in the shadows was a large mahogany wardrobe on one side of the room, and on the other, below the one window, a chest of drawers. There was, besides that, one chair and a desk, both lost in the darkness. In Fitzgerald's experience this room typified the New England Puritan aesthetic. By Southern standards it was quite spartan.

24

Fitzgerald, twenty-five years old, had been an officer in the Virginia Militia since his seventeenth birthday. None the less, his present rank of major was owed almost entirely to his family's place in Fairfax County society and their friendship with the man who now commanded the Army of the United Colonies. Unlike many others in the Militia who had fought in the last war, Fitzgerald had done nothing more dangerous than drill and parade.

If anyone had so much as insinuated to Fitzgerald that his commission was based on influence alone, he would have called that person out and would most likely have killed him. That fact notwithstanding, Fitzgerald was well aware of his shortcomings in the military line. He had hunted fugitives and runaway slaves, he had fought duels and brawls, but he had never, for all his eight years in the Militia, been in a real battle or a military engagement of any description.

This fact had annoyed him in Virginia; in Massachusetts, in the siege of Great Britain's ministerial army in the city of Boston, it tormented him. The New England militiamen, as far beneath him as they might be in rank or wealth or social standing, had seen combat and he had not. There were here many veterans of the last French War, and those too young to have fought in that conflict had fought at Concord and Lexington and Bunker Hill. He was an officer, and he had not been in combat, and he felt like a fraud.

So until he had the chance to prove himself in combat, Major Fitzgerald intended to prove himself through hard and competent work in his position as adjunct to the general. For this reason he would never allow the commander in chief to wake before him.

But it was more than just pride that drove him. He worshiped Washington, and he believed fervently in the cause of American independence, perhaps even more than the general himself, who still hoped for a reconciliation with Parliament and the king.

The major pushed himself off the low bed and rustled through the dark shadows until he found his breeches. Not quite fully awake, balancing as best he could, he stepped into the legs then buttoned the waistband.

He had never imagined that being an aide to Gen. George Washington, a man nearly his father's age, would be so exhausting. Their time in Philadelphia, and the trip to Massachusetts, had been madness. Fitzgerald had hoped that the pace might slacken once the general arrived and took command of the troops encircling Boston. It had not. Now the hours before breakfast were taken up by an inspection of the American lines of defense, all six miles of them.

Fitzgerald sat back down on the bed and pulled his silk stockings over his feet and calves and buttoned the knees of the breeches. A twinge of anxiety drove him to dress faster; shirt, buff waistcoat, and belt and sword.

He pulled his boots on. The spurs were still attached; he and Washington spent so much of their time in the saddle that it was not worth removing them. A love of horses was one of the many things that he and the general shared. Washington had once declared that Fitzgerald was one of the best horsemen he had ever known. The major had been taken quite aback by the kind words. Washington was *the* best horseman Fitzgerald had ever known.

Last he pulled on his long blue coat with buff facing and snatched up his cocked hat. He stepped out of his small room into the more brightly lit hallway. It was an elegant home, once solely the residence of Mr. Samuel Langdon and now on loan as the army's headquarters. "Is the general awake?" he asked the servant, the same one who had attended to him, as the man emerged from Washington's room.

"He's just about dressed now, sir. I'll send the boy to fetch the horses."

Fitzgerald stood in the hallway, trying to strike a pose somewhere between casual and martial, and waited for Washington to emerge. He felt in his pocket for paper and pencil; one of his primary duties was to make notes on the numerous thoughts that the general had while they rode the American lines. There was the better part of a pencil and three sheets of paper, one mostly covered with yesterday's notes. That would serve for the morning.

The door to Washington's room opened and the general stepped softly into the hall, his spurs making a sound like small bells on the hardwood floor. Fitzgerald snapped to full attention and saluted smartly, sweeping his hat from his head and looking up at the general's face. At six feet tall Fitzgerald was not used to looking up at anyone. It was still an odd sensation to stand next to a man whose height exceeded his own by more than two inches.

"Good morning, Major," Washington said, nodding by way of returning Fitzgerald's salute.

"Good morning, sir. I trust you slept well?"

"Well enough. This damned humidity. Have you ever visited Massachusetts in the summer?"

"No, sir, I've never been to Massachusetts at all. I've never been north of Maryland, for that matter. But sure you've been here before?" Washington was one of the most well traveled men in Virginia.

"Only once, some time ago. I'll own I didn't count on this miserable weather. I somehow imagined it was always cool this far north."

The two men walked down the hall as they spoke, treading softly in the quiet house, then stepped through the front door and out into the heavy morning air.

In the predawn light the various heights surrounding Boston were no more than black shapes against the dark gray sky to the east. The occasional sound of a frog or a bird only accentuated the stillness of the morning. Somewhere to the west a rooster took up his raucous call. Cambridge and Boston were still asleep. Nothing indicated that in this place two armies faced each other, save for the horrible odor carried on the morning breeze.

Fitzgerald made no comment about the offensive smell, since it was a source of great irritation to the general, but Washington brought it up himself, as Fitzgerald knew he would. "For God's sake! I've been harping on them to build decent privies for a month, and still we're assailed with this! Do the officers here pay the least attention to general orders?"

"When they find it convenient, sir, I believe they do."

"That won't do. Someone must be held accountable."

"Well, sir, I had an idea regarding that. Perhaps we should require every officer to keep a book containing each order you issue. That way they can't plead ignorance. Otherwise they act as if they never received them."

"That's an excellent idea, Major. Jot that down please." Fitzgerald fished the pencil and a clean sheet of paper out of his pocket and in the dim light wrote down the first note of the day.

The stableboy appeared leading the horses, and without a word the two men mounted and rode off north toward the left flank of the American line, through the growing light of the morning and the ubiquitous odor.

"It's beyond comprehension," Washington said at last. "Can you imagine a Virginian tolerating this . . . this stench? What kind of a people are these Yankees?"

"I'll own it's beyond me," Fitzgerald replied honestly.

"It's beyond comprehension."

The two men rode on in silence, casually inspecting the various encampments through which they passed. Most of the troops were still asleep. Not until the sentries could see a thousand yards in any direction would the soldiers' day officially begin.

The living quarters of the New England militia, from which a few early risers were now beginning to emerge, were the most eclectic collection of shelters Fitzgerald had ever seen. Some men lived in hovels nailed together from odd scraps of lumber, some lived in proper tents, and some in lean-tos that looked more as if they should house a band of Red Indians.

Fitzgerald's idea of a military encampment was neat rows of identical tents and campfires and fine uniforms such as the Virginia Militia displayed on their training exercises. This seemed more a massive, semibarbaric hunting party. But the men were well fed, and crude though they were, the shelters seemed to be doing their job.

"Major, you're familiar with the fringed hunting shirts often worn by our woodsmen?" Washington asked. "They're generally made from deerskin or tow cloth."

"Yes, sir."

"I've a mind to have some made, about ten thousand, I should think. They're inexpensive and they'll serve as a uniform of sorts. What are your thoughts on that?"

Washington was sincere in his request for counsel, and Fitzgerald was flattered to be asked. "I think the men need some type of uniform. As it stands, each company dresses after the fashion of their hometown. That has to hinder discipline and any sense of common purpose."

"Just so. These men have to start thinking of themselves as the Army of the United Colonies, not a tag-and-rag bunch of New England militia. That's the only way they'll fight like an army."

"And the only way they'll accept taking orders from a Virginian?" The Yankees, some of them, still did not care to have a Southern commander in chief, and that sentiment was often made obvious.

The general swiveled around in his saddle, and Fitzgerald was glad to see that he was smiling. "Just so. Make a note about the shirts."

As the major wrote, Washington continued his thoughts. "We must order a new supply of cartridges today, as well. That can't wait. Incidentally, you recall that report we received in New York, the one from the Committee of Safety here about the Bunker Hill action?"

"I do, yes, sir."

"That note mentioned a desperate need for gunpowder, but I've since been informed that there's three hundred or so barrels . . ."

"Three hundred and eight, sir."

"Just so, three hundred and eight in the storehouse, which is more than enough for anything beyond an extended artillery duel. We'll have to find out the truth of this matter when we see the quartermaster about the cartridges."

"Very good, sir," Fitzgerald said, committing the thought to paper.

The road tended uphill now as the two men rode into the hills just south of the Mystic River that comprised the left flank of the Americans' far-flung line of defense. To the west they could see the redoubts on the high ground, made much more formidable since Washington's arrival. The commander in chief, with much help from Generals Charles Lee and Horatio Gates, had managed to spur the New England militiamen into greatly improving the earthworks. Discipline and the strategic situation were better now than ever before, and much improvement was yet to come.

"Halt!"

Fitzgerald was startled by the challenge. They had just turned onto the path leading to the defenses at Prospect Hill. To the east the sun had broken free of the horizon, and up and down the American lines the morning guns sounded.

"Who's there?" the sentry called out as he stepped onto the path. His feet were bare and the loose breeches that came down to his knees were tattered to the point that the cuffs looked like fringe. He wore a torn linen waistcoat over his bare chest and on his head a round hat with one edge of the brim pinned up. His musket was pointed somewhere between the two officers.

"This is General Washington," Fitzgerald said.

"Uh-huh," the sentry said, and said nothing else. Fitzgerald felt his anger spark like a flint on steel. They had encountered this sort of thing before.

"Yes, Private, this is General Washington. Step aside please," Fitzgerald said, biting off the words. The commander in chief did not care for displays of anger.

"I got no way of knowing that, do I?" the sentry said at last.

"Oh, for God's sake . . ." Fitzgerald would gladly have leapt off his horse and run the man through with his sword. Washington held up his hand and Fitzgerald fell silent.

"You've done your duty, Private. Now please let us pass."

"I can't let you pass unless I gets—"

"Please call your commanding officer," Washington cut the sentry off.

Never taking his eyes off the Virginians, the sentry yelled over his shoulder, "Hey, John, step up here, would ya?"

"Sir, this is absurd. This idiot knows full well who you are. He's only baiting us—," Fitzgerald said in a loud whisper, but Washington interrupted him.

"Is this the commanding officer?" he asked the major, indicating another soldier walking slowly down the path. The new arrival was dressed almost identically to the sentry, save for the shirt he wore under his waistcoat. In place of a musket he carried a beef bone from which he was chewing the last bits of meat.

"Yes, sir, that's an officer."

"How the devil can you tell?"

"The cockade on his hat, sir," Fitzgerald answered, indicating the remnants of a green cockade that the man wore on the upturned brim of his round hat. "It's hard to see."

"What is it, Billy?" the officer asked the sentry.

"Fella here says he's Gen. George Washington."

The officer took a long look at the two men on horseback. "I reckon I wouldn't know," he said at last. With his fingers he tore a piece of meat off the bone and put it in his mouth, chewed it, then fished it out again, examined it, then tossed it aside with a sour look on his face. "I reckon I wouldn't recognize any General Washington."

"What's your name and rank, sir?" Washington's manner was calm; Fitzgerald feared he was going to let the militiamen get away with their insolence.

"Lt. John Fuller, mister, First Medford Militia."

"Major, make a note to have Lieutenant Fuller arrested for insubordination pending court-martial. The private is to receive a dozen lashes." Washington spurred his horse and pushed past the startled men. "I mean to make a pretty good slam among these people," he said as much to himself as to Fitzgerald.

Beyond the defenses, campfires were flaring up in front of the usual odd collection of tents. Washington spurred his horse past the encampment. They climbed the steep path to the redoubt that crowned Prospect Hill, past the position of Col. John Glover's Twenty-first Massachusetts Regiment from Marblehead.

Fitzgerald noted again, with some amusement, the great tents that the regiment from that coastal town had formed out of discarded sails. The 21st Massachusetts were sailors to the bone. They dressed in the mariner's baggy pants and blue jackets and tarpaulin hats, and they had the laconic, sneering attitude with which seamen the world over viewed soldiers and soldierly discipline. It irked Fitzgerald greatly.

Even more irritating, for all their disdain the Marblehead men were among the best soldiers on the American lines. The hardships of the camp, Fitzgerald imagined, were nothing in comparison to what the sea could serve out. The men of the 21st were used to obeying orders, used to a chain of command. Just being able to sleep a full eight hours undisturbed was a luxury to these men. What was more, they treated their camp with a sailor's fastidiousness. They were hard and disciplined, at least with their own officers. And they hated the Parliament, whose acts had virtually destroyed the shipping and fishing trades, as much, and perhaps more, than any other regiment on the line.

Fitzgerald and Washington arrived at last at the crest of Prospect Hill. From their position atop their horses the officers could see the land below and beyond the fortification. The sun was clear of the horizon now. A mile away and nearly lost in the blinding light was Charlestown, and rising behind it, Breed's and Bunker Hill. A significant portion of the British army was encamped on those heights, their redoubts plainly visible.

South of there lay Boston, more like an island than a peninsula. To the east of the city the ships of the British navy swung at their anchors. And south of that lay Roxbury. Though he could not see it, Fitzgerald knew that there stood the Roxbury line, the southern flank of the American defenses, six miles away.

Washington was silent as the two officers surveyed the lovely harbor and the green hills that stretched out below them. At length the general spoke. "There is an unaccountable kind of stupidity among the lower class of these people that prevails too generally among the officers here," he said, choosing his words carefully. "They don't seem to consider themselves officers at all, they're nearly of the same kidney as the privates." He paused again, then smiled. "That will change, I assure you," he said, and, wheeling his horse around, called out, "Come, we've much more to see," and trotted back down the path, Fitzgerald taking up position at his side.

They rode north until they could swing around the far left flank by the Mystic River and inspect the encampments beyond the high ground. It was half past six in the morning and the day's routine was well under way. Washington stopped to speak to, and congratulate, a colonel of the Second Winnisimmet Militia, whose troops were actively digging privies downwind of the camp.

They continued south, through the center of the American lines, and then back up to Cambridge to cross over the Charles River. In the distance they could see General Lee and his entourage, riding at full gallop, off to the American lines in Roxbury, the general's beloved dogs racing beside him. Washington and Fitzgerald followed at a more leisurely pace south to the Roxbury Heights.

It was eight o'clock, and already hot, when they arrived at the southern flank. They sat on the edge of the redoubt there and ate breakfast, looking out over Boston, now north of their position. The men of a Rhode Island artillery unit, known officially as the United Company of the Train of Artillery of the Town of Providence, were busying themselves around the fieldpieces in the embrasures.

Like everything else about the Army of the United Provinces, the field artillery was an odd assortment, consisting of four-, six-, twelve-, and twenty-four-pound guns in various states of health. But the men of the artillery unit were more uniform than most, and the officers in their brown coats with red facing and distinctive leather caps had as military a bearing as one could ask.

"Good morning, sir. Morning, Edward." Maj. John Crane, in command of the United Train of Artillery, joined the two officers on the earthworks. "I hope you find everything in order."

"I am well pleased, Major," Washington replied. "I could only wish all our companies had your discipline and, shall we say, appreciation of the dangers at hand."

"It may be easier for us to appreciate them, General, since we're looking at that all day long." Crane nodded his head north. Just a mile away, on Boston Neck, the strip of land connecting Boston to the mainland, and squarely facing the Americans, were the formidable British defenses. The artillery behind the British earthworks was visible even without a telescope. Fitzgerald imagined that the British artillery did not consist of a smattering of different calibers and weapons of dubious integrity.

"Whatever the reason, Major, I hope your example spreads like camp fever," Washington replied.

The daily inspection of the American lines complete, the two officers rode north back to Cambridge to begin the more administrative chores of the day's routine. Fitzgerald had filled another page of notes, and they would be lucky if they were able to act on a quarter of them before nightfall.

"I can't put off corresponding with Congress for a moment longer," the general said as they once more entered the town of Cambridge, "and I think we should prepare a general letter to the colonial governors regarding the tow cloth for the hunting shirts."

"Sir, you had in mind to order some cartridges as well," Fitzgerald reminded him.

"Just so, just so. Let's take care of that matter right away," and with that the commander in chief swung his horse around and made for the quartermaster general's office.

Fitzgerald was mildly surprised to find John Pierce Palmer, the quartermaster general, at work. It being now past noon he imagined the rotund quartermaster would be in some tavern well away from any military goings-on. He knew that the commander in chief was looking to replace Palmer, who had been given his position by the Massachusetts legislature three months before.

Palmer stood as the two men stepped into his office, and his smile looked more like embarrassment and agitation then delight. "General! How very good of you to stop by! Good afternoon, Major." Palmer shook both men's hands. Palmer's coat lay crumpled on a table in the corner. His waistcoat was unbuttoned and his shirt was wilted in the heat. Large perspiration stains stood out on his chest and under his arms.

"Good afternoon, sir," said Washington, and wasting no time with small talk continued, "I haven't heard any complaints of late regarding the bread. I trust that situation has been resolved?"

"Bless you, sir, yes. Once I conveyed to the bakers your . . . ah . . . promise of reprisals."

"Just so," said Washington. It still annoyed Fitzgerald that the commander in chief had had to step in and sort out so silly a problem as inadequate bread. If Palmer could not handle the issuance of bread, he should certainly not be in charge of powder and shot.

"We need more powder distributed," Washington continued, "enough for at least ten cartridges per man. That should be adequate for the time being."

"Ah, yes . . . well," Palmer stammered. Fitzgerald could see the perspiration standing out on his forehead, more even than was warranted by the heat.

"Is there a problem? I was informed we had . . . what was it?" The general turned to Fitzgerald.

"Three hundred and eight barrels, sir," Fitzgerald supplied.

"Just so. Is that number not correct?"

"Well, sir, as it happens . . ." Palmer chuckled nervously. "As it happens, that number, the three hundred and eight barrels, sir, was the amount of all powder that had been collected ever, do you see? Some of it, naturally, has been spent, what with the fighting. At Bunker Hill, and all."

Washington tapped his fingers on the quartermaster's desk. Fitzgerald knew how much he loathed such equivocating. "All right, man, how much powder do we have?"

"Well . . . sir, we have as of now in the storehouse . . . thirty-six barrels."

The words sounded as loud as an artillery barrage in the small room. Washington drew himself up to his full height, his face impassive save for a slight frown, the expression that the general took on when presented with the gravest of disasters.

Palmer coughed and shuffled uncomfortably, but the General stared silently out the window and took no notice of him. Fitzgerald roughed out the figures in his head; thirty-six barrels, about nine thousand pounds. Less then nine shots per man.

At last Washington broke his silence. "Thirty-six barrels among all these men," he said softly as if speaking to himself. "My God, my God, what if the British were to discover this? It is terrible, terrible even in the idea."

CHAPTER
4

The Farm in Bristol

IT WAS THE LIVESTOCK THAT BROUGHT ON THE MEMORIES. IN THOSE rare times that he was around such things—the bleating of cows and sheep, the smell of animals and dirt—Biddlecomb could not help but see images of his childhood, despite his best efforts to anchor them in the backwater of his mind.

He stared across the *Charlemagne*'s quarterdeck to the sloping bank of Conanicut Island. A dozen of the brig's men were ashore, herding a number of sheep and several cows toward the water's edge. Many of the crew being farmers by trade, they drove the animals with an expert hand. Only Rumstick hung back and looked awkward in his efforts to help.

It was September, more than two months since the *Charlemagne* and the *Katy* had taken the *Diana* back, and still the *Charlemagne* remained attached to the upstart Rhode Island navy. Biddlecomb had not yet had the courage or opportunity to ask, but it did not appear to him as if William Stanton had any intention of sending the brig off privateering.

He looked down at the *Charlemagne*'s waist where the men who remained on board were herding a variety of livestock forward. During the past month he had gone from the sick terror of having to offer up the lives of these men to the dull ache of carrying out this silly mission of depriving the *Rose* of fresh meat. It was like being a spectator at his own failure, watching his ambitions of privateering and the concomitant

37

riches of that profession atrophy and die, always with the possibility that he might again find himself under the guns of the *Rose.*

"Damn this nonsense," he said out loud. He turned his back to the scene and rested his hands on the *Charlemagne*'s taffrail, trying to suppress his annoyance. He did not want to think about the old days, the memories he had more or less ignored for sixteen years, but the caterwauling of the sheep and the cows and the smell of the rich earth warmed by the August sun stirred up that mental sediment. He stared off at the distant shore, a low hill beyond which had once stood a small farm, ten miles from where the *Charlemagne* now swung at her anchor. He had lived there once, before the sea had become his home.

Isaac was more than a year old when he first saw his father, though of course he did not remember that. He was five years old when his father came home to stay. It was the summer of 1751 when John Biddlecomb returned from Nova Scotia and packed away the blue broadcloth uniform, the tomahawk, and bayonet with which he had fought in the company of Gorham's Rangers. With his six years accumulated pay and bounty from Indian scalps, he purchased the small farm outside of Bristol, near where he had been raised, and settled happily, contentedly, into the life of a farmer. He never spoke of his years as a soldier in the northern wilderness.

But he never forgot the soldiering either, not completely. The Biddlecombs' farm held a welcome for any of the Rangers who were passing through, going north or south. Isaac remembered them well; big men, like warriors from a storybook, who often were guests in their home. His father enjoyed their company, and his mother tolerated them and maintained a good humor.

These men, his father and his father's friends, would sit for hours in the kitchen, drinking rum and whiskey and talking about their adventures in the north woods. The Rangers knew that John did not care to have his wife and child hear stories of his former trade, but when he was not around, they told Isaac tales of his father's prowess as a soldier. They called him Fighting John or Viking John.

There was one story, told to him by three different men on three separate occasions, in which his father had attacked a French encampment single-handedly, mistaking Gorham's signal and thinking the other Rangers were at his back. He had killed five men, blinded with a fighting madness, by the time his surprised comrades joined in. Isaac enjoyed the stories, but he envisioned some mythic warrior acting out those deeds. He could not place his father, the soft-spoken, gentle farmer, in that image.

In the rare times that Biddlecomb thought about his childhood on the farm, thought back through the ache and the loss, the memories were vague and happy; his mother and father, the small house, the woods and the fields as vast to a young boy as the great wilderness beyond the Appalachian Mountains.

And there were the ships. From his earliest memories he was transfixed by the ships. He would run the mile to where their neighbor's fields touched on Narragansett Bay and watch the ships working in and out of Bristol and down from Providence and dream long dreams of the distant places to which they were bound.

One night, after their supper and pudding, his parents said they had a surprise for him. Isaac sat in silence. The fire in the oven was left burning to defend against the chill of the early-spring evening. It was May of 1758, and he was twelve years old when his mother told him that she was going to have another baby. Isaac remained silent. The implications of this statement were outside the small sphere of events comprehensible to his young mind.

"You're going to have a little brother or sister," his mother said with her comforting smile.

In the following months he began to understand, as the baby grew inside his mother, and with it the sense of anticipation that pervaded their home. Conversation around the dinner table centered on the upcoming event. And names. It had not occurred to Isaac that he and his mother and father had to pick out a name for the baby, just pick it out of thin air, the name by which God himself would know this new person. Thomas if it was a boy, Katlin if it was a girl.

Then came the first days of December, cold and bitter, and the long wait was over. The northeast wind pounded the house, and in the next room Isaac could hear the midwife giving loud orders to her assistant, could hear his mother screaming in pain. His father told him that it was normal, that all women screamed that way when giving birth, but Isaac did not think he sounded very certain. He saw fear in his father's face. It was something he had never seen before, and it made him afraid in turn.

And then they told him that his mother was gone, and Katlin was gone. The men from the neighboring farms used picks and adzes to dig their graves in the frozen ground.

Isaac held his father's hand, huddled against him, seeking some shelter from the buffeting wind, as he watched them lower his mother's coffin into the hard earth. The tears streaming down his father's cheeks were blown away by the wind. Isaac held tighter to his father's hand and pressed closer against him. He thought that his father must be half-frozen; he had left his coat and hat behind.

For the next week John Biddlecomb said little and Isaac stayed out of his way and roamed the frozen fields alone. Then one day he came home from watching a merchantman beating north against a howling gale to find his father had laid out his blue broadcloth coat, the leggings, and the odd blue hat like the Scotsmen wore. He was holding his bayonet, the bayonet that had been packed away for eight years, and polishing it with a chamois cloth.

"The Rangers are forming up, up in Halifax," he said. "Pack what you need in the haversack I put on your bed."

Isaac stared at him for what seemed a long time, but his father went on polishing the long blade. At length he looked up at his son.

"Go on, boy, get your gear packed. If we don't leave tonight, we'll miss the transport," he said harshly, and Isaac burst into tears.

"Papa?" he cried, and flung himself into his father's arms. John Biddlecomb laid the bayonet aside and hugged his son, hugged him for a long time. Isaac's tears made a dark spot on his father's shirt. "This is something I have to do, Son, and I have no kin to leave you with," John Biddlecomb said finally, by way of explanation.

Isaac drew back and looked into his father's eyes. His father was not going to Nova Scotia. He was running away from Bristol. Even at twelve years old Isaac understood that, and he understood that his father would not be stopped. And he realized then, truly understood, that he would never see his mother again. They were alone in the world, he and his father, and his father was taking him away from everything that was familiar. The tears came again and he cried with complete abandon.

It took them two days by coach to reach Boston. The trip was rough and cold, a procession of small, dead-looking towns wrapped in their winter mantle, and between them frozen roads and deep pine forests.

At last they rolled down Roxbury Heights and across the strip of land that connected Boston to the rest of Massachusetts. Isaac peered out of the window of the coach. He had never seen a city like Boston. The carriage pushed on through the crowded streets and then jerked to a halt. The driver's face appeared in the window. "Rowe's Wharf," he said. "I'll get a boy to carry your dunnage."

"That won't be necessary," John Biddlecomb said, stepping out of the carriage and stretching to his full height, his uniform making him look even more imposing.

Isaac clambered out of the carriage and looked eagerly around. It seemed as if there were a thousand people doing a thousand different things. The carriages rolling through the streets, people rushing past, the cry of gulls and vendors, the ring of hammers, made a cacophony such as Isaac had never heard before. It was a new and extraordinary world.

"Here you go, Son." His father held out his haversack. Isaac took it and slung it over his shoulder as his father paid the driver of the coach. The driver climbed back into his seat, and with a flick of the reins the horses were under way.

"The transport's there," John said, nodding his head toward a place on the other side of the carriage. The vehicle drew away, like a curtain pulled back, and fifty feet away the merchant ship *Providence* lay tied to Rowe's Wharf.

In later years Isaac would see the *Providence* and think her a clumsy and awkward vessel, but to his young eyes, closer now than they had ever been to a real ship, she was the finest vessel afloat. Her masts seemed to rise up forever, the tallest things Isaac had ever seen. He was transfixed by her beauty, the curve of her bow, the slight tumble home of her sides. He stood in the road and stared.

"Come along, Isaac," his father said. "I'm here, there's no call to be afraid."

He took his father's hand and they crossed the street and walked up the icy brow of the *Providence*. He was twelve and a half years old, and for the first time in his life Isaac Biddlecomb set foot on the deck of a ship.

"On deck!" the voice of the lookout perched in the main topgallant shrouds shook Biddlecomb from his memories. He looked aloft.

"Deck, aye!" he shouted, knowing full well what the lookout would say next.

"There's the *Rose*, sir, just beyond Prudence Island!" he cried. Biddlecomb turned automatically and looked in that direction, though he knew that the frigate was nearly ten miles away, hidden by the island, and would not be visible from the deck.

"And again . . . ," he muttered to himself. It was an old game by now. The *Charlemagne* or the *Katy* would discover the frigate's position, then begin removing livestock from some island as distant from the *Rose* as was practical. When the man-of-war got too close, they would up anchor and go, depositing their unhappy cargo on Block Island.

It had been exhilarating at first, like a deadly game of tag, but now it was just dull. There was no chance that the *Rose* would catch them; it would be another two hours before she arrived at their anchorage, and he would be gone in another thirty minutes.

He felt the breeze on his face. About ten knots and out of the northeast. He picked up his speaking trumpet and turned toward the field on Conanicut Island opposite the quarterdeck. Rumstick and five seamen were there, trying to persuade a reluctant cow into the *Charlemagne*'s launch.

"Mr. Rumstick!" he called across the water. "Half an hour, we can't tarry any longer, then we must be under way!"

Rumstick waved his acknowledgment, then turned back to the cow. "Mr. Sprout," Biddlecomb addressed the boatswain in the waist. "Please see to buoying the cable in case we must slip it." If for some reason there was no time to raise the anchor, the buoy would mark it's location for retrieval later. But that had not been necessary yet, and Biddlecomb doubted it would be necessary now. They were in no real danger from the *Rose*.

"Aye, sir." Sprout saluted and hurried forward.

Biddlecomb took one more look in the direction of the unseen frigate, then turned his back again. It was all so silly. Stanton was clearly opting for patriotism over profit, intending to keep the *Charlemagne* on loan to the Rhode Island navy, and that meant that Biddlecomb's carefully planned life was hard aground. Rather than working toward owning a merchant fleet of his own, he was festering away in this unprofitable obscurity, tortured at night by vivid dreams of carnage, and in daylight by boredom, failure, and the consideration of his inadequacy as a naval commander. It could not go on. He could not recall any time in his life when he had been more miserable.

And then he remembered, yes, there had been a time, a time of much greater misery. And the first step toward that misery had been, ironically enough, his first step aboard the *Providence*, his first step toward the sea.

No sooner had Isaac and his father come aboard the transport than John Biddlecomb was surrounded by his comrades, the men of Gorham's Rangers. Their uniforms were like his father's, if a bit more worn, and like John Biddlecomb they were big, hard-looking men. Isaac recognized a few who had visited them at their home in Bristol. The faces of the Rangers had a severe quality that eight years on the little farm had erased from his father's countenance.

"Sorry about your loss, John," Isaac heard one of the men say softly, and heard the others mutter their concurrence. "We all liked Sarah very much," said another.

"Thank you," John Biddlecomb replied, and no more was said about it.

Isaac Biddlecomb only half-heard the greetings of the Gorham Rangers. He stood fixed as if nailed to his patch of deck, his eyes moving in every direction, trying to take in all at once the wondrous surroundings. The ship smelled of tar and wet wood mixed with the salty and fishy smell of the waterfront. The masts and rigging that towered above him were coated in ice, except where the seamen, working high aloft, trampled and shook the lines. Bits of ice fell to the deck, shattering like broken glass.

Isaac was certain he had never seen so many lines in his life. Watching the ships from a distance as they tacked and wore up the bay, they had seemed so simple, each evolution silent and unhurried. Now, staring aloft, he wondered how anyone was capable of understanding such complexity. The sailors, he concluded, must be very, very smart men.

"And what's your professional opinion of this ship, son?" a voice intruded on Isaac's awe. He looked up at the man who spoke, a man about his father's age, though not as tall or lean. He was buried in a long blue wool coat. A cloth was wrapped around his ears and a cocked hat pushed down over that.

'It's beautiful, sir," Isaac said with such sincerity that the man laughed.

"You're a natural-born sailor-man, I can see that, and you have a fine eye for ships. I'm Capt. William Stanton, owner and master of the *Providence*." The captain extended his hand and Isaac shook it. He felt as if he were being presented to King George. "I'm sorry about your mother, son," he added softly.

"You knew my mother?"

"We met. I'm from Bristol, like you, though I'm at sea more often than not."

Isaac stared and nodded his head. He could not think of anything to say.

"Well, if there's anything you or your father need, just ask. And keep a weather eye out. A ship can be a dangerous place if you're not careful. And them foremast jacks love to jerk soldiers a bit." With that the captain turned and walked aft, leaving Isaac to stare after him. Not one word of Stanton's final bit of advice had made sense to him.

"Come on, Isaac, let's get our dunnage below stairs," Isaac's father called to him.

Isaac picked up his haversack and threw it over his shoulder. "Papa, what's a 'weather eye'?"

His father considered this as they stepped toward the scuttle. "I don't know, Son."

For the next ten days the *Providence*, bound away for Halifax, struggled to run her eastings down through the wintery north Atlantic. For Isaac they were the most extraordinary days that he had yet experienced in his short life, though tempered at first with concern for his father. Despite the thrill of feeling the ship heave and pitch underfoot, like a living thing, his father's face was a color quite unnatural, and what little he ate he soon vomited over the ship's side. Isaac panicked, terrified that he would loose his father as he had lost his mother, but his father assured him it would pass, and after a few days it did.

Concern for his father now alleviated, he gave full vent to

his curiosity. Every day he was up before dawn watching the sailors shake out the reefs they had tucked at nightfall, and mouthing to himself the strange phrases the sailors used. "Let go and haul, let go and haul . . .," he was softly repeating when a seaman approached him from the weather side.

"Studying for your mate's berth?"

Isaac looked up with an embarrassed smile. "Hello, Mr. McKeown." McKeown was a foredeck man whose thick gray beard made him look as old as the sea itself. His voice still carried more than a trace of his native Ireland.

"I've been watching you, boy, and thinking you might have an inkling to be a sailor-man."

Isaac smiled and nodded. This was the first time any of the sailors had spoken to him, and McKeown was the best hand in the forecastle.

"Do you know the parts of the rig?"

Isaac turned to the bow and pointed. "Bowsprit, jibboom, foremast, fore topmast. The fore topgallant mast and yard have been sent down, sir . . ." Isaac began the litany of his knowledge. When he was finished, he stopped and frowned, suddenly aware that he did not know very much at all. But McKeown seemed to hold a different opinion.

"Damn me, boy, you done all right, and no one teaching you a thing. Come on, it's my watch below so let me start educating you on the particulars of ships such as this."

Within two days it became the chief sport of the forecastle to teach Isaac the mysteries of seamanship and to marvel at the speed with which he learned. John Biddlecomb and his comrades in the Rangers showed no interest in the workings of the ship and little even in going up on deck, and Isaac would spend just as much time with them as he felt was necessary to satisfy his sense of filial obligation, then race topside to continue his lessons.

The sailors took him through basic sail evolutions, the theory of tacking and wearing, standing and running rigging, the names and uses of the deck furniture, and knotting, hitching, and splicing. Nor were the afterguard, Captain Stanton and the mates, willing to be left out of the fun. They introduced him to the charts and the log line and the octant and to the concept of sun sights and deduced reckoning. Isaac's thirst was insatiable.

Finally, and with his father's grudging approval, McKeown took Isaac aloft. The old sailor was careful and thorough in his instruction, and Isaac, with the agility of his years, took quickly to working high in the rigging. Four days later, from the main topsail yard where he had laid out with the other sailors for the morning routine of shaking out the sail's deep reef, he caught his first sight of Nova Scotia.

The land was blue-green under the overcast winter sky and stretched from the northern horizon south. As the seaman at the yardarm cursed and fought with the recalcitrant reef earring, Isaac breathed deep and reveled in the biting, whistling wind, the beauty of the gray sea and sky, the landfall beyond their bow, and the motion of the ship rolling sixty feet below him. In that short passage north he had come to love the life on shipboard. He wished it would never end, he wished he could go on sailing forever. And in his boyish dreams he never stopped to consider the events that might make that wish come true.

"I can see her now, sir, with royals flying," Weatherspoon said.

Biddlecomb followed the midshipman's pointed finger north up the bay. At the extreme end of Prudence Island he could just make out the tiny patches of white sail moving south, all the canvas that the frigate *Rose* would carry. "Wallace must be getting sick of this."

"I should imagine so, sir."

"I hope he's half as sick of it as I." Biddlecomb picked up the speaking trumpet and called to Rumstick ashore. "We had best be getting under way, Mr. Rumstick. I think just those two sheep and we'll weigh. I'd prefer to not slip the anchor if we can avoid it."

Rumstick waved his arm and continued to drag the sheep

down to the water's edge, and Biddlecomb returned to what he had been doing, which was nothing at all.

"Who in the hell is that?" Captain Stanton called down from the quarterdeck of the *Providence* to the boat alongside. It was June and Isaac Biddlecomb had turned thirteen years old. For five months the *Providence* had laid at anchor in Halifax, waiting for the fleet to assemble and for the ice to go out, and now, finally, the assembled transports and ships of the British navy were well into the theater of operations. They had sailed as a convoy, not for the open ocean but for the wide, fast-moving St. Lawrence River, bound away for Quebec.

"Frenchy pilot," the midshipman in the boat called back. "The lead ships ran up Frenchy colors and tricked a covey of them into coming out. We're setting one aboard each ship to bring them through the channel up ahead."

Stanton gave a short, mirthless laugh. "I'll be damned if any Frenchman'll give orders aboard my ship. You can have him back for one of your men-of-war."

"The channel's quite treacherous, you know. This fellow says the French won't risk anything above one hundred tons displacement through there."

"Well, bully for the French," replied Stanton, turning his back on the midshipman and closing the argument.

The river was over a mile wide at that point, and the impenetrable forest came right up to the edge of the steep banks on the north and south shore. And on that river there were more ships than Isaac had ever seen in one place. The British navy was represented by twenty-nine ships of the line, twelve frigates, and two bomb vessels. Sandwiched between squadrons of the navy were the transports, eighty in all, carrying between them almost nine thousand soldiers. From the *Providence*'s main truck Isaac could see several miles of river in either direction, but he could still not see the beginning or end of the attacking fleet.

The water was breaking white over sunken hazards to larboard and starboard as the ships pushed their way southwest through the Île d'Orléans traverse, the last hazard before reaching Quebec. Once through the treacherous channel the transports anchored in a close-packed group on the south shore of the Isle of Orleans, away from the guns of the enemy, and began discharging their martial cargo. Brilliant red-coated soldiers, blue-coated artillery officers, horses, and cannon streamed ashore until the brown, tilled fields of the island opposite Quebec were alive with men, and tents sprouted like the summer's corn.

The siege of Quebec had an aura of excitement, a pervasive atmosphere of many important things happening at once. The great invading army moved with surprising efficiency. Isaac saw General Wolfe one afternoon as the commanding officer was rowed around the transports. Those last days of June in 1759 had about them the spirit of some great event in the offing, and only the sailors, swaying out equipment from the holds and ferrying men ashore, looked upon the "tin soldiers" with amused disdain.

Not all the troops, however, reacted like machines to shouted orders. In addition to the British regulars and the Royal Americans there were the Ranger units, men who had fought with Rogers, and Gorham's Rangers. They were humorless men, men more at home in the woods than in the encampment, men who did not shy away from the most brutal aspects of warfare. Accustomed to a short chain of command, they were not given to taking orders from officers who had not earned their loyalty through hard use. Isaac saw the respect with which his father's unit was treated. Officers did not shout at the men in the blue broadcloth coats the way they shouted at the regulars, and even the sailors displayed a certain diffidence in the Rangers' presence.

"Isaac, let me show you the lay of the land here," his father said after breakfast. It was the first day of July and the morning was already warm.

"Let's go aloft, where we can really see," Isaac said, pointing to the main topgallant mast. He had hoped, in the way of thirteen-year-old boys, to discomfort his father, but his father would not give him the satisfaction.

"All right, Son, you lead." They clambered into the main shrouds.

Though denied the pleasure of his father's refusal to follow him aloft, Isaac at least had the pleasure of admonishing the old man for holding on to the ratlines rather than the shrouds, and the pleasure of beating him to the topmast crosstrees by more than a minute.

He was seated on the crosstrees in a feigned attitude of relaxation when his father pulled himself over the futtock shrouds. John Biddlecomb moved slowly through the unfamiliar rig, but the climb of nearly one hundred feet had not caused him the least difficulty, nor was he breathing any harder than he had when standing on deck.

He found his footing and looked around. "My God, this is a famous view. I had no notion you could see so far from here. I can see the chief of the enemy's defensive works."

Isaac was also taken by the vista spread out below them. The deep green forest, reaching to the horizon in any direction, was cut in two by the wide St. Lawrence. The river as well continued unbroken until it could no longer be seen, a deep blue band the color of the navy officers' uniforms, picked out here and there with white flashes of turbulent water. The lighter blue of the sky formed a dome over the entire scene. Below and to their right the British forces were deploying on the Isle of Orleans, the uniforms and tents and artillery making points of bright color among the browns and greens.

His father stood in silence for a moment and surveyed the scene. "Let me show you how things lay. You see that high banking on the river there?" He pointed to the north shore of the St. Lawrence. Mud flats poked through the surface of the water revealing the shallows that ran up to the steep banking. "The French have entrenched all along there, from the St. Charles River there"—he pointed to the mouth of a river broad on the larboard bow—"to the Montmorency there." The second river was broad on the starboard bow. The French entrenchments were almost six miles long.

"That would be a hard place to attack, with the shallow water and mud and all." Isaac pieced together his opinion from the bits of military knowledge he had picked up from the Rangers' conversations. "And any frontal attack'd be exposed to enemy fire all the while."

"Good, very good. We'll make a soldier out of you yet," his father said, slapping his son on the back. "And you see how their right and left flanks are anchored down to rivers? It would be impossible to turn them."

They stood for a moment, taking in the scene and thinking of the deadly struggle that would soon take place on that peaceful landscape. "Quebec's there, you can just see it over the high ground on Point Levis." His father pointed over the larboard side. Across the channel in which the *Providence* was anchored, the mainland jutted far out into the river, terminating in a high ridge that looked down on the St. Lawrence. Along the river at the base of the ridge and huddled together as if shrinking from a rising tide, were the many buildings that made up the city of Quebec. Larger buildings, including high-spired churches, were spread out along the high ground. "Do you see the walls of the Citadel there, just over the ridge?"

Thrusting up above the trees was the Citadel of Quebec. Isaac could see the gray walls and the high roofs of a dozen buildings, seeming to rise out of the deep forest. It looked magnificent, impregnable. "Damn me," he said without thinking. He looked up at his father, expecting an admonishment for his sailor's language, but his father was staring at the distant fortifications and seemed lost in his own thoughts.

"You can't see the half of it from here," he said at last. "I've been past it on the river; it's unassailable from this side. And on the landward side, across the Plains of Abraham, well, it's pretty much unassailable from there too. Unless the French come out and fight on open ground, which they won't if they're smart."

"So how will General Wolfe ever take it?"

"We'll take the heights there on Point Levis and put artillery across the river from the city." His father indicated with a sweep of his hand the high wooded ground between the *Providence* and the city of Quebec. "From there we'll pound them into rubbish if we must. We go over tomorrow." His father looked at him, a half smile on his lips. "Gorham's Rangers are the first in."

Isaac's eyes went wide, and he felt his stomach convulse. Up until that point the siege had been an amusement, like a camping trip with thousands of men and a million different and exciting diversions. It had not really occurred to him that the soldiers might have to fight. Might have to die. That his father was one of those soldiers.

He flung his arms around his father's waist, forcing John to grab for the topgallant shrouds to steady himself. "No, Papa! Why?" he asked, the words muffled as he buried his face in his father's coat.

"Come on now, Isaac. You know why. I'm a Ranger." He gently pushed his son away until they were looking into each other's eyes. "Look, I was just running away when I joined up with the Rangers again, I've smoked that now, and I think you knew it all along. I had no call dragging you clear up to Quebec. But I'm here now and I've got my duty. I can't back out. When this is over, I'll resign again, and we'll go back to the farm, you and me."

"Why can't you resign now? Just tell 'em you're sick, or something. Why can't we go back to the farm now?"

"This is important, what we're fighting for, Isaac, and I can't just let my friends do it all and me not help. You know that. Sometimes a cause is more important than the life of one man."

For the first time since leaving Bristol, Isaac began to cry. He hugged his father tighter. "But, Papa, what if . . . something happens?"

"There's nothing to worry about, the point's not defended by above a thousand riflemen and Indians. I've been in worse, much worse." Once again he pried his son away until he was looking into his eyes. "I'll come back."

* * *

Biddlecomb was looking aft now, at the *Rose*'s topgallants, visible without a telescope but growing more distant as the *Charlemagne* made her easy escape down the bay, crowding on sail. "I'll come back . . . ," he thought. His father had come back all right. He had come back carried between two of his fellow Rangers, a hole the size of a shilling in his chest where the rifle ball had struck.

His father had been right about one thing. The resistance on Point Levis had been minimal; fewer than thirty of the attackers had been killed. But John Biddlecomb was one of them. He lay on the cot in the hospital choking up blood and cradled in his son's arms for three hours before he died. If he was conscious during that time, no one ever knew. He never said a word.

A week later Captain Stanton signed Isaac on to the ship's company as an apprentice seaman. It was another two years before he knew any home other than the *Providence*.

Now, he turned and looked forward, down the neat rows of guns to starboard and larboard. The deck was crowded with terrified livestock, bleating, mooing, and defecating on the scrubbed planking. "You were the military man, Father, you were the hero. Not me," he said softly.

"Beg pardon, Captain, what was that?" asked Rumstick, standing near him on the quarterdeck.

Biddlecomb looked up in surprise. He did not realize he had spoken out loud. "What was it, Ezra, that the soldier says to King Harry? 'I am afeard there are few die well that die in battle. . . . Now if these men do not die well, it will be a black matter for the king that led them to it.' "

"I don't know what you mean, Isaac, but I reckon you ain't been elected king yet."

"It's Shakespeare. *Henry V*. The old man knew what he was talking about." Isaac looked back at the livestock, summoning the courage to tell Rumstick of the course to which he was now resolved.

"I've quite had it, Ezra." This was the end. He had loaded his last cow, he had fled for the last time from the *Rose*. He would not let his career atrophy this way. He would not continue to pretend he was a naval officer when he was nothing of the kind and could not be. His father was the fighting man, and Biddlecomb had seen in Quebec what that had got him. An anonymous, penniless death. "I don't believe Stanton has any intention of setting up to privateering, and I have no intention of continuing with this absurd Rhode Island navy charade. I can lead men at sea, but I cannot lead them to their slaughter. The next time I speak with William, I intend to resign my command."

CHAPTER
5

The Article of Powder

MAJOR FITZGERALD AND GENERAL WASHINGTON WERE HALFWAY BE-
tween Roxbury and Cambridge when they heard the musket
fire on their right. They wheeled their horses to a stop, throwing up great clouds of dust from the dry road, and stared
down the hillside toward the American lines. The brown earthworks made just enough contrast with the grass and scrubby
brush to be visible three-quarters of a mile away. The American Line was right at the water's edge, at the point where the
muddy Charles River widened into the pea green water of
Boston Harbor's Back Bay.

The two men sat in silence and listened. Two more muskets
went off in rapid succession, followed by a third. Then it was
quiet again.

"What in the hell do they think they're shooting at?" Washington asked.

"Rabbits, perhaps. Or squirrels," Fitzgerald suggested.

"I should be happier if that were the case, but you know as
well as I do that the idiots are shooting at the British lines.
Without the slightest hope of hitting anything." Washington
prodded his horse's flank with his heel and Fitzgerald did
likewise to his mount.

The two men rode the next half mile in silence. They were
alone, their only accompaniment the buzzing of the insects in
the surrounding fields. The sound seemed to make the warm

morning air feel warmer still. "The troops here are quite insensible to our crisis in the article of powder," Washington began. "How many orders must I give before they'll stop wasting it?" Since Palmer's revelation of a week before the subject was always foremost on the general's mind.

"There's no way to convey to them the seriousness of the situation without alerting the enemy as well. They have too much intercourse with the people in Boston. Even with the enemy pickets. Too much by half."

"Of course you're right. God save us from amateur soldiers." The general was silent for a moment, then said, "I'll issue yet another general order concerning the use of powder. I'd better include some kind of threat this time, though it's beyond me why I must threaten my own troops just to get them to do the sensible thing. Here, write this down."

Fitzgerald fished out paper and pencil as the general began his dictation. "It is with indignation and shame," Washington said in the tone of voice he reserved for dictating general orders, "that not withstanding the repeated orders which have been given to prevent the firing of guns in and about the camps, that it is daily and hourly practiced, and that soldiers are firing at a distance where there is not the least probability of hurting the enemy."

Washington paused as Fitzgerald finished scribbling the words. "Make a note there that the commanding officer of each regiment is to see his men acquainted with these orders," Washington continued. "I think perhaps we should order every man's ammunition examined at evening roll call, and anyone found deficient be confined. Just note that down, we'll work out the wording back at headquarters."

Fitzgerald finished writing and stuffed the pencil and paper back in his pocket.

The two officers continued on. The Charles River came into sight, running roughly parallel to the road, the water moving sluggishly toward the harbor. Nothing seemed to move fast on those humid summer days.

Fitzgerald gave his horse a nudge with his heel and drew

up next to the commander in chief. "Sir, there's a thing that's been troubling me . . ." He faltered, uncertain of how to present his thoughts to the general.

"Please, Major. I'm always interested in your opinions."

"Well, sir, it's this powder situation. We've discussed the possible consequences of the British finding out how little we have. Now, as long as the only stories going around are vague rumors, I think we need not worry." Fitzgerald paused. This was the difficult part. "It's that idiot they call a quartermaster general. Palmer. If the British get intelligence from a highly placed officer like Palmer . . . God knows what kind of infernal tool he is. I shouldn't be surprised if he's passing it all on to the British, either through duplicity or stupidity."

Having thus committed himself, Fitzgerald sat like a statue in his saddle and waited as Washington considered the implications. "You could well be right, Major," the general said at last. "I have my concerns about him as well, though I doubt we'd ever find enough evidence to court-martial him. He'll be replaced as soon as I receive word from Philadelphia. But you know that."

"Yes, sir," Fitzgerald said, relieved that the commander in chief was not upset about his challenging the loyalty of a superior. "But if we do get evidence, then that would suggest that it's too late, that he's already passed information to the enemy. Of course we can't lock him up beforehand. However, there may be a more . . . immediate solution, sir."

Washington reined his horse to a stop and Fitzgerald stopped as well. "What do you have in mind, Major?"

"I have in mind to dispatch him, sir," Fitzgerald said boldly, committing himself. "I could easily contrive to have him insult me, sir, in public, before witnesses. I could call him out and kill him. Swords or pistols, either way. It's been done before," he added in a lower tone.

Washington stared into Fitzgerald's eyes. The major sat rigid in his saddle and held his commander's gaze, bracing himself for whatever reaction might come, satisfied that his suggestion was at least worthy of consideration.

"Major, if I had just one grand division of men with your zeal and dedication to this enterprise, we should see the ministerial army out of Boston by next week. Unfortunately, I don't see Palmer as the dueling sort, and in all fairness we need more proof than an uncomfortable feeling before we kill the man." Washington wheeled his horse around and continued on toward his headquarters in Cambridge. "However, I don't dismiss your plan altogether."

The stableboy was waiting to take the horses when the two men finally arrived at their headquarters. Just a week before, Washington had moved his operations from the relatively cramped Langdon House to the luxurious mansion of John Vassall, a loyalist who had fled Cambridge for the protection of the ministerial army in Boston. Fitzgerald could feel the dust from the road clinging to his skin and chaffing under his uniform as he and Washington strode down the hall to the general's office. He longed to strip his clothes off and pour buckets of cold water over his head.

"Tell me, Major, what do you hear from your spies in Gage's camp?" Among Fitzgerald's duties was the gathering of information that flowed from Boston. People who worked and lived close by the British army—tradesmen, clerks, chambermaids, even American wives of British soldiers—all had access to important information, and they passed that information on to Fitzgerald.

"Little this week, sir, save for the ongoing shortage of fresh food. Morale in the ministerial army is low and getting lower; many of the soldiers apparently have to take second jobs at night to earn their living. And incidentally, General," he added, smiling, "we don't call those people spies, we call them patriots."

"A subtle distinction, indeed," Washington said, stepping into his office.

A dozen men were sitting in the chairs that lined the hall, waiting for an audience with the commander in chief. "The general will see you shortly," Fitzgerald reassured them, then shut the door and took his place at the big table that served as Washington's desk. He arranged his quill holder and sander and inkpot and a fresh supply of paper while the general sorted through the various documents piled before him. It was their daily routine and had continued uninterrupted, seven days a week, since their arrival in Cambridge.

"As you can imagine," Washington began when all was settled, "I have been giving a great deal of thought to the situation concerning the article of powder. I've heard a number of propositions on the subject, but there's one here that has some weight with me, as well as with the general officers to whom I've proposed it." He pulled a letter out of the stack and laid it on the desk in front of him. "This is from Nicholas Cooke in Rhode Island."

"Acting governor now, is he not?"

"Just so. I've had a great deal of correspondence with him, as you know. A good man, much given to the American cause. He points out that on the island of Bermuda there's a sizable cache of gunpowder. It's lightly guarded; the British don't see a threat to it. Cooke suggests dispatching an armed vessel to the island and taking the powder by force. What are your thoughts, Major?"

"Where does Governor Cooke propose we get an armed vessel?"

"He's spelled it all out here," said Washington, pointing to the letter. "Rhode Island apparently has a navy of sorts, two vessels. Cooke and a few others have been discussing this. Metcalf Bowler, the Speaker of the House of Representatives, and a man by the name of William Stanton are taking the lead in this matter."

Washington handed the letter to Fitzgerald, who quickly read through it. "This seems well thought out, sir," Fitzgerald said when he had finished. "Cooke and his people seem to think the citizens of Bermuda will be disposed to help us. Do you feel the same?"

"If they won't become principals in the enterprise, I believe at least they'll acquiesce in the measure. In any event I could write a letter to the citizens of the island to rally them to our cause. I'll instruct that it be used as a last resort."

Fitzgerald looked over Cooke's letter once more, considering the plan as it was laid out there. "It seems quite feasible to me. No extraordinary risk and the possible rewards are great. And as they seem to be offering their ship and their services for free, Congress should be delighted."

"That was my thinking. We'll draft the orders and the letter to the people of Bermuda, then I need you to deliver them in person to Governor Cooke. This is too important by far to trust to the mails."

"Of course, sir." Then another thought occurred to Fitzgerald. "There needs just the right man to command on this mission."

"Ah, to that end they have made a suggestion as well." Washington handed another letter to Fitzgerald. "This came with the governor's letter. It's from William Stanton, the fellow I mentioned. He has the governor's utmost confidence."

Fitzgerald took the letter. It had been sealed with a great wad of red wax, into which was pressed a seal bearing the motif of a fouled anchor. He began to read.

William Stanton, Esq.
Stanton House
Bristol, Rhode Island

General Washington,

I would like to bring to your attention the name of a master currently in my employ, a man of known activity and spirit, whom I would recommend for commission as Captain of the Army of the United Colonies in order that he might take command as an official representative of the Continental Army of the brig *Charlemagne* on her proposed cruise to Bermuda. His name is Captain Isaac Biddlecomb . . .

CHAPTER
6

Virginia Stanton

FOR TWO DAYS THE *CHARLEMAGNE* AND THE *KATY* LAY AT ANCHOR far up the Providence River, just south of Sabin Point, less than one hundred yards from shore in water too shallow for a frigate to navigate. From the bow of each vessel a heavy anchor cable ran forward and disappeared into the blue water. From their aftermost gunports a spring line ran along each ship's side and was in turn attached to that ship's anchor cable. Hauling on the spring lines would make the ships swing at anchor and allow them to present a broadside to a threat from any direction. At night the men slept at quarters, and guard boats patrolled the water, their crews straining to hear any sound that would alert them to a cutting-out expedition.

They could see the *Rose* during the daylight hours, tacking back and forth in the deeper water farther south. She reminded Biddlecomb of a frustrated hound, running in circles around a hole down which a rabbit has disappeared. But until the frigate gave up her vigil or was called away on other business, there was little that the Rhode Island navy could do, beyond wait. There was little that Biddlecomb hated more than waiting.

He stood on the quarterdeck, his arms folded across his chest, his dark blue coat and cocked hat flung carelessly over the binnacle box. It was hot and becoming hotter still. His collar was open and he had long since dispensed with his neck cloth. He considered, for the fifth time that morning, packing his gear,

61

going ashore, and giving his resignation. But if he did so, he would have to endure Rumstick's protests and disapproval until he was clear of the brig, and he did not feel up to that. He would have to wait until he was summoned to Stanton House.

Two hundred yards upriver a small fishing smack tacked smartly and settled on a course that brought it alongside the *Katy's* larboard side. He watched the skipper hold the tiller with his knee and lower the gaff away as his one-man crew let the jib sheet fly. The boat came up into the wind and eased against the fenders that the *Katy's* crew had let down. She was as innocent looking a vessel as one could find on Narragansett Bay, but Biddlecomb knew she carried dispatches to Commodore Whipple from the Rhode Island Committee of Safety.

He hated that name, Committee of Safety. Safety for whom? Certainly not the men who were expected to go up against the *Rose*.

Rumstick stepped up to the quarterdeck and saluted. He was not smiling. "Reckon we'll clear for action and drill with the guns after lunch, Captain."

"As you wish."

It had not been a good day thus far, starting at sunrise when Biddlecomb had woken in his sweltering cabin with a pounding head and a taste in his mouth like copper pennies. His dreams had been among the worst yet: vague and bloody images, gunfire and men screaming, and then he himself screaming. He had come to with a start and lay in his cot, listening, wondering if he had actually screamed out loud. There were no footsteps overhead, no sound of the anchor watch pacing the deck. Had they stopped short at the sound of his bloodcurdling cry? What kind of a madman did they think he was, screaming like a lunatic?

A half a pot of steaming coffee had gone far toward restoring him to sociability, and he was almost prepared to be civil when Rumstick had knocked and entered.

"Morning, Isaac," he said, making a rhumb line to the coffeepot and pouring a mugful. On a good morning Biddlecomb found

Rumstick's energy uplifting. On a bad morning it was annoying in direct proportion to the foulness of Isaac's mood.

Had Rumstick been any other first officer, Isaac might have invited him to breakfast once a week if he did not much like him, two or three times if he did. He would certainly not have invited him on that morning.

But Rumstick was far from any other first officer. They had met fifteen years ago, when Biddlecomb was in his second year as an apprentice aboard the *Providence* and Rumstick had signed aboard as an ordinary seaman.

They were just boys then, the youngest in the merchantman's crew, and together they mastered the intricacies of ships and the sea, mastered drinking and whoring in distant ports, mastered the Darwinian life in a forecastle. Three years later they left the *Providence* and shipped out together aboard the *Lucy Stanton*, both rated able-bodied. A year after that, when Biddlecomb was promoted to third mate over the heads of many more experienced men, Rumstick included, his friend was the only one in the forecastle to greet the promotion with enthusiasm and goodwill.

Rumstick had had two fights that voyage. On the first occasion he had fought with an older seaman, the cock of the forecastle, and he had beaten him half to death. The second fight was with the same man and a younger sycophant, and though Rumstick had not fared as well—he had had his nose and several ribs broken—he ultimately doled out as much punishment to the two men as he had to the one. Biddlecomb never knew for certain, but he long suspected that the fights had been over questions of his own competence as third mate.

For most of their lives at sea they had sailed together, Rumstick eventually as boatswain, Biddlecomb as third mate, then second mate, then first and captain. Rumstick seemed to have an unwavering and, in Biddlecomb's opinion, wholly unrealistic regard for his friend's abilities.

It was because of this history, and this friendship, that Isaac now gave Rumstick a standing invitation to breakfast. And it was because of this that Rumstick could not, while in the privacy of the great cabin, be silenced like any normal subordinate.

His monologue, uninterrupted since he'd entered the cabin, continued on, something about the lead of the throat halyard, and Biddlecomb grunted at the appropriate places, swilling coffee as quickly as he could. It had been two days since he'd told the first officer that he was going to resign his command. Since then Rumstick had chosen to ignore that statement, and Isaac had not had the courage to repeat it. But that could not go on.

At last breakfast was brought in: eggs, ham, toasted bread, and butter and jam, fresh food being one of the advantages of remaining on Narragansett Bay.

With his hunger sated Biddlecomb grew more willing to speak, even if his mood had not greatly improved. Rumstick moved on to his thoughts on recaulking the quarterdeck, and Biddlecomb marveled at how Rumstick could be at times so garrulous and at others so taciturn.

He knew this man so well, respected him, and counted on his friendship. That was why he owed him an explanation of the course of action to which he was resolved, and why it was so difficult to give him one.

"Right under the binnacle box is the chief of the problem," Rumstick was saying. "I reckon—"

"Ezra," Biddlecomb cut him off. "I was quite serious when I said I was leaving the *Charlemagne*. Do you understand? There's no call to tell me about the maintenance needed, I'll be gone within the week."

Rumstick stopped talking and leaned back in his chair. In the absence of his voice, which seemed like cannon fire in the small cabin, it was very quiet indeed.

"This should not be a surprise, Ezra. I said as much the other day."

"Well, yes, you did. I reckoned you was just saying it."

"When do I ever just say something I don't mean?" Biddlecomb asked, then to deny Rumstick the opportunity to answer the question added, "I was quite serious. I cannot continue on this way. I signed on to command a privateer, but it's clear now that Stanton has no intention of sending the *Charlemagne* out on that mission."

"Privateer? What the hell good is a privateer?"

"What the hell good is running a cattle ferry? Risking men's lives to get sheep safely to Block Island?"

"We're denying supplies to the enemy," Rumstick said, holding up his hand to stop Biddlecomb's objection, "and don't say they ain't the enemy. It's not just talk now. There's been bloodletting, at Lexington and Concord and Bunker Hill. General Washington's got the Continental Army holding the ministerial army up in Boston. Ethan Allen and his men have taken Fort Ticonderoga. What in God's name more do you need before you see it's time to choose sides?"

Biddlecomb threw his napkin on the table and stared out the stern window at the wooded shoreline. This was the only subject that he knew of that could make his friend this angry. "I don't have to choose sides, Captain Wallace and his frigate did that for me." He turned and looked Rumstick in the eye. "Why're you so insistent? I'm far from the only sea captain around here that will answer."

"There's things you can do that no one else can," Rumstick said, his tone calm and reasonable, his anger held at bay. "It's what made you the best merchant captain in Rhode Island. Sure there are others that are as good seamen as you, some maybe better, but there's none that's as clever. I've seen it a hundred times. That time in Jamaica, with the customs man. Or the way you used to trick Glacous in your molasses deals in Barbados. And the way you led the mutiny on the *Icarus* and held that bunch together all the way back here. It's brains we need now. We're fighting for our lives."

Now, two hours later, Isaac clasped his hands behind his back and stared across the water at the *Katy*, considering again that conversation. He was the only man he knew of, disposed to the American cause, who had commanded a man-of-war, if a king's ship in a state of mutiny could still be called that. And he had led them in combat, an experience no one else in

Rhode Island, possibly in all the colonies, shared, save for those who had gone privateering in the last French war. He had led them in combat, led them to their deaths. As tortured as he was by the thought of resigning his command, that memory still tortured him more.

"I'm sorry, Ezra. I'm not a man-of-war's man," he had said in final response to Rumstick's angry questions.

"What the hell is it?" Rumstick asked.

Biddlecomb wondered if their friendship would be another casualty of these hostilities. "It's personal."

"Are you afraid, is that it? Are you afraid of being killed?"

He had been startled by this suggestion. He had never really thought of his own death. He did not want to die, but fear of his own death was not what fueled this. "No, I'm not afraid to die, no more than any sane man."

"Then what is it?" Rumstick was insistent.

"You want to know? Fine, Ezra, I'll tell you. I have enough damned blood on my hands. Wilson's blood and the *Icarus*'s bosun, what was his name, McDuff and the rest. I as good as killed them all. I don't mind killing an enemy, I've found, particularly when they're trying to kill me, but I can't and won't lead any more men to the slaughter."

Rumstick was silent for a moment, surprised, apparently, by this unexpected announcement. "They went of their own accord, Isaac," he said at last, the argument that Biddlecomb had expected. "Just like this lot here."

"This lot here volunteered because they don't know what it's like. They don't know . . ." Images from that night when the *Rose* beat the *Icarus* to death floated in his head, and he felt the sweat bead up on his forehead.

"Signal from the flag!" Weatherspoon said, jarring Biddlecomb from his memories. "Captain to repair on board!"

He looked across the narrow stretch of water that separated the two American ships. "Why in the hell must he use those infernal flags? He could yell across just as easily."

"I don't know, sir."

"Turn out the boat's crew, Mr. Rumstick."

"Aye, sir," Rumstick said, failing for once to salute, and stamped off forward. They had not reached any satisfactory conclusion that morning. If Rumstick understood at all how Isaac felt, he had not let on, had not yielded an inch in his determination that Isaac should stay. But he knew he could not and told Rumstick as much, and since then the first officer had been seething with anger and frustration. If this decision meant the end of their friendship, and Biddlecomb feared it might, then he would grieve for that, but so it had to be.

The crew of the *Charlemagne*'s gig scrambled down the side and into the boat, already in the water. Weatherspoon followed, then Biddlecomb, and with a word they were under way.

The boat pulled around the stern of the fishing smack and the *Katy*, and Weatherspoon at the tiller steered for the boarding steps in the sloop's starboard side. Biddlecomb ran a professional eye over the little man-of-war, noting her condition, trying to drive his friend's anger from his thoughts.

The *Katy* looked better than he had ever seen her. Whipple had managed to recruit nearly an entire crew of prime seamen, and it showed in the *Katy*'s appearance. He thought of his own crew, at least half of whom were farmers or clerks. He had made precious little effort to turn them into seamen, he realized with a twinge of guilt.

"Toss oars!" Weatherspoon called, and the four oars that propelled the boat came up in ragged order and the bowman grabbed on to the *Katy*'s chains with the boat hook.

Biddlecomb took hold of the boarding steps and stepped onto the second rung. His face was a foot above the deck; he was staring at Whipple's heavy calves stuffed into white wool stockings when the sailors manning the side burst forth in a discordant shriek of bosun's calls in what was meant to be a salute to the captain coming aboard. He hurried up the three steps; setting foot on deck was the only way to make the cursed noise stop.

"Captain, Captain, welcome aboard!" The portly commodore's greeting was effusive. Despite the heat Whipple was missing not one part of what he considered to be his uniform. This included his coat and waistcoat, with the ruffles of his shirt peeking out from under his heavy chin and his neck cloth all but lost from sight. His sword with its intricate brass hilt and pommel hung at his side. Biddlecomb shook Whipple's proffered hand.

"Captain Biddlecomb, this here's Captain Walpole," Whipple continued, taking the skipper of the fishing smack by the arm and pulling him forward. Walpole was young, perhaps twenty, and dressed in loose trousers and a plain shirt and waistcoat, his sleeves rolled up, a cocked hat on his head.

"Captain Biddlecomb, it's an honor, sir," Walpole said, doing his best to snap to crisp attention and elegantly sweep his hat off in salute. Biddlecomb did not return the salute; rather, he extended his hand, which, after a second's confusion, Walpole shook.

"It's a pleasure to meet you, Captain Walpole. And thank you for your good work."

"Oh, hell, sir, my good work ain't nothing against what you done, that British brig, sir, and all—"

"Indeed, thank you, sir," Biddlecomb cut the young patriot off. He could not bear being the object of hero worship at that moment. The last thing he felt like was a hero.

"Well, Biddlecomb, I'd like to invite you below for a glass, but there ain't time," Whipple continued. "Captain Walpole brung me a note from Captain Stanton, and he requests your presence at a meeting at his house as soon as is convenient. And as you know, when the gentlemen say that, it means now, and no tarrying about. He says there's no need to pack a bag, you won't be ashore long."

"Humph," Biddlecomb replied. He was going to meet with Stanton. He wanted to pack, wanted to take everything, but he couldn't now, not without admitting to Whipple that he was going to resign, and he did not have the courage to do that. "Have you any idea what it's about?"

"None. But I hope it don't mean I'm going to lose you to some other mission."

"Well, nothing in this world is permanent, sir."

"Amen to that. Now, Captain Walpole here has orders to convey you to Bristol. You'd best be under way. You can leave instructions for Rumstick with your midshipman."

Biddlecomb leaned over the bulwark and looked down at Weatherspoon in the boat. After he resigned his command, he could not return to the *Charlemagne*, he knew that. It would be intolerable. He would get word to Rumstick to send ashore the few personal possessions he had left in the great cabin. The few that had not been destroyed by the *Diana*.

"Mr. Weatherspoon, I'll be going ashore in the fishing smack. I'll be meeting with Captain Stanton. Tell Mr. Rumstick that I don't know when I'll return and he's to carry on. He'll understand."

Weatherspoon nodded. "Aye, sir." The midshipman idolized Biddlecomb, as a boy might an older brother. He did not know if he would see Weatherspoon again. The young man deserved some kind words, some encouragement or thanks for his good service.

"Very good, Mr. Weatherspoon. Carry on," he said, cursing himself for his cowardice.

"Now, sir," Walpole said, "I'll precede you into the boat, as is proper with you being senior officer." The smell of old fish, accentuated by the hot sun, wafted up from the smack. Biddlecomb wondered where Walpole and Whipple had picked up so much naval etiquette.

He turned to Whipple and again extended his hand. "Thank you, sir, for everything," he said, pumping the commodore's hand.

"Er, you're welcome, I'm sure, Biddlecomb. I fancy I'll see you again by nightfall."

"Indeed. Good-bye, sir," he said, and followed Walpole down into the fishing smack.

Major Fitzgerald was certain that he had found the right house. He reined his horse to a stop on the fine trimmed lawn that covered at least an acre and looked up at the house that sat in the center of that lawn. It was three stories tall and the same white clapboard construction with dark green shutters that he had come to associate with all houses in New England. On the gravel-covered drive in front of the porch stood two coaches. Those parts of their polished surfaces that were not coated with a fine dust from the roads glinted in the afternoon sun. The horses stood in their traces, contenting themselves with feed bags as the liverymen brushed them down. This had to be Stanton House.

"Are you a tourist, sir, or have you business here?" Fitzgerald heard a woman's voice behind him and almost leapt in surprise. He twisted around in his saddle and turned his horse to face the newcomer.

She was beautiful, and she was riding a tall chestnut horse, a noble animal. His eyes moved from woman to horse and back again, and uncertain of which was more worthy of comment, he said nothing.

And then the woman laughed, a happy, humorous, and slightly mocking laugh. She tossed her head back, and her long hair, nearly the same chestnut color as her horse and bursting out from under a riding hat, tumbled over her shoulders and a wisp fell across her face. She was not riding a sidesaddle. "Are you struck dumb, sir?" she asked, brushing the hair from her face. "Is it my beauty or that of my horse that has rendered you thus?" She was still smiling, flashing white teeth, a transfixing smile.

"I beg your pardon, ma'am." Fitzgerald knew he was blushing and that annoyed him. He was generally not awkward around women, quite the opposite in fact. He removed his hat and bowed in his saddle. "It's rare indeed that one is greeted by such beauty all at once. It's a bit staggering."

The woman regarded him curiously, and Fitzgerald saw her run her eyes over his uniform. "You're no Yankee, sir, you are too charming by half for that. Might I ask your business?"

"Please forgive me, ma'am. I am Maj. Edward Fitzgerald of General Washington's staff."

"General Washington's staff. I am impressed," the woman

said in her half-kind, half-mocking tone. In another woman it might have been annoying, but in this woman, with her slightly sunburned cheeks and their smattering of freckles, her slender body perched with great authority on that fine horse, Fitzgerald found it most seductive indeed. "I'm a great supporter of the American cause, sir, and the fight for independence." Now there was nothing flip in her tone. "You have my thanks for your good work toward that effort."

"Thank you, ma'am." Fitzgerald wondered if she would be so impressed if she knew he had never yet fired a shot in that fight. "And might I ask your name?"

"I'm Virginia Stanton."

Virginia Stanton? Fitzgerald thought. William Stanton's daughter, or his wife?

"I'm William Stanton's daughter. I take it you're here for this meeting?"

"I am. That's a fine animal you have." He nodded toward the horse. He was trying to make conversation. He did not want to leave this woman's company.

"Thank you, Major. We've had him since he was a yearling, which was some time ago. I still like to give him a run now and again. He does excellent work as a stud." Fitzgerald was certain he heard a playful, even flirtatious note in her voice.

"It's good work to have," he replied, and gave Virginia just a hint of a smile. "Is he much troubled by that hock?" He could see the animal shying away just slightly from his left rear leg.

"He is a bit and has been this past year or so. You know a great deal about horses, sir."

"Horses are a passion with me, ma'am."

"And with me as well. I've used a hot mustard compress to some effect, but when the weather's cold, there's little I can do."

"There's little to be done when they get on in years. This is a fine estate your father has. Perhaps we could go for a ride? I've had little chance to enjoy New England."

Virginia smiled again and wheeled her horse around. "I'm

71

sorry, Major, but your duty calls and I have someone to meet." She paused and held his eyes in hers. "Good-bye," she said, and with a nudge of her heels the chestnut horse broke into a trot, then canter, heading off across the lawn toward the stables. Virginia rode with an ease and confidence that, in Fitzgerald's experience, few men could match. She was an extraordinary woman, absolutely extraordinary.

They ran south along the shore, Walpole keeping the shallow-draft smack a half a cable from the wooded bank. That close, they were surrounded by the ubiquitous smell of the pine trees and the call of the birds hiding there, as if they were walking through the woods rather than sailing past them. Soon the *Charlemagne* was far astern and the North Point of Popasquash Neck loomed ahead.

"Captain Stanton reckoned it'd be quicker to set you ashore here, sir," Walpole explained. "There'll be a horse waiting." He pushed the tiller over and the smack rounded up into the wind. The deckhand tossed the anchor over the bow and paid out the line as the smack gathered sternway, easing the boat up close enough to the rocky point for Biddlecomb to step ashore.

"Very neatly done, Captain. Thank you," he said, concentrating more on his footing than his words.

"My pleasure, Captain. It's an honor." Walpole saluted and Biddlecomb in turn waved good-bye, then made his way ashore.

He stepped over the rocks and onto a dirt road that disappeared into the shadows of the pine forest. He could hear the horses and imagined that Stanton's stable boy was waiting just out of sight. He frowned. He hated horses, and with the little riding he had done he could never feel comfortable on one. He wondered if Stanton had sent the horse just to annoy him, as a kind of practical joke. It was only a mile to the house.

He stepped into the shadow of the road, and to his surprise he saw not the stable boy but Virginia Stanton holding the reins of the mounts.

"Virginia! This is a surprise," he said, feeling suddenly foolish. Was that a stupid thing to say?

"Welcome home, Isaac." She smiled, her teeth brilliant.

"I, ah, had reckoned on the stableboy."

Virginia cocked her head and gave him a coy look. "So did Daddy, but it was such a fine day I decided to come myself. Besides, I can never resist seeing the great Captain Biddlecomb conning a horse. 'Conning' is what you sailors do, is it not?"

"Among other things. So, in faith, you've come to amuse yourself with my discomfiture."

"Never in life, Isaac," she said in a perfect imitation of sincerity. Biddlecomb loved talking to her. It was exciting to him in a way that few things were, far more exciting than any of the other women he had known in most of the ports touched by the Atlantic Ocean. It was exhilarating, like tricking an otherwise savvy merchant into a deal that was greatly to his own advantage.

"Here's your horse," Virginia said, passing the reins to Biddlecomb, who took them in his uncertain grip. "I brought Pallada for you. She'll be gentle." She was enjoying this very much.

He placed his foot with some difficulty into the stirrup and pulled himself up onto the horse. Virginia found her own stirrup and swung herself up into the saddle with a flurry of petticoats. Biddlecomb made a halfhearted attempt to avert his eyes.

"You're not using a sidesaddle," he observed, a bit scandalized but far from surprised. "I think your father wouldn't approve."

"That's because my father has never tried riding with one of those damned things." Virginia pressed her heels into her horse's sides and headed down the road.

Biddlecomb then pressed his heels into Pallada's flanks, though the animal had already started moving without any command from him.

The road soon emerged from the woods and ran into fields of grass and tall corn. The sky above, no longer hidden by the trees, was pale blue, and the horizon was lined with high cumulus clouds. The water of the bay in the distance was a great blue valley between the steep, green islands and the mainland.

He loved the smell of the earth, loved immersing himself in the scene. They rode slowly, and Pallada was as gentle as Virginia had promised, so that he managed to enjoy himself. For a man who had spent the better part of the last sixteen years at sea, the countryside was as refreshing to him as it might be to a city dweller. It reminded him of a happier time.

But more than anything he loved to be with Virginia. Something crackled between them, like Saint Elmo's fire in the rigging.

"I love it here," he said, and turned to Virginia. He reined his horse to a stop and Virginia did likewise. Their eyes met and they smiled at each other, and Biddlecomb knew that he was making the right choice, giving up the *Charlemagne*. It made no difference that there was no merchantman for him to command. He could use some time on the beach. He could use some time to be with Virginia.

"What do you think of this situation in Boston, Isaac?" Virginia asked, nudging her horse into a walk. "I would love to hear your opinion, someone in the fray."

"What situation is that?"

"The siege of Boston? The Army of the United Colonies surrounding the ministerial army in the city?" she prompted, and in answer to his still-confused look added, "The war? Lexington and Concord, Bunker's Hill? You've heard of Bunker's Hill?"

"I've been a bit preoccupied this past month, what with Wallace wanting to hang me and all," he explained, hoping to hide the fact that he had not given the situation sufficient thought even to form an opinion. "And I've had my cattle-ferry service to operate."

Virginia smiled at him. "Of course you have."

Stanton House was in sight now, rising like a great white rock from a sea of grass, the freshly painted clapboard shining brilliantly in the afternoon sun. Crowning the steep roof was a cupola and widow's walk that commanded a view from Bristol Harbor to the far end of Prudence Island. The widow's walk was a sad irony; Stanton's wife had died eleven years ago, leaving the merchant to raise their daughter alone.

"It looks like we're in good company," Biddlecomb observed, nodding his head toward the two coaches and four that stood in the semicircular drive in front of the house.

"Some very important people who have come here to meet with the great Captain Biddlecomb," Virginia teased, and with a flourish wheeled her horse to a stop. Biddlecomb did likewise, though with much less flair.

"Isaac, there's something I want to say . . . while we're alone," she began, her usual bold playfulness deserting her.

Biddlecomb felt himself flush with excitement, felt the soles of his feet tingling. Some confession of love or desire was coming, he knew it.

"I'm . . . I'm so proud of what you're doing for Rhode Island, and all of the United Colonies, Isaac. These are hard times and we need men like you." She looked away, summoning the words, then looked back at him. "I'm so afraid sometimes, for you . . . this fight for independence, God knows how long the war will last."

That was not what he had expected. "'Fight for independence'? Come now, you must have been talking to Rumstick."

"Why must I have been talking to Rumstick?" The warmth was gone from her voice, like a sudden drop in temperature. "Do you not think me capable of forming my own opinion?"

"Yes, of course you are." Their conversation was veering off course. "It's just that . . . independence, war, those are pretty radical thoughts. We're still Englishmen, you know. We still share the same monarch with those in England." He was on a precarious footing here, but he continued anyway. "We have grievances, sure, worth fighting for, but I don't know who actually wants independence."

Virginia's mouth hung open. She could not have looked more surprised if Biddlecomb had just admitted to pederasty.

" 'Same monarch'? 'Don't know . . .' Whose side are you on? What in all hell are you fighting for?"

"Well, come now . . ." He was flailing, like a bug in wet paint, trying to get himself out but only getting more stuck. "The Parliament has not dealt fairly with the colonies, no one is more aware of that than me. Recall I have lost everything I had, been pressed into the British navy. But I, and many others, I might add, think . . ." What the hell did he think? He hadn't given it enough thought to think anything, and now he had to make it up. "I think there can be some . . . reconciliation. I mean . . . to say we're at war . . ."

"We *are* at war, Isaac, God damn it! Men died at Concord and Lexington. Men died at Bunker Hill . . ." She was near to shouting, and her anger in turn dispelled the sweet affection that Biddlecomb had been nurturing. No one, least of all her, would tell him about war.

"And men died aboard the *Icarus*, Virginia!" he yelled, surprised at his own anger, surprised at his need to shout. Rumstick had pushed him to the brink, and now she was pushing him over the edge. "Men died on those decks, my friends, God damn it to hell! You don't know what it's like. Don't you sit there and lecture me on war, because you don't know what in all hell you are talking about." This was not going at all as he had hoped it would.

"Isaac, I don't know who you are. I thought . . ." His anger had taken her aback. Tears were welling up in her eyes, then running fast down her cheeks. "I don't know who you are," she said again, then wheeled her horse around and pounded off toward the stable, leaving Biddlecomb in a cloud of fine dust.

He tried to recall her words, the words that had made him so angry, but all he could remember were the tears, and the hurt and confusion in her parting words. And there he sat, feeling like the biggest son of a bitch in the Western world.

CHAPTER
7

A Captain's Commission

BIDDLECOMB LEFT HIS HORSE WITH THE STABLEBOY AND WALKED UP the familiar path to the front door of Stanton House. Virginia had left him on the road and had not looked back; he did not know where she had gone and assured himself he did not care. He climbed the three steps and crossed the wide porch. The front door swung open and he was greeted by Ebenezer Rogers, the butler of the house and sergeant in Stanton's Bristol Militia.

"Welcome, Captain Biddlecomb," Rogers said, and Biddlecomb saw the hint of a smile play across his face; it was perhaps the most emotion he had ever seen Rogers express. "Please come in." The butler opened the door wider and made a sweeping gesture with his arm.

Biddlecomb was nearly blind in the dark foyer after the bright sunlight outside, but he could not be disoriented in that house. Excluding various forecastles, mate's and captain's cabins, Stanton House was the closest thing to a home that he had known since he and his father had left for Nova Scotia. He had taken residence in the great house between voyages, and he was regarded by Stanton more as family, more as something of a prodigal son, than as a guest.

"The gentlemen are waiting in the drawing room, sir," Rogers said, pulling open the double doors. Light spilled into the foyer from the huge window on the eastern wall. There were four or five people sitting or standing in the elegant, book-lined room. He stepped through the doors and felt as if he were stepping onto a stage.

"Ah, Isaac!" Stanton's face lit with genuine pleasure as he crossed the room and clasped Biddlecomb's hand between his own. "It's good to see you again!" Stanton was just past sixty years old, but he had the vitality of a man half his age. Sometimes Biddlecomb felt as if Stanton were the younger of the two of them. He wore his long white hair straight and tied in a queue, a vestige of his days at sea.

Virginia was passing a tray with various small cakes around to the other three men in the room. He wondered how she had made it there so quickly.

"It's good to see you too, William," he said, turning his attention back to Stanton. He felt a twinge in his stomach; he doubted the old man would be so pleased with him after he resigned his command.

"I trust all is well with the *Charlemagne?* And Rumstick is well?"

"Both were fine when I left. William, could I have a word with you in private?"

"Of course, of course. But here, first let me introduce you around. My guests are most anxious to make your acquaintance." Stanton took Biddlecomb by the arm and guided him forward as he made the introductions.

"This is Mr. Nicholas Cooke, deputy governor of Rhode Island, whom I reckon you know has been functioning as acting governor in preference to Governor Wanton, who proved too . . . loyalist in his sentiments." Biddlecomb shook hands with Cooke. He had never met the acting governor before, but he was perfectly familiar with his record. Everyone in Rhode Island was familiar with Nicholas Cooke. The acting governor was around Stanton's age, perhaps a bit younger. His clothes were well made but plain, giving no hint of his financial status.

"Your servant, sir," Cooke said.

Biddlecomb nodded. "And yours, sir."

"Virginia of course you know," Stanton said. Biddlecomb

nodded to Virginia, who in turn gave a shallow curtsey, not meeting his eyes.

Another man, who appeared to be around Cooke's age, was sitting in Stanton's reading chair, a book open on his lap. Isaac had seen him before; he was one of the leaders of the radical movement in Rhode Island, and like Cooke one of the most prominent men in the colonial government, though Biddlecomb could not recall his name. His red coat was trimmed out in gold, and his waistcoat, tailored to perfectly envelop his slim midriff, was richly embroidered. He stood and set the book aside as Stanton led Biddlecomb across the room. He gave a quick and elegant bow—the carefully structured hair on his wig did not so much as stir—and extended a hand.

"Isaac, this is the honorable Judge Metcalf Bowler, Speaker of the House of Rhode Island," Stanton said. "He's been the prime mover behind the business we're here to discuss."

The Speaker waved his hand as if to dismiss Stanton's praise, then proffered it once again. Biddlecomb took the extended hand and shook it. "Your servant, sir."

Bowler nodded his head. "And yours."

Now Stanton directed Isaac to the other side of the room. The man who sat there was younger than the others; he guessed they were about the same age, and he was dressed in a simple but impeccable uniform of deep blue with buff trim and plain silver buttons. He stood and extended his hand. Biddlecomb was surprised at his height; six feet at least, two inches taller than himself.

"This is Maj. Edward Fitzgerald, of the staff of Gen. George Washington. He just arrived from Cambridge, sent here by the general himself," Stanton said, evidently delighted to have the man in his home. Biddlecomb took the major's hand; his grip was as firm as he imagined it would be.

"Your servant, sir." The major's accent was soft, almost lilting, not the harsh accent of New England.

"And yours, sir. You're from the South. North Carolina?"

"Virginia, sir." Fitzgerald smiled.

"Virginia, beautiful country." Biddlecomb glanced at Stanton's daughter, but she was ignoring him. "I've had the opportunity to navigate the Potomac on several occasions."

"Then you've been a stone's throw from my home, sir."

"Yes, well, there's not a moment to lose," Stanton interrupted. "Isaac, please sit here." He directed him to an unoccupied chair, the request for a private audience apparently forgotten. Once he and the others were seated, Stanton continued, "Judge Bowler, this being your idea, perhaps you'd like to begin?"

Bowler waved his hand again in his dismissive gesture. "I prefer to remain in the background, really, Stanton. I think Governor Cooke, perhaps?"

"Certainly, Mr. Speaker," said Cooke, nodding to Bowler. "You see, Captain, the American forces encamped around Boston currently find themselves in something of a predicament. As it happens, they're quite short of gunpowder—"

"'Quite short'? An understatement, sir, I'd say," Bowler interrupted. "They're damn short, not above forty barrels left, or thereabouts. That's a secret, by the way, Biddlecomb."

"Yes, indeed," Cooke continued. "Now we have it on good authority that there's a significant store of gunpowder on the Island of Bermuda—"

"Nothing like a decent guard over the stuff," Bowler interrupted again. "British don't expect anyone to attempt to move on it, you see. Please continue, Governor."

"We've reason to believe that the people of Bermuda will be disposed to help our cause . . ."

Biddlecomb drew a deep breath. They were trying to draw him even further into the war. It was time for him to speak up, to resign his command before this went any further, even if he had to do so in the presence of these men. He had not expected this. Now the young major was talking.

"Captain, I have here a commission for you." Fitzgerald held up a sealed envelope. "This will officially make you an officer in the Army of the United Colonies of North America with the rank of captain. I have as well . . ."

This was terrible, worse than he could have envisioned. Fitzgerald was still speaking, but Biddlecomb did not hear the words. For the past two months he had tortured himself, brutally and uncharacteristically, over the morality of leading those unsuspecting calves on the *Charlemagne* to their deaths. He had finally made a decision, and he had come here ready to face Stanton and to resign his command and endure the ignominy of that decision. And now they were offering him a commission.

"A captain in the Army? Of the United Colonies?" he asked, incredulous. He saw the first signs of surprise cross the men's faces. He knew that Virginia was looking at him, but he could not return her gaze.

"It's an Army commission simply because we have no navy as of yet," Fitzgerald explained. "You would of course be a ship's captain . . ."

"Young man," Cooke said with a tone usually reserved for recalcitrant children. "We've gone to great lengths to secure this for you. There are others who would kill for such an opportunity."

Then let them do so and be damned with them, sir, Biddlecomb thought, but he remained silent.

"I am assuming," Fitzgerald began again, "that you are interested in a commission. That your ambitions are . . . military in nature?"

Before he could answer, Cooke answered for him. "Of course he has military ambitions! What did I just tell you he's been doing for the past two months? Biddlecomb's the one who captured that British brig, he's the one who took back the *Diana* from Wallace."

"My ambitions aside, sir," Biddlecomb said, ignoring Cooke, "I am not certain I am the man you want."

"And why not, Captain?" Fitzgerald asked.

Isaac paused and ran his eyes over the model of the *Virginia Stanton* that stood on the sideboard, the ship that was supposed to be his next command. He thought of the time he had cowered in the hold of a merchantman, waiting while the British press gang searched for him, knowing the inevitability of his capture. He had the same sensation now. A decision that had taken him two agonizing months to make had been swept away in as many minutes. Even as the protests formed in his mind, he knew that he would not refuse this commission. He could not be so craven. But neither could he entirely ignore his doubts.

"My fidelity to your cause, as I understand it, is intact, sir," he began slowly. "But I am not certain I possess the right . . . martial qualities desirable in a man-of-war's captain."

There was a silence in the room, an unhappy silence as if he had said something shameful. Biddlecomb looked up from the model and met Fitzgerald's eyes. The major was staring at him, but his expression was not the anger or contempt that Isaac expected. There was interest there, and perhaps a touch of amusement.

"Gentlemen, and Miss Stanton," Fitzgerald said to the others, "I wonder if you would give the captain and I leave to speak in private," and before anyone could answer, he crossed the room and graciously showed Biddlecomb the door.

The two men stepped out onto the porch and then down to the lawn that stretched away for hundreds of yards in all directions. They walked in silence, side by side across the grass. With no thought as to where he was going, Biddlecomb made his way toward the sea, walking up the gentle slope of lawn that terminated in a high bluff looking out over the harbor of Bristol and the reaches of Narragansett Bay beyond.

On the crest of the grassy height stood a gazebo, painted an immaculate white, as was nearly everything at Stanton House that did not move. The gazebo was in the center of what was once a fine garden with gravel paths winding among various stands of brilliant flowers, bushes, and hedges.

It was his favorite spot on dry land. He had spent hours there, over the years, just looking out over the water and thinking. He could not stand there now without thinking of Rachel Stanton, Virginia's mother, on hands and knees, lovingly tending her plants. He knew that William secretly wished that Virginia would take over the gardening as her mother had, but

Virginia's sole interest was horses, and William apparently did not want to hire some stranger to toil in that holy ground. And so the areas that once were lush with exotic plants were now no more than patches of neatly manicured grass, hardly distinguishable from the other acres of lawn that surrounded the house, save for the gravel paths that intersected it and the white gazebo in the center.

He stepped over to the gazebo, his shoes crunching as he walked, and leaned against the structure. Before and below him was Narragansett Bay, his beloved Narragansett Bay. He could name every island, every point of land, every rock upon which his eyes fell.

"This is an odd sort of garden," Fitzgerald commented.

"It was nicer than this once."

The two men stood in silence for a long minute. "We cannot," Fitzgerald began at last, "tolerate any longer the tyranny of Parliament, their willfully ignoring our natural rights. This way we are no better than slaves."

"If you say so." Biddlecomb had no intention of being lectured about the righteousness of a cause for which he had already sacrificed so much. "You Southern gentlemen know far more on the subject of slavery than I."

To his surprise Fitzgerald looked at him and smiled. "Marvelous *dérobement*."

Biddlecomb smiled as well at the major's fencing allusion. "You're a swordsman, sir?"

"A bit. I'm a soldier. And I'm trying to understand your attitude."

"Don't. It goes way back."

"I'm aware that you've been ill-used by the Royal Navy."

"Ill-used isn't in it. The Royal Navy has taken from me everything I ever had. I've been more brutalized by the Parliament's butchers than you, and I hate them as much, and with more reason, than any American. And that has nothing to do with my feelings about this commission."

"What, then?" Fitzgerald sounded genuinely curious.

"It is, as I said, no business of yours, but it's clear I'll get no peace until I tell you." Biddlecomb paused, organizing his wild thoughts, then took a deep breath and began. "Many men died on the *Icarus*, and they died because they followed my orders. It's not an easy thing to live with, not for me. And"—he cut off the objection that Fitzgerald was trying to present—"and don't tell me they volunteered. No one volunteers for the kind of slaughter the men of the *Icarus* were put through. Those people on the *Charlemagne* don't know what they're in for."

Fitzgerald stared out over the water and for a long moment said nothing. "Well, this is a new one, Biddlecomb," he said at last. "If you said you were afraid for your own life, it would make more sense."

"I don't relish the idea of ordering men to their deaths like . . . like cattle. Perhaps you can. Perhaps that's why you can lead men into combat."

"Perhaps."

Biddlecomb saw the flicker in Fitzgerald's eyes and knew he had hit a sore spot. "You *have* led men into combat, have you not?"

"No, Captain, I have not." The words sounded much like a confession.

Then you don't know what it's like, Biddlecomb thought, but he did not say it. He did not have to.

"I can't empathize with you, Biddlecomb, because I haven't been there. I'll admit it, though it's a source of some shame for me. But I'll say this: when it comes my time, I won't send men in to fight, I'll lead them in. I'll take on more risk than any of them. Just like you did. That's the difference. That's what gives me the right, even though the orders given might cause men to die."

The two men stood in silence, both staring out over the water, both lost in thought. Then Fitzgerald spoke again. " 'The king is not bound to answer the particular endings of his soldiers, the father of his son, nor the master of his servant, for they purpose not their deaths when they propose their services.' "

Biddlecomb smiled, despite himself. It was Shakespeare. King Harry's answer to the soldier. "Nobody thinks on their death when they offer their services. That's because they don't know how easily it can happen."

"You will, of course, accept the commission." It was not a question, it was an observation.

"Perhaps. I'm not certain."

But what other choice did he have? He was close to losing Virginia's love, and Rumstick's was most likely lost already. To maintain his moral stance, to keep his hands clean of further innocent blood, would mean the loss of his friends, his home, his country. It meant staying ashore, it meant giving up the sea he loved. No ship other than the *Charlemagne* was available for him to command, nor, with the British searching for him, would he be safe in anything but a well-armed vessel. More than just rocks and shoals, wind and high seas, were waiting for him now.

He looked out at the water, flashing tiny points of light in the sun. Fear for his own safety played no part in his decision, he knew that, but others would not, or they would not believe him. He would be branded a coward. Again he smiled at the irony; he did not have enough courage in his convictions to stand being thought a coward. He had to fight for them. He had no choice.

"Don't be coy, Captain. You knew the moment I showed you the envelope that you would accept this commission. You're too proud to run away from such a thing, and more important you're too practical. You'll never be allowed any peace as long as the British are here, and you know it. The only way you'll ever be able to go back to your old life is if we win this war."

"You are one of those who advocate independency, then? You're not looking for a compromise with Parliament?"

"There is no compromising. If we compromise, then we'll have to fight this war again and again. So, yes. I am one of those."

Biddlecomb knew the major was right on one point, at least.

Isaac was a part of the war now. He had become a part of the war the moment he had defied Captain Wallace, and now his life depended on the outcome. He had not wanted it that way, quite the opposite, but there it was.

"It's a noble thing, being so worried about risking other men's lives, and I mean that sincerely." Fitzgerald stared out over the water for a moment. "We have it on good authority that you're a man of activity and intelligence, Biddlecomb, which is why we've gone to these lengths to recruit you. Now I want you to understand why this mission is so important."

He paused, then continued in a lower tone. "It is no exaggeration to say that we are desperately short of gunpowder. We have less than nine shots per man right now, and that's if we don't employ artillery. If the British decide to attack, we'll be routed, slaughtered, and the chance for Americans to resist British tyranny will be lost forever. Our entire cause now rests on our having gunpowder. This is important, Captain, more important than any man's life."

Biddlecomb looked down at the grass at his feet. Fitzgerald's quiet words rolled over him like the concussion from a rippling broadside. His father had said those words, standing on the crosstrees on the *Providence*'s main topmast, looking out over the Citadel of Quebec. In the end his father had not wanted to go with the Rangers, he had wanted to stay with his son. But he had gone in anyway and fought beside his comrades. Because he had to.

Was his father's death at the heart of this reluctance to lead men into combat? Was it moral cowardice? The question made him uneasy, but it did not matter. He could not decline this commission any more than he could ever have placed his shipmates and his vessel in jeopardy by declining to lay out on a yard and reef sail in a howling black gale.

"Well," he said at last, looking into Fitzgerald's dark eyes, "I guess I better go get you some gunpowder."

CHAPTER
8

Bound for Sea

BIDDLECOMB COULD JUST BARELY HEAR FOUR BELLS RINGING OUT
from the *Charlemagne*'s deck. It was ten o'clock at night and
the men in the longboat had another half a mile to cover before
they reached the brig. The crew, which consisted of Rogers
and the stableboy, were taking advantage of the light wind to
sail rather than row him back to his command.

Rogers sat in the stern sheets with his hand on the tiller and
Biddlecomb sat beside him. At his feet was a leather haversack,
stuffed quite full, that Fitzgerald had given him with instructions that it be opened only in the privacy of the *Charlemagne*'s
great cabin.

The stableboy held a lantern in the bow. Though the light
hurt their ability to see in the dark, Biddlecomb did not want
the guard boat to think they were making a clandestine approach. It would be ironic indeed, he thought, if he were shot
by his own men after deciding to stay with them.

He peered out into the night, searching the darkness for the
armed men in the guard boat rowing their patrol, but he could
see nothing beyond the lantern's glare.

"Bring to! What boat's that!" a voice came out of the dark,
close by, and Biddlecomb jumped in surprise.

"*Charlemagne!*" Rogers answered, to indicate that he had the
brig's captain aboard. Biddlecomb doubted that the men in the
guard boat would take Rogers's word for it.

"Bring to!" the voice shouted again. Rogers turned the bow of the longboat into the wind until the sails flogged gently in the breeze. The guard boat appeared in the circle of light cast by the lantern. Gardiner was at the tiller.

"Toss oars," he called, and the oars came up and the guard boat eased alongside the longboat. "Hello, sir," Gardiner said as he saw his captain in the stern sheets. "Odds my life you gave us a hell of a scare. We never actually had a boat approach at night before."

"Well, if the British come, let's hope they also have the courtesy to carry a lantern," Biddlecomb replied. "All's well aboard the *Charlemagne?*"

"Yes, sir," said Gardiner. "But Mr. Rumstick said you was . . . ah . . . yes—" Gardiner aborted his sentence with a cough.

"Very well, Mr. Gardiner, carry on."

Ten minutes and two more challenges later the longboat bumped against the *Charlemagne*'s side. Biddlecomb climbed the few steps to the brig's deck. There was no side party, no squealing bosun's calls. He looked for Rumstick and saw him at last, leaning against the capstan. Despite now being an officer, Rumstick seemed physically incapable of remaining on the quarterdeck where he belonged.

Rumstick said nothing by way of a greeting, but stood up straight and stared, a black scowl on his face. He had apparently given up, resigned to the fact that the *Charlemagne*'s captain would not join him in his fight, and he was giving his anger free rein. At last he pushed himself off the capstan and ambled over. He had a hulking, menacing quality, and Biddlecomb suddenly understood why men were so often afraid of him. "Come to get your gear?" he asked, his tone bitter and sarcastic.

Biddlecomb stood perfectly straight and still, clasping his hands behind his back, and held Rumstick's eye. "You will address me as Captain Biddlecomb, thank you."

Rumstick lifted an eyebrow. " 'Captain' Biddlecomb?" he

asked, but his expression did not change. "Not captain in the Rhode Island navy?"

"Captain of the Army of the United Colonies, in command of the United Colonies brig *Charlemagne*," he said sharply, and watched both of Rumstick's eyebrows shoot up.

"The United Colonies . . . ?" he began, his expression softening, but Biddlecomb turned and marched to the after scuttle.

"Carry on, Mr. Rumstick," he said, and disappeared below. He would let the first officer stew in his curiosity and contemplate his behavior. He hoped things would improve by first light.

The night was warm, and the many candles strewn about the drawing room made it almost intolerably hot, and Virginia knew that if she was not careful, she would fall fast asleep.

Isaac was gone. He and Major Fitzgerald had returned to announce that the captain would accept the commission, and then after a flurry of handshakes and back slapping he had returned to the *Charlemagne*. She had not had the chance for a private word with him.

She thought of the fight she had earlier picked with him, and the memory made her sick. She had become furious, irrational. She had stormed off like a petulant child without giving him the chance to explain himself, to explain to her what he was feeling. Now he would dismiss her from his thoughts, consider her no more than a silly girl, and he would not be far wrong. And things had been going so well.

The four men—her father, Cooke, Bowler, and Fitzgerald, who had since returned—sat around the room, droning on. Their discussion had moved from war to commerce, and Virginia was sufficiently bored that she did not bother to listen. As the lady of the house she felt it her duty to see them off, and she hoped it would be soon.

Metcalf Bowler was talking now, and Virginia watched him with some curiosity. Bowler was wealthy; Virginia knew him to be among the wealthiest men in Rhode Island, as was her father. As, for that matter, was Governor Cooke. It amazed her that men so rich could so concern themselves with becoming richer still, but here they were discussing just that thing, as they so often did.

Twenty-five years ago, eight years before she was born, Virginia's father had worked for Metcalf Bowler as the master of one of the three vessels in his fledgling fleet. Most men never reached the position of master, and of those who did, most were content to stay there.

William Stanton was not one of those men. He saved every penny he earned, living the life of a pauper while ashore until he had enough saved and enough borrowed to buy his own vessel, the tubby *Providence*. Two years later he married Virginia's mother, and a year after that he had a daughter and a second ship.

It was now sixteen years later, and William Stanton was at least as successful as his former employer. Virginia often wondered how that sat with the judge. She had the impression that he found it a great irritant. But again, Judge Bowler seemed to find the world a great irritant.

Now Cooke was speaking and the subject, a favorite, was the deplorable state of commerce in the colony since the arrival of the *Rose*. Though Cooke was also very wealthy, Virginia suspected that Bowler's wealth and her father's exceeded that of the acting governor. Cooke had once tried to recruit Biddlecomb to be master of one of his vessels, had offered him a large share of the ship and cargo, but Biddlecomb had refused to leave her father's service.

These three men: brothers in arms and enemies in trade. She often wondered what animosities ran beneath the surface of good cheer. They had been rivals for years. Were they really able to set that all aside for a common cause?

Virginia shook off her thoughts. The men were standing and making arrangements to meet again, and Virginia realized that the meeting was over. She stood as well and walked over to the drawing-room doors and pulled them open.

Stanton escorted his guests into the foyer. "Rogers, tell the coachmen that the gentlemen will be under way directly," he said.

Stanton and Virginia said their good-byes to Governor Cooke and Major Fitzgerald, and Bowler stepped into the foyer and they said good-bye to him as well.

"In a month, then, when we've had word from Isaac," Stanton said, shaking the men's hands one last time. "Good night, gentlemen, thank you all." Bowler and Cooke walked across the drive and climbed into their respective coaches, and a moment later they disappeared down the dark road.

"Good-bye, sir, it was an honor," Stanton said, extending his hand to Major Fitzgerald. "Please give my regards to General Washington."

"I shall, sir. And thank you for the loan of your ship and your help in this matter. Your country is grateful."

"Bah," said Stanton, but Fitzgerald turned his attention to Virginia.

"Good-bye, ma'am."

"Good-bye, sir." Virginia extended her hand. Fitzgerald took the offered hand and pressed it to his lips and kissed it gently, caressing her skin.

"Until we meet again," he said softly, so that only she could hear, then turned and stepped out the front door.

Virginia stood in the doorway, watching the major mount his horse. Her father had returned to the drawing room and she could hear him rustling around his desk. "Rogers, be so good as to fetch a candle," he called. "I've a note to write to Captain Martin and I'll thank you to take it to him."

"Yes, sir," Rogers said.

Virginia stepped out onto the porch, staring into the dark where Fitzgerald had just disappeared. She could still hear the sound of his horse's hooves as he made for the edge of their property.

He had refused the invitation to stay the night, saying that he wanted to cover some distance back to Boston before morning. Virginia was disappointed, and as she stared after him, she caught herself thinking certain thoughts about him, thoughts that had hitherto been reserved for Isaac.

As eight bells rang out the following morning, Biddlecomb reached for his pewter mug and swallowed his last gulp of cold coffee. He had already been at his desk for two hours, reading and rereading the various documents that Fitzgerald had enclosed in the haversack. He stretched his arms and glanced around his great cabin. It was in reality not so great, about the size of one of the big walk-in closets in Stanton House, though the great cabin had only five foot four inches of headroom, as opposed to the closet's ten feet.

The morning sun streamed in through the broad windows and tiny quarter galleries that formed the after end of the cabin, and undulating reflections from the water below danced on the cabin's brilliant white paint. The windows, as well as the bulkheads and furniture in the great cabin, were either crudely rebuilt or crudely repaired; the raking broadsides from the *Diana* had made kindling of the fine joinery work done by the *Charlemagne*'s original shipwrights.

His desk was still serviceable, despite a long gouge in the top and one broken leg that had been fished like a miniature spar. The official papers were spread out across the surface. There was his own commission as captain of the Army, filled out and signed by George Washington two weeks prior. There were his official orders and instructions, three pages of them. There was also a letter from Washington to the inhabitants of Bermuda, to be used only if the natives proved reluctant to aid the Americans in liberating the powder. There was a lieutenant's commission, signed by the general and left blank for Biddlecomb to fill in the name of the fortunate soul. And there was a flag.

He stood and stretched the cloth out on the settee. It was a substantial size, nearly a fathom on the hoist, and consisted of a white field with a green pine tree in the middle and above that the words AN APPEAL TO HEAVEN. "An appeal to heaven indeed," he muttered to himself. "We could well use one."

There was a knock on the cabin door. "Come," he said. Rumstick pushed the door open and ducked into the cabin, bending low under the deck beams and saluting in his half-crouched position.

"You sent for me, sir?" Rumstick had failed to show up unannounced for breakfast, nor had Biddlecomb expected him to, after last night. Now he stood just inside the door, his face a mask of pure contrition, calling Biddlecomb "sir" even though no one else was present. The crouched position forced on him by the low overhead made him look more contrite still. There was an awkwardness between them such as neither had ever before experienced.

"Yes, Ezra, sit down please." Biddlecomb waved toward a much injured chair in front of the desk. Rumstick eased his two hundred and fifty pounds gently down, and Biddlecomb took his seat behind the desk.

"I have been given a commission as captain in the Army of the United Colonies in order that I might command the *Charlemagne* in a more official capacity." Rumstick sat quite still and listened. Biddlecomb could see in his face his growing discomfort. "I want to—"

"I was one goddamned big ass, Isaac, and I can only apologize," Rumstick interrupted. "I like to think we're friends, beyond being captain and mate, and I wasn't much of one. I'm sorry."

Biddlecomb leaned back in his chair. He felt the tension burn away like an early-morning mist. "And I apologize for my part in this." The former awkwardness was replaced now with a mutual embarrassment. Isaac cleared his throat and picked up the orders on his desk.

"I wanted to inform you of our mission, but it's to go no further than this cabin, understood?" Rumstick sat more upright and nodded. "We're to sail to Bermuda. It seems the Continental Army around Boston is desperate for gunpowder, and they have it on good authority that there's a large supply on the island, poorly guarded. We liberate the powder and bring it to General Washington. Simple."

"Sounds simple enough." Rumstick's eyes moved over to the flag stretched out on the settee. "You've accepted a commission as captain in the Army?"

"Yes, as there's no navy. Stanton's loaned the *Charlemagne* to Washington, so we're officially the, well, I suppose the Navy of the Army. Seems the general has an appreciation for sea power."

Rumstick was grinning like some kind of fool. "Congratulations! Damn me all to hell!"

"I might yet. There's also a lieutenant's commission, for whomever I choose as first officer."

"Well, there's plenty of good . . ." Rumstick looked at Biddlecomb and the realization hit him like the first punch of wind from a squall. "Oh, no . . . oh, no, I ain't taking a commission," he said, holding up his hands as if to ward off the evil spirit of responsibility.

"Come now, Ezra, we both know you're the second most experienced man-of-war's man in New England." There was little attempt at persuasion in his tone; he was not giving Rumstick a choice.

"I'm a bosun, Isaac. I was a bosun on *Icarus*, I've always been a bosun. I don't even own one of them damn neck cloths and them frilly shirts like you officers wear."

"I only on occasion wear frilly shirts, and then never without a waistcoat. I hold you largely responsible for my being in this position, and I expect you to do your part." Isaac dipped his pen in the inkpot and scratched Rumstick's name across the commission. "I wish you joy on your promotion, Lieutenant Rumstick." He smiled and Rumstick smiled back, half mirth and half resignation. "I regret you won't have a chance to lay in a stock of neck cloths and frilly shirts as I hope to sail at slack water tonight. How are we provisioned?"

"Food, powder, and shot's all laid in. If we spend the chief of the day wooding and watering, we should be ready to get under way by nightfall."

"Excellent. Tell off some parties for those chores, if you would, Lieutenant."

"Very good, Captain." Rumstick stood, grinning and saluting. "One more thing. We got a volunteer, came out in a boat this morning. I wanted to get your approval before I entered him in the books."

"Is he a seaman?"

"I don't know. He's a strange bird, anyway. Some kind of foreigner."

Biddlecomb snatched up his hat. "Well, let's have a look," he said, and followed Rumstick out of the tiny cabin.

The two men stepped up on the quarterdeck and Biddlecomb cast an eye over his command. The *Charlemagne* looked vastly better for his twelve-hour absence. Rumstick had restowed the sails and squared the yards and had the brass polished until it shone brighter than it had in months. The guns gleamed with fresh blacking, and the falls of the train tackles were neatly flemished. The men on deck and working aloft moved with a purpose that they had lacked under Biddlecomb's careless leadership. Well, I'm back now, he thought, and I'll make Rumstick look like a slacker.

"Mr. Gardiner," he called out. Gardiner was forward, clapping service on a new truss for the spritsail yard. Gardiner let the serving mallet hang and hurried aft, saluting once he had gained the quarterdeck.

"Mr. Gardiner, you are now officially acting second lieutenant." Gardiner nodded. "Get a wooding party together and lay in all the firewood you can by nightfall. Mr. Rumstick will see to the water. Then I need the two of you to ready the brig for sea. Slack water's just before midnight, I wish to sail then. Questions?"

"Can I finish serving my bowsprit truss, sir, while the wooding party's getting together?"

"Certainly." Biddlecomb grinned as a joke formed in his head. "As Milton might have put it, 'They also serve who only stand and serve,' " he said, chuckling at his allusion.

"Yes, sir," said Gardiner with a stoic face.

Biddlecomb looked at Rumstick, whose face showed a similar lack of amusement. "You see, the joke of it is, what Milton actually said . . . ," he began, then changed his mind. "Very good, Mr. Gardiner, carry on."

Gardiner saluted again and hurried forward.

"You're familiar with the poet John Milton?" Isaac tried again, but Rumstick gestured to someone forward and said, "This here's the new hand I mentioned."

The man who approached the quarterdeck was dressed in black, from the broad-brimmed hat on his head to his scuffed shoes, save for a white collar around his neck, after the fashion of the more conservative religious sects of New England. His expression was somber, and were it not for the light coating of dust on his clothes, and his generally unkempt and scruffy appearance, Biddlecomb might have taken him for a preacher at a Quaker meeting house.

The strange volunteer removed his hat with a military-style flourish and held it before him. He nodded a greeting to the quarterdeck. "Good day, sir. My name is Jaeger. William Jaeger." His voice had a heavy Germanic accent, and he pronounced his name "Villiam Yayger."

With his hat off and the morning sun illuminating his face, Biddlecomb could see that he was older than he had first appeared; forty years at least, and from his worn and battered look they appeared to have been hard years. He was standing ramrod straight, and his eyes did not meet Biddlecomb's but were fixed on a point just over the captain's left shoulder.

"Where're you from, Jaeger?"

"Riverside, sir," he said, indicating with his thumb the small cluster of houses half a mile away on the shore.

"No, I mean originally."

"Prussia, sir."

Prussia. Biddlecomb doubted he had ever met anyone from Prussia. "What brought you to the colonies?" This line of questioning had no bearing on Jaeger's fitness for a position aboard *Charlemagne*, but he was curious.

"Religious reasons, sir."

Biddlecomb's attention was drawn again to the curious black clothing. "Are you a Quaker, or some such?"

"Dutch Reformed Church, sir."

"Dutch Reformed Church? Hmm." Biddlecomb considered that information. "You people aren't particularly known for using the sea, are you?"

"No, sir."

"Am I to take it you're not a seaman?"

"Yes, sir. I am not a seaman."

"Why are you interested in serving aboard *Charlemagne?*"

"I have always been of a mind to go to sea, sir. I seen you anchored here these past few days and thought I would ask to join your ship."

Biddlecomb had hoped for a more enlightening answer. Still, familiar or not with the ways of the sea, the strange, unkempt Prussian Dutch Reformist displayed more military bearing than he was used to seeing among the more free-spirited, native defenders of Rhode Island. He found it encouraging. "One moment. And, ah, at ease, I suppose."

Jaeger's expression did not alter, nor did his eyes move, but his hands, still holding his hat, moved automatically behind his back and he took a wider stance.

Biddlecomb drew Rumstick aside. "What do you think, Ezra?"

"He could make a good hand. Them Puritan types all take their discipline serious, like this one, and they're damn hard workers to boot."

"That was my thinking. He's not exactly macaroni, but if he knows how to put in a day's work, we could use him, even if he isn't a seaman. You don't think this religious thing will be a problem with the men?"

"I reckon not. It ain't like he's a papist or something."

"Now, Ezra, this is Rhode Island. Religious tolerance, and all that." Biddlecomb stepped up to the break of the quarterdeck. "Very well, Jaeger, Mr. Rumstick here will enter you onto the books as a landsman. The pay is six and two-thirds dollars per month, less anything you draw from the slop chest. Prize money's . . . well, Mr. Rumstick will explain. Any questions?"

"No, sir. Thank you, sir." The Prussian saluted and followed Rumstick aft.

The sun was an hour from setting when the last of the wood and water was brought aboard and stowed down. Biddlecomb issued an extra tot of rum, saw the men fed, then stood them down to an anchor watch. One by one the men staggered up from the hot tween deck, supper finished, and collapsed in exhausted heaps on the deck. Soon the snoring was loud, fore and aft, and the sound put him in mind of the *Charlemagne*'s days of hauling livestock.

He had taken special note of Jaeger as the Prussian came and went with the wooding party. He hoped he had made the right decision; the *Charlemagne* was already shipping more landsmen than he was quite comfortable with. But Jaeger seemed attentive and willing and able to learn, and he turned to the tasks with a will, his face always set in its stony countenance. That was as much as Isaac could ask of a landsman.

The day had been warm, the men engaged in the hot work had stripped to their waists, and Jaeger again proved to be the oddest sight on board. His skin was pale white, as white as the scrubbed deck planks, in startling contrast to the black breeches, stockings, and shoes he wore from the waist down. But his back, chest, and arms were sinewy and strong, and the hard, defined muscles and numerous scars, some quite wicked-looking, stood out as Jaeger carried across the deck loads that had taken two men to lift from the boat.

Biddlecomb was still thinking about the Prussian as seven bells rang out on the *Katy*'s quarterdeck, fifty yards away and just visible in the light of the crescent moon. Half an hour to midnight. He picked up the lantern and an oak chip from on top of the binnacle box, leaned over the taffrail, and holding the lantern above the water threw the chip into the river. The wood bobbed in the stream and headed north, slower than the last one. By the time the sails were ungasketed and the anchor was at short peak, they would have slack water.

A gentle offshore breeze was blowing across his face, just

enough to waft them down the bay to the sea. If the British did not stop them first.

He stepped over to where Rumstick was sleeping, flat on his back, his mouth open, and snoring in a most unofficerly manner. He nudged the lieutenant awake with his toe.

"We'll loosen all plain sail and get the anchor to short peak, please," he issued the orders once Rumstick was sufficiently awake. "I intend to sneak down Sakonnet Passage, so I'll want our best man with a lead in the chains."

"Aye, sir," Rumstick said through a yawn, then stood and trotted off forward, rousing the sleeping men in a manner far less gentle than he himself had been woken.

As Biddlecomb watched the activity of getting the brig under way, he was forced to admit that he had utterly failed in training the men under his command. They had been the crew of the *Charlemagne* for the better part of two months; still Gardiner was forward, showing the foredeck men once again how to rig the messenger for hauling in the anchor cable, and Rumstick was shouting instructions to the hands aloft. Men who had sailed for two months should know better, there should be no need for shouted orders. And now he was taking the ship to sea, where both the British navy and the open ocean were waiting for them, either of which might make Biddlecomb pay for his lethargy with his life.

Ten minutes later the sails were hanging in their gear, the messenger rigged, and men stationed at capstan and nippers. Ten minutes after that the anchor, dripping and crusted with mud, was hanging from the cathead, and the *Charlemagne* moved slowly down the river under slatting topsails.

"*Charlemagne!*" Biddlecomb was startled by the hail in the night. He had already forgotten the *Katy* as the sloop disappeared astern.

"Good luck and Godspeed!" Whipple's voice called again.

Biddlecomb picked up his speaking trumpet. "Godspeed to you too, Commodore!" He wondered if Whipple knew of the Bermuda mission, or if he was simply choosing discretion over curiosity by not questioning the *Charlemagne*'s departure. Isaac turned his back on the *Katy*, and on the first part of what was becoming, through no design of his own, his career as a naval officer.

Capt. James Wallace sat in his great cabin, the great cabin of His Majesty's frigate *Rose*, and stared at the darkness through the windows. It seemed so odd to him to be riding here at anchor, idle, knowing that Biddlecomb was out there in the deep water, in the Sakonnet Passage no doubt, beyond the protective shallows of the Providence River.

He could hear his ostensible guest sitting at the table behind him and helping himself, to Wallace's great irritation, to more of the excellent claret that he had been carrying since the West Indies. It was the first time he had met the man; their prior intercourse had been through letters passed in the most clandestine manner. It was better that way. Their present meeting was not a good idea. His guest was known as a leader in the Americans' rebellious movement, and if he was seen, he would be recognized.

Wallace had attained his rank because he was a fighting sailor and an uncompromising disciplinarian. But now he was learning that warfare was more than just gunnery and seamanship. It included, among other things, cooperating with men such as his guest.

He heard the man put the bottle back down on the table. "Can I refresh your glass, Captain?"

"No, thank you." No matter how rich or educated the Americans might be, they all sounded like ignorant backwoodsmen to Wallace. "I should say again that your king and country are most grateful to you," he added when his irritation had subsided.

"Well, if you're so bloody grateful, perhaps you'll consider not choking our business to death. I shall be lucky to clear any profit at all this year."

"Blame the rebels, sir, not the navy," Wallace said, and was greeted with a dismissive wave of his guest's hand.

"It should be clear by now where my loyalty lies, Captain.

And when these hostilities are over, I assume my help will be remembered."

"Most assuredly." Wallace fell silent, knowing that the American would continue. He seemed to loathe quiet.

"I hope you've made sufficient arrangements so that we'll see an end to this," he said, waving his hand toward the after windows and the dark night beyond. "I've taken considerable risks and expense arranging things, you know." He shifted uncomfortably, and Wallace realized that despite his facade of assurance the American was not well pleased with what he was doing.

"And I assume Biddlecomb will be treated fairly? I don't need that on my conscience as well. He's as much a victim of circumstance as any of us."

"The *Glasgow* sailed last night. She'll reach Bermuda a good four days before Biddlecomb." Wallace had been hesitant to dispatch the frigate, particularly on an errand suggested by this man, but if things worked out, it would be well worth the trouble. "And be assured Biddlecomb will be treated with the dignity befitting any captured officer."

Wallace had finally admitted to himself that he would never catch the Yankee captain on Narragansett Bay. The man's local knowledge and the skill with which he drove his brig would keep him out from under the *Rose*'s guns indefinitely.

And even if Wallace did contrive to trap him, his capture would put the colony in an uproar, a greater uproar than it was already in. It might alienate those still loyal to the king. And the danger was that much greater since Wallace had every intention of hanging Biddlecomb once he caught him, his assurances to the contrary notwithstanding.

"You sent the information with which I provided you to Boston, I take it? The general is aware of how little gunpowder the rebel army possesses?"

"He's aware."

"And will he do something? The rabble is practically lying at his feet, defenseless."

"Don't count on Gage to do anything bold; those farmers

on Bunker Hill scared him half to death. I don't care if Mr. Washington himself told Gage of the lack of gunpowder, he won't attack unless he has another ten thousand men." And then realizing that he was disparaging his own people in front of the colonial, he added, "I've no doubt he will do the best thing, from a military standpoint."

The great cabin was silent again, save for the lapping of the water under the windows and the soft footfalls of the officer of the watch pacing overhead. "You are sensible, I assume," the American spoke at last, "to the great danger to which I subject myself. My life, sir, should be at risk if this were to be revealed."

"There is no one here who would have the desire or opportunity to compromise you." Wallace knew the man was going to ask for money next. In his letters he always couched his requests for money in a reminder of the risk he was running, and Wallace was certain that he had requested this meeting to press his fiscal demands in person.

"I hope that your commander in chief is as sensible. I think it only right that something handsome be done by way of compensating me for my risks."

"I'll see that the proper authorities are apprised of your request." This man was one of the wealthiest men in Rhode Island. He was one of the leaders of the treasonous mob. And now he had his hand out to the crown as well.

Wallace turned and again looked out the window into the darkness. Biddlecomb was out there, somewhere, headed for the open sea. And the funny thing of it was, he respected the rebel son of a bitch. As much as he wanted Biddlecomb caught, tried, and hung at the yardarm, as much as he despised any man who would rebel against his king, Wallace had come to respect the American's bold and clever moves and his skill as a ship handler.

At the same time he loathed the man sitting in his great cabin, drinking his wine, selling out his countrymen. It was an odd situation; he had to kill the man he respected and embrace the traitor he loathed. The irony of that was not lost on him.

"It's late, sir, and we both have a great deal to do come the morning." Wallace stood.

The American stood as well. "Yes, well, thank you for your hospitality, Captain, and your sense in this matter."

"Certainly. And I think it would be best if we did not again meet in person. Safer for you. Will there be any problem in continuing to pass correspondence through Truax, my coxswain?"

"There shouldn't be. Your man has been diligent in his post thus far, and I will continue to use him. If things work out, I mean, as far as your commander's consideration of my efforts."

"No doubt you'll be satisfied." Wallace then shouted, "Sentry, pass the word for my coxswain." The cry of "Captain's coxswain" sounded around the ship, and twenty seconds later the man knocked and entered.

Truax was a powerful man in a powerful position. His muscular frame and his worn blue jacket, his long clubbed hair framing a weathered, bulldog face, bespoke nearly a lifetime at sea. He performed many duties beyond coxing the captain's barge. Serving as a conduit for those people ashore who wished to pass information to Wallace was just one of them.

"Truax, please escort Mr. . . ." Wallace stopped. He had intended to say the traitor's name out loud and to enjoy the man's discomfiture, but that was poor sport and doing so would yield more trouble than pleasure. "Please escort my guest to the gig," he said instead, "and see him safely ashore."

CHAPTER
9

Crossing

IT WAS WHAT BIDDLECOMB LOVED ABOVE ALL ELSE, THE LAND WELL down over the horizon and the deck lively beneath his feet. After five landlocked months he reveled in the pleasure of standing at the weather rail of the quarterdeck in the peace of the early morning with nothing but ocean to be seen beyond the confines of the ship. The sun was an hour above the horizon, the sky was light blue, and the sea through which they plowed their mile-long furrow was the mesmerizing aqua of the Gulf Stream. All plain sail, and weather studdingsails as well, were set in the twenty knots of wind just aft of the starboard beam. He was in a tremendous mood, and even watching William Jaeger vomiting over the leeward rail and collapsing in the scuppers like a broken doll could not alter that.

Rumstick stepped up to the quarterdeck, having relieved Gardiner of the watch, and saluted. "Morning, sir."

"Morning, Mr. Rumstick." Their brief animosity was gone now, the last trace washed away by the joy that they mutually felt at being on the big ocean again, and it was only before the men that they maintained something like a stiff formality.

Rumstick nodded toward Jaeger, who was now lying facedown and still. "Looks like our Prussian's done with puking. Reckon he's seasick?"

Biddlecomb considered the crumpled figure in the scuppers.

"I was just wondering that myself." The *Charlemagne*'s motion had not changed for four days, not since they had cleared Rhode Island Sound, and Jaeger had been fine up until that morning. It was odd to see a man suddenly become seasick after four days. "Let's have a look," he said, leading the first lieutenant down into the waist.

They were a full five feet away from the prone Jaeger when they first smelled the rum. "Christ, he smells like a bloody distillery," Rumstick said. He put a foot under Jaeger's shoulder and rolled him over on his back. His once-black shirt was stained and torn, and it appeared as if he had vomited on himself.

"Ferguson, fetch a bucket of water," Rumstick called out to one of the watching seamen. "And the rest of you, if you ain't got something to do, by God I'll find something." The Charlemagnes scattered like roaches, certain that whatever he found for them to do would not be pleasant.

Ferguson appeared with a full bucket of seawater and on the first officer's cue dashed it across the supine figure. The water drenched him, splaying his hair out on the deck and soaking his clothing until it appeared its original black. Jaeger revived and slowly wiped the water from his face with the back of his hand and then, as if exhausted from the effort, lay still for a moment in the puddle.

"Damned Gulf Stream water's too damn warm to do any good," Rumstick muttered.

"Jaeger, what in the hell are you thinking?" Biddlecomb knelt beside Jaeger and shouted in his ear. "What do you have to say for yourself?" It was not uncommon for a sailor to have an extra nip now and again, or to hoard his tots of rum until he had a more substantial amount, but when a man became incapacitated and unable to do his duty, it fell to his shipmates to do his work for him. With the exception of stealing there was no greater crime on shipboard.

Jaeger flinched from the captain's harsh words. He sat up, clutched his head, and turning his bleary eyes toward Biddlecomb's face, muttered, *"Decretum horribile."*

Biddlecomb looked up at Rumstick. "What in the hell is that supposed to mean?"

"I don't know, sir."

"What's that supposed to mean, Jaeger?"

The landsman had started groaning, softly and rhythmically. "It's my burden, sir,—" he muttered. He sounded as if his tongue were too big for his mouth. "It's my burden . . ."

Biddlecomb stood up. "Well, he's as useless as a steaming pile of horse dung, in any language. Stuff him below for now and go through his kit, toss any drink you find overboard."

"Aye, sir," Rumstick said, taking Jaeger's arm in his massive hand and dragging him across the deck as easily as if he were a small child, bouncing him off various pieces of deck furniture on the way to the forward scuttle.

Biddlecomb regained the quarterdeck and watched Rumstick and Ferguson maneuver Jaeger below. If the *Charlemagne* had been a ship of the Royal Navy, then Jaeger would have been flogged the next morning, a dozen lashes at least.

He felt a growing and greatly disturbing uncertainty. Should he order Jaeger flogged? Could he? As a merchant captain he had rarely encountered such lapses in discipline, and when he had, the threat of setting the perpetrator ashore at their next landfall and never shipping him again was usually enough to discourage further incidents. If it happened again, then he simply made good on the threat. To accept a man's offer to serve aboard the brig, to risk his life for his country, and then beat him half to death was abhorrent to him. But then again he had agreed to be a navy officer, so what the hell kind of navy officer was he being?

Rumstick and Ferguson emerged from the scuttle, each holding two bottles of rum, which they tossed over the side. Biddlecomb smiled at the Charlemagnes' expressions of longing as they watched the bottles disappear in the brig's wake. Then Rumstick stepped up to the quarterdeck.

"You found his rum, I see."

"Aye. Rum's pretty near all he had in his kit too. A couple of pistols, a Bible, a wool coat, and the rum."

"So much for our sober, God-fearing hand. I guess that's why he wanted to go to sea."

"No doubt. I'll wager getting paralytic drunk is frowned on by them people. Calvinists ain't known for drinking men."

"Calvinist? He said he was . . . what did he say? . . . Dutch Reformed."

"Same thing. All them reform churches, Puritans, German Reform, they're all bloody Calvinists."

"You astonish me, Lieutenant. I had no notion you were such a scholar."

"So what're you going to do with Jaeger, Captain?" Rumstick asked in an apparent effort to divert attention from his surprising knowledge of comparative religion. "Flogging?"

"I'm not certain." Rumstick clearly had no moral dilemma concerning corporal punishment. During their time on the *Icarus* they had learned a great deal about flogging. Handed out indiscriminately, it would destroy a crew's morale quicker than stopping their rum. But doled out correctly, applied to the men who deserved it, it was an effective punishment and deterrent. Any real man-of-war's crew—and Biddlecomb was determined that the men of the *Charlemagne* should be just that—accepted it as a part of that life. They did not grumble when men were flogged who deserved to be flogged. And Jaeger deserved to be flogged.

"His rum's gone now. I believe I'll give him another chance. If there's another incident, then we'll make an example of him."

"Yes, sir." Whether Rumstick approved of his decision or not, Biddlecomb could not tell. He stepped aft to the binnacle box and read the numbers scrawled on the slate. The *Charlemagne* was doing eight knots at the last cast of the log, and it looked as if they would run close to two hundred miles during the twenty-four-hour period between yesterday's noon sight and today's.

"Mr. Rumstick, I believe we'll have sail drill directly." This would come as no surprise; they had done little else for the past four days. Since the shores of New England had disappeared below the horizon, they had tacked the *Charlemagne* and wore around, boxhauled, hove to, set sail, doused sail, reefed and fisted sail; courses, topsails, topgallants, royals and skyscrapers set flying from the deck, spritsail, studdingsails and driver, night and day. They had launched and retrieved the boats, roused out cable, rigged the messenger, even fothered a sail over an imaginary leak. The men grumbled at first, and they grumbled still, and Biddlecomb knew they would always grumble, but he could see their pleasure as once clumsy maneuvers were done quickly and precisely, with no orders shouted from the deck and no confusion aloft.

His eyes moved down to the main deck and ran along the lines of six-pound guns that were poised behind their gunports. Every time he looked at them he was reminded that for all of the training the men were receiving in sail evolutions, they had not yet exercised with the guns, not even so much as loaded them.

And he knew perfectly well why that was. He had no confidence in his ability to train them. He knew more than any man aboard about naval gunnery, and what he knew was next to nothing.

The smell of fresh coffee filled the *Charlemagne*'s great cabin, overpowering even the ubiquitous smell of tar and linseed oil. Biddlecomb pushed aside his thoughts of Virginia Stanton and thought instead of William Jaeger. The Prussian had been sober for two days now, since Rumstick and Ferguson had tossed his rum overboard, and Isaac was satisfied that that simple expedient had solved the problem.

Rumstick, sitting opposite him at the desk, refilled the pewter mug that Biddlecomb extended, then poured the remainder of the pot into his own mug. The two men sat in the dim circle of light cast by the lantern hanging from the deck beams, taking advantage of the predawn quiet to finish the paperwork that plagued all ship's officers, merchant or naval. The desk, which now doubled as their breakfast table, was strewn with logbooks, provision lists, muster bills, plates of toasted bread, and pots of jam.

Biddlecomb sipped his coffee and ran his eyes over a list of provisions. "It appears we'll have to open another beef barrel before dinner."

"Yes. And I'm afraid the rats have got at the bread, more than usual," Rumstick added.

"Hmm. Let's empty out the bread room in the forenoon watch and see if we can slow them down. How're you doing on the quarter bill?"

Rumstick grunted and fished through the papers on the desk. "I reckon it's all right, though I'll own I ain't got a clue what I'm doing." He handed the lined sheets to Biddlecomb. On them were listed every man aboard and their stations and duties during battle, down to the weapons they would carry if boarding an enemy ship. "I wish I'd paid more attention when we was aboard the *Icarus*."

"We had other things on our minds, then," Biddlecomb said, taking a bite of toast and looking over the lieutenant's work. "This should answer famously. You recall how on the *Icarus* we used to clear for action before dawn every morning? Barrett said it was a standard practice in the British navy in times of war."

Rumstick nodded his head. "Damn good practice too, I reckon. It's sometimes a hell of a surprise what you see when the sun comes up."

"I agree. We'll do that, starting this morning. And I think we'd better start exercising with the guns and small arms."

Rumstick frowned. "I reckon you're right. But I don't know how much help I can be. I know pretty well how to load and fire a gun, but I don't know anything about training a whole crew at gunnery."

"We'll just have the gun crews load and shoot until they're as fast as they can get, maybe set out a barrel for a target, and pray that's enough."

Rumstick grunted again. "I guess the praying will be a big part of it."

By the time the *Charlemagne* was cleared for action Biddlecomb doubted that even the most fervent prayer would save his ship if they were forced to exchange broadsides with a British man-of-war. The sun had broken free of the horizon, illuminating what was, thankfully, an empty ocean, by the time the last gun crew announced themselves ready.

It had been closer to low comedy than anything he had seen off the stage or outside the harvest fair. The men had literally fallen over themselves, had spilled shot and even, to his distress, gunpowder on the deck, and had been unable to locate half the tools they needed to operate the great guns. During those fine days on Narragansett Bay there had never been any particular need to rush, and clearing for action had been a leisurely process, generally consuming an hour or more. He might have laughed, would have laughed, if it had been any crew but his own.

"Silence, fore and aft!" Rumstick bellowed, and the men fell silent. Biddlecomb could see them shifting nervously, some eyes now cast down toward the deck. They were well aware of how substandard their performance had been.

"Listen up, you men," Biddlecomb began. "It took us forty-eight minutes to clear this brig for action. That is inexcusable. And in a fight that could well mean the death of every man aboard." He paused, letting the words register, then continued in a different key, "This is as much my fault, more my fault, than anyone else's. Now, the watch below can take their breakfast, and when they're done, we'll exercise the great guns. Mr. Rumstick, dismiss the men."

Rumstick dismissed the men. The *Charlemagne* settled back into her daily routine, plowing through the Atlantic, heading south by east. The rig above creaked under the strain of hundreds of square feet of canvas, and below them the sea rushed down the length of the brig and slapped occasionally at the *Charlemagne*'s side. Along the deck the men talked quietly, their voices mixing with the sounds of the wash pump being rigged and holystones broken out, and William Jaeger, at the leeward rail, retching into the sea.

CHAPTER
10

The Artilleryman

"Good God, is that son of a whore drunk again!" Rumstick shouted. Biddlecomb could see the lieutenant's hands clench into fists, fists like sledgehammers, and he could imagine him pounding the life out of Jaeger. He had seen Rumstick lose control before, had seen him beat the *Icarus*'s powerful boatswain half to death.

"Avast, there!" Biddlecomb called. Rumstick was halfway down the ladder to the waist when he stopped. "We're two days out of Bermuda. We'll put him ashore there. There's no need to punish him if he's not staying with us."

Rumstick frowned. "Humph," was all he would say as he stamped back to the quarterdeck.

Biddlecomb looked at Jaeger, once again crumpled on the deck. He should flog him, he knew that. Letting the man get away with drunkenness could not be good for discipline. He thought of the floggings he had witnessed aboard the *Icarus*, the flesh torn from men's backs, the shrieks of agony. The memory made him clench his teeth.

The clanking of the deck wash pump distracted him from his thoughts. Four men of the starboard watch worked the pump handles up and down as Nathanial Sprout, the *Charlemagne*'s bosun, directed the stream of water over the deck.

"Mr. Sprout," Biddlecomb called out across the deck.

"Sir?"

"Hose Jaeger down over there to sober him up some and set him to scrubbing," he ordered, pointing to the Prussian lying in the scuppers.

The boatswain grinned. "Aye, sir!" he said, turning the hose on Jaeger's supine form. The men working the pump grinned as well and redoubled their efforts, and soon the water was flowing with terrific force, washing the inebriated Prussian up against the bulwark, where he held up his arms to fend off the assaulting spray.

"Hold up there, lads," Sprout said to the men at the pumps, and they ceased their frenetic pumping.

The boatswain grabbed up a couple of brooms and ambled over to where Jaeger lay. He grabbed Jaeger by the shirt and jerked him to his feet, leaning him back against the bulwark for support, then thrust one of the brooms, none too gently, into his chest. The Prussian took feeble hold of the handle as Sprout used the other brush to poke him in the chest.

"Come on, you drunk bastard," Sprout said. "Clap on to that and earn yer peck, you useless whore's son."

Biddlecomb stood and watched the little drama from the quarterdeck. Jaeger held his brush at the base of the handle, as a child might hold a sword that is too heavy to lift, then showed no inclination to move further. Sprout poked him again in the chest with his own brush. "I said get scrubbing, you useless bastard."

And then Jaeger did a surprising thing. He held his broom up, handle first, and as Sprout moved to poke him again, he knocked the boatswain's broom away in a perfectly executed fencing move, a defense in the sixth position: arm cocked, a quick move of the wrist, and the broom handle slashed down and to the left. Sprout's handle was knocked aside and Jaeger swept his own broom around in a wide arc, locking it with Sprout's, jerking the broom from the boatswain's hand and flicking it across the deck in a flawless *de armement*. Then he let the handle drop to the deck and, dragging it along, ambled off to join the other scrubbers who had gathered to watch the fun.

Biddlecomb realized, to his embarrassment, that his mouth was hanging open, but he could not recall when anything had surprised him more.

An hour later, when Sprout was at last satisfied with the level of perfection in the deck planks and the brass and the gun tackles and began to hand out the morning's work, Biddlecomb was satisfied that Jaeger was sober enough for further investigation. "Weatherspoon!" he called out, and the midshipman, who had been standing obediently at the leeward rail, practically leapt across the deck and saluted.

"Sir!"

"Weatherspoon, you know where my foils are, in my cabin?" The midshipman nodded. "Good. Nip below and fetch them up. Quickly."

Weatherspoon disappeared through the scuttle as Biddlecomb struggled out of his heavy coat and tossed his hat aside. "Mr. Sprout, please send Jaeger aft, will you?" he shouted.

"I hope you're intending to skewer that bastard, Captain," Rumstick said from the leeward side of the quarterdeck.

"Perhaps, Mr. Rumstick. Or perhaps Jaeger will surprise me further."

In a moment Weatherspoon was back, carrying the two long canvas sleeves that held the foils. Biddlecomb took one and drew out the long, thin weapon. The steel blade glinted in the sun, and the grip felt familiar and comfortable in his hand. The foils were useless against the heavy weapons used in real combat; still, he could not bear to leave them ashore, rare though it was that he found someone with whom he could fence.

He drew the other foil from its canvas sleeve and handed it to Jaeger, who had gained the quarterdeck and was standing on the leeward side. Jaeger took the weapon by the grip, holding it out straight so he could sight down the blade, then grabbed the tip and flexed it over his head. Then he took a few uncertain lunges and parries at the air.

"Is a good blade," he mumbled at last. "Good steel."

"Thank you," Biddlecomb said, taking a step back and assuming an *en garde* position. *"En garde."*

Jaeger assumed an *en garde* position as well, as naturally as a man standing up from a chair, feet at right angles, foil held loosely in his right hand, right arm cocked, left arm at his waist. Biddlecomb stepped forward, extending the tip of his foil in an exploratory jab, and Jaeger in turn stepped back, maintaining the distance between them. Biddlecomb stepped again, this time slashing down and to the right, but Jaeger easily parried the blow, knocking the attacking foil aside and lunging forward, forcing Biddlecomb to jump back to avoid the tip of Jaeger's blade.

The Prussian was off-balance, having committed to the lunge, and Biddlecomb exploited that. He parried Jaeger's still extended foil, knocking it aside, then stepped in for the attack. He could see his adversary's chest, exposed, unprotected, and he lunged for it.

But Jaeger was faster than he could have imagined such a sodden wretch could be. Jaeger stepped back, recovering from his lunge and sweeping Biddlecomb's sword aside in a great arcing parry. Biddlecomb used the momentum to keep his foil coming around, attacking again, and again Jaeger's weapon was there to stop him. The thin blades clashed and blinked in the sun as the two men stepped forward and back, foils moving by instinct.

Biddlecomb feigned to the left. Jaeger parried and lunged. Biddlecomb leapt back, swept the attacking blade aside, throwing Jaeger off-balance, then stabbed his foil into Jaeger's chest. The cork tip struck Jaeger's breastbone and the thin blade bent under the force of the thrust.

Jaeger straightened, nodded his head toward Biddlecomb, and saluted with his sword, bringing the blade up and down with a flourish. Biddlecomb returned the salute.

"Well, kiss my arse," said Rumstick. "Who'd have thought that drunk bastard was a swordsman?"

"You are very good, Captain," Jaeger said. "Excellent point control."

"And you. You are very good yourself. Wherever did you learn to fence like that?"

"Bah," said Jaeger, making a sour face. "I was good, once. It was many years ago."

Biddlecomb was a bit taken aback. If Jaeger's performance did not constitute "good," he was hard-pressed to imagine what good was. "You didn't answer my question, Jaeger. It's not often we see people of your . . . faith who can handle a weapon."

"I used to be a soldier, sir." Biddlecomb could hear the pride beneath the words. "Before I was shown the light, sir, I was a soldier in the Grand Army of King Frederick of Prussia."

Rumstick stepped up beside them, now apparently interested in what Jaeger had to say. "You were in the Prussian army? Why didn't you tell us?"

Jaeger shrugged. "When I came to the Dutch faith, I give that up, forgot it. That is why I come to America."

"This makes no sense," Biddlecomb said. "You find religion, so you left the Prussian army and came to America?"

"*Ja.* Yes."

"So why did you join the *Charlemagne?*"

"I thought perhaps going to sea would be good for me. I was not so welcome among the others of my faith in America." Jaeger stiffened and looked Biddlecomb in the eye, mustering what pride he had left. "I drink, you know."

"I know."

"If you left the army to get away from all that," Rumstick asked, "why'd you ship out in a man-of-war?"

The Prussian looked around, looked down at the line of guns. He shrugged again. "I know nothing of boats. I thought this was a . . . how do you call a boat that carries cargo?"

Biddlecomb and Rumstick looked at each other, amazed. Such a mistake seemed incomprehensible to two men who had spent the better part of their lives at sea.

"You thought it was a merchantman?" Rumstick asked, incredulous.

"What did you think when you saw all the guns?" Biddlecomb added.

Jaeger shrugged once more. "Merchantman carry guns, do they not?"

"Sure," said Rumstick, "but not this damn many."

"I may have been drinking when I decided to join you, I don't remember. I know nothing of boats."

"Tell me," Biddlecomb said. "What did you do in the Prussian army? Infantry?"

"No, sir." A thin smile appeared on Jaeger's lips as he saw some happy vision of his past. "No, sir, I was an officer, a captain, like you. A captain of artillery. With the great Brummer battery."

The two Americans looked at each other once again. "A captain of artillery, you say?" Biddlecomb asked.

"*Ja.* Yes."

"Mr. Rumstick, you have the deck. Mr. Jaeger, please step into my cabin. I'd like to continue this conversation."

Biddlecomb led the way to the great cabin, sitting himself down behind his desk and gesturing for Jaeger to take a seat. The Prussian sat carefully in the wounded chair, his eyes surveying the obvious repairs.

"You were in a fight, *ja?*"

"Yes, about two months ago. Believe it or not, we won. Now listen here. You'll not be surprised when I tell you that I'm less than pleased with your work."

Jaeger looked the captain in the eyes and stiffened. "*Ja,* I have not done my duty well."

"I had every intention of leaving you off in Bermuda. I considered it an alternative to flogging you, which is what I should do. Have you been to Bermuda? Do you know anything of the island?"

"No, sir, I know nothing of it."

"It's no paradise, I assure you. But I'm willing to offer you this one chance to redeem yourself. The fact is that we need someone aboard who knows about artillery and can train the others. Mr. Rumstick and I have precious little experience. Could you train the men?"

Jaeger considered this. Biddlecomb could see in his eyes that he was going back, back to some past of respect and glory, to a past when he was more than just a drunk outcast of a severe religious sect. "I have trained many men, many men, in artillery," he said at last. "But I do not do that now. I renounced that. I am a man of God."

Biddlecomb considered pointing out that he did not look much like a man of God, lying in the scuppers covered in vomit, but he opted for a different approach. "I was also reluctant, damn reluctant, to take up arms in this fight. But we're both Englishmen, living in America, and the time has come that we must fight for the rights that are ours. And not least of all the right to worship as we wish. No one could understand that more than an officer of Frederick of Prussia."

He held Jaeger's gaze. He could see the Prussian wavering, see the conflict, like an artillery duel, in his eyes. "I cannot," he said at last.

Biddlecomb let out a sigh. "Very well, Jaeger, then I have no choice but to set you ashore in Bermuda. You're . . . what? Roman Catholic? Isn't that what you said?"

"No, sir. I am of the Dutch Reformed Church."

"Oh. Indeed. Well, that's a little awkward. Bermuda is a Spanish colony, like the others in the Caribbean. Papist to the core." This was an outrageous lie, even for him, and he doubted he would get away with it. "But you'll manage. After all, what's the difference, really, between one religion and the other?"

Jaeger's expression remained unchanged, but Biddlecomb saw his eyes grow just perceptibly wider. "Spanish Catholic, you say, sir?"

"Yes, and I'm sure they'll show you every respect. I believe that they're quite done with that inquisition nonsense. You may go, Jaeger. Report to Mr. Sprout." Biddlecomb turned to some paperwork on his desk.

For half a minute Jaeger did not move. "Sir," he said at last, "what you said about the rights that are ours, about freedom to worship . . . perhaps you are right."

Twenty minutes later Biddlecomb was again at the break of the quarterdeck, waiting as the men assembled in the waist to hear his words from on high. He could see eyes darting over at Jaeger, who stood at his side. The Prussian looked considerably better than before, dressed out in clean slop trousers and shirt and he stood stiffly, with his head up. Biddlecomb imagined that the men watching believed they were about to witness Jaeger's flogging. He smiled. The men were in for a surprise.

He nodded to Rumstick, who stood on his other side. "Silence, fore and aft!" Rumstick shouted, and instantly the Charlemagnes fell quiet. Biddlecomb cleared his throat. This would be interesting, if nothing else.

"Men, you all know William Jaeger here, who joined us just before we sailed. Now, I know, and you know, that he hasn't always been the best hand aboard—"

"Amen, brother!" an anonymous voice shouted from the crowd, and the men broke into laughter.

"Silence! Silence fore and aft! Bosun, get that man's name!" Rumstick fairly screamed, the muscles on his neck standing out. The noise died down again, with the occasional chuckle or whisper still heard in the festive atmosphere.

"Now, as it happens, Mr. Jaeger here is a former officer in the Prussian army, a captain of artillery, and an expert in the use of cannon." Biddlecomb paused, letting the words sink in. The watching men were silent now. "If there's one thing we need aboard the *Charlemagne*, it's someone with experience in artillery. Mr. Rumstick, Mr. Gardiner, Mr. Sprout, and myself have been able to teach you seamanship, and we've been damn pleased with what you've learned. I am promoting Mr. Jaeger to gunner, and he will begin this morning training you in the use of the guns."

Seventy-four protests exploded from the waist and the shrouds. The wave of noise washed aft over the quarterdeck as the men of the *Charlemagne* reacted to this most unexpected development. Rumstick glanced at Biddlecomb; the lieutenant wanted to order the men to silence, but Biddlecomb gave a quick shake of his head. He would give the men a moment to digest this.

"I know a lot of you are thinking Jaeger is the last man that deserves promotion," he said after the shouting had tapered off. "And you're right. But we need what he knows, and in turn Mr. Jaeger has agreed to square his yards and behave like a warrant officer should. Any comments?" he asked in a tone that did not invite comment. "Good. We'll exercise the guns until the first dogwatch. Mr. Rumstick, see the guns cast off."

Rumstick bellowed the orders that set the men running to the great guns. "Very well, Mr. Jaeger, here's your chance. You think you can train these men?"

"*Ja.* I have trained much worse."

Biddlecomb looked down into the waist. The men were stationed at their guns, holding rammers, sponges, and handspikes and waiting for orders. They glanced at each other and muttered in low tones and shot black looks aft at the quarterdeck. They were not happy about this new development, not happy about having a drunken foreign Puritan suddenly promoted to gunner. Too bad, Biddlecomb thought. They don't have to be happy, only I do.

"Carry on, Mr. Jaeger." Jaeger snapped to attention, saluted crisply, then stepped down the ladder to the waist. He watched the Prussian as he began making his rounds of the guns. It was a gamble; Jaeger might have been drummed out of the Prussian army for being a worthless drunk, or he might never have been in the army at all. He had only Jaeger's word and his swordsmanship to go by. If he had made the wrong decision in promoting the Prussian, then his own authority would be compromised as well.

The Charlemagnes were silent now, all eyes on Jaeger. The only sounds to be heard were the working of the vessel and the clump of Jaeger's shoes as he walked slowly, deliberately down the line of the great guns.

From the quarterdeck Biddlecomb could feel the tension as the men chafed and exchanged meaningful glances and waited for their new warrant officer to say something. Anything. But Jaeger continued his slow inspection, seemingly oblivious to the hostility around him.

Biddlecomb could see what the Prussian was doing. By making the men wait for him, Jaeger was setting in their minds the idea that he was in charge now. If it worked, it would be damn effective. Isaac was impressed.

Jaeger made his way to the forwardmost gun on the larboard side, then crossed over to the starboard side and began to work his way aft. The tension on deck was reaching a breaking point, Biddlecomb could feel it. A gun captain muttered something to another man in his crew. In a moment the men would be talking among themselves, their attention gone. He was about to call for silence when Jaeger spoke up.

"Who is the gun captain here?" he demanded, pointing to number five gun starboard side, his voice loud enough to be heard around the deck. All attention was once again on the Prussian. "Who is the gun captain here?"

"I reckon I am," a man said, stepping forward, his tone confrontational.

Jaeger stepped closer until his face was inches from the gun captain's. "Your match is out," he said, his voice more quiet than before.

The gun captain leaned back and shrugged his shoulders. "I reckon it is." He wore a stupid grin on his face.

Jaeger was silent, but his eyes continued to bore into the gun captain's. The man leaned farther back, glanced down at the deck, then looked up again, meeting Jaeger's stare. "You reckon it is," Jaeger said softly. "When, pray, were you planning on lighting it again?"

The gun captain shrugged again. "I dunno. When I needed it. When we get some gunpowder in them guns," he added with a smirk.

"You need it now," Jaeger said in the same even tone, thrusting his face closer to the gun captain's. The man leaned back, clearly uncomfortable, trying to get away from Jaeger, but Jaeger continued to lean into him. "You need it now. You need it every time the guns are in use."

The two men stood like swordsmen with locked blades, every eye on them, Jaeger leaning farther and farther into the man, his voice firm and quiet. "You need it now."

Biddlecomb saw the gun captain take half a step back, saw him glancing around. Jaeger had chosen this man, a man with a reputation as a bully, as his example. By Biddlecomb's count he had already walked past three other gun captains whose match was not lit.

It was like watching a fuse burn toward a powder keg. The Prussian was unnerving the man, staring him down, actually frightening him with his mechanical instructions and merciless stare. "Light your match. Light it now."

And then the gun captain's hand shot out and grabbed at Jaeger's shirt, but Jaeger seized the hand before it could get a hold and twisted it to one side. The man's eyes went wide and his mouth hung open as if to scream, but he made no sound. Jaeger twisted farther, easing the gun captain down to the deck. He went down on one knee, then the other, then in one fluid motion Jaeger released his hand and kicked him in the chest, sprawling him backward against his gun.

"Light your match," Jaeger said again, as if nothing had happened. To Biddlecomb's surprise the gun captain, with no further comment, crawled to the tub, snatched up the linstock that held the match, and touched the extinguished end to his neighbor's burning match.

Jaeger turned and walked over to the capstan. "Is everyone's match lit? Is everyone's match lit?" he shouted, and was greeted with a sea of nodding heads, including those of the few men who had just hurriedly lit theirs. Biddlecomb could sense the relief among the men that the confrontation was over, could feel the tension diffuse.

"All gun captains, hold up your match! Hold up the linstocks!" Jaeger shouted, and fourteen linstocks rose in the air, and on each was the smoldering match. "Blow on the match, keep it burning!" he shouted next, and fourteen men blew on their match until the ends glowed bright orange. "A gun is useless, useless, without a lit match! It is imperative that you learn to keep your match lit! It must always be on your mind!" Jaeger paused and looked around, letting the words sink in. "Now," he said at last, "you may put down the linstocks. We will now begin to drill by the numbers."

From the quarterdeck the officers watched the scene in silence. "Damn me, sir, he's good," Rumstick said at last as the men hauled the guns inboard.

"Indeed. I'll warrant the reputation of the Prussian army is well deserved. You searched his kit again?"

"Aye, Ferguson and me gave it a good going over, his mess area too. I don't know where he had his rum hid so we couldn't find it before, and if he's got more, then damn me if I can find it now."

As the gun crews wrestled their charges inboard, Jaeger stepped up to the break of the quarterdeck. "Mr. Rumstick, are the gun crews assigned their numbers?

Rumstick glanced at Biddlecomb and an embarrassed look crossed the lieutenant's face. "Uh, what exactly do you mean by 'their numbers,' Mr. Jaeger?"

"You know, sir. Gun captain is designated number one, points, primes, stops vent. Second captain is number two, attends the apron and what you call train tackle on a boat, and so on."

"Well, Mr. Rumstick?" Biddlecomb asked as innocently as he was able. This was the first that either of them had heard of such organization.

"Ah, no, Mr. Jaeger, the men ain't been designated by their numbers. I never did seem to get around to it."

"Very well, sir." If the artilleryman had any opinion of such oversight, he was too good a subordinate to betray it. "May I have permission to assign numbers now?"

"Yes, by all means, as you wish," Rumstick said, and Jaeger saluted, turned on his heel, and marched forward again. Then Rumstick turned to Biddlecomb. "Did they do that on the *Icarus?*"

"Not that I recall."

Gunnery Officer William Jaeger made the rounds of each gun, assigning the men their numbers and informing them of what was expected. The smoldering anger was still there on the men's faces, but they were respectful, superficially at least, and none dared to show Jaeger their formerly open disdain. It was a start.

For the remainder of the afternoon Jaeger marched fore and aft, instructing the men, working them, shouting orders, admonishments, and praise as the crew of the *Charlemagne* ran the six-pounders in and out. They worked like machines, mechanically following his shouts of "Number one, stop your vents!" and "Number four, sponge out!" and "Number three, load!"—pretending to handle cartridges and shot in a dumb show of loading and firing the guns.

The men stripped down to their waists and cursed and sweated under the hot sun, and judging by the undercurrent of growling and complaining, none seemed to notice the steadily increasing speed of their operations, or the fact that Jaeger on occasion failed to call out an order, and the gun crews, now well used to the rhythm of loading and firing, performed the omitted step anyway.

At three bells in the afternoon watch on the following day, after the dripping men had loaded and run out the guns in dumb show three times in two minutes, Jaeger pronounced them ready for live firing.

Biddlecomb could see smiles fore and aft as the men anticipated actually shooting the guns. Since Jaeger had first mentioned during their meeting in the great cabin the importance of live firing, Isaac had been uneasy about this. The *Charlemagne*'s magazine had a full supply of gunpowder, and in two days, with any luck, their hold would be full as well. Still, gunpowder was the most dear substance on earth to the struggling American forces surrounding Boston. It was the whole reason for his mission, and he was loath to expend it firing round shot into the empty sea.

Of course, if they had to fight their way back to Massachusetts, which was more than likely, all the powder in the world would not help them if they could not work their guns faster and better than their opponent. If Jaeger said they had to expend powder to properly train the men, then, Biddlecomb decided, he had best take him on his word.

As he had with the initial training, Jaeger began the live firing drill slowly, building precision and speed, until soon the men were firing three live rounds in two minutes and the *Charlemagne* was wreathed in smoke, despite the ten knots of wind over the starboard beam. The men who moved like shades in the fog were grimy and black, their hair matted with sweat, their soot-covered backs glistening. But on their blackened faces Biddlecomb could see wide smiles. They were like children, like little boys allowed to fire their father's muskets.

Eight bells rang out, signaling the start of the first dogwatch, but the men were now unwilling to end the fun of shooting the big guns. Instead, the *Charlemagne* was hove to and Weatherspoon was sent off in the gig to set a barrel adrift two cables away. The natural competition among the men was heightened by the captain's promise of an extra tot of rum for the first gun crew to hit the barrel. One by one the guns went off, churning up the sea around the target. Halfway through the second broadside, the barrel burst into a hundred fragments, and the crew of number three gun cheered as the other men sulked and cursed.

"Deck there!" the lookout called from the main topmast crosstrees.

"Deck, aye!" Biddlecomb shouted, knowing what was coming next.

"Land, ho!"

"Very good." So high was his mood that he could not bring himself to admonish the lookout for his negligence, though twenty minutes before, and from the quarterdeck, he had seen the round green hills of Bermuda through the smoke of the *Charlemagne*'s guns.

CHAPTER
11

Bermuda

"ON DECK!" RUMSTICK'S VOICE SOUNDED CLOSE, THOUGH HE WAS calling from the fore topmast crosstrees, ninety feet above the deck.

Biddlecomb tore his eyes from the sandy bottom of Bermuda's Great Sound, clearly visible beneath seven fathoms of water, and looked aloft. They had spent the night hove to three miles off the Bermudian coast so that they could approach the island in daylight. Biddlecomb had seen at least half a dozen ships rip their bottoms out on the coral reefs that surrounded the island like a carefully laid underwater defense, and despite the chart, the lookout in the main topmast crosstrees, Rumstick in the fore, and Ferguson in the chains with the lead, Isaac was still nervous.

"Deck, aye!" he shouted back. Rumstick was peering through a telescope that rested on a topgallant ratline.

"Captain, you may want to look at this."

"On my way." He tossed his hat on the deck by the binnacle box and wriggled out of his coat. Though the sun was only two hours old, it was already quite warm, and Biddlecomb did not relish the climb to the crosstrees. That in turn led to his cursing himself for a fat and lazy lout and reminding himself that the climb would do him good and might even help contribute to a better fit for his breeches, which were becoming snugger by the week. As a ship's captain, one was not wont to get much exercise.

"Mr. Weatherspoon, I'll take the signal glass, if you would be so kind." Weatherspoon was relashing the edge of a wide canvas strip, painted black and run from the *Charlemagne's* bow to her stern, covering the gunports on both sides. Thus disguised, and with no ensign flying, the brig was indistinguishable from any of the many merchant vessels that visited the island. Still, behind the canvas and the bulwarks forty men were hunkered down beside their loaded guns, and forward, Jaeger was supervising ten more men as they sewed and filled cartridges of gunpowder. "Mr. Gardiner, you have the deck."

Weatherspoon unslung the big telescope that he kept over his shoulder ready for reading signal flags. The midshipman was good about caring for the instrument, and Biddlecomb was both pleased and amused by this. He wondered if it had ever occurred to Weatherspoon that there was virtually no one with whom they could exchange signals.

By the time he reached the head of the fore topmast, his breath was coming fast, much to his annoyance, and looking up into Rumstick's idiotic grin did nothing to relieve his mood. He pulled himself up onto the crosstrees and stood there catching his breath and ignoring the lieutenant. "What is it, Ezra?" he said at last.

"Look there, right up the harbor, in front of the town."

Biddlecomb scanned around the horizon, getting his bearings again. They were well into the Great Sound, which made up most of Bermuda's western end, and were standing in toward Hamilton Harbor, ghosting along at three knots in the light breeze. To the north, over the larboard beam and half a mile away, was Spanish Point, and arcing forward from the point, all the way around to the starboard beam like a broken castle wall, was the scattering of small islands that sheltered the entrance to the harbor.

Rumstick stepped aside and Biddlecomb took his place, aiming the signal telescope at the town of Hamilton, a mile and a half away. The town was a great white smudge in the unfocused lens, bordered above by the green of the thick vegetation in which it sat, and below by the aquamarine harbor over which it presided.

He twisted the tube until the island was in sharp focus and the white smudge resolved into individual whitewashed, stucco buildings. He moved the glass along the row of houses and over the unmoving water of the harbor. Two small vessels came into view, sloops riding at anchor, no flags flying from their ensign staffs. He paused, then continued to sweep west, then paused again.

"Oh, damn it. Damn it to hell," he whispered as his glass fixed on the next vessel in the anchorage. It was a frigate. There was no doubt about it. If the gunports had been closed, he might not have been so certain, but as it was, they were gaping open and even from a mile away he could see the vicious muzzles of the guns thrust out from the black gundeck. He felt his stomach tighten with disappointment and frustration and fear, churning together, felt the telltale tingling on the soles of his feet. A frigate. He hated that word.

He looked over at Rumstick. "Damn it."

"That was my feeling."

"I don't recognize her, do you?"

"No. She ain't the *Rose*, and I don't think she's the *Cerberus*."

"Well, we can thank God for that small favor."

"That's the truth. I don't know if I ever seen her before. It's hard to identify 'em with their rig down like that."

"Humph," Biddlecomb grunted in reply, putting his eye to the telescope once again. Her rig *was* down, completely down, and he felt like an idiot for having missed, in his panic, this most obvious fact. All of the frigate's yards were gone, as well as the topgallant masts, topmasts, jibboom, and mizzen gaff. All that was left of her running rigging was a gantline on each mast, and all that was left of her spars were the lower masts and bowsprit, stumpy looking in the absence of the top-hamper. The rig was sent down to a gantline and he had not even noticed, a fact that he was not going to admit to Rumstick. He felt his frustration and fear dissipate.

"She's not going anywhere soon," he said at last.

"Maybe they're going to heave her down," Rumstick suggested. It was possible. When the bottom of a ship became fouled with marine growth, as it did rapidly in the tropics, the only cure was to run her up on a beach on a falling tide and roll her on her side, cleaning the exposed bottom when the tide went out. On the next tide she was floated, turned, and then heaved down again on the other side. This laborious process meant emptying the hold of stores and guns and dismantling the entire rig.

"You could be right," Biddlecomb agreed. "In any event, that frigate isn't company I care to keep." He turned and called down to the deck, "Mr. Gardiner!"

"Aye, sir!" Gardiner called back from the quarterdeck.

"Put her about please, heading north by west. Just the hands on deck, keep the gunners hidden. I'll be down directly," Biddlecomb called, then training the glass toward the frigate again, he said to Rumstick, "Let's see if we have their attention."

The two men carefully adjusted their positions on the cross-trees, keeping their eyes directed at the frigate as the *Charlemagne* turned under them. The brig's about-face seemed to occasion no excitement aboard the man-of-war; Biddlecomb could see no movement at all on her decks.

His initial surprise ebbed and he realized that the strange frigate presented no immediate threat to them. He looked back at the sloops. There was no way to tell if they were merchantmen or naval vessels. Not that it mattered; they were too small to do any harm to the *Charlemagne.*

"It don't look like anyone's seen us, and even if they did, I don't think they'll reckon us for a Continental man-of-war," Rumstick observed.

Biddlecomb smiled. "Continental man-of-war" sounded so absurdly grandiose, especially when applied to their little brig, which, with gunports covered up, was indistinguishable from any of the many merchant vessels that visited the island. "It'll be two days at least before that rig is all sent up again, that's if they start working on it now," he said, "and it doesn't appear that they are. We should be able to snatch the powder and be hull down by the time they're under way."

Below their feet the *Charlemagne*'s yards squealed around as she settled on the opposite tack. Both men again raised their telescopes to their eyes and swept the harbor. The town of Hamilton was directly astern of them now as the *Charlemagne* retraced her course back out of the Great Sound. The scene in their lenses was the very picture of island tranquillity; the only visible activity was the few boats that moved lazily between the frigate and the shore.

"It doesn't look like we've got anyone's hackles up here," Biddlecomb said at last. "I imagine St. George's Harbor should answer our purposes just as well, and we'll be less visible there. What do you say?"

"I reckon we'll be all right if we can fetch the powder quick and be gone like, well, like thieves in the night."

"Well put. Let's lay back to deck." Biddlecomb slung the signal telescope over his shoulder and reached out for a backstay, then looked down at his stockings, the last good pair that he had. "I think I'll take the long way," he said, and swung his foot down to the topmast ratlines below.

For the next three hours, with Rumstick aloft once again to con the *Charlemagne* through the ship-killing reefs, Biddlecomb drove the brig north by east along the coral-strewn north shore of the island. They poked past Two Way Shoal and Elbow Shoal, making no more than three knots in the light air, but that was fine. If there was a chance of hitting coral, he preferred to do it at three knots rather than ten.

Stretched out along the starboard side was the low green island of Bermuda, and half a mile away was St. Catherine's Point, the steep hill that formed the northeast corner of the island, where they would turn southwest and run through the narrow gap in the reefs to Town Cut Channel and the entrance to St. George Harbor.

"On deck!" a voice cried, and Biddlecomb realized that for

the first time in three hours it was not Rumstick hailing but the lookout at the main topmast crosstrees.

"Deck, aye!"

"There's some people on shore, sir, looks like a lot of them!"

Biddlecomb picked up his telescope and trained it on the shore, less than half a mile away. There was indeed a crowd of people there. They stood on the sandy beach by the water's edge and seemed to be staring back at him.

"Well, damn, it looks like we have some friends here after all."

"Sir?" said Weatherspoon.

"Mr. Weatherspoon, I think it would be proper to show these people the ensign of the . . . well, I guess the Continental Army's navy. The white one with the pine tree. Run it aloft, if you would."

A minute later Weatherspoon broke the big white ensign out at the mainmast head, but the light air did little to lift the heavy cloth and the flag hung limp in a particularly undramatic fashion. Still, Biddlecomb was surprised at the effect that it had on the people watching from the shore. Through the signal telescope he could see figures pointing toward the brig, and others turn and hurry off inland behind the high, grassy dunes.

Finally the last of the islanders disappeared from sight. Biddlecomb looked past the bow to the shoreline in the distance. St. Catherine's Point was a quarter mile away, and beyond that headland was the entrance to the narrow channel between the reefs.

"On deck!" Rumstick sang out.

"Deck, aye!"

"I can see the reefs now, sir, off St. Katy's Point and past that, about half a mile away!"

"Very good, Mr. Rumstick. Now take us through!"

An hour passed before Biddlecomb noticed the tension in his shoulders, and he was quite surprised by the degree of pain that the knots were causing him. He looked away from the coral reefs, just thirty feet off either beam, that held him mesmerized and flexed his shoulders. They had rounded St. Catherine's Point and turned southwest and now they were sailing down the Narrows, the channel between the reefs. Rumstick had not called out a helm command for five minutes.

He looked past the starboard bow. The narrow Town Cut that opened up into St. George Harbor was clearly visible a mile away, but over that intervening mile the water above the coral was less than a fathom deep. To avoid ripping the *Charlemagne*'s bottom clean out, they had to maintain their course until the Cut was directly abeam, then turn right and shoot straight in, as if turning a corner on a city street.

Overhead the topsails flogged and hung limp, and the huge mainsail boom swung lazily inboard. The wind had dropped and was dropping still, and he was considering his next move when the *Charlemagne*'s bow began to swing to starboard, setting down on the sharp coral heads.

"Steady as she goes, damn it!" he turned on the helmsman as Rumstick shouted a warning from aloft, but the helmsman, his eyes wide, already had the tiller hard over.

"No steerage, Captain!"

No steerage. The *Charlemagne* was going too slow for the rudder to grip, and now they were caught in a flooding tide that was sucking them onto the reef. "Sweeps!" Biddlecomb shouted. "Hands to the sweeps! By gun crews! Mr. Sprout, break out sweeps!" Men leapt from their crouched positions by the guns and took up station at the row-ports. On Sprout's orders four men began pulling the long oars from the booms and passing them to anxious hands lining the bulwark.

Biddlecomb felt the brig lurch, and from the starboard bow he could hear the horrific sound of yellow-pine planking grinding against unyielding coral. "Mr. Sprout!" he shouted, but the boatswain had anticipated his orders and was leading a gang of men forward, a spare topgallant mast held between them at chest height, looking for all the world as if they were storming a castle gate. They thrust the spar over the bow, jamming it against the coral head, and threw their weight against it.

The *Charlemagne* was swinging now, pivoting on the grounded bow and setting down on the reef. "Sweeps! Run 'em through the after row-ports!" Biddlecomb shouted. "There! And there, run 'em out!"

The men rushed to obey, running the sweeps out through the aftermost of the small row-ports pierced through the bulwark. "Backwater now! Backwater!" Biddlecomb shouted, but this was one thing they had not practiced. To starboard the crew backed their sweeps, but on the larboard side one sweep went back and another forward and the two struck each other and tangled, knocking half the men to the deck.

Then Rumstick was there, sliding down the topgallant backstay in a controlled plummet. He hit the caprail with both feet, bounded off, and landed on the deck, grabbing up a sweep in his powerful arms and bellowing orders. "Backwater, you motherless bastards! Like this!" he shouted, even as he pulled the sweep aft, pulling the rest of the crew with him. The other men grabbed onto their sweeps and followed his lead, forcing the blades forward through the water.

Again Biddlecomb heard the crunching sound of wood on rock, but now it was the sound of the forefoot coming off the coral. He saw the spar yield under the pressure of Sprout and his gang. On either side men ran more sweeps out and joined in the effort as the *Charlemagne* moved backward, like a Roman galley backing off to ram her victim again.

"Thank you, Lord," he breathed to himself, and then, as the sweeps came dripping from the water for another stroke, called, "Starboard side, toss oars!" Rumstick and four other oarsmen obeyed, their oars hanging motionless over the side, but the rest, accustomed to the steady rhythm, brought their oars aft and down ready for another stroke as Rumstick shouted, "Toss oars, starboard side, you whoreson idiots! Toss oars! Don't move!" Thus enlightened, the men along the starboard side stood frozen as the larboard sweeps swept forward, turning the brig straight down the channel.

"Mr. Sprout, we'll sweep forward now, if you please," Biddlecomb called, and Sprout replied, "Forward, aye!" stepping up onto the fore fife rail and facing aft, like the galley's slave driver. "Sweeping forward now," he called, "just like rowing a boat. Good, all together now, and strooooke!" The sweeps came down in reasonable coordination and the *Charlemagne* gathered momentum again.

Rumstick stepped up to the quarterdeck. "This should be much to your liking, Isaac, playing it the great Caesar on his galley."

"*Et tu Brute?*"

"Beg your pardon?"

"Never mind. Back to the foremast head with you and bring us in. We'll go in under sweeps."

"Aye, sir." Rumstick hurried off forward, then flung himself into the fore shrouds and raced aloft.

Five minutes later Town Cut Channel, which opened into St. George Harbor, drew abeam of the *Charlemagne*, and Biddlecomb swung the bow east, making for the narrow entrance, maneuvering to pass between two thin markers that delineated the channel. Water swirled around the base of the markers, laying them over on their sides so they seemed to be pointing the way into the cut. The tide was flooding at full force, setting hard through the tiny channel and sweeping the *Charlemagne* into the harbor.

"Mr. Sprout, double time please!" he called. The brig would have to go faster than the flood if the rudder was to have any effect at all.

"Double time, aye, sir!" Sprout shouted, and with the next stroke he increased the cadence of his chant until the sweeps were moving at twice their former speed. Biddlecomb could see the sweat pouring off the men's faces and soaking their shirts, and here and there blood dripped from raw hands, making dark spots on the white deck.

The steep banks of the channel rose up on either side, almost to the level of the mainyard, and the *Charlemagne* was swept forward on the flood. Biddlecomb felt the ship slew to one side, and the helmsmen thrust the tiller in the other direction. The sweeps came down and pulled aft and the brig shot forward, and then they were through, the lovely, still water of St. George Harbor, enveloped on all sides by lush green hills, opening up before them.

"You may slow it back down, Mr. Sprout," Biddlecomb shouted, and an audible sigh of relief rose from the men at the sweeps. "Mr. Gardiner," he called to the second officer, who was sweating at number four sweep, "please prepare to anchor."

As the *Charlemagne* moved slowly across the harbor, Biddlecomb stared through the telescope at the town of St. George, a quarter mile away. It looked like a smaller version of Hamilton, and along the quay he could see a crowd of people, the same crowd, he imagined, that had come to the beach to greet them. A knot of men were gathered around a small cannon, mounted on a field carriage.

"Mr. Jaeger," he shouted. "Please prepare to return a salute from the shore."

"Salute, yes, sir," Jaeger called aft.

The *Charlemagne* was a cable length from the quay when Biddlecomb ordered the sweeps to backwater and Gardiner to let go the anchor. The best bower splashed down and the anchor hawser slowly paid out and they came to rest, floating motionless in the still harbor.

He turned his attention back to the shore. The men at the fieldpiece were standing to either side of the gun, and even without the glass he could see the match come down on the touch-hole. The gun leapt back, spurting smoke, and before he heard the gun's report he felt the round shot smash into the hull beneath his feet.

"Good God, they're shooting at us!" he shouted in surprise. He looked over the side of the brig. A six-pound ball, now badly deformed, was embedded in the planking. He looked up at the quay again, just in time to see the last of the people fleeing into the streets of St. George.

CHAPTER
12

St. George

IT WAS NOT THE WAY HE HAD ENVISIONED THEIR RECEPTION IN BERmuda, and it evidently was not what General Washington or Governor Cooke had in mind either. The sun was an hour away from disappearing in the west when the *Charlemagne's* longboat ground up on the beach and the boat crew tucked their oars away and leapt out onto the sand. Biddlecomb stood up from his place in the stern sheets and made his way forward until he was able to jump clear of the surf. He adjusted the cutlass that hung from a sling across his shoulder, then looked up at the town of St. George.

The streets, which had been deserted after the one-shot salvo was fired from the old fieldpiece, were deserted still, and there were no signs of life. He considered his situation, and that, in turn, led to a series of muttered curses. He had perhaps two days before the frigate on the far side of the island could be made ready for sea, and for safety's sake he had to assume that it would be. If he did not receive help from the islanders, then he would never be able to locate and liberate the cache of gunpowder in that short time.

The twenty armed men of the boat crew and landing party grunted as they heaved the longboat farther up the beach. Biddlecomb touched his hand to his breast, checking that General Washington's letter to the people of Bermuda was still tucked in his shirt. He was to use the letter only as a last resort, but as things were unfolding, it appeared that the last resort might be the only resort.

"All right, you men, form up behind me, double file," he said to the men who were milling about the beach. "Ferguson, you stay and keep an eye on the boat. That means stay with the boat. The rest of you come with me. All guns on the half cock. Mr. Weatherspoon, up here, if you please."

He pulled the cutlass from the sling, held the blade up, and waved it toward the town. "March!" he called, and the sailors headed across the sand in two ragged, unsoldierly files, toward the cobbled roads that branched out from the beach.

The town of St. George was lovely. The narrow cobblestone streets ran between stucco buildings, the whitewash of their upper stories tinted pink in the fading light, the ground floors lost in the deep shadows of the hills behind the town. Brilliant wildflowers cascaded from planters on the many balconies. The road sloped gently up, then down, like the swells of a placid sea. Biddlecomb divided his attention between the town and the sailors at his back. The men gawked at their strange surroundings, but they kept to their ragged files and seemed in no danger of misbehaving.

The landing party moved on. Soon the narrow street opened up into a square off of which ran three more streets like unevenly placed spokes on a wheel. Biddlecomb held up his hand and brought the men to a stop. He stared at the roads for half a minute and had settled on the second when he heard the sound of approaching men.

It was difficult to tell how many there were, or even from which direction they were coming. The Americans behind his back began to murmur, and he called for silence.

The sound of the strange mob grew louder. "Stand ready," he ordered, and the men spread out in the square, muskets in their hands, fingers curled around flintlocks and triggers. He heard a lock snap into the cocked position.

"Half cock, damn it, half cock," he hissed. "Mr. Weatherspoon, check that all muskets are on half cock. If one man fires before I give the word, he gets two dozen lashes at first light!" Even as he made the threat, he wondered if he could carry it out. Yes, he realized, he could. And would.

Then a mob of men, at least twenty that he could see and with muskets much in evidence, burst from the street to his left. Biddlecomb's surprise at seeing them was nothing to the surprise of the Bermudians at seeing the American landing party. Some shouted, some ducked behind the building on the corner, and more than a few leveled their weapons at the sailors.

At his back he heard several locks click, his men forgetting or ignoring his orders. With two quick steps, and before he could think about it, he advanced toward the Bermudians, his hands held up, palms out. "Hold your fire! For the love of God, hold your fire!" he shouted.

No shots came, but he could see that the muskets were now leveled at him. He turned to his own men. "Hold your fire! Put up your guns!" Slowly, reluctantly, the Americans pointed their muskets toward the sky.

Biddlecomb turned back toward the Bermudians. "We don't wish a fight with you," he said in as calm a tone as he could muster. "We didn't come here to fight."

"No, of course you didn't, you blackballing whoreson!" replied a portly gentleman who seemed to have hastily dressed in a silk shirt, embroidered waistcoat, and breeches, incorrectly buttoned. He held a musket at chest height and stepped forward from the mob of armed islanders. " 'Cause you didn't expect a fight, just figured you'd come and take our livestock and take our water, like always! Well, we've been ill-used by you for the last time, *Captain!*" He said the last word with a sarcastic flourish, and through the gathering dusk Biddlecomb could see smiles on the faces of the islanders.

"You have the advantage of me, sir," he began, but the portly man was not through with his harangue.

"First your damn frigate cleans out the livestock at Hamilton, then the sloops take what they want, and now you come here because the rest of the island's picked clean! Well, we won't stand for it, sir!" The man's volume increased until the last words were practically shouted. Behind him the Bermudians nodded and murmured their agreement, and more men stepped from the street into the square.

And suddenly Biddlecomb understood the mistake and he smiled. "We're Americans, sir, not British. We represent the Continental Army of the United Colonies of America, not the British navy."

The portly man opened his mouth, apparently ready to further lambast the intruders, but his expression brightened like a lantern unshuttered. "Americans? Americans, did you say?"

"Yes, sir. We are representatives of the Continental navy. Well, actually the army, sort of the navy branch of the army . . . it's still a bit unsettled." He stepped toward the big man and shook his eagerly proffered hand.

"Americans, you say?" the portly man said again. "Well, that's something else all together! Your colonies have been as ill-used as ours. An honor, sir, an honor. Dreadfully sorry about this, calling out the militia and all. Bloody navy's been helping themselves to our livestock, our crops, our water . . . water's damn precious here, you know, no source but rainwater on this island. Been sucking us dry."

"We share many of the same grievances, sir, with Parliament and the arrogance of the military." Biddlecomb considered the note from Washington; apparently it would not be needed after all. "In fact, it is just that matter that brings us to your island. Could you direct me to the chief official here?"

"You're looking at him, man, you're looking at him! I'm the Right Honorable William Cornwall, Mayor William Cornwall, mayor of St. George and colonel of militia."

"Mayor, it's an honor. I'm Capt. Isaac Biddlecomb, of the Continental brig-of-war *Charlemagne*. The matter I have to discuss is, well, perhaps better discussed in private."

"Of course, of course, I am certainly sensible to military secrets."

"I would be honored if you and your officials would be my guests. Aboard the *Charlemagne*."

"We'd be delighted, Captain . . . Biddlecomb, did you say?

Biddlecomb!" Turning to a middle-aged man who held a musket at his side and whose silk stockings had fallen down around his ankles, the mayor continued, "John, please call together the Committee of Safety. Captain Biddlecomb here has invited us aboard the Continental man-of-war. Captain, is there anything we can provide for your vessel, anything at all?"

Biddlecomb considered the offer. "I'm hesitant to ask, what with your recent depredations, but fresh food, meat, and vegetables are always welcome on shipboard. And fresh water if you can spare it."

"Of course we can spare it, brothers in arms and all that," the mayor said, smiling in the sincere pleasure of generosity. "And of course rum, Bermuda rum, the best in the world!"

"Ah, well, actually we have rum, really, all we need. Perhaps it would be best if we just imposed on you for the meat and water . . . ," Biddlecomb said, but before he could finish his sentence, the mayor was issuing orders.

The town's officials who made up their Committee of Safety, so Biddlecomb came to discover, consisted of every citizen in St. George of any wealth or note, nine in all. The *Charlemagne*'s longboat was filled nearly to capacity as they were rowed out to the brig.

"Dreadfully sorry about the cannonade when you came into the harbor," Mayor Cornwall said for the third time. "We did think you were British, and, you know, that white ensign can be misconstrued if you don't see it full."

"Truly, an honest mistake and there's no harm done to the *Charlemagne*. I see the carpenter's already repaired what little damage there was," Biddlecomb said, indicating the patch of fresh wood on the *Charlemagne*'s side.

"Well," Cornwall said, and then after a pause added, "I'm right glad," in a tone that sounded more like disappointment than relief.

The longboat came alongside the *Charlemagne*, and one by one, and with varying degrees of difficulty, the officials of St. George made there way up the brig's boarding steps and straight into the blast of the side party's bosun's calls. Rumstick, on seeing the loaded boat pulling back to the *Charlemagne*, had organized all available pomp.

Biddlecomb waited in the longboat. As captain he should have been first aboard his own command, but in this instance he was glad to distance himself from the caterwauling topside.

The last of the city officials clambered aboard and the captain followed him up and the piping ceased. "Gentlemen, please follow me," he said, and led the procession down the scuttle and aft.

The great cabin, which seemed crowded when Biddlecomb entertained the *Charlemagne*'s three officers, was now packed to capacity. The city officials stacked their muskets in one corner and with much difficulty arranged themselves on various seats. Weatherspoon was sent to gather up a sufficient number of cups to serve wine to all the ship's guests, and soon they were drinking a toast to their common cause, some from wine glasses, some from pewter mugs, and some from tin.

It was a warm night, and inside the tiny cabin, with the close-packed men and four lanterns illuminating the space, it was soon sweltering. Biddlecomb could feel the sweat beneath his coat and he tugged at the stock around his neck. He longed to pull the stock off, and his coat as well, but as a representative of the Continental Congress he felt that some formality was called for. He mopped his brow with his handkerchief as discreetly as he was able.

"And now, Captain, how can this Committee be of assistance?" Cornwall asked after the toast was completed.

"Well, sir," Biddlecomb began, "it's no secret that we in America have initiated what might become a long struggle for certain of our rights. We have shed blood at Lexington and Concord, and at Bunker Hill . . ." He paused, struggling for the words, hoping to sound sincere and not melodramatic. It occurred to him that he had never before had to plead for or even explain the American cause.

"Right now the Continental Army, under the command of Gen. George Washington, has encircled the British Parliament's ministerial army stationed in Boston." He looked around the cabin. The men were listening intently and nodding their heads. "We are in a good position, save for one thing. There's a serious shortage of gunpowder."

He took a deep breath and launched into the heart of the matter. "We have it on good authority that the British have a store of gunpowder on the island, and that it is lightly defended. My mission is to liberate that powder, employing my own forces, and joined by your militia if you wish, and to bring it back to General Washington."

He stopped and leaned back, trying to guess what the mayor and the others were thinking. Cornwall spoke first.

"It's a capital plan. You know we've had our eye on that powder ourselves, would have taken it too if we had any place to put it. Certainly, we'll—"

A Committee member seated on Biddlecomb's sea chest in the corner cut the mayor off. "My pardon, Bill, but I think I best speak to this." The man turned to Biddlecomb. "I'm afraid you're too late, Captain, just barely, but too late none the less. That frigate over in Hamilton cleaned out the powder stores two days ago. First thing they did after they came to anchor, took all the powder on board. As you see, I haven't even had the chance to inform my fellow Committee members."

A murmur ran through the great cabin as the Bermudians discussed this new intelligence. Biddlecomb felt his stomach tighten into a knot. Of all the cursed luck! If he hadn't wasted all that time on the crossing, drilling his woolgathering crew, he would have made it in time to fulfill his mission. But now he would have to return with his hold empty and explain why he had wasted so much precious powder exercising his gun crews. He felt like a fool, and he knew that the humiliation he felt then was nothing to the way he would feel explaining it all to Fitzgerald and Washington.

"Well, that's the damnedest luck," Cornwall said, echoing Biddlecomb's thoughts. "But there's no chance of taking it now, I fear, even with the help of the militia."

Biddlecomb stared out of the quarter gallery window into the darkening evening. Something about the committeeman's report bothered him. "Pardon me, sir," he said, turning to the man perched on his sea chest, "you said the first thing the frigate did on arrival was to clear the powder out of the storehouse and load it aboard? Do you mean that they actually brought the powder on board? They didn't store it under guard ashore?"

"They brought it on board. That much I saw with my own eyes."

"And then they struck their top-hamper?"

" 'Struck their top-hamper'? I'm afraid I don't follow your sea jargon, Captain."

"They took down their masts and sails? After they loaded the powder on board?"

"Yes. Actually, as I recall, they were doing both together."

Biddlecomb frowned as he considered this. It made no sense. If they were dismantling the rig to heave the frigate down, then they would be taking stores off of the ship, not bringing more aboard.

"Is there a problem, Captain?" the mayor asked.

"No, Your Honor, none," Biddlecomb said, shaking off his contemplations and standing up, "but I'm afraid there is little we can accomplish now, so we had best sail on the first ebb tomorrow. Damned unfortunate. Another round of wine with you?"

"With pleasure, sir," Cornwall said. "Damned unfortunate indeed, about the powder." He extended his glass. "Fortunes of war, and all that."

Biddlecomb made every effort to remain pleasant and conversational as he offered up two more rounds of wine to his guests, consuming in the process five bottles and an hour and a half. He was anxious for the men to leave, but in the name of diplomacy he tried not to let his anxiety show.

At last Cornwall rose to leave and the others followed his example. "Sorry again about the powder, Captain," he said. "I hope in future we can be of some assistance."

"I thank you, sir," said Biddlecomb, extending his hand to the mayor. "I thank you personally, and in the name of Gen-

eral Washington and the Congress of the United Provinces."
Then through the open door he called, "Mr. Weatherspoon!"
and, when the midshipman appeared, said, "Please see the
longboat prepared to bring these gentlemen ashore."

Twenty minutes later he and Rumstick stood together on the
quarterdeck, watching the longboat pull away as Weatherspoon took the St. George Committee of Safety ashore. In
the light of the new moon Biddlecomb could see flushed and
glistening faces and stupid grins scattered among the *Charlemagne's* company.

"They sent rum aboard, didn't they?" he asked softly.

"Yes, sir, along with the fresh meat and vegetables them
gentlemen had sent over. Gardiner and me tried to stop the
hands getting at it, but . . ." Rumstick's voice trailed off into
an embarrassed silence.

"Never mind, just see the hands don't get any drunker than
they are. We have greater concerns."

"About the powder? Is there a problem?"

"No, the powder won't be any problem for us," Biddlecomb
said bitterly, the humiliation of his failure rising to the surface
again, "because the British already have it. Took it on board
the frigate the moment they arrived here."

"Damn it all!" Rumstick cursed softly, then fell quiet, and
Biddlecomb knew that the lieutenant's mind was moving
down the same path as had his own. "That don't make sense,
though," he said at last. "Do you mean they took it on board
or they're just guarding it?"

"Took it on board apparently, as soon as the hook was
down."

"If they're getting ready to heave down, why would they
take the powder on board?"

"I don't know."

"Maybe they ain't heaving down. Maybe they're setting up
new rigging."

"Maybe, though this is kind of an odd place for that. You'd
think they'd go to Halifax or Antigua, someplace with a dock-
yard and a rigging loft."

"You'd think."

"Tack or wear, I have a bad feeling about this, and I don't care to wait for the answer. Our mission's ruined in any event. I want to be under way on the first of the ebb."

As if on cue, both men leaned over the bulwark and peered down at the water alongside. The current was making little ripples as it streamed down the length of the hull, as if the *Charlemagne* were already under way.

"Tide's ebbing now," Rumstick observed, then looking out over the water added, "Might be enough moonlight to work through the coral heads tonight."

Biddlecomb considered this. He could try to work his way through at night with a half-drunk crew and only the moonlight to reveal the murderous coral, or wait twelve hours, until noon the following day, for the next ebb tide. "I think we'll wait for morning, Ezra, and get under way at slack water. The hands aren't dead drunk, are they?"

"Ah, no, sir. They ain't too far gone, not at all. Except . . ."

"Please don't say . . ."

"Excepting for Jaeger."

It was an hour before dawn when Biddlecomb stepped up onto the quarterdeck, a steaming mug of coffee in his hand, and fifteen minutes after that that Mr. Sprout began waking the hands. He was none too quiet or gentle in his treatment of the men; his shouts and kicks were as much for the sake of punishment as to see that they were properly awake and sober. With many a groan and clutching of an aching head, the men fell to, sweeping and scrubbing down the deck.

Biddlecomb swallowed the last gulp of coffee and set the mug on the binnacle box. The tide was near full flood, the water pouring in through the narrow Town Cut Channel, which was their only exit to the open sea, and the *Charlemagne* swung on her anchor until the jibboom was pointing directly east, pointing at the rising sun.

There was nothing to do but wait. Though the light wind was out of the northwest and fair for leaving the harbor, they could not make headway against that tide, and Biddlecomb felt his impatience mounting. He pulled off his greatcoat and snatched up the signal telescope. "Mr. Rumstick," he said as he stepped up onto the bulwark, "I'm going to the masthead to look around," then began the climb aloft, eager for any activity to pass the time.

He climbed on the larboard side, facing south, admiring the brilliant light blue water of St. George Harbor and Castle Harbor beyond that. From the main topmast crosstrees Bermuda was even more beautiful than it was from the deck. The view from aloft accentuated the brilliance of the water where it met with white sand and green forest along the shoreline. He turned and looked north. The town of St. George, again bathed in the pink light of the low-hanging sun, looked warm and comforting.

He swept his glass past the town, past St. Catherine's Point, and out toward the stretch of water over which they had passed only yesterday. He moved the telescope west, staring out toward the horizon, and suddenly his circle of vision was filled with a ship, just over a mile away. He gasped in surprise, almost dropping the glass. He twisted the tube and the vessel resolved into sharp focus.

It was the frigate. It was the frigate, driving hard along the northern shore, heading to round St. Catherine's Point. Her towering rig, which the day before had been dismantled, was set up again, save for her topgallant yards. Through the glass Biddlecomb could see the light spars swayed aloft, and the topgallant sails, already bent on, were set and drawing even before he had recovered enough to speak.

CHAPTER
13

Flood Tide

"MR. RUMSTICK!" BIDDLECOMB SHOUTED DOWN TO THE DECK, AND the urgency in his voice made every man look aloft. "Please prepare to cut the cable. I want sweeps out immediately!"

"Aye, sir!" Rumstick replied, then turned to issue orders to the men forward, but they were already acting on Biddlecomb's commands, assembling by gun crews at the row-ports and passing out the sweeps. They knew by now how much real danger it took to make their captain sound that anxious.

Biddlecomb put the glass to his eye again and took one last critical look at the frigate before laying back to the deck. She now had all plain sail set, and weather studdingsails as well, and appeared to be making six knots at least in the light wind. Her gunports were closed, but he did not need to see the row of big guns to know they were there.

He moved the glass up along the edge of the driver. There, partially obscured by the frigate, was another vessel; Biddlecomb could just see a long boom jutting out over a transom, and above it the peak of a gaff with another ensign fluttering from a halyard. It was one of the two sloops that he had seen in Hamilton Harbor, and there was no question now as to their being vessels of the Royal Navy.

That was all that he needed to see. He slung the glass over his shoulder and reached out for a backstay, sliding to the deck and turning his last pair of silk stockings into tar-stained and shredded rags.

He reached the caprail on the quarterdeck and from that vantage point surveyed the scene forward. The men had run the sweeps out the row-ports and now stood ready. Sprout and Rumstick, with the parsimony bred of cumulative years as boatswains, were leading a gang of men at hauling in as much of the cable as they could before it was cut.

"That's all you get, Mr. Rumstick," Biddlecomb shouted. "Mr. Sprout, do your duty."

Sprout nodded, picked up his ax and brought it down on the thick cable, cutting the strands with powerful strokes. The cable parted and the *Charlemagne* began to drift to larboard, pushed by the flooding tide. "Sweeps, give way!" Biddlecomb shouted, and with more coordination than they had displayed the day before, the men brought the sweeps down and aft and the brig gathered way, nosing forward against the tide. 'Straight for the cut, take us right out of here," he said to the man at the tiller.

"Straight for the cut, aye," the helmsman replied.

After the frenetic manner in which the brig was put under way, the *Charlemagne* seemed positively tranquil as Sprout took up the cadence and the men settled into the monotony of working the sweeps. But Biddlecomb could see the anxiety on their faces, could see the furtive glances over the sides as they searched for the cause of their hasty departure. They did not yet know of the frigate racing along the north shore, less than a mile away on the other side of the narrow island. But they would, and soon.

Rumstick stepped up to the quarterdeck, crossed to the weather side, and saluted formally, making an obvious effort to restrain his curiosity.

"Beg pardon, sir, but . . ."

"The frigate, the one we saw in Hamilton, is just north of the island, just over there," Biddlecomb said, pointing over the larboard side. "Rig sent up, all sail to weather studdingsails set. They were just crossing topgallants when I saw them. One of the sloops is with her."

Rumstick sucked in his breath and scowled. Biddlecomb could see the veins bulging in his neck as he considered this news. "The rig's sent up? That was pretty fucking fast, wouldn't you say? How in the hell did they do that?"

That was a question that Biddlecomb had been asking himself, one of a growing number of questions. He looked over the larboard side, then down at the water, ignoring Rumstick for the moment. They were making progress, but with the flood tide their speed was half of what it should have been with the effort the men were putting into the sweeps.

"I think it could be done," he replied at last, "if the rig was taken down and laid out with the intention of sending it up again fast."

"What purpose would that serve? Why would anyone do that?" Rumstick demanded, becoming increasingly angry.

"This is a trap," Biddlecomb said, realizing it even as he spoke the words. "The frigate wasn't here by accident, it was waiting for us, and they sent their rig down so they wouldn't appear a threat and scare us away. Why else would they have loaded the powder aboard first thing, unless they knew that's what we were coming for? I can think of no other logical explanation." He felt his anger rising to match Rumstick's. They had been betrayed, and they would be damn lucky to escape, if they could escape at all.

"Son of a bitch . . . Some damned Judas . . . but who could have done this? What infernal tool knew what we were doing?"

"I don't know, and right now we have bigger worries than smoking the traitor. If we don't clear past the Cut and get into open water before that frigate blocks us in, then it won't matter much who betrayed us. Even if we get clear first, we'll be hard-pressed to escape now."

The two men looked north to the shoreline, then east to the Town Cut Channel that led back to the open sea. They were almost past the town of St. George, but their progress was growing slower as they approached the swifter moving water flowing through the Cut.

"I don't know if the men can sweep against this current, Captain," Rumstick said.

"I don't imagine that they can. We'll have to kedge out of the harbor. I want every anchor on board forward and ready to go." Biddlecomb's mind began working through the problems at hand, and he issued orders as he went. He could feel his fear and anger settling into something benign as he envisioned solutions to their predicament. Taking command always had a cathartic effect on him.

"Bend cables to the anchors that don't have them and get the boats ready to go over the side. Get Mr. Sprout and take whatever men you need, one man from each sweep. I want everyone on deck. I don't see the cook or the cooper; I want them on the sweeps as well. And where in hell is Jaeger? Get that useless piece of rubbish up and aft."

Rumstick hurried forward, issuing orders on the run. One man from each sweep left off, and soon a gang of men was preparing to put the gig and the longboat over the side, while a second gang, jumping to Sprout's orders, were wrestling the sheet anchor, stream anchor, and kedge anchor forward.

It was going to be a nightmare trying to get the brig out of the harbor against the flood tide, and once out of the harbor they still had to make it through the reefs before they could attempt an escape. But if they managed to get out, Biddlecomb could try to shake the frigate with a game of follow-my-leader through the coral reefs surrounding the island. And if the frigate made it to the Cut before they were through? They would be trapped in a harbor on an island, and there was no place to run.

"Beg your pardon, sir," Jaeger's slurred voice cut through Biddlecomb's morbid thoughts.

He turned and regarded the gunnery officer. His face had a gray pallor and his dark hair was projecting wildly in all directions. His larboard shirttail was hanging out, and the rest of the shirt was marked by various unidentifiable stains. "Jaeger, you look like . . . God knows what, like something on a stable floor. You're a disgrace, an utter disgrace, and if we're not prisoners of war by this time tomorrow, I'll set you ashore the first chance I get. Is that clear?"

Jaeger clutched his head with one hand. "Yes, sir. Aye, sir," he corrected himself.

"I am going to give you yet another chance to redeem yourself, if that's still possible. I want you to handpick a crew and man the forwardmost gun on the larboard side. When we emerge from the channel, you should have a target, perhaps two. Do you understand?"

"Aye, sir."

"Good. Get on with it," Biddlecomb said, then turned his back on the Prussian.

They were making virtually no headway now. Biddlecomb stared over the side at the water as it ran down the hull. It rushed along the waterline, swirling and making eddies around the ship. From that perspective it appeared as if the *Charlemagne* were moving at a tremendous rate, but it was the flood tide moving past the hull, not the hull moving through the water, that created the illusion. A quick glance at the fishing boats anchored nearby confirmed that fear. They were still a cable length away from entering the cut, and they could no longer make headway with the sweeps.

They would have to kedge, have to move the brig forward by taking an anchor out ahead with a boat, dropping it, then winching the *Charlemagne* up to it with the capstan.

"Mr. Rumstick, Mr. Gardiner, Mr. Sprout, we'll have to start kedging now," Biddlecomb called out from the break of the quarterdeck. "We'll put the gig in the water with the kedge anchor. I want the men to remain at the sweeps until the first anchor is holding."

At his command the gig lifted off the booms amidships and swung outboard as the men at the sweeps continued their exhausting effort. Just beyond the reach of the long oars the gig dropped in the water, and less than two minutes later Gardiner, in charge of the small boat, had the kedge anchor hanging from the davits over the transom and was pulling away from the *Charlemagne.* The anchor cable stretched from the brig's bow to the anchor on the stern of the gig, and forward Rumstick's gang was feeding slack out of the hawsehole.

Biddlecomb stared at St. Catherine's Point, trying to imagine where on the other side of that high ground the frigate was now. Were they becalmed there, or had they already made it into the narrow channel between the reefs and were now moving to block the *Charlemagne's* escape? He felt his stomach tighten, felt the soles of his feet tingle with the fear of the pending battle.

He thought of the night six months before when the *Icarus* had been pounded to a wreck under his feet, the decks slick with blood, men screaming, crushed by wreckage falling from aloft and pinned under the fiery hot muzzles of overturned guns. He thought of Bloody Wilson, the man he had made second officer aboard the *Icarus.* His friend. He remembered the stupid look on Wilson's face as he died contemplating his own guts, torn from his body and spilling over the deck, steaming in the cold night.

He shook his head and cursed himself for a coward and a fool. He would not have to worry about causing the deaths of any more men if he paid attention to his duty and got them out of the harbor before the frigate came up to them. Or if he had not agreed to this fool's errand. Or if he had not been betrayed.

He looked forward, past the bow, just as Gardiner let slip the anchor and it disappeared below the crystalline blue water.

"Up oars!" Biddlecomb called out, and the sweeps rose from the water and hovered motionless in the air. The *Charlemagne's* forward momentum was gone and she hung still for a second before gathering sternway. Then with a subtle jerk the brig came to a stop as the anchor cable took up the strain. "Anchor's holding," Rumstick called aft.

"Unship your sweeps!" Biddlecomb said to the men in the waist. "Run 'em in there and lay them on the booms! Man the capstan, let's go!"

The long sweeps were run inboard and were laid indelicately on the spare spars amidships as men rushed to take their positions at the capstan bars. Biddlecomb would have liked to keep the sweeps manned, to sweep and kedge together, but he needed the capstan and both boats manned, as well as one gun at least, and even a man-of-war did not carry enough men for all that.

"Heave away the capstan!" Biddlecomb shouted as the last of the men ducked under the swifter and held a bar to his chest. Slowly the capstan turned, then faster and faster as the cable came inboard and the men at the hatch fed it down to the cable tier below.

"Mr. Rumstick, get these idle hands ready to put the longboat in the water and tell off the boat crew," Biddlecomb called, forcing back with further activity the gruesome shades of his memories. "Mr. Sprout, you will take charge of the longboat. We'll set the second bower next."

He looked toward the anchored fishing boats and was gratified to see that they were astern of the *Charlemagne* now. The brig was making progress, real progress, out of the trap and toward the Cut and the open sea.

"Short peak!" Rumstick called, indicating that as much of the anchor cable had been hauled in as could be without breaking the anchor out of the bottom. Now they would have to pull the men away from the capstan to get the bigger boat in the water.

Biddlecomb tapped his foot with impatience as the longboat was got over the side and manned. And though the Charlemagnes could not possibly have done it fast enough to please him, still it was no more than three minutes before the second bower was loaded aboard and the longboat swept forward, taking the anchor out far ahead of the brig.

And that was how it would work; haul the brig up to one anchor as the second is set, then haul up to that and reset the first, as many times as they had to, until they were prisoners or they were free.

At the larboard bow Jaeger and his picked gun crew were

clearing away the number two gun. Jaeger had cleaned himself up a bit, Biddlecomb could see, and he moved with the calmness and efficiency that the guns seemed to evoke in him.

Beneath the clacking of the capstan pawls and the creaking of the cables and the shouted orders and grunting of the straining men, Biddlecomb heard a low rumble, like far-distant thunder, but higher pitched, and realized with a start that it was gunfire.

He felt the panic explode inside, like a submerged volcano, and thought for a second that he would be sick. Was the frigate already through the Narrows, already blockading the Town Cut Channel through which they were trying to kedge? He jumped up onto the bulwark, steadying himself with the backstay, and aimed his glass east through the cut. There was a ship there, but it was not the frigate. The sloop was gliding past the entrance. The little vessel must have gone ahead, more confident among the reefs with its small size and shallow draft, and now they were taking potshots at the *Charlemagne* with their tiny guns.

Biddlecomb felt the panic ebb, felt an overwhelming relief, even as the sloop fired another of her guns. They were sailing past the Cut, and it would take them a while to find water deep enough to tack and work their way back. And even if they did, even if they stood in the *Charlemagne*'s way, it was only a sloop, flimsy scantlings, four-pound guns at best and not many of them. The *Charlemagne* could blow them out of the water, pound them to kindling. His men were drilled with the guns and they were fast and steady. He could reduce that sloop to flotsam and it would not even slow him down.

He realized, to his surprise, that he was grinding his teeth and savoring the vision of destroying the enemy's vessel. He had never experienced such blood lust in his life. He thought of his father. Fighting John Biddlecomb. Viking John.

He smiled at the idea of himself as a warrior, a *berserker* as the old Norsemen called those who were overwhelmed with fighting madness. Just a moment before, when he thought that the frigate was up with them, he had been ready to puke from fear. He was a fair-weather Viking, to be sure.

He was still smiling at the thought when he hopped back down to the deck and Rumstick called out, "Short peak!"

Short peak. One anchor was ready to break out, and then they could haul the ship up to the next, which was already set, haul themselves closer to the open sea.

"Heave away!" he shouted, and the men leaned into the capstan. The jibboom was already extending into the Cut, and with a few turns of the capstan the *Charlemagne* would be into that narrow gap. The sloop was nowhere to be seen; her captain had no doubt sailed past the entrance and was now looking for a place to come about. If he did not make it back before the *Charlemagne* was clear of the land, then he would be very sorry.

Something was wrong. Biddlecomb no longer heard the fall of the capstan pawls, and the sound of the men heaving was now a low and desperate groan. He looked down at the waist and met Rumstick's eyes.

"Anchor won't break out!" the lieutenant called. "Must be hung up on something."

"Cut it away! Just cut it now!" Biddlecomb said without a second's hesitation. He had envisioned this happening, that was why he had had every anchor aboard brought up to the bow. "We'll use the stream anchor next, that's already got a cable bent," he continued as Rumstick brought the ax down on the cable, parting the six-inch line in two strokes. The short end of the severed cable flew out of the hawsehole and the *Charlemagne* slewed astern until the cable from the kedge anchor took up the strain.

The men at the capstan stamped around once more and the *Charlemagne* moved slowly into the Town Cut Channel.

The steep banks rose up on either side of the brig, and the smell of the vegetation and the sound of the many insects there mixed with the familiar sounds and smells of the brig. The water roiled along the sandy banks and made eddies around any imperfection below the surface. The current held the brig in its grip and pointed the bow straight out of the Cut. The men at the capstan grunted and strained as they hauled her forward against the terrific press of water. By the time they hauled up to the next anchor, they would be clear of the Cut, surrounded on three sides by the open ocean. But then they still had to clear a half a mile of coral reefs before they could run for safety.

"Short peak!" Rumstick called again.

"Heave away!" Biddlecomb called, and the men leaned into the capstan bars. The anchor came free of the ground and again the *Charlemagne* slewed back until her sternway was snubbed by the other hook.

They were in the Cut, surrounded on both sides by the steep banks, and beyond the land Biddlecomb could see the open ocean, the long swells and the corduroy ripples that indicated a soft breeze over the surface.

It was maddening not knowing where the frigate was, not knowing if it was an hour from coming up with them or a minute. The tip of the jibboom was now clear of the Cut and jutting out into the open water; from there he would be able to see the enemy. But he had no business at the end of the jibboom. His place was on the quarterdeck, pretending to be unflappable as he led his men through the madness.

The hell with that, he thought, pulling off his coat and hat and dropping them on top of the binnacle. He snatched up his telescope and made his way forward, skirting past the long capstan bars and stepping onto the heel of the bowsprit and through the knightheads. He clambered outboard, up and out over the water, searching with his foot for a secure hold as the angle became increasingly severe. The water twenty-five feet below was like molten glass, and the white sand and scattering of rocks and kelp and coral were visible under the crystal stream that flowed over them and bubbled around the *Charlemagne*'s cutwater.

He reached the end of the jibboom and with his hand on the fore topgallant stay pulled himself up until he was standing on the narrow spar. From that point, as far forward on the brig as one could go, the island was astern of him and in front water stretched away in every direction. He took a breath and looked northwest along the shore.

The frigate was there, less than a mile away and turning into the Narrows, having weathered St. Catherine's Point. They were under topsails and jibs alone, moving slowly in the light air, feeling their way through the coral. Biddlecomb felt some tiny sense of relief. It was a race now, and a close one, but there was still a chance.

He heard Rumstick's ax fall as the lieutenant cut away another fouled anchor. We're losing anchors at the rate of three per hour, he mused. But anchors were easier to replace than ships.

And then the frigate fired, let loose her first terrible broadside. The air was filled with the shriek of flying metal, and Biddlecomb found he was falling, flailing in the air, his support gone. He lashed out and caught something solid and gripped it with both hands, regaining his balance. The fore topgallant stay, with which he had been steadying himself, had parted, cut in two by a lucky shot from the frigate, and he had managed to grapple the royal stay before falling off the jibboom into the water below.

The boats! Biddlecomb whirled around, fearing that the fragile boats had been blown apart in the fusillade, but they were intact and still rocking from the turbulence created by the round shot's striking the water.

He reached out with his toe until he found the jibboom horse, and a minute later he was stepping back through the knightheads and onto the heel of the bowsprit.

"Sir?" he heard Jaeger's thick accent. "May I have permission to fire?"

"Of course, Jaeger, fire at will."

The Prussian leaned down over the gun, peering along the muzzle and out of the gunport to the frigate in the distance. "Handspike, here," he said, and one of the gun crew stepped up and muscled the gun to the left.

Biddlecomb stepped back between the knightheads. The bow

of the *Charlemagne* was now past the land, and from his position Biddlecomb could see the frigate clearly. The big ship was into the Narrows, running the tricky gauntlet of reefs that would lead them to the *Charlemagne,* the same gauntlet that the *Charlemagne* had run yesterday. Few of the frigate's guns would bear now, which was a good thing, but they would also be closing in on the brig, which was not.

Biddlecomb pulled the glass from his breeches and put it to his eye just as Jaeger's gun went off with a roar. He saw wood fly from the frigate's bulwark amidship.

"Excellent shot, Jaeger!" His voice sounded strange to him and far away after the deafening cannon blast.

"This gun pulls to the left when it's cold," Jaeger said as the barrel was sponged out.

The *Charlemagne* inched along, slowly forward, the men at the capstan pulling her against the tide while three-quarters of a mile away the frigate bore down on them.

"Run out!" Jaeger called, and the gun crew laid back on the side tackle and the gun was thrust from the port.

"Handspike, here! Move!" Jaeger called, his voice calm and urgent all at once. "Good!"

Biddlecomb was ready for the shot this time, with his outboard hand training the glass on the frigate and an inboard finger in his ear. The gun went off, leaping back with the recoil. Aboard the distant man-of-war he could see wood shattering along the quarterdeck rail and figures thrown to the deck.

The frigate yawed to larboard, swinging out of control. He watched, transfixed, as the bow turned away from him. And then the man-of-war stopped, shuddering along its length, its masts swaying like saplings in a gale, and Biddlecomb knew that she was on the reef.

CHAPTER
14

HMS *Glasgow*

IF JAEGER WAS AWARE THAT HE HAD JUST SHOT OUT THE FRIGATE'S helm, an extraordinary shot at that extreme range, then he did not show it. Even before the gun had come to a rest against its breech ropes, he was stopping the vent and ordering the sponge run down the muzzle, giving hardly a glance to the fall of the shot.

Biddlecomb was not nearly as stoic. He smiled as he watched through the glass the bedlam on the frigate's quarterdeck. Blue uniforms and red scattered like leaves in the breeze, and men swarmed over the deck. Before Jaeger's crew had run the gun out again he saw the frigate's longboat hoisted aloft, and he imagined that they would try to kedge off the reef, try to pull the frigate astern in the same way that he was pulling the *Charlemagne* forward.

A half a mile to starboard the sloop had tacked and was working her way back. None of the *Charlemagne*'s guns would bear on the sloop, and if her captain was smart, he would keep it that way. Once we're clear of this damned reef, Biddlecomb thought, we'll pound that little bastard into driftwood.

"Short peak!" Rumstick called. The *Charlemagne* was out of the Cut now, and nothing but the unbroken surface of the water was between the frigate, the brig, and the sloop. But one glance over the side belied the freedom of the open ocean. Even from the deck Biddlecomb could see the reefs that held them as tightly as the banks of a narrow river. They still had half a mile to kedge before they were free of the land.

"Heave away!" he shouted as he stepped aft to the quarter-deck. "Mr. Weatherspoon, pray fetch the ensign and run it up to the mainmast head."

As Weatherspoon fished around for the flag, Biddlecomb focused his glass on the frigate. Her sails were clewed up now and the boat was in the water, its crew assembling on the deck and clambering down the side. And then Jaeger's gun went off and the boat exploded into fragments, sending men and oars and shattered planks flying in all directions.

"Well done, Mr. Jaeger, well done!" he shouted. The loss of the boat would set the frigate back precious minutes, enough minutes, he hoped, for the *Charlemagne* to get clear of the reef. The gig was taking the kedge anchor forward again, its ten oars moving in a slow and graceful rhythm. The sloop was less than a quarter mile away now, but the *Charlemagne* would soon be clear of the reefs able to deal with the diminutive man-of-war.

He was still watching the scene beyond the bow and bathing in the warm pleasure of a narrow escape when the frigate fired her full broadside. The hull shuddered with the impact of the iron, and the gig, which a second before had been a thing of grace and symmetry, was cut in two, broken like a bird shot in flight. The shrieks of agony from the boat's crew reached Biddlecomb's ears at the same moment as the muted roar of the frigate's guns.

"God damn it!" he shouted, and slammed his fist down on the caprail. Sprout, in command of the longboat, had turned his boat toward the wreckage and was now pulling the gig's crew, living, wounded, and dead, into the larger boat.

"Sir, shall I still hoist the ensign?" Weatherspoon asked, the flag a great bundle of cloth in his arms.

"Yes, Mr. Weatherspoon." He turned the glass back to the frigate just as her cutter emerged from under the counter, an anchor hanging from davits over the stern. They had launched the boat over the far side, safe from Jaeger's marksmanship.

"Mr. Jaeger, you see your target, the cutter?" he shouted, and Jaeger waved his acknowledgment.

"Sir?" Rumstick called from the waist. "We'll have to get the kedge anchor up now."

The kedge anchor, which had gone down with the gig, was now under the bow. There was only the sheet anchor to spare.

"Cut it away, we don't have time to get it aboard." With only one boat it would be slower going; he had to take the risk of running out of anchors.

The frigate fired again, only a few of her guns, the iron whistling overhead. Sprout maneuvered the longboat alongside, and the men on deck helped their wounded shipmates aboard. And then the dead, the three that were recovered, were handed up and carried below.

Biddlecomb watched the last of the torn bodies disappear down the scuttle, but his mind was wrestling with the problems of kedging with the one remaining boat. He was aware of his dispassion and startled by it, but in the madness of trying to escape, and in his anger at his complacency, his pity for those who had died had all but fled. It would come later, he knew, and in spades, but now he could not think about it.

"Short peak!" Rumstick shouted. Sprout had positioned the longboat under the sheet anchor, and the gang at the bow was lowering it into the boat.

"Wait for Mr. Sprout," Biddlecomb shouted, and Rumstick nodded. Sprout would have to set the second anchor before the first was broken out of the bottom.

He turned to the frigate again. The four forwardmost guns had been moved, almost twelve tons of iron pulled from the bow and run aft, and one look at the frigate's waterline told him that it had worked to lift the bow higher and most likely off the reef. The frigate's captain, whoever in hell he was, knew his business.

Sprout, almost a cable length ahead of the brig, pushed the anchor off the boat's davits and into the clear water.

And then the sloop fired, her four-pounders sounding high-pitched and insignificant after the frigate's throaty broadside.

Round shot hit the hull, and one of the deadeyes on the starboard fore shrouds was smashed to slivers. But the longboat was unscathed, and Sprout's crew was driving it back to the *Charlemagne* as fast as they were able, returning to retrieve the next anchor.

Biddlecomb looked aloft, trying to gauge the strength and direction of the wind. His eye caught the big white ensign hanging from the mainmast head. It's pine tree was hidden in the folds of cloth and it looked like the white French ensign. Or a flag of truce.

He looked north just in time to see the frigate come free of the reef, slip the cable out of a stern port, and set the fore topsail. Then Jaeger's gun went off and the after end of the frigate's cutter was torn away and the boat filled with water and capsized. Biddlecomb took a grim satisfaction in the spectacle, but it was too late to do the Charlemagnes any good.

"Mr. Jaeger, please concentrate your fire on the frigate now," he called, hoping that Jaeger would be able to take out something vital, but doubting that the *Charlemagne*'s little six-pounders would affect much damage.

He tried to ignore the nearly continuous fire from the sloop and the screams of the wounded men coming up from below as he stared out past the bow. They were kedging up to the stream anchor now, and Sprout was heading back for the sheet anchor. And that would be it. One more cast of the anchor and they would be free from the reef, free from the grip of the land and able to elude pursuit among the reefs, able to hold off the enemy until dark and then disappear.

But the frigate was moving fast through the Narrows, her captain recklessly crowding on sail—courses, topsails, topgallants—in a wild effort to cut the Americans off before they slipped from his trap.

Jaeger stepped back from his gun and brought the match down, and the *Charlemagne* and the frigate fired in the same instant. The frigate's guns sounded devastating, like the wrath of God, with the distance between the two vessels now cut in half. One of the shots struck amidships, overturning number eight gun, but no one was in the way and Biddlecomb gave silent thanks for that.

And then he became aware of the shouting. The men had abandoned the capstan and were peering forward. He followed their gaze out across the water, twenty yards ahead of the *Charlemagne*.

A shot from the frigate had torn the bow clean off of the longboat. The boat crew, most of whom Biddlecomb imagined could not swim, were shrinking from the rising water, climbing aft as the longboat sunk by the bow. In a second the boat would capsize.

"Get back to the capstan, God damn your eyes! Get back to the capstan!" Rumstick shouted. The boats were gone and the only way to rescue the men in the water now was to kedge the brig up to them.

He grabbed a man by the collar and the belt and hurled him across the deck toward the abandoned capstan. That demonstration was enough for the others. They peeled away from the side like a startled flock of birds and resumed their former station, urged on by Rumstick's curses and blows. The *Charlemagne* gathered way once more, hauling up to the wreckage of the longboat.

" 'Vast heaving!" Biddlecomb shouted, his eyes fixed on the sinking boat and the men clinging to it. Rumstick snatched up a line, calling for others to do the same. He flung the coil across the water and the rope was taken up by eager hands clinging to the overturned longboat. The boat was hauled alongside and the boat's crew, those who were left, were helped up on deck.

Biddlecomb watched as the last of them came through the entry port, then turned back to the business of their escape, while there was still a chance.

And then he saw that, as far as the possibility of escaping through Town Cut into the deep water, there was no chance at all. The frigate was crossing their bow, the row of guns thrust from the side, silent now but able to crush the brig under their weight of iron.

The man-of-war was clear of the Narrows. Her yards braced around and the ship turned and hove to, coming to a stop between the *Charlemagne* and the open sea beyond.

"Short peak!" Rumstick called. Biddlecomb had not heard the first officer pass the order to haul away, but apparently he had and now the anchor was ready to break out. This was the point where Biddlecomb was to have cut the cable and fallen off under topsails, gathering speed and running away between the reefs. And he still could, except now the frigate was there, hove to, ready to destroy them if he tried. He stared at the big ship, twisting his hands behind his back, ready for the next broadside.

No shot came, but rather a request, amplified through a speaking trumpet. "Ahoy, *Charlemagne!* Do you strike?" the voice called across the water. Biddlecomb wondered vaguely if that was the frigate's captain speaking, and how he knew the brig's name. He dallied with those meaningless considerations for a few seconds, then turned to the only question that was of importance at the moment. Do you strike?

And his choices were . . . what? Cut the cable and run back into St. George Harbor? That would be easy enough with the flood tide. He might even ground the *Charlemagne* in time to get his men ashore before the frigate stopped them. And then what? They were on an island. They could hide out, maybe elude pursuit for some time, but one by one they would be hunted down and taken. The British might even find some sport in it, riding to the hounds and all that; perhaps they were hoping that Biddlecomb would do that very thing.

But he would not. Might he instead try to run past the frigate before the frigate sunk them? He had tried that with the *Icarus,* under the guns of the *Rose.* And his men had been butchered and he had been carrying that with him all these months. He had wanted to surrender then, but Wallace had not allowed him the opportunity, he had not offered quarter until so many lay dead that the offer was meaningless. Not like the captain of the frigate under whose guns he now lay.

"Ahoy, *Charlemagne,*" the voice came again, this time with a peevish note. "Do you strike?"

Biddlecomb realized that he was in that unhappy position, generally relegated to gods and ship's captains, of having the fates of men resting on his decision. He considered the uncertainties that attended being a prisoner of war as weighed against the certainty of slaughter under the frigate's guns. He knew what slaughter was like. He had been forced to choose it before. If his men were prisoners, at least they would still be alive.

Biddlecomb looked up at the white ensign hanging from the masthead. "Haul it down, please, Mr. Weatherspoon," he said bitterly.

She was the frigate HMS *Glasgow,* Capt. William Maltby commanding, and His Majesty's sloop *Ant* with lieutenant something or other in command. That much Biddlecomb had learned in the five hours that he had been aboard the frigate. He had been treated kindly; the man-of-war's officers seemed to regard him more as a guest than as a prisoner, but their politeness only accentuated his miserable condition.

He had given his parole and been allowed the run of the ship, and now he stood at the break of the frigate's quarterdeck, on the leeward side, and the other officers aft were considerate enough to leave him alone. There was no time for him now in any case; they were entering Hamilton Harbor, and the ship was a bedlam of activity as the 160 men aboard prepared to moor. In the waist he could see some of the Charlemagnes standing miserably together in a clump. His crew had been split up among the three vessels, and British sailors had been placed aboard the *Charlemagne* to guard and augment the diminished crew.

The three ships were sailing in line ahead, with the *Charlemagne* between the *Ant,* which led the way, and the frigate bringing up the rear. Biddlecomb looked over at the *Charlemagne;* sandwiched between the British vessels she looked like a prisoner being led between two guards, which was, in fact, her present situation. The white ensign with its pine-tree device was still flying at the masthead, and above it the ensign of the Royal Navy. He read the words: AN APPEAL TO HEAVEN. There was something sad, martyrlike about them now.

They had been betrayed. There was no doubt about that, and Biddlecomb tortured himself trying to deduce who their Judas was. He had been led to believe that only the four men he had met at Stanton House, and General Washington, knew of the Bermuda plan. And, of course, Virginia.

Virginia Stanton. He had not thought of her since they had raised Bermuda. He could not recall another time in the past year that he had gone four days without thinking of her. The last time he had seen her had been in the crowded drawing room at Stanton House, where he had been denied the opportunity to speak privately with her, to explain his fears and his behavior, to apologize for his actions and see if she could understand. And now it seemed possible, if not likely, that he would never see her again.

He was certain that his childish and cowardly behavior had led Virginia to dismiss him from her thoughts. He felt an overwhelming despair as he considered that, and he found no relief in the thought that if the British did find out that he was the one who had led the *Icarus* mutiny, then he would soon be hung and his misery ended.

He had done everything in his power to prevent their finding out. Even as Weatherspoon was hauling down the ensign, Isaac had torn the great cabin apart, seeking out every official document there—orders, commissions, signal books, muster rolls, anything with a name or an order on it—and burned the lot in a bucket before flinging the ashes out the stern windows. No record was left of his name nor of the men who served as officers aboard the *Charlemagne*. If the frigate's captain knew anything about them, then he knew it already, and that would give Biddlecomb some idea of the depth of the treachery.

Virginia Stanton. She was, as far as he knew, the only person who knew of this venture other than the men who organized it, and somehow, of all of them, she was the one he most trusted. William Stanton of course would not betray him, but sometimes the old man did foolish things, and he might have let something slip. As for the others, he did not know them at all. But one of them was the traitor. If he was to die betrayed, then he wanted that vermin exterminated as well.

A cable length ahead, the *Ant* rounded up into the wind and dropped anchor. The *Charlemagne*, under the command of the *Glasgow*'s first officer, rounded up as well, dropping the sheet anchor from the larboard cathead. Maltby gave a quiet order to the helmsman that turned the *Glasgow*'s bow into the wind. The topsails came aback and the frigate stopped, then gathered sternway, and the best bower plunged into Hamilton Harbor. Twenty minutes later the three vessels were moored, riding at their anchors as if they had not moved for years.

Biddlecomb was not surprised, ten minutes later, when a midshipman approached him, began to salute, then thought better of it and scratched his face instead, saying, ''Beg pardon, sir, but Captain Maltby's compliments and would you grant him the honor of an interview?''

The great cabin was airy and neat. Captain Maltby sat behind his desk, flanked on either side by his clerk and his steward. ''One moment, please,'' he said as he scratched away with his quill at the document before him.

Biddlecomb searched his face, searched his mannerisms, for some indication of the man concealed within. Maltby was older than him, but not by much; he placed the captain at thirty-one or -two. He was good-looking and had the aristocratic bearing that Biddlecomb had observed in most officers of the Royal Navy. Whether he owed his position to family influence or not, Biddlecomb had already seen enough of his work to know that he was more than competent at his job.

Maltby signed his name with a flourish, replaced the quill in the inkpot, and sprinkled sand over the paper. Biddlecomb stood more erect and assumed his dispassionate quarterdeck expression. He had long ago trained himself to keep the appearance of unperturbable calm regardless of what he was actually feeling. He had done it during a hundred negotiations for ship's cargoes. He had done it while ships under his command had been torn apart by hurricane conditions hundreds of miles from shore. He had done it while smuggling molasses under the nose of the Royal Navy, and he would do it with Captain Maltby.

"I am sorry to keep you waiting, Captain Biddlecomb. Please, sit." Maltby gestured toward a chair in front of the desk.

Biddlecomb sat, his body taking on an attitude indistinguishable from genuine calm. "You have the advantage of me, sir. I'm afraid that I don't know what help I can be to you."

"I imagine you'll be precious little help to me," said Maltby not unkindly, "but nonetheless, as you are my prisoner, I am duty-bound to interview you."

"You say I am your prisoner, sir, but you have yet to indicate what I have done to warrant that honor."

Maltby smiled, not a devious smile but one of genuine mirth. "All right, Captain, we had best be out with it. I don't want you to waste your legendary eloquence. I know who you are, I know about the *Judea* and the *Icarus*. I know about your gunpowder mission, such as it was."

Biddlecomb was silent for a moment, staggered by the depth of the treachery to which he had been subjected. Had there been no gunpowder mission at all? Was it from the outset a plot to get him to Bermuda to be captured?

"I'm flattered, to be sure, by the lengths to which you people have gone just to bring me into custody," he said at length. "But I'm certain that you overestimate the threat that I present to you."

"It's not so much that you're a threat, Captain, as it is . . . your example that's a threat, if you follow my meaning." Maltby leaned back in his seat and regarded Biddlecomb with a look of curiosity. "Flaunting the authority of the British navy is one thing, but the mutiny on the *Icarus,* and the destruction of the *Swan* and your open defiance of Captain Wallace, well, that can't go unpunished. It's too much. It's an ugly thing, Captain, but an example must be made."

"I would like to know what's to become of my crew."

"And what's to become of you, of course, though you are too much the gentleman to ask." Maltby smiled again, the same genuine smile. "I understand that a number of your men are former English seamen, and they will be taken into the navy. A few have already volunteered."

That was a farce; Biddlecomb knew it and he was certain that Maltby knew it as well. Every man aboard the *Charlemagne* was an American, and few were former sailors of any description. And none of them would have volunteered without some drastic coercion. Maltby was just trying to justify the illegal impressment. He wondered why the British captain even bothered to play these games.

"As for the rest, and for you and your officers—"

"My officers? How, pray, do you know who the officers were? I don't recall any uniforms, and I know you didn't find any commissions. I must insist that no one be singled out from the men for punishment based on their being an officer."

"I'm afraid that not all of your men are as noble as you when it comes to shielding their shipmates. Several of your men, in fact, were quite free with their information in exchange for some little considerations. Though you can take comfort that it was none of your officers who told tales."

Biddlecomb sat silent for a moment. He could not argue with that. Now Rumstick and Gardiner and probably Sprout would pay for his arrogance. And Jaeger, poor Jaeger, who didn't even know he was signing aboard a man-of-war.

"Some of your men," Maltby began again, "I'll send along to Newport tomorrow, in the *Fox*, the other sloop there, along with these damned reports. You and your officers and the rest of your men will remain aboard one of the three vessels here. Ultimately I should think you'll all end up in England for trial for . . . uh"—Maltby hesitated—"trial for treason, I believe is the charge they intend to make."

England for trial on charges of treason. They had undeniably participated in acts of rebellion against the Crown. If the British wished to call it treason and not legitimate war, then there was nothing to stop them. As prisoners of war they could expect some slight consideration. As traitors they would be hung.

What had he done? He had made a decision that he hoped would save his men, and now they were to be battened down in a transport and sent to some hellish prison in England, there to await a farce of a trial and execution. Theirs would not be the clean death of a musket ball, or the relatively quick death of an infected wound. Their deaths would take months to come, but in the end it would come just the same. He had started them on that road to the gallows the moment he had ordered the colors struck.

"We'll be rendezvousing with a convoy bound for Boston," Maltby was speaking again, "with military goods and fresh troops, in about three weeks' time. Until then we stay here at anchor, and I'm afraid it will be a bit of a bore for all. I wish I could send you along tomorrow, for your own sake, but I'm afraid you're a bit of a risk."

"You've gone to so much trouble to capture me," said Biddlecomb with a thin smile, "even I would hate to see me escape."

Maltby smiled again. "Just so. When we fetch Boston, you'll all be held there until there's a ship bound for England."

There were so many considerations in this situation; they would be in Boston for a while. They were escorting a convoy, a convoy of military supplies, including, no doubt, gunpowder. Biddlecomb smiled to himself. He was still thinking of gunpowder for Washington when in all probability he would be a prisoner for the next three months, and then he would be dead.

"I trust the wardroom has made you comfortable, Captain," Maltby broke the silence. "You have the run of the ship as long as I have your parole, but I'm afraid I can't allow you to go ashore. Is there any other way in which I can be of service?"

There was something else, one last thing that needed doing before he was put to death. There was a traitor back home, a traitor who would be responsible for killing him and Rumstick and most of the Charlemagnes. He wanted that person to pay;

more than anything else he wanted that Judas dead. And that meant alerting someone.

"Perhaps one thing," he began slowly, the ideas forming as he spoke. "I . . . I was to be married, and I must give my . . . my bride-to-be some indication, some note of what's happened. I appeal to you, Captain. I can't endure the thought of her wondering, not knowing what's become of me. You said the other sloop was bound for Newport tomorrow; let me send my betrothed a letter."

Maltby frowned. "Hmm, this is damn awkward, Captain. I couldn't allow such a note to be sent unread, there are military considerations here, but it's hardly proper for me to read another man's . . ."

"Oh, I quite understand, sir, and I'll gladly give you leave to read the letter before it's sent. If it doesn't meet your approval, then we'll tear it up. I'm certainly sensible to your situation."

"Well, if you give leave for me to read the letter first . . . ," Maltby said, though he did not sound any happier about the arrangement.

"Thank you, sir," Biddlecomb said before Maltby could voice further objections.

An hour later he was again sitting in the great cabin. He waved the completed letter in the air to dry the ink, then handed it to the captain for inspection.

"Please forgive the time I took with this letter, sir."

"Not at all, not at all." Maltby took the proffered sheet, laying it on the desk before him. "I'm certain it was not easy to write. And I'll confess, I'm not comfortable reading so personal a missive . . ."

"Please, Captain, don't think on it. You are kindness itself in allowing me to post it at all. You have your duty."

"Yes, well . . . ," said Maltby, then fell silent as he read.

Biddlecomb watched the emotions play on the captain's face. He was frowning, but Biddlecomb could not tell if it was discomfort or suspicion. That and the occasional muted "humph" or "well" was all the reaction that the captain had as he read the words. Finally he straightened and handed the letter back.

"Your reputation for eloquence is well deserved, Captain. It's rare that we see such gifts in men who follow the sea."

Or in Yankees? Biddlecomb thought, but instead replied, "You flatter me, sir."

"Go ahead and address it and I'll send it over to the *Fox* with my dispatches this afternoon."

"Thank you, sir." Biddlecomb folded the letter into a square. He pulled the quill from the inkpot and across the front of the note wrote, "Miss Virginia Stanton, Stanton House, Bristol, Colony of Rhode Island."

"Johnson!" Maltby called to his steward through the door. "Fetch a candle and some sealing wax in here." Then turning to Biddlecomb, he said, "Truly, Captain, that was a beautiful letter."

"Thank you, sir," said Biddlecomb. "It was the most difficult I have ever had to write." And that, at least, was the truth.

CHAPTER
15

My Beloved Virginia . . .

IT WAS MID-OCTOBER. THE LAST TRACES OF SUMMER HAD DISAP-
peared weeks ago, and in their place came the cold and health-
ful air of autumn. The sugar maples that had for months been
lost among the green pines now stood out in brilliant reds and
yellows. Tall brown stalks of corn were lashed in bundles and
stood in the fields like soldiers in loose ranks. Wood smoke
was carried on the breeze, every house adding its part to that
familiar and comforting smell.

This was the time of year that Virginia Stanton loved best,
when her boots crunched across the early-morning frost as she
made her way to the stables, and her horse's breath and her
own came in small gray clouds as they rode hard across the
fields bordering Stanton House.

She sat atop her chestnut mare, next to the gazebo in the
remains of her mother's old garden. This spring, she vowed,
she would plant it as her mother had, as she knew her father
would like her to. Her eyes moved out over the deep blue
water of Narragansett Bay. A small packet was beating north
against the cold wind, the only traffic moving on the bay. How
many times, she wondered, had she sat like this, watching for
Isaac's ship to return?

It had been almost a month since she had seen him. There
was nothing unusual about that; generally his voyages took
him away for three months at least. She had missed him be-

172

fore, but not in the way she missed him now. He had noticed her at last, had shown an interest in her. She had not just imagined it. Their relationship had grown from tolerance on his part to friendship, affection, and would have turned into love, she was certain.

And then it had gone all wrong. She had made a fool of herself, losing her temper, not listening to what he had to say. She remembered galloping away, remembered the crowded drawing room, the look that he had shot at her before he left. That look, that expression, as Fitzgerald herded him out the door for the last time. What was it? Not anger. Apology, then? Contempt?

"Son of a bitch," she said out loud, certain no one would hear her. She was not used to feeling confused, as if she had lost control, and it made her angry.

The long rides through the country were the most cathartic activity she could find, and that morning she chose the fields south of the estate, far from the worrying eyes of her father and Rogers. She turned her horse off the road and charged across a now barren cornfield, weaving between the bundled stalks and leaping the stone wall at the far end. She prodded the horse's flank with her spur and pulled the reins over and turned hard to the right, pounding down the familiar road on the far side of the wall, then turned off the road again and raced up a small hillock, pulling the young mare to a stop at the crest.

They were both breathing hard, horse and rider, and Virginia could feel the sweat under her shift, despite the cold. She looked up at the sky and took in great gulps of air, then looked down the dirt road that led from Stanton House to Bristol.

The road was visible for half a mile before it wound behind a stand of pines, and Virginia could see that someone was coming, a horseman, riding hard. She tied her unruly hair in a loose knot, adjusted her clothes as best she could, then walked her horse down the hillock and onto the road in hopes of intercepting the messenger, if such he was.

He came around the bend in the road, a quarter mile away, pushing his big horse down the hard-packed road, charging toward Stanton House.

It's from him, I know it is, Virginia thought. In the past two weeks, since the time that Biddlecomb had been expected to return, she had been certain that every visitor to the house had come to bring word of him, and now she reminded herself of those previous disappointments.

The horseman was closer now, and she could see that it was Gideon Oray, whose small farm abutted the Stanton property. He was riding his plow horse, and Virginia grimaced to see how hard he was making the old mare work.

Oray was one hundred yards from Virginia when he noticed her and slowed to a trot and then to a walk as he approached. Virginia could see that he was heaving for breath, as was his horse.

"Mr. Oray, your poor old horse cannot take such treatment!" she called out. "Her racing days are over, I fear."

"This old gal's racing days was over the day she was sired, Miss Stanton," Oray said between gasps. "And I'll warrant we're both of us getting too old for such rushing around."

"Then why, pray, are you doing so?" Virginia asked, concealing with some effort her curiosity.

"I got a letter for you, miss, and I was told it's from Captain Biddlecomb, so I reckoned it must be important."

Virginia felt the excitement well up and she redoubled her effort to project only a casual interest, wondering at the same time whom she was trying to fool, Gideon or herself. "For me, you say? Sure if it's from Captain Biddlecomb, it's for my father."

"No, ma'am." Oray reached into his waistcoat and pulled out a much rumpled letter. "It's addressed to you, and you can see for yourself if it's the captain's writing."

She took the letter and looked at the address. "Miss Virginia Stanton, Stanton House, Bristol, Colony of Rhode Island." There was no doubt that it was Biddlecomb's writing. It was a hand that she knew well.

"Thank you, Mr. Oray," she said, realizing that she had been staring stupidly at the letter. "Will you come to the house for some dinner? I know my father would be happy for your company."

"Bless you, Miss Stanton, but no. Mrs. Oray will have dinner waiting for me already. Please give Captain Stanton my best regards, and the best to you, miss."

"Thank you, Mr. Oray, I shall. And thank you for bringing the note."

Oray waved and wheeled his horse around and headed back down the road, bound for home at a more leisurely pace.

Virginia held the letter in both hands, reading her name over and over, afraid to open it. Her anxiety formed a knot in her stomach, and it grew in size as she considered what might be written within. Why would Biddlecomb write to her and not to her father?

"Oh, for God's sake, what's the matter with me?" she said out loud, breaking the seal and unfolding the letter.

My beloved Virginia,
Before all else, I must tell you that I love you, as I have always said I love you, and as I will always love you.

She looked up from the letter and breathed deep and laughed out loud. He loved her! All of the angry thoughts that she had entertained, all of the times that she had tried to convince herself that he was no gentleman, were swept away in the flood of those words. True, he had never actually said that he loved her, as he claimed there, but such a mistake was a trifling in the light of his saying it now.

She took another deep breath, wrapped in happiness, and plunged into the letter again. She read the rest of the page, down to the final profession of love. She read it again, her joy changing to fear and anger. And confusion.

Biddlecomb was a captive of the British, or so the letter claimed. But how could she know if that was true or not? The letter made no sense to her. She felt the tears forming in the corners of her eyes. This letter was no profession of love. It was lunacy.

The sun was almost down before she returned to Stanton House, no less angry and no less confused. She walked her horse back and forth over the worn grass, cooling it down, and reading the letter over and over in her mind. She could not imagine what Biddlecomb was thinking, and she concluded, again, that he was mad. No other explanation made sense.

With her horse at last stabled, Virginia headed back toward the house. Light shone from the windows of her father's study, casting long dull yellow patches over the lawn. There was light in the kitchen as well, and Virginia imagined that Rogers was waiting there, ready to fetch her anything she might want. She wanted to be alone, desperately, but she knew that it would not be so easy to sneak past two men whose primary occupation was doting on her.

She stepped quietly onto the porch, putting each boot down slowly and stepping around the boards that long practice told her would squeak underfoot. She eased the big front door open, just far enough for her slender frame to squeeze through, then closed it behind her.

"Virginia?" William Stanton called from his study, and she heard his chair scrape on the floor as he pushed himself away from his desk. At the same time she heard the kitchen door open and Rogers's shoes in the hallway.

"Virginia, you're back! You missed supper, I was beginning to worry," Stanton said as he stepped through the double doors from his study.

"Is there anything I can get for you, Miss Stanton? I kept your supper warm," said Rogers, coming into the foyer.

"Honestly, can't I come into my own home without being pounced on like . . . like something in a pack of wolves?" Virginia said, regretting the words and the tone even as she was saying them.

"Virginia?" Stanton took her gently by the arm and turned her face toward the light from the study. She had hoped to avoid this, she had hoped to keep her pain to herself. "My Lord, girl, have you been crying? Rogers, look here, she's been crying. Whatever is the matter, dear?"

Virginia looked into her father's face, his features becoming clearer as her eyes adjusted to the light. Biddlecomb was like a son to him; he would have to know.

"I received a letter today . . . from Isaac," she said at length.

"From Isaac? My God, what is he about? What does he say? Where is he?" The questions spilled out of Stanton.

"It seems he's been captured by the British, but . . . I don't know. The letter is nonsense," she said, struggling to explain as she resigned herself to enduring her father's questions. "You had best read it yourself, perhaps it will make some sense to you." She stepped away from her father and walked into the brightly lit study. "You may as well hear this too, Rogers."

She pulled the letter from her bodice and flopped down in the winged easy chair, sprawling out and ignoring the disapproving glance that flashed between her father and Rogers. She began to unfold the letter again, then stopped.

"Here, Daddy, you best read it. I can't bear it anymore."

William Stanton took the letter, and Virginia could see the concern on his face. "Well, this is passing strange. I always thought you rather liked Isaac," he said as he took the letter and adjusted the spectacles on his nose. "It's addressed to you, I see."

Did you think I was lying? Virginia thought but kept silent. Stanton began to read out loud:

My Beloved Virginia,
 Before all else, I must tell you that I love you, as I have always said I love you, and as I will always love you.

"My goodness," Stanton said. "I had a notion Isaac fancied you, but this . . ."

Virginia let out a sigh of exasperation. "That's not the bad part, Father, that's the part I had hoped for."

"Hoped for? Isaac's a fine boy, but you don't—"

"Please, Daddy, read on."
Stanton turned his attention back to the letter.

The day of our nuptials was to be the day of my greatest joy, the fulfillment of all I longed for, but now God has seen fit, for my sins, to deprive me of my chief desire. I have been made prisoner by the British, by means which I cannot here disclose. Suffice to say that I shall not make our appointment with the Right Reverend Henry on the fifth. Please express my regrets to those ones who have been so kind to me, Messrs. Cooke and Bowler and Fitzgerald. They are all still in Rhode Island, though one, I believe, is Cambridge.

" 'Is Cambridge'? He must mean 'is *in* Cambridge.' Still, this is passing odd. Who is 'Reverend Henry'? What in the hell is this 'nuptials'? He didn't actually have the gall to—"
"No, Father, he had precious little gall, less gall than I might desire." Virginia's tone indicated how little she wished to discuss it. "Please read on."

They are all still in Rhode Island, though one, I believe, is Cambridge . . . is in Cambridge.

Stanton continued, "That must be Fitzgerald. I don't see why he wants you to express his regrets. He only met these men but once, and he was damned rude to them then."
"They're the men who put the Bermuda venture together, sir," said Rogers. "Perhaps he wishes to apologize for not being able to fulfill the mission."
"Perhaps. Damned odd way to start, with this stuff about marrying my daughter," Stanton grunted.
"Father, please finish the letter so I can get to bed."
"Yes, of course, dear."

. . . one, I believe, is Cambr—is in Cambridge. Please see he gets the greeting I should give myself, if I were able.

I know not when I will again hold you in my arms, and feel your warm love against a cold night. I love you, please understand, despite all that might seem madness, I truly love you.

Yours,
I. Biddlecomb.

Virginia felt the tears welling up again, and she waited for her father to say something sufficiently foolish to distract her from the hurt.

"I am frankly scandalized by this," Stanton said. " 'Feel your warm love . . .' The rascal! I shall give him some warm love when I see him next."

"May I, sir? Miss Stanton?" asked Rogers, holding out a hand for the letter.

"Certainly, Rogers," said Virginia. Rogers took the letter, holding it up to a candle, and read it again.

"It's an odd letter, to be sure," he said at last. "But I can't say I've ever known the captain to ramble like this. Why should he tell us where these men are? We know where they are, and he knows that we do."

"It makes no sense. The man's gone mad," said Stanton with finality. "And to think he should profess love to my daughter!"

"Oh, Daddy, damn it, will you stop saying that, like professing love to me is such an unthinkable thing!"

"Well, really, I—," Stanton blustered until Rogers interrupted him.

"Biddlecomb is a prisoner of war, that much seems clear. We don't know the particulars of his capture, and he says here"—Rogers scanned the letter—" 'by means which I cannot here disclose.' Why couldn't he disclose them?"

The room was silent for a moment and the question hung in the air. "Because his mail was being read," Virginia said at last, slowly. "Because the British posted the letter and he knew that they would read it. It was obviously written after he was captured."

"That would make sense," said Rogers.

"Then why did he write the damn thing at all?" asked Stanton. "If he couldn't say anything useful, except some damn nonsense to Virginia, why bother writing at all?"

"That's the question, then," said Rogers. "Why did he write the letter? Certainly there is nothing wrong with professing love for Miss Stanton—"

"Thank you, Rogers," Virginia interrupted. "I'm glad someone recognizes that."

"Well, I suppose if we wish to take this line of thought to its end," said Stanton, "then it might help us understand the nature of the thing. If Biddlecomb is a prisoner of war, and his mail is being read, then this is just the type of letter he might send. I mean, they're not going to let him write to General Washington now, are they? But to one's betrothed? If the officer who has charge of him is anything of a gentleman, he would allow a letter to a woman that a man was about to marry."

He was right, Virginia knew that he was right, and it completed her unhappiness. Biddlecomb's professions of love had not even been wild ramblings, they had been a subterfuge to get a letter to her father. They were a calculated lie.

"An excellent point, sir. It would be the only way for the captain to get word to us. But what about the rest, the part that seems like nonsense?" Rogers looked at the letter again. " 'I shall not make our appointment with the Right Reverend Henry on the fifth,' " he read aloud.

Something in the words, that combination of words, that phrase, was familiar to Virginia, something ignited a spark of recognition. Reverend Henry on the fifth, she thought to herself, Reverend Henry on the fifth . . .

Henry the Fifth. Of course, that was why the words had a familiar tone. They just happened to mimic the name of a king. Or a play, no more.

"And the names as well," Rogers continued after a moment. " 'They are all still in Rhode Island, though one, I believe, is . . . is *in* Cambridge.' We're in a better position to know where they are than he is, why tell us?"

Is *in* Cambridge, Virginia thought. No, he didn't write that at all, he wrote "one, I believe, *is* Cambridge." Was it just a simple mistake? She frowned and stared into the fire and suddenly another thought was upon her.

"Bah," said Stanton at last. "It's nonsense. Madness."

But perhaps, perhaps, Virginia thought, as another possibility occurred to her, there is method in't.

CHAPTER
16

Siege of Boston

It was, by now, quite familiar to Major Fitzgerald, like a part of the Virginia estate that he had known since childhood. The sun was nearly free of the eastern horizon, and the dirt redoubts on Cobble Hill, and the general and his horse, and Bunker Hill and Boston in the distance, were washed in various shades of pink and gray. The first part of their morning ride was over; the rising sun revealed, as always, a military situation essentially unchanged since the Virginians had arrived almost four months before.

Fitzgerald grabbed the edge of his cloak and wrapped it farther around his body. The very faintest odor of an open latrine assailed his nostrils, but the smell was more a memory than an irritation. The general's orders were finally being honored more in the observation than the breach. The encampments encircling Boston looked more military by the day, the latrines were properly dug, general orders obeyed, and the traditional military chain of command more readily followed. The men, the soldiers, were beginning to think of themselves as the Army of the United Colonies, not a conglomeration of New England militias, and were increasingly able to accept a Virginian as their commander in chief.

Fitzgerald shivered, and his view of Boston Harbor was obscured for a second by the cloud of his own breath. Just as things were beginning to function properly, the weather had turned cold, and their once-pleasant morning rides were becoming increasingly bitter. It was quite beyond him why anyone would, by choice, live in New England.

Way off to the south a gun fired and was answered by another, fifty feet away, the sound like Jove's thunder in the morning, like a messenger from the heavens proclaiming that the nighttime quiet was over and the loud work of the day begun. Up and down the six miles of American defenses the morning guns went off, calling the men of the Continental Army to arms and the weary sentries to bed.

Washington turned in his saddle and looked at Fitzgerald, his expression one of sadness. "We must issue a general order today," he said as Fitzgerald pulled his paper and pencil from his pocket, "putting a stop to the morning guns."

The major paused in his writing. "Really, sir? A stop to the guns?" Washington loved the morning guns, loved the martial air they gave to the beginning of each day. Nothing reminded the men that they were in a military encampment, waging a war, and not on a great frolic, as much as the morning guns.

"Yes, I'm afraid so. And I'll tell you my concern. It's not that the guns are such a great waste of powder; they do use a prodigious amount, but I think it's worth it. My fear is that one morning the gunfire will set off an artillery duel with the British, and then where should we be? Either use all our supply answering them, to no good end, or ignore the bombardment and as much as admit we don't have the powder to fight back. No, you know how much I hate to stop the practice, but it must be done."

"Yes, sir." Fitzgerald turned the paper on its side and wrote in the space remaining at the margin.

Washington pulled his reins to one side and started his horse back down the hill, Fitzgerald's horse following with only the slightest encouragement from its rider.

"We've no word from Philadelphia yet on that powder they promised?" Washington asked once they were clear of the redoubt and walking their horses back toward Cambridge.

"Not yet, sir."

"That's far from surprising. We must send yet another message to the Congress on the article of powder. It can't be that they're completely insensible to our needs here."

"One wouldn't think so, sir, with the fair warning you've given them."

"I hate to think that we might lose this war just as it's started, through no effort of the British but through the parsimony of a few politicians. Incidentally, did I mention to you the article I saw in the last newspaper we had from Philadelphia?"

"No, sir."

"It was about that powder on Bermuda that we sent that Rhode Island fellow for. The notice said it had been removed some weeks ago. I should think it was done a week at least before . . . what was his name?"

"Capt. Isaac Biddlecomb, sir."

"Just so. A week before Captain Biddlecomb arrived."

"Damn it all. Begging your pardon, sir. But that's the damnedest hard luck."

"It most certainly is. We might have solved this whole thing but for a week's delay."

"It's been how long now since Biddlecomb sailed?" Fitzgerald asked, running back over the weeks. "Sometime in September, four or five weeks ago at least. It's not more than a week there and a week back, and he would have had no need to tarry more than a day or two on the island. It's strange we've had no word."

"I hope he hasn't run into any misfortune. This Bermuda venture may have been a failure, but we still have a real need for naval people."

The two men rode on in silence. "I hope," Fitzgerald said at last, "that it was only misfortune that kept the powder from Biddlecomb's hands."

"What do you mean, Major?"

"Well, sir, perhaps I'm over fearful"—Fitzgerald paused—"because of this thing with Dr. Church."

He was loath to mention it; only a few weeks before it was

discovered that Dr. Benjamin Church, ostensibly a devotee of the American cause, one of the Whig leaders from early on, was supplying the British with information on troop strength and placement as well as Washington's military plans. Church's treason made Washington furious like nothing Fitzgerald had ever seen. "I just hope that there was no treachery involved here, sir. Not that I have any reason to suspect there was, it just seems an awful coincidence."

"Let's hope it's exactly that."

The two men continued south, past Cambridge and along the familiar road to Roxbury, as overhead the gray dawn sky turned the vivid blue of autumn. At length they reached the redoubts on Boston Neck, the Americans' southern flank. This was the point where British and Americans faced off, the bottleneck through which the British army would have to pass to turn the Americans' right flank in an overland assault. But if the British had learned one thing at Bunker Hill, it was that the Americans would not be easily routed.

Two hours later, their inspection of the lines complete, they returned to the Vassall House and handed their horses over to the stableboys who waited for them. During the summer months Fitzgerald had hated to step from the hot grounds into the much hotter house; now he was glad to get indoors where he knew fires would be blazing to keep the Southern commander in chief warm.

Washington walked directly through the door to his office, ignoring the pleading stares of the men who waited to have a word with him. Fitzgerald, walking behind the general, paused, ready to make his usual announcement that the general would see them as soon as he was able, when his eye caught a face, a familiar face but not one that he knew from the lines around Boston. The man wore civilian clothes, not elegant but not the clothes of a working man or a farmer either. He wore tall boots, and a boat cloak like the sailors wore was folded on his lap. Fitzgerald paused, trying to place the man.

"I know you, sir, but from where?" he asked finally.

"Ebenezer Rogers, Major, sergeant of the Bristol Militia," the man said, standing and extending his hand. "We met at Captain Stanton's house, where I serve as his butler. Captain Stanton from Bristol, Rhode Island, sir."

"Of course, of course," said Fitzgerald, shaking Rogers's hand. Not an hour before he had been thinking of that big house. And Virginia, the lovely Virginia, whom he had thought of often since meeting her. "What brings you up here?"

"We've received word from Captain Biddlecomb, sir. I really can say no more. It's quite sensitive. I'm here to see General Washington on the matter."

"Very well, come in then. We were just discussing Biddlecomb. I'm certain the general will wish to hear this." Fitzgerald ushered Rogers past the others, ignoring the angry glances shot at him for showing a civilian preferential treatment.

Fitzgerald guided Rogers into the office and shut the door behind him. "General, this is Sgt. Ebenezer Rogers. He is an associate of Capt. William Stanton of Bristol, who loaned us the ship for the Bermuda venture. Sergeant, General Washington."

"It's an honor, sir. A great honor," said Rogers with genuine sincerity, pumping Washington's hand.

"Thank you, Sergeant. The honor's all mine. Please, have a seat. What may we do for you?"

"Last week we received word from Captain Biddlecomb, sir. Actually, Captain Stanton's daughter, Virginia, did."

Virginia. How odd to hear someone pronounce that name, here in Washington's office, where Fitzgerald had so often daydreamed of her. Was there something between her and Biddlecomb?

Fitzgerald was suddenly aware that the room had gone quiet, and he had not heard anything that Rogers had said.

"Please, Sergeant, proceed," Washington prompted, but Rogers shifted uncomfortably in his chair.

"It's a private matter, sir. Very private. I have instructions that it's for you alone."

186

"Major Fitzgerald has my every confidence," Washington said.

"Very good, sir," Rogers said, glancing at Fitzgerald, clearly still not comfortable with his presence. "I have a letter here"— he held up a well-worn, folded paper—"which, like I said, was sent by Captain Biddlecomb to Captain Stanton's daughter, Virginia."

Rogers handed the letter to Washington, and as the general read, he continued, "It seems that the captain was captured, though he doesn't say how. A good part of the letter seems to be nonsense, and Miss Stanton, you'll remember her, sir," he said to Fitzgerald, "Miss Stanton felt Biddlecomb was trying to send a message, a message that he was the victim of some treachery."

"Indeed," said Fitzgerald, leaning forward in his chair.

"Please take a look at this." Washington handed the letter to Fitzgerald. The major took it and ran his eyes over it. The first lines were adamant protestations of love, and after that a reference to an upcoming wedding.

"Hmm," Fitzgerald said. They were engaged to be married? Why did he find that vaguely annoying? "I was not aware that Captain Biddlecomb and Miss Stanton were betrothed."

"They're not, sir," Rogers said. "That's the strange thing— one of them, anyway."

"Indeed?" Fitzgerald read quickly through the letter. He saw his own name in the neat handwriting. He read the sentence again.

"This part, where he mentions these names, am I to presume that these are the men he thinks are the traitors?" he asked with a flash of anger.

"Yes, sir. It would appear so," said Rogers.

"It's hard to know," Washington said. "The note is cryptic at best. I guess I don't see what the message is."

"It was Miss Stanton that smoked it, sir," Rogers took up the explanation. "You see in that first paragraph, where he talks about their coming nuptials? The one you just mentioned?"

"Yes, here," Fitzgerald said. "Their meeting with the Right Reverend Henry . . ."

"Quite right, sir," said Rogers. "But the thing of it is that there is no Reverend Henry, at least not that any of us know of. And the Captain says 'on the fifth,' but not even Miss Stanton knew of any wedding. They were never engaged, like I said, not even courting. Miss Stanton was the one who put together *Henry the Fifth*. She thinks the captain was making reference to the play by Shakespeare."

"I see . . . ," said Fitzgerald, staring at the letter again and picturing the play in his mind. He liked the play very much and was quite familiar with it. He had, in fact, quoted a part of it to Biddlecomb. "But I fail to see any hidden meaning."

"Further along," Rogers continued, "where Biddlecomb lists those names of people to greet and where they are."

Fitzgerald looked down the letter to the list of names, staring again at his own name along with Cooke and Bowler. " 'They are all still in Rhode Island,' " he read aloud, " 'though one, I believe, is in Cambridge.' That would be me, I take it," he added dryly.

"The thing of it is, sir," said Rogers, "and Miss Stanton smoked this, that he didn't say 'is *in* Cambridge,' he said '*is* Cambridge.' I know little about Shakespeare, sir, and nothing of the play *Henry the Fifth*, but . . ."

"Cambridge," said Fitzgerald softly. "I see what you're saying! Cambridge, the traitor, the one who tried to sell out King Harry to the French. One of them *is* Cambridge, *is* the traitor! It looks like a mistake, but perhaps it isn't."

"That was how Miss Stanton saw it, sir."

Fitzgerald stared at the list of names. "These are the only men, beyond the general, Miss Stanton, and myself, and you, Sergeant, who knew of the Bermuda venture. Biddlecomb therefore assumes that if there is a traitor, it is one of these men. I should point out that Captain Stanton was also one of those who knew of the venture.

"Captain Stanton is not a traitor, sir," Rogers stated flatly.

"That's why Captain Biddlecomb did not include him in the letter."

"Treason is not something one makes generally known, Rogers," Fitzgerald replied.

"Captain Stanton, sir, is not a traitor," Rogers said again, a keen edge to his voice, and Fitzgerald knew that if he pressed the point further, he would be fighting a duel in the morning.

"Stanton dispatched you, I take it?" he asked instead.

"No, sir. Captain Stanton thinks I'm in Providence with family. Miss Stanton asked me to come here. She didn't tell Captain Stanton what she smoked from the letter; the captain is sometimes . . . less than subtle, if you catch my meaning. If he knew of this and started looking into it himself, well, he'd most likely chase this traitor into hiding. Miss Stanton felt it best to warn the general and let him investigate those suspects as he saw fit."

"Myself included among them?"

"Yes, sir," said Rogers as if acknowledging a request for tea.

"You believe," Washington asked, "that Biddlecomb knew the letter would be read by the British, that's why he was so circumspect?"

"Yes, sir, it was Miss Stanton who figured that out. And it stands to reason if he posted it after he was taken that his captors would read it."

"Just so," said Washington. "Particularly when one considers that if the letter is not some sort of code, then it is meaningless."

Fitzgerald tried to imagine a situation in which Biddlecomb would know that he was betrayed. "He must have fallen into some type of obvious trap," he concluded, "obvious after it was sprung, that is, if he's so certain."

"I should imagine so," agreed Washington. He turned to Rogers. "Sergeant, you have done us a great service coming here, as has Miss Stanton in dispatching you. Your country is grateful."

"Thank you, sir," said Rogers as Washington pulled a piece of paper from a stack, dipped a quill in the inkpot, and began to scratch the feather across the sheet. "I am writing you a letter, Sergeant, instructing all under my command to help you in any manner you need. Food, clothing, whatever you need."

"Thank you, sir. If you have no further need of me, I'll be returning directly. Shall I leave the letter with you?"

"Major, what do you think?" asked Washington.

"I think we've seen all we need to see. Pray, give it back to Miss Stanton, but ask her to show it to no one else."

"Yes sir," said Rogers. "And, sir, about this traitor?"

"We shall look into it, Rogers, never worry about that. I am as anxious to smoke him out as you." Washington handed the letter to Rogers, then stood and extended his hand.

Rogers stood as well and shook the general's hand. "Thank you, sir. Thank you. I've known Captain Biddlecomb a long time, sir. He's a brave man, and he's a patriot, even if it took him some time to come around. Anyone who betrayed him, sir, I'd be happy to kill with my own hands."

"Thank you, Rogers. I hope you get the chance," said Washington.

Fitzgerald stood as well and offered Rogers his hand. "One last thing. How was this letter delivered?"

"It passed hands a few times from Newport to Bristol, but as I understand it, it came in on a British navy sloop with dispatches. I don't know from where."

"Thank you, Rogers, and thank Miss Stanton. And please give her my best," said Fitzgerald. "And not a word of this to anyone."

Rogers snapped to attention and saluted the officers, who returned his salute, somewhat less formally, then he stepped out of the door and was gone.

"Well, Major, what do you really think about all this?" Washington asked after the two men had regained their seats.

"This 'is Cambridge,' 'is in Cambridge' thing isn't much, but it makes sense the way Rogers explained it."

"It does make sense, it makes a damn lot of sense," said Washington bitterly, and Fitzgerald looked up, surprised by the change in the general's tone. "Damn it all to hell! First this damn business with Church and now this." The commander in chief shifted in his seat and stared out the window at the brown grass in the yard. "I think that Biddlecomb's message is clear, and if Biddlecomb thinks there's a traitor, then he's probably right. He would be in a position to know. I want to find this son of a bitch. Any thoughts on who it could be?"

Fitzgerald considered that. "No, sir. If a trap was set, then the betrayal must have come from a well-placed source. I don't think the British would have acted on anything else, so it must have been one of those men who had a hand in putting the thing together. It's not me, and I imagine it's not you, but beyond that I have not a clue."

Washington's expression lightened a bit and he nodded. "No, it's not me. But Rogers thought that it might be you, as did Biddlecomb. In all fairness, they don't know your record."

"If Biddlecomb's letter came in on a British navy sloop, that would explain how he knew it would be read." Fitzgerald looked at the date on the top of the letter. "This was written over two weeks ago, so it came from some distance, Bermuda most likely. If a trap was set, it had to be set before Biddlecomb sailed, which is more proof that the traitor is one of the men who knew of the plan from the beginning. One of the men Biddlecomb mentions."

"You have met them all. Is there anyone that you suspect?"

"At this moment I suspect everyone, sir."

"That's no doubt a good policy. Though I'll admit it's hard for me to think of any of them as traitors. In any event I think we can eliminate this Virginia Stanton. If it was her, then I doubt she would have sent Rogers. And if it was Rogers, I doubt he would have come. Beyond that it could be any one of the others."

Washington turned and stared out the window again for a long moment before he continued. "I want this traitor business dealt with, and dealt with quickly. And I want it done discreetly as well; no trials, no newspapers, we don't have the luxury of all that. Our cause is at a delicate place, and this business with Dr. Church has already compromised us greatly.

We can't afford to have it come out that yet another highly placed individual is a traitor. I don't think we could survive that at this juncture."

He paused, then continued on in a lower tone. "Major, I need you to go to Rhode Island and look into this thing. When you've smoked the traitor, when you are certain, deal with it swiftly, and quietly, however you see fit. Do we understand each other?"

Fitzgerald stared at his commander in chief. The man was fairness itself; Fitzgerald had found his sense of justice at times exasperating. Now Washington was asking him to deal with a problem in his own way, the way he had wanted to deal with other problems in the past, the only way he could imagine dealing with a traitor.

"Oh, yes, sir," Fitzgerald said softly. "We understand each other passing well."

CHAPTER
17

His Majesty's Sloop Ant

BIDDLECOMB LEANED AGAINST THE LEEWARD BULWARK OF THE SLOOP *Ant*, just aft of the single mast and forward of what was considered the quarterdeck on the little flush-decked man-of-war. He stared absently across the gray, choppy water toward his former command. The *Charlemagne* was a beautiful sight, despite the damage she had suffered in her race through the Town Cut Channel two weeks before. He could not look at her without marveling at how quickly fortunes could change. His own life, for example, had gone with meteoric speed from the joy of commanding that handsome vessel to the nightmare that it was now.

Fifteen feet aft, Biddlecomb heard Lieutenant Shave, the officer in command of the sloop, begin to clear his throat with a long growling noise, like a shovel scooping up gravel. He knew what would come next and gnashed his teeth and fought down the desire to scream.

For the two weeks that they had lay at anchor in Hamilton, Biddlecomb had lived aboard the frigate in a wardroom of gentleman officers, but when the time had come to sail, Captain Maltby had transferred him to the sloop *Ant*, apparently fearing, though he would not say as much, Biddlecomb's influence on the frigate's crew. It was ironic to Biddlecomb now, and not humorously so, to recall how miserable he had been aboard the *Glasgow*. It had not occurred to him then that things could get a great deal worse.

Lieutenant Shave's throat-clearing built in intensity as the copious phlegm that resulted from his constant tobacco chewing was worked into a wad of spittle in his mouth. Biddlecomb twisted his hands behind his back. Only with great effort did he avoid cursing out loud. He heard the rush of air as Shave spit the great wad of tobacco juice and mucus on the white planks of the *Ant*'s deck.

"Admiral's steward! Lay aft!" Shave roared with a joviality in his voice that made Biddlecomb cringe. He picked up his bucket and stepped aft.

Lieutenant Shave was one of those rare types who had entered the navy as a ship's boy, the lowliest of creatures, and through a combination of luck, cunning, and meanness had worked his way up from the lower deck to master's mate and then managed to pass for lieutenant. He would never make the step to post captain, but for a man like Shave that did not matter. He had a command, and small though it was, it was his kingdom to rule with his own perverted brand of despotism.

Biddlecomb felt his gorge rise as he knelt down on the deck and mopped up Shave's mess. Having prisoners on board was, for Shave, a perfect opportunity to mete out degradation to those who had no recourse. His game of "Admiral's Steward" was just one example.

At least twenty of the *Charlemagne*'s men, Biddlecomb knew, had been forced into the Royal Navy and were divided among the crews of the *Charlemagne* and the *Glasgow*. Ten had been sent to Newport on the sloop that he hoped had carried his letter. Ten more were prisoners aboard the frigate. The rest, about thirty-five men, including Rumstick, were still prisoners aboard the brig that had once been theirs. Maltby apparently preferred to keep their poison contained, risking the loss of a prize rather than a commissioned vessel.

Seven Americans were on board the *Ant*—Biddlecomb, Weatherspoon, and five of the Charlemagnes—and all were forced to take their turn mopping up after the lieutenant. Biddlecomb had refused at first, refused despite the beatings and despite the reduction of his rations. But when Shave had reduced rations for all of the American prisoners to one among six, and all the Americans were denied exercise on deck, he had relented. Now Shave was directing all of his efforts toward him.

"Hurry it up there, Brother Jonathan," Shave said, prodding Biddlecomb with his boot. "I don't want no Yankee bastard back here where the officers is any longer than it takes to wipe up after me, you hear?"

Nor did Biddlecomb care to be back there any longer than necessary. Anger and humiliation mixed together in him and made a lethal brew. Where had he got this notion that surrendering would somehow secure decent treatment for him and his men? He could not recall any decision that he regretted more.

He wiped up the last of the mess until only a light brown stain remained on the planks, then tossed the rag in the bucket and stood and walked forward.

"Hold up a second, Jonathan," Shave said, and reluctantly Biddlecomb stopped and turned around.

"Yes, Lieutenant?"

"Captain! You call me *captain* you whore's son!" Shave shrieked. Biddlecomb regarded him with a face devoid of expression. It was a poor revenge at best, needling Shave thus, and he knew that he would pay for it, but he could not resist.

"Yes . . . Captain?"

"You been eyeing my sword, ain't ya?"

He stared at the lieutenant's face. Shave had several days' worth of beard, and his fat cheeks and forehead had a greasy quality, a sort of a sheen that extended up to his matted black hair. Biddlecomb's eyes moved down the stained waistcoat to the sword that hung from the belt. He had never seen a naval officer wear a sword except for ceremony or battle, but Shave was never without his weapon. There were, no doubt, too many people aboard his own vessel that wanted him dead.

"I've noticed it," he said at last.

He had indeed noticed it. It was not the clumsy butcher's tool he would have expected Shave to carry, but as far as he could tell, a finely crafted weapon, and his eye was drawn to it.

"Well, here, Jonathan, take a closer look." Shave drew the sword from its scabbard and presented it to Biddlecomb, hilt first. "Go on, take it up."

Biddlecomb grabbed onto the hilt and took the sword, holding it tentatively with his arm extended and twisting his wrist around to get a sense for the weapon's balance.

It was a finer weapon than he had imagined, far finer, and the balance made it feel as if it were floating. He grabbed the tip and flexed the blade. It bent and sprung back with the quality of the finest steel. The grip was wrapped in wire thread, and the guard swept down from the pommel and split into three separate legs, forming a simple basket to protect the hand.

Biddlecomb was transfixed by the sword's beauty; not ornate but simple, even stoic, a sword that needed no baubles to draw attention to its quality. He took a few tentative lunges at the air.

"She's a beauty, ain't she, Jonathan?" Shave asked in that mocking tone in which he couched all of his words, and then, when Biddlecomb did not answer, asked again, "Well, ain't she?"

"Yes, it's a fine weapon."

"Thank you. I took it from a damned Yankee whoreson who didn't have no need for it no more. Know why he didn't have no need for it no more?"

Biddlecomb had a fairly good idea of why that was, at least of the reason that Shave would give, but he also knew that he had to ask to shut Shave up. "Why?"

"Why, *sir*, you Yankee rascal."

"Why, sir?"

"Because I killed the son of a whore."

"Indeed," said Biddlecomb in a noncommittal voice.

"You'd like to run me through with that, wouldn't you?"

Biddlecomb smiled to himself as he lunged at an invisible adversary. "Well, wouldn't you, you worthless Yankee sodomite?"

Biddlecomb lowered the sword and looked at the lieutenant, who smiled back at him with filthy teeth. Yes, he would love to run the man through.

He gripped the hilt harder and his eyes moved automatically to Shave's chest. Shave spread his arms and grinned wider. Biddlecomb felt the tingling in the soles of his feet, felt his stomach tighten with the threat of impending action. Shave was certain he would not do it, that was why he was taunting him that way. Well, wouldn't he be surprised. They would hang him for it, but they were going to hang him in any case. He might as well do it.

The muscles in Biddlecomb's right arm were tightening and he was describing small circles in the air with the point of the sword. He was going to kill the filthy man in front of him.

"On deck!" the lookout called from the masthead, and the tension on the quarterdeck collapsed like a sail braced to a shiver.

Shave took the sword from Biddlecomb's hand and slid it back into the scabbard, grinning his idiotic grin. "You'll never get a chance like that again, you blackballing coward."

"On deck!" the lookout called again.

Shave pulled his eyes from Biddlecomb and looked aloft. "What is it?" he shouted.

It was the convoy. For the past two days they had been tacking back and forth, waiting for the convoy that they were to accompany to Boston. And now, on the wide Atlantic, convoy and escort had found each other, and another mile marker was past, to Biddlecomb's thinking, on the road from Narragansett Bay to a gallows in London.

But despite what the convoy's arrival meant to him, he had to admit that it was an impressive sight. There were sixty sail in all, and even as the first lumbering merchantman came up with the three men-of-war, the tail end of the convoy was still hull down.

This was the real might of England, this and the rest of the great merchant fleet, the ships that brought England's goods to the world, and the world's wealth back to England. With these ships the British could move their armies up and down the American coast, striking at will, while the Continental Army slogged along decrepit roads. The Americans could build men-of-war to fight the British navy, they could issue letters of marque, they could fight the British army on land, but they could not do this.

Biddlecomb recalled the first convoy he had seen, at the siege of Quebec so many years ago, and the effective use to which it had been put. And that thought in turn made him even more depressed.

And mingled in with his despair was the frustration of missed opportunities. The *Charlemagne* was built for privateering. If he had not been talked into the Bermuda venture, talked into it, in fact, by some traitor for the sole purpose of his capture, then he might be preparing to attack this very convoy.

The thought of that betrayal led to thoughts of his letter to Virginia Stanton, and soon his shoulders were aching with tension. Did she ever receive it? Perhaps Maltby smoked the secret message, perhaps that was why he had been placed aboard the *Ant*. And if she did get it, would *she* smoke it? The message was cryptic at best, and though he knew Virginia to be an admirer of Shakespeare, he did not know if she was familiar with *Henry the Fifth*. At first he had worried that the message was too obvious, but since Maltby did not catch it, he now worried that it was too subtle. The thought of dying while the man who had betrayed him lived was abhorrent to him.

Then he realized that he was no longer thinking about the letter, but about Virginia; about the way she looked stepping out of the front door of Stanton House to greet him, the flash of amusement in her eyes. And the flash of anger. And the way she matched him quip for quip, her penchant for playing the devil's advocate with unshakable reason. Virginia.

At worst, she would think that the letter was insanity, or at best a manipulation of her to get a letter to her father. But there was more to it than that. He had tried to include in the note the fact that he did deeply, honestly love her. But as he thought of the words he had written, the personal words directed to her, he felt certain that they were too vague, too obscure for her to catch. Now he was as miserable as he could be.

"Our number, sir!" Biddlecomb heard the *Ant*'s midshipman report to Shave. Isaac turned and looked back toward the quarterdeck. The midshipman was peering through his telescope across the water at the frigate. "Take station ahead of convoy, sir."

"Right, then." Shave hitched up his slop trousers and looked furtively about. Numbered among Shave's many sins was the fact that he was a terrible seaman. He did not enjoy any type of sail evolution, and he did not do them well. Watching him try was Biddlecomb's sole source of amusement in an otherwise desperate situation.

The convoy and the men-of-war were sailing opposite courses, passing each other like wagons on opposite sides of a highway. The convoy was downwind of the men-of-war and close-hauled, sailing north by west, beating against the prevailing westerlies. The men-of-war were sailing east on a dead run and passing quickly down the line of merchantmen. The wind had been building steadily, and now it was blowing twenty-five knots with choppy seas. Such conditions had little effect on the larger ships, but aboard the *Ant* they would make any evolution that much more difficult.

Biddlecomb watched as the *Glasgow* rounded up into the wind, turning onto the same course as the merchantmen and racing for the head of the line. The *Charlemagne* turned as well and resumed her position to leeward of the *Glasgow*, where she would remain just under the frigate's guns.

"Hands to stations! Ready to brace up, starb—larboard tack!" Shave shouted, and the Ants moved grudgingly to their lines. Shave ran his narrow eyes over his command. The *Ant* was running with the wind astern and her long boom jutting out over her starboard side. "All right, put your helm down," he shouted at the helmsman.

The *Ant* began to swing up into the wind, the bow turning away from the convoy, and the wind came over the larboard quarter and then the larboard beam, and she began rolling hard as her side was presented to the waves. The afterguard hauled away on the mainsheet, pulling the long boom inboard as the sloop turned into the wind, turning from a broad reach to the close-hauled course of the convoy. Shave looked around, a smirk of satisfaction growing on his lips, then noticed the ensign staff still made fast to the taffrail.

"Oh, bloody hell!" he fairly screamed. "Get that ensign staff down before the fucking boom hits it!"

The boom was not about to hit the ensign staff; it was incredible to Biddlecomb that Shave did not realize as much. The men at the mainsheet made the line fast and scrambled aft to attend to the staff, which was now more threatened by their awkward ministrations than it was by the main boom.

"Oh, hold on, belay that," Shave called tentatively as it dawned on him that the boom would not swing past the centerline of the vessel. The *Ant* settled on her new course paralleling that of the convoy, her bow plunging up and down in the chop and sending up great bursts of spray.

Another gun went off from the frigate's leeward side. "Oh, beg pardon, sir," the midshipman said, once again staring at the frigate through his glass. "Signal is 'Take station *astern* of convoy.' I didn't—"

Biddlecomb could not determine what the midshipman did not do, as a second later the young man was lying supine in the scuppers, Shave having knocked him there with a backhand to the jaw. The young man curled up as the lieutenant delivered a series of kicks to his stomach.

"Stupid bastard! Stupid bastard, why don't you look next time!" Shave shouted. Then he left off kicking the midshipman and turned to the men forward. "Right, you bastards, we're going to come about!" he shouted, then turning to the helmsman said, "Keep her coming around!"

Instead of turning the *Ant* back the way she had come, Shave was going to keep turning, going to tack the sloop and then turn downwind. What looked to be a disappointingly normal evolution was now becoming more interesting.

"Hands to sheets and braces! Lay into this mainsheet!" Shave was shouting orders with confidence now. Biddlecomb smiled; his confidence was a bit premature. For one thing the ensign staff, which had been fine before, was now in the way, and Shave, looking forward, had forgotten it.

Shave took his eyes from the bow long enough to catch Biddlecomb's glance, and Biddlecomb smiled as he watched the heavy main boom swing amidships, behind the lieutenant's back, and strike the ensign staff. The force was not enough to sheer the pole off, but enough to crack it. At the sound of breaking wood, Shave spun around like a dancer, shouting orders as the staff began to lean to leeward like a drunken sailor.

"Get that damned thing!" he shouted, and the men tending the mainsheet ran aft and pulled the broken staff and the ensign inboard, depositing them in a heap on the deck.

The *Ant* was through the wind and still turning. The main boom, now free of the ensign staff, had swung far over the larboard side and was held there by the stiff breeze.

Biddlecomb looked up at the leech of the big mainsail. They had turned so far that the edge of the sail was starting to flutter. In a second the wind would catch the sail on the wrong side and they would be in an uncontrolled jibe. Then the long boom would sweep across the quarterdeck with enormous force.

"Send that up to the gaff," Shave said, his entire attention directed at the men who were removing the ensign from the broken staff. He looked aloft, and his expression changed from confusion to panic as he realized what would happen next.

"Oh, bloody hell," he said, and then the wind caught the big mainsail on the other side and the boom swept across the deck with a devastating force.

The helmsman, who stood six foot two inches tall, was

knocked clean over the tiller and came to a stop only when he slammed into the starboard bulwark. The main boom hit the traveling backstay and did not pause in its arc, tearing the ringbolt from the deck and sending bits of debris flying in all directions. The boom slammed into the after shroud on the leeward side, and Biddlecomb could hear the channel shatter as the chainplate was wrenched from the side of the vessel.

"Amidships!" Shave shouted to the helmsman. "Amidships, you . . . ," Shave cried again, and only then noticed that the helmsman was a bloody heap in the scuppers. The *Ant* swung past her course and began to round up into the wind again as Shave grabbed the tiller himself. He pushed the helm to weather, turning the *Ant* off the wind and settling her down on her old course.

A tense silence hung over the deck as Lieutenant Shave ran his eyes over the damaged rig, then over the transom toward the frigate and the *Charlemagne*. Biddlecomb watched him, waited until his back was turned, then scrambled down the scuttle to the tween decks. He did not care to be on deck, sitting on the hatch and grinning, when Lieutenant Shave exploded.

CHAPTER
18

Rhode Island

MAJ. EDWARD FITZGERALD, GIVEN A CHOICE, WOULD HAVE AVOIDED travel by boat altogether, though he understood that that was not realistic if one wished to do business with a naval officer. He clung to the gunnel of the *Katy*'s launch and gritted his teeth and stared out over the confused water of Narragansett Bay, trying to ignore the growing discomfort in his stomach.

He hated boats and ships and waterborne vehicles of all description, and they were one of the few things on earth that frightened him. But he had resolved to speak to Capt. Abraham Whipple, and this was the price he had to pay.

It had been a long day's ride from Cambridge to Providence, a long, cold, and meditative ride, during which he had thoroughly considered the treachery and fixed on his best hypothesis of how it had been done. From there had come the first dim vision of the trap he would lay for his traitor, whomever he might be. But he still needed answers for some important questions, answers that would tell him if his idea was plausible. He hoped that Captain Whipple could help him.

Fitzgerald tore his eyes from the shoreline and looked south. He could see a vessel riding at anchor, a sloop that he took to be the *Katy*. He turned to ask the midshipman who sat beside him in the stern sheets if it was indeed the *Katy*, but decided against it. He did not entirely trust his voice and figured it would be better for him to keep his mouth firmly shut. Speaking would both reveal his ignorance and serve as an invitation for his stomach to revolt.

On either side of the boat ten oarsmen stroked with a steady rhythm, and despite what seemed to Fitzgerald to be very choppy conditions indeed, with waves breaking white over the steel gray water and on occasion sloshing over the gunwales, the sailors seemed unconcerned and even in some cases a bit bored.

In an effort to take his mind from what he was certain was a fairly perilous situation, Fitzgerald began once again to mentally examine his list of suspects, those people in a position to betray Biddlecomb and the cause: Cooke, Bowler, Stanton, Rogers, Virginia. All could have betrayed the captain, and all seemed equally unlikely to have done so. But it was one of them, he was certain. Judas, he recalled, had been something of a surprise to the disciples.

Fitzgerald was a believer in swift and terrible justice, but in his philosophy, and more importantly in Washington's, the swift and terrible was subservient to the justice. There would be no court in this case, no lawyers and witnesses and judges. It was only him, and when he made a move, he had to be right.

"Toss oars!" the midshipman cried, and to Fitzgerald's surprise the sailors on either side of the boat pulled their oars from the water and held them straight up. He looked past the oarsmen. The *Katy* loomed over them as the launch swept up to her side. So lost had he been in his thoughts that he had not been aware of their arrival, and he felt a warm sense of relief when he realized he could get out of the boat and onto the more stable ship.

The launch pulled up alongside, and a man in the front grabbed on to the sloop with a hook. The midshipman turned to Fitzgerald. "You first, sir," he said, indicating the few steps up the vessel's side.

"Oh, thank you," Fitzgerald said, standing unsteadily and putting a hand on the midshipman's shoulder as he pushed his sword out of the way. He grabbed on to the step and, as the boat rose on a wave, stepped up. His head reached the level of the deck, and suddenly his ears were assaulted by a horrible discordant screeching. He looked up in startled surprise and saw that the screeching was coming from a party of men standing on either side of the entranceway and that this was some sort of formal greeting. He took the next two steps quickly and stepped onto the *Katy's* deck, and the caterwauling stopped.

"Major Fitzgerald?" A portly man in a cocked hat, blue coat, and white breeches stepped forward, hand extended. "I'm Captain Whipple, of the Rhode Island sloop *Katy*."

Fitzgerald took the big, callused hand and shook it. "An honor to meet you, sir. Your servant."

"The honor's mine, Major, all mine . . . an officer from General Washington's staff. I received your note just in time. We're to sail on the tide tomorrow. Unless you bring more urgent business, that is."

"No, I won't interfere with your sailing. I desire only some intelligence from you."

"Well, I'm pleased to see the army will credit us poor sailors with any intelligence at all. No, no, I'm joking, Major, please, no offense. If you'll step below, we'll have a glass and you'll tell me how I might be of assistance."

The captain's quarters aboard the *Katy*, the "great cabin" as Fitzgerald understood it to be called, was a tiny affair; Fitzgerald could not even begin to stand upright; but it was neatly appointed and had a cheerful and homey aspect.

He found himself seated in a comfortable winged chair lashed to ringbolts in the deck, a glass of good wine in his hand, and his host seated opposite him. Whipple seemed an amiable man, like a kindly uncle. Fitzgerald had to remind himself that this was the same man who had led the party that stormed and burned the *Gaspee* and shot her commanding officer, one of the most daring and offensive actions yet taken by any colonist. This man had taken back a colonial sloop captured by the black-heart Wallace and had been depriving Wallace of stores, whisking cattle away right under the frigate's guns. This was a man whose dedication to the cause had been demonstrated by bold and daring action, not mere words, and Fitzgerald trusted him. What was more, he knew nothing of the Bermuda venture.

"Now, Major, how may I be of assistance?"

"Have you had any word of Capt. Isaac Biddlecomb?" Fitzgerald asked first, probing.

"No. The last I saw of him was when *Charlemagne* sailed . . . what? . . . a month ago? But how is it you know Biddlecomb?"

"I had a hand in the work he was doing. It was a special task for the general, very secret. In any event, we have it on some authority that Biddlecomb was captured by the Royal Navy."

Fitzgerald could see in Whipple's face the effect that that news had on him, like hearing of the death of a good friend. Apparently this Biddlecomb engendered some love and loyalty among those who knew him to a degree that Fitzgerald found surprising.

"I am very sorry to hear that, Major," Whipple said at last. "If the British know who he is, what he's done, I reckon it will go hard for him."

"There's worse news, I fear. We have reason to believe that he was betrayed by someone well placed in the American cause, that his destination was made known to the navy in order that they might lay a trap for him."

Fitzgerald took a sip of wine and let the captain consider the implications of that statement, then continued his speech, one he had been rehearsing for the past hour. "In my position on the general's staff I work with a number of people friendly to our cause, people quite highly placed in the administration of the ministerial army in Boston. I am kept informed of what happens there, and for that reason I am quite certain that the orders for setting this trap did not come out of Boston. And since Captain Wallace has more reason than anyone I know of to wish Biddlecomb caught, it stands to reason that he was the one who set the trap, and that the traitor is having intercourse with him."

Whipple nodded his big head. "That stands to reason, Major,

though if you're here to ask me who this traitor might be, I can assure you that I have no notion. And if I did, I can assure you he wouldn't live long enough for you to speak with him."

"No, I didn't imagine that you knew the man I'm looking for. But you know more about naval affairs than any man in this colony. If the traitor is in Rhode Island, as I suspect he is, then he's sending word to Captain Wallace. No one besides Wallace would have the resources to set such a trap as caught Biddlecomb. I need to find out—"

"One moment, please." Whipple held up his hand. "I think I know where you're bound with this and I think I know the man for you to talk to." He stood and walked to the great-cabin door. He opened it and peered out, then yelled, "Lieutenant Trevett, would you step in here, please?"

A moment later, Lieutenant Trevett, a tall, lanky dark-haired man in his late twenties, stepped through the door and saluted in an awkward, crouching stance. "Lieutenant Trevett, this is Maj. Edward Fitzgerald. From Gen. George Washington's staff."

"An honor, sir," Trevett said, shaking Fitzgerald's hand.

"Sit, Lieutenant," Whipple said, waving his hand toward a chair. "Lieutenant Trevett is from Newport, Major, which Wallace calls his home port. He's the man that knows what goes on in that town, knows the ins and outs. He's the one you should speak with."

"I thank you, Captain," Fitzgerald said, then turning to Trevett continued, "We have reason to believe that someone well placed in the American cause is betraying us, and I believe Wallace is the one getting the information. Have you any idea how someone might be passing word to him? I have to believe they wish to be secret about it."

"Sure, I know damn well how that black-heart bastard gets word from his infernal tools, beg your pardon, sir."

"That's quite all right, Lieutenant, I share your sentiments." Fitzgerald was encouraged by this news. "Please, go on."

"Wallace has this coxswain, named Truax, a big, nasty son of a bitch. It's well-known around town that Truax's the one'll get a message to Wallace. There's a shameful amount of information sent through him, but we've always figured it was from small fry, shopkeepers and such wanting favors. We never figured anyone important was sending word. They give their notes to barmaids and whores and such, we don't know who exactly, and they pass them on to Truax."

"Has there ever been an attempt to get Truax to say who the notes are from?"

At that Lieutenant Trevett smiled and shook his head. "We reckon it'd be a waste of time to try and get Truax to talk. There's no one man alive could beat it out of him, and besides, he gets the notes from a go-between. Probably don't know himself who they're from. We thought about killing him, but that wouldn't do any good, and it would just give Wallace an excuse for more of his tyrannical ways."

"Is there any other way, do you think, that people might be sending word to Wallace?"

Trevett thought about that, then slowly shook his head. "Newport may be a bit backward in its loyalty, but it still ain't too safe to be seen communicating with Wallace. There's enough folks there that see our point of view and might . . . object, if you catch my meaning. Truax's the most discreet messenger the Tory's have, and I don't reckon there's any other."

Fitzgerald considered these words. They were just what he had hoped to hear. Now that he knew how word was passed, he had only to find out who was passing it. "Tell me, how can I find this Truax?"

"Well, you can ask just about anyone in Newport, but there's no need. Just go to Captain Lillibridge's Tavern on the Parade, just about any night, and he'll be there."

"Just about any night? How does he manage that?"

"Well, sir, Wallace gives his officers and some hands a run ashore of an evening when they're in port. Truax is in charge of the boat. And since he's become something of a message boy, I reckon Wallace is even more willing to let him go ashore and make himself seen."

"And how will I know him?" Fitzgerald asked.

"You'll know him," Trevett said, smiling. "Believe me, one glance at that ugly son of a bitch and you'll know him."

It had been an interesting two days since the men-of-war had rendezvoused with the convoy, a nonstop flurry of tacking and wearing and sending signal flags aloft and firing guns as the *Glasgow, Ant,* and *Charlemagne* attempted to shepherd sixty ships driven by sixty uncooperative merchant captains. Biddlecomb took every opportunity to watch the evolutions, trying to lose himself in the technical considerations of convoy escort, but in the end it did little to assuage his misery. Nor would Shave give him a moment's peace.

"Ain't that a sight, Brother Jonathan?" Biddlecomb was sitting on the knighthead in the bow, as far away from the quarterdeck as possible in an attempt to escape from Shave, but the lieutenant had followed him forward.

"I said, ain't that a sight, Jonathan?" Biddlecomb could hear the note of irritation carried on Shave's fetid breath.

"What would that be, Lieu—Captain?" he asked reluctantly.

"The convoy, you stupid whoreson," the lieutenant answered with a smile. "Bound away for Boston, enough men and arms to murder every Yankee rascal there, and then some. There, you see that big bastard of a ship, third from the end in the weather line?"

Biddlecomb looked in the direction that Shave was pointing. "Yes."

"That there's the *Lord Dartmouth,* troopship. She's carrying part of the Eighteenth Regiment of Foot and the Seventeenth Light Dragoons. Bloody animals, them Light Dragoons, bloody murderers. They'll have their way with them Yankee bitches after they bloody slaughter your American mobs."

"You mean like they did at Bunker Hill?"

"And that other one, just ahead of the *Dartmouth,* the *Sussex,* that's the bastard you want. Loaded with powder and small arms, enough to kill every Yankee rascal a few times over.

Powder, that was what you was after, right? That's why you come to Bermuda?''

Biddlecomb clenched his fists, fighting down the urge to lash out, verbally or otherwise. Shave knew exactly which strings to pull to make him angry and disgusted and took great delight in pulling them. He had to credit the lieutenant with that; few men had been able to successfully goad him in that manner.

"Ain't that why?'' Shave asked again, determined to get a response.

"Yes, it is. You know, you'd get more speed out of this tub if you'd check away the mainsheet and headsails a fathom or so,'' he added, but his attempt to needle Shave was halfhearted and had no effect on the lieutenant.

"Don't you worry about how I sail my ship, you Yankee son of a bitch.'' Shave then continued his inventory of the ships and cargo. "The one just to leeward of the *Sussex*, they got more troops on board, the rest of the Eighteenth Regiment as well as artillery.''

Biddlecomb half-heard the words. His eyes were fixed on the *Sussex*, fourth from last in the weather line. She was a large ship, high sided and clumsy looking, no different from a hundred merchantmen he had seen. But she was loaded with powder. Powder and small arms. Powder had been at the forefront of his thoughts for so long that even now the word excited him, and he looked at the *Sussex* with something akin to lust in his heart.

"Damn me, this convoy alone should be enough to crush all you Yankee vermin, shouldn't it? Your mother live in Boston? She gonna give a piece of it to them lads? A bit of bulling with old mum?''

Biddlecomb turned and looked at Shave. The lieutenant's big head, with its crown of greasy hair, was a foot away, and he was grinning wide enough that the filth between his teeth was clearly visible. "Well, Jonathan?''

Biddlecomb was silent, but he knew that he had to answer or he would never be rid of the swine. He was about to make some offhand remark when a gun from the frigate banged out, a mile and a half away at the head of the convoy. The *Ant's* midshipman, who, since his beating, had displayed much greater alacrity in reading signals from the *Glasgow*, sang out, "Signal from the frigate, sir! All vessels tack in succession!"

"Time to tack your boat, Captain," Biddlecomb said softly, and smiled at Shave.

"We'll talk later, Jonathan, I like our little talks." Biddlecomb had the satisfaction of seeing a glimmer of uneasiness in Shave's eyes as he turned to go aft.

The frigate fired another gun, then put her helm up, and her sails began to flutter as she came about. The forwardmost ships of the convoy did the same, and on down the line the heavy merchantmen tacked one after the other.

Then the ship two ahead of the *Sussex* missed stays. She flew up into the wind and hung there, her sails aback as she drifted astern, and the ship behind fell off just in time to miss smashing into her stern. In just a few seconds the entire after end of the convoy was in disarray, and signal flags and guns erupted from the *Glasgow* and the *Charlemagne*.

It was like this every time Maltby tried to tack the convoy in succession. Biddlecomb wondered when he would figure out that a bunch of undermanned merchantmen could not carry out the same fancy evolutions one might expect of a squadron of fully manned naval vessels.

The merchantman that had missed stays was falling back onto the old tack, and the *Sussex* managed to duck to leeward of it and come about. Biddlecomb watched the ship turn and felt the same longing he had experienced earlier. Delivering a ship full of powder and small arms to General Washington would wash away any taint of failure. But just as he was starting to bask in the warmth of his fantasies, he was brought up short once again. He was a prisoner on board a British man-of-war. There was nothing he could do; he could only wait until others did unto him, and when they did, he knew that it would not be pleasant.

"On deck!" the lookout at the *Ant's* masthead cried out.

"What the hell is it?" Shave called back.

"Sail to leeward, sir, just hull down now!"

Just hull down. That meant the stranger had been overhauling them for some time, and the lookout had not noticed. Biddlecomb waited for Shave to explode in anger, but the lieutenant was too preoccupied with the convoy to notice the lookout's negligence.

"Here," Shave said to the midshipman, "skip aloft with your glass and tell me what you see." The midshipman snatched up his glass and leapt into the shrouds, as anxious, Biddlecomb imagined, to get away from Shave as he was to swiftly carry out his orders.

"Ready about! Stations for stays!" Shave screamed, and the Ants moved to their stations for tacking. Biddlecomb knew what would happen next and grabbed on to the forestay for support. Shave was of that breed of seagoing idiot who believed that trimming sails meant hauling them in as tight as he could, and as a result the *Ant* was pressed down hard to leeward. Biddlecomb could hear her timbers strain, and he wondered that Shave had not yet torn the rig out of her.

"Helm's alee!" he cried, and the sloop shot up into the wind, rolling forty-five degrees as the sails spilled their air, turning out of control. She spun through the eye of the wind and around on the other tack, and the headsails, which still had not been cast off, now came aback.

"Cast off those goddamned headsails!" Shave shouted. The sails flew off to leeward, flogging like thunder close overhead. The *Ant* ceased swinging wildly to larboard under their influence, but instead began swinging wildly back to starboard under the pressure of the mainsail.

"Sheet in those headsails, you motherless idiots!" Shave screeched from the quarterdeck, and the foredeck men struggled to haul them in on the larboard side. Biddlecomb was grateful for the loud flogging of the sails, which masked his laughter, and it was only with great effort, as the canvas was subdued, that he was able to keep silent. The *Ant* settled down on the starboard tack, overburdened as she had been before, and the uncomfortable silence that generally followed the sloop's botched maneuvers hung over the deck.

"Biddlecomb!" Shave shouted from the quarterdeck. "Biddlecomb, lay aft here!"

Biddlecomb hopped down from the knighthead and walked aft. He could just imagine what would come next; any humiliation that Shave received would be returned with interest. He crossed the imaginary line that marked the quarterdeck, and Shave turned and spit a great brown wad of tobacco on the white planks. "Clean that up."

"On deck!" the midshipman called out from the masthead.

"What!" Shave shouted.

"It's a ship, sir!" the midshipman reported. "Studdingsails aloft and alow!"

Biddlecomb knelt down on the deck and began to swab up Shave's mess. Studdingsails aloft and alow. Whoever this stranger was, he was trying hard to catch up with the convoy. He could think of only three possibilities. It was either a British man-of-war coming to assist or a British merchantman hoping to join the others. Or it was an American privateer. He felt a pinprick of hope, felt his misery subside just that tiny bit.

"You think that's another Yankee?" Shave asked in his ironic tone. "You hope to have some more company when they hang you, is that it?"

Once again he had found the right string to pull, and he was pulling it hard. Biddlecomb dropped the rag back in the bucket, ignoring him, but the lieutenant nudged him with his toe. "I said, is that it, you Yankee bastard? You think that's another colonial son of a whore?"

"Yes." With that word Biddlecomb snuffed out any hope that was smoldering in his mind. It did not matter in the least, as far as his fate was concerned, what ship that was on the horizon. Even if that stranger was an American privateer, as far as being an agent of his rescue, there was not one damn thing that they could do, or would.

CHAPTER
19

The Admiral's Steward

BIDDLECOMB STOOD AND LOOKED INTO SHAVE'S RED-RIMMED EYES. "Hadn't you better signal the frigate about that strange sail?"

"I'll signal the frigate when I'm bloody ready, you son of a bitch!" Shave shouted, then smiled and said, "You just take your place over there, Jonathan. I think you've earned the right to be admiral's steward this next hour."

Biddlecomb retreated to the leeward side, fighting to keep his anger and humiliation in check. Weatherspoon was on deck, as were the other Charlemagnes, and that only made the degradation of Admiral's Steward worse, a fact that was not lost on Shave. The lieutenant turned his attention to the midshipman aloft. "Get your arse down here and signal the frigate!" he shouted.

The entire convoy had come about and settled down on the starboard tack, more or less in good order, by the time the *Glasgow* acknowledged the *Ant*'s signal. The frigate was near the head of the line, a mile ahead of the *Ant*. The acknowledgment broke out at the *Glasgow*'s yardarm as Maltby was putting his helm down, turning and running downwind past the lines of merchant ships. High aloft once again, the *Ant*'s midshipman shouted, "Signal from the frigate, sir. Maintain station on convoy!"

Five minutes later the *Glasgow* passed the *Ant*, sailing the opposite course, charging away downwind to investigate the potential threat that had appeared over the eastern horizon.

The frigate was a magnificent sight, running with all plain sail set, the white foam curling around her cutwater and rushing down her sides, vivid against the slate gray of the ocean. Biddlecomb watched her go by, less than two hundred feet away. He had allowed himself to hope that it was an American on the horizon, even indulged the fantasy that the stranger might be their salvation, but now he stowed all hope away. If it was an American naval vessel, it would be too small to take on the frigate. If it was a privateer, it would not fight, regardless of its size. Privateers were not in the business of fighting frigates, or even of helping fellow Americans. Wasn't that the reason he had wanted to get into privateering himself? he thought bitterly.

Weatherspoon stepped up beside him, and together they watched the frigate running away downwind. Biddlecomb wondered how far the *Glasgow* would chase the stranger. Every foot the frigate lost to leeward would have to be regained through an exhausting beat back to weather.

"On deck!" the lookout called.

"Deck! What's acting?" Shave called back.

"Stranger's hauled his wind, sir! Running for it!"

And that was an end to it. The strange sail most likely was an American privateer, and just a glance at a British frigate was enough to make him turn on his heel and run.

"Too bad, you poor, sorry Jonathans!" Shave called out so all on deck could hear. "No rescue today!"

The *Glasgow* wasted not a moment before she also spun on her heel and resumed her course, close-hauled, heading back for her station at the head of the convoy. The *Ant* was at the very end of the windward line of ships now, and the frigate was half a mile downwind of her. Even with her vastly superior speed it would take the *Glasgow* a few hours to regain the position she had lost in just a few minutes.

An hour later the lookout reported that the strange sail had disappeared below the eastern horizon. Biddlecomb stared over the leeward rail at the *Glasgow*, now less than a cable astern of the *Ant*. Maltby was pushing the frigate hard trying to regain his proper station at the head of the convoy. The wind had built to twenty-five knots now, and the bow of the man-of-war pounded into the chop, sending spray as high as the foretop. Maltby was going to pass down the leeward side of the *Ant*, and very close by the looks of it, as he pushed past the other vessels.

It was a bold move, passing between the sloop to windward and the convoy to leeward, but it was the fastest way back to the head of the line. Maltby was a hard driver and an excellent ship handler, willing to take chances. He had proved that much in Bermuda.

Biddlecomb tore his eyes from the frigate and looked forward. The *Charlemagne* was close by as well, a cable length ahead of them, having just chased another merchantman back into line. He could see men milling about in the waist and wondered if they were members of his old crew taking their air on deck. He looked over the crowd. Yes, there was Rumstick, his hulking frame unmistakable even at that distance, and he could make out Sprout and Jaeger as well. His old shipmates were so close that he could have talked to them if he had a speaking trumpet. The thought made his loneliness and despair even more acute.

"You wish you was back on board her, don't you, Jonathan?" Shave called out.

"God damn you to hell, you bastard," Biddlecomb muttered, so softly that even Weatherspoon did not hear him. Shave was always watching, always waiting for an opening he could exploit.

"Maybe they'll use her to transport you to England for your hanging. How would that be?" By the time Shave had finished his harangue, the *Glasgow* was starting to overhaul the little sloop.

Both vessels were healing hard to larboard, pressed down by the building wind. The sea boiled down the *Ant*'s side just four feet below where Biddlecomb stood. He could see the

Glasgow's jibboom and topgallant masts bending under the pressure of the sails as Captain Maltby pushed his ship back to the station from which he was best able to protect his flock.

Biddlecomb looked up at the *Ant's* huge, straining mainsail and the jib and staysail. The canvas looked like a solid thing with the sails hauled in taut, much tauter than was right. As it was, the mainsail was exerting tremendous leverage on the sloop, trying to force the bow up into the wind, and that pressure was balanced by the headsails, trying to force the bow off the wind. The result of these conflicting forces was a tremendous strain on the rig of a vessel that was being pushed too hard.

Biddlecomb looked aft at Shave, swaggering around the quarterdeck and looking aloft as if he knew what he was looking at. He felt a loathing deep inside, a desire to strike out at the swine who was tormenting him. He looked away before Shave caught his eye and started in again.

He turned his attention back to the frigate. The tip of the jibboom was almost up with the *Ant's* transom; in a minute or two the vessels would be side by side and only fifty feet apart, as if in a race that the *Glasgow* was winning. Biddlecomb gave his fantasies free reign and found some slight pleasure in the exercise. He envisioned the destruction of the British ships. In his mind he visited horrible accidents upon them, spars snapping like twigs, vessels out of control, destruction and ruination. And escape.

And suddenly he relaxed his grip on the caprail. He felt the soles of his feet tingling and the concomitant convulsions in his stomach. He looked around, up at the *Ant's* rig and back at the frigate overtaking them. It was madness, what he was thinking, and even as that thought occurred to him, he knew that he would go through with it nonetheless.

It was well past dark, and too late for any official visit, by the time the *Katy's* boat delivered Fitzgerald to Providence and he found a suitable public house in which to stay. He had breakfast before dawn the next morning, sitting with his eggs

217

and chops and strong coffee as close as he could to the big fire in the front room of the inn.

When at last the sun came up, it revealed, through the distorting glass of the windows, an overcast sky and a howling wind that blew the last tenacious leaves from the trees and sent them swirling along the cobbled streets. Fitzgerald wrapped his cloak around his freshly pressed uniform, asked the publican for directions to the offices of the colonial governor, and stepped into the cold morning air.

It was a short walk uphill to the governor's offices. Fitzgerald pushed open the door and stepped inside, taking his hand off his hat for the first time since leaving the public house.

The waiting room was lined with chairs, most of which were filled with men wishing for a moment of Nicholas Cooke's time, and by the door to the inner room was a desk piled high with paper and behind it a clerk. Fitzgerald smiled to himself. It was just like the general's headquarters, except that now he was the one waiting.

"May I help you?" asked the clerk in a tone that indicated how little he wished to do so.

"I'm here to see acting Governor Cooke," said Fitzgerald, removing his hat.

"Governor Cooke is no longer acting governor. He was made the official governor a week ago," said the clerk, clearly contemptuous of anyone who did not know that. "Please take a seat and the governor will see you if he has time." The clerk pulled a quill from its stand and poised it over a sheet on the desk. "What name shall I put on the list?"

"Forgive me, but I'm on urgent business." Fitzgerald did not have time to wait, particularly as it appeared that waiting would be an all-day affair. "I'm from the headquarters of—"

"I am genuinely not interested in where you're from. You'll have to wait like the others. Name, please?"

Fitzgerald felt his anger mounting. He was silent as he unbuttoned his cloak and pulled it off his shoulders, revealing his perfectly tailored uniform, the blue coat and buff-colored lapels and the brilliant silver buttons. He ignored the clerk's look of surprise. "Major Fitzgerald, of General Washington's staff."

"One moment, sir. Please have a seat," said the clerk, more obsequious now. He backed away and disappeared through the door behind him.

The major remained standing, and less than half a minute later the clerk returned. "The governor will see you now, sir."

"Thank you," said Fitzgerald as he brushed past the man. He disliked such histrionics, but the haughty clerk had annoyed him, and as he stepped into the governor's office, he made a mental note to have more patience with the men who were waiting for General Washington.

"Major Fitzgerald, how wonderful to see you again," Cooke said, stepping around the table that served as his desk and greeting Fitzgerald in the middle of the room. Fitzgerald took the proffered hand and shook it warmly. He had always liked Cooke, and he reminded himself of the job he was there to perform.

"The pleasure is mine, sir. And General Washington sends his warmest regards."

"Please, sit," said Cooke, gesturing toward a chair and stepping back around the table. "Can I get you anything? Tea? Coffee? Something to eat?" The governor looked old, older even than he had looked a month before, and more tired. Fitzgerald knew that he had taken on the duties of governor only after much prodding from the leaders of the colony. "Nothing, thank you, Your Honor," Fitzgerald said as he took his seat.

"How is the general? And how do things go on in Boston?"

"Little is changed since your visit, sir. We watch the British, they watch us. Discipline has improved, to be sure, and the various militia are more of a Continental Army than ever before. Our powder situation is still quite desperate." There was no harm in saying the last. Whichever of these men was the traitor, he was already well aware of the shortage of gunpowder.

"Is that what I owe the pleasure of your visit to?" Cooke

asked with a slight smile. The general was forever pleading with the colonial governors for powder.

"In a way, sir, yes. Actually, my visit concerns the past Bermuda venture, the one on which Captain Biddlecomb was dispatched." He was on a fishing trip now, casting around for a bite, and despite the casual attitude projected by his relaxed tone and posture, Fitzgerald scrutinized Cooke's face for any flicker of doubt or fear, but there was nothing. The governor was either very good or he was innocent.

"Yes, I've heard nothing on that line. Has he returned? What do you hear?" Cooke asked, his voice more animated now.

"Biddlecomb was captured, sir. In Bermuda, we believe."

Cooke's face fell. "Oh, dear," he said at last. "Such a promising young man, even if his behavior was a bit odd. Stanton had great faith in him. Do you know how it happened?"

"We don't have all the details, but it appears he was the victim of some treachery. Someone familiar with the voyage alerted the British."

He said the words and let them hang in the air. Cooke held his gaze for a moment, then let his head sink down to his chest and let out a sigh. "This is too much, too much," he said, the weariness back in his voice. "Is it not hard enough that we must take on the British, without Americans betraying each other?" He looked up and met Fitzgerald's eyes once again. "I was one of the few that knew of the voyage. I presume that I am a suspect?"

"No, sir," Fitzgerald lied, "you're not a suspect. No man has done this country greater service than you. That's why the general wished for me to inform you of the traitor's existence. And there is more to the story, sir, about Biddlecomb. You see, he sent us just a short, cryptic letter written apparently after he was captured. It was later confirmed by the captain of another American ship that was in Bermuda at the same time. This other fellow had some interesting things to say. He told us a great deal about the subsequent events that we hadn't known, what happened after Biddlecomb wrote the letter."

Fitzgerald leaned forward, as did Cooke, and in a low voice

Fitzgerald related to the governor this new information concerning Biddlecomb's whereabouts. It was new information indeed, information that not one other man on earth knew, for just that morning Fitzgerald had made it up.

Biddlecomb forced himself to be calm, and doubt swept over him again. His plan, if it could be called such, was insane. Even if it worked, it might be no better than suicide.

Then he heard Lieutenant Shave begin again his long and protracted throat-clearing, summoning up from his lungs some horror for Biddlecomb to clean. He felt the rage building, felt the insanity take charge. There was only a minute to get things ready, to think through the anger. He felt his hands shaking with excitement, felt his muscles tense as he gripped the caprail, fighting to control himself. The warrior was waking up.

"Weatherspoon, come here," he said in a loud whisper, and the midshipman, who was always hovering about, stepped up to him.

"Yes, sir?"

"If you want to try an escape, we'll do it now."

"I'm with you, sir," said Weatherspoon, no equivocation in his voice.

"Good. There's five more of our men over toward the bow. When all hell breaks loose, grab them and . . ." Biddlecomb looked around the deck. He was making his plan up even as he was issuing orders. There was no time. "Grab them and snatch that grating off the small hatch, the one just forward of the mast, and carry it aft. All of you run aft to the quarterdeck. Understand?"

"Yes, sir," said Weatherspoon, and Biddlecomb was grateful that the boy did not ask for further explanation.

He looked around, waiting for the moment, steeling himself. The frigate's jib boom was overlapping the *Ant* now by half its length; he could see Maltby on the weather side of his quarterdeck with the *Glasgow* not forty feet downwind of the sloop. He was taking a risk to the point of arrogance passing so close, and now he would pay. Biddlecomb felt the madness overcome him.

And then Shave let fly with his wad of spittle. "Here, admiral's steward, come wipe this up!"

The tingling in his soles grew stronger, and Biddlecomb felt his body tense, but he was not afraid, and that surprised him. He picked up his bucket, considering his own emotions raging inside, like a doctor examining a patient. He even managed a smile as he sauntered aft.

"Here, what the fuck are you smiling about, you whore's son?" Shave shouted, and in response Biddlecomb flung the bucket of filthy water into the lieutenant's face.

"What the hell!" Shave sputtered. Biddlecomb leapt forward, wound up with the bucket, and smashed it into the side of Shave's head. The lieutenant staggered back, falling, and Biddlecomb grabbed the hilt of his sword and jerked it from the scabbard.

The weapon was magic in his hand; the second it was free of the scabbard, it felt old and familiar. He caught a glimpse of the helmsmen's expressions of shock, but they were wrestling to keep the overburdened vessel on course and could not let go of the long tiller to help the lieutenant.

Shave was down and Biddlecomb raced aft to where the mainsail sheet ran from the long boom to the weather side of the sloop. The sheet, a two-inch-thick line, was under an extraordinary strain as it held the big mainsail in place against the tremendous press of the wind. He could hear the fibers of the line popping as the rope stretched under the pressure.

He slashed at it with the sword; the sensation was like chopping wood. He slashed again and the rope snapped and whipped through the blocks. The boom and its mainsail swung away to leeward, beyond control, spilling its wind and smashing all in its path, tearing out the after shroud that had just yesterday been repaired.

He turned and looked forward. The jib and staysail were still set. With the wind spilled from the mainsail, and the balancing pressure of that sail gone, the bow was starting to swing wildly downwind. But the helmsmen were still at their stations, pushing the tiller over, trying to counteract the pressure of the headsails. They were leaning into the helm, fighting with everything they had to keep the sloop on course.

Biddlecomb saw the lead helmsman look with bulging eyes at the frigate less than a boat length to leeward. Isaac smiled as he hopped over the tiller and stepped forward.

"You there," he said, and when the lead helmsman looked up, Biddlecomb smashed the beautiful hand guard of his sword into the man's startled face, sending him reeling to the deck. Lieutenant Shave was on his knees and awkwardly regaining his feet when Biddlecomb turned to the one remaining helmsman, who was straining to hold the tiller to leeward.

"Run," said Biddlecomb, prodding the helmsman with the point of the sword, and the terrified sailor released the tiller and raced forward.

Shave had just managed to stand when the helmsman let go of the tiller. The long wooden bar swept across the deck, catching the lieutenant just above the knees and throwing him against the weather bulwark. Biddlecomb saw blood spray from his scalp as his head smashed into the pinrail, and then the lieutenant rolled drunkenly onto his side.

The *Ant* was beyond human control. The big headsails had charge of the vessel now, and her bow was swinging wildly downwind, straight into the path of the hard-driving frigate. Biddlecomb was aware of shouting fore and aft, of men running in a disorganized panic, and he was suddenly afraid that someone would cast off the headsail sheets, or that the *Glasgow* would react in time.

Two of the *Ant*'s men charged for the bow, racing to cast off the jib and staysail sheets and stop the sloop's wild swing. He took a step in their direction, but he knew he could not reach them in time.

And suddenly they were down on the deck, knocked flat, with Weatherspoon standing over them, a handspike from the windlass held like a club in his hands.

The convoy seemed to sweep past the bow as the *Ant* spun

out of control. Then the *Glasgow* was there, looming overhead, as the *Ant* turned right across her path, so fast that the *Glasgow* could not avoid them. The two vessels hit and Biddlecomb was knocked to the deck by the impact.

The frigate struck the sloop at a right angle just aft of the mast. Her long jibboom sailed over the *Ant*'s deck, tearing up the larboard shrouds and piercing the mainsail like an arrow. It fetched up on the *Ant*'s gaff, bent, and shattered in a shower of splintered wood.

Biddlecomb pulled himself to his feet and looked up at the frigate towering over them, quickly becoming one with the sloop. The *Glasgow*'s fore topgallant mast collapsed as if shot clean through, and he caught a glimpse of the main topgallant mast going as well. The frigate's bowsprit was directly overhead, its cap caught on the *Ant*'s mast, threatening to break one or the other.

Next the frigate's cutwater struck the side of the sloop. The *Ant*'s low bulwark collapsed under the impact, and the deck was stove in almost to the main-hatch combing. The sloop rolled away from the frigate, and for an awful second Biddlecomb thought the frigate would roll right over them, taking them all to the bottom. But the *Ant* came upright again, rolling back into the frigate, the rigging of the two vessels becoming a hopeless tangled mess as both men-of-war, quite beyond control, began to fall off to leeward.

Biddlecomb tore his eyes from the destruction. This was only half the plan accomplished, the predictable half. He saw Weatherspoon and the five Americans hurrying aft, holding the grating over their heads, all but ignored by the frenzied British sailors.

The *Charlemagne* was still near the end of the convoy, but not as close as she had been. Biddlecomb ran over to the binnacle box and snatched up the speaking trumpet, cursing himself for wasting precious seconds enjoying the destruction he had wrought. If the *Charlemagne* was beyond hailing distance, then he and the other Americans would die a foolish death.

A crowd of men were leaning over the *Charlemagne*'s bulwark, watching the excitement he had created, and he hoped fervently that one of them was Rumstick.

"Rumstick!" he shouted through the trumpet with all the volume his lungs could muster, volume born of years of trying to outshout the howling wind. "Rumstick! Take the brig! Take the damned brig! Take it now!" He could hear behind him the sound of shattering wood and running and shouting men, and he knew that he could not remain aboard the *Ant* much longer.

"Take the brig, Rumstick!" he shouted one last time, then threw the speaking trumpet into the sea and turned and looked down the length of the deck.

Aboard the frigate they were clewing up sail as fast as they could, but the two vessels were now locked together and spinning off downwind. It would be hours before they were disentangled, and more before they were repaired. Weatherspoon and the Americans were standing by the starboard rail, resting the grating on the bulwark. Forward, the British sailors were clustering together, and Biddlecomb could see fingers pointing aft. It was time to go.

He was stepping over to the Americans when he saw the look of surprise on their faces, caught the shadow of a motion from the corner of his eye. He ducked and a belaying pin grazed his skull and swept past, gripped in a hairy hand projecting from a blue sleeve. Biddlecomb spun around and leapt back. Lieutenant Shave was facing him, the wooden pin in his hand, his face smeared with blood, his expression something less than human.

"Come on, you bastard," Shave growled, "I'm gonna tear your head off for this! I'll rip your fucking lungs out, you whore's son!"

He swung at Biddlecomb and Biddlecomb sidestepped his attack. The two men circled around, facing each other. Biddlecomb stared into Shave's narrow eyes. He remembered how the lieutenant had looked, standing above him and grinning as he wiped up the man's spittle, and he saw the lovely vengeance that would now be his.

Shave took a wild swipe with the belaying pin. Biddlecomb knocked his hand aside with the sword, drawing the blade down across his arm, ripping through cloth and flesh. The lieutenant dropped the wooden pin and grabbed at the torn limb, blood oozing between his fingers. And then Biddlecomb fixed his eyes on Shave's chest and lunged.

The point of the blade was less than an inch from Shave's chest when Biddlecomb turned his wrist and impaled the lieutenant half a foot above his heart. Though the quirk of Biddlecomb's conscience had saved Shave's life, it did little now to preserve his shoulder as the blade drove through flesh until the point hit bone.

"You bastard! You stupid bastard!" Biddlecomb realized that he was screaming at the top of his lungs, screaming even louder than Shave's shriek of pain. He twisted the sword and pulled back, jerking the dripping point of the blade from Shave's shoulder. The lieutenant fell to his knees and doubled over as the blood spread across his filthy shirt. His mouth opened and closed and Biddlecomb could hear his whimpering over the sounds of breaking wood and shouting and the wind through the tattered rigging.

"Sir! Come on, sir!" Weatherspoon was shouting. In the *Ant*'s bow Biddlecomb could see the British sailors grouping for a rush aft, belaying pins and sheath knives in hand. He looked over the rail toward the *Charlemagne*. There was activity on her deck, furious activity in fact, but he could not tell if Rumstick had effected anything or if the British lieutenant was preparing to come to the aid of the stricken vessels.

"Throw that overboard!" Biddlecomb shouted to the Americans, pointing to the grating with his sword. "Throw it out as far as you can!"

The Americans flung the grating outboard. It spun through the air and splashed down ten feet from the sloop. "Okay, men, I intend to jump! Who's with me?" He saw glances and nods among the six Americans. "Good! Go, I'll cover your backs!" he shouted. The first of the Americans stepped up onto the bulwark and leaped into the cold water as Biddlecomb turned to face the angry mob of sailors. They were making tentative steps aft, bolstering each other's courage in the face of his sword, but when they saw the first American jump, they broke and rushed aft in a frenzied attack.

"Go! Go!" shouted Biddlecomb as Weatherspoon stood on the bulwark and jumped. The British sailors were at the quarterdeck and running now. He turned and hopped up on the bulwark, balanced awkwardly for a second, then launched himself out over the water. He was in midair, plummeting down toward the gray sea ten feet below, the British sailors shouting at his back, when it first occurred to him that this might have been a very bad idea.

CHAPTER
20

Collision at Sea

BIDDLECOMB'S FIRST THOUGHT, EVEN BEFORE HE REGAINED THE SUR-
face, was of how very cold the water was. He kicked his way
up, broke through, and drew in a big gulp of air and seawater.
He felt his muscles contract and his flesh stand up in goose
bumps as the frigid ocean quickly seeped under his dry, warm
clothes. He gasped at the shock of it, clenched his teeth to stop
them from chattering, then struck out for the grating. He was
not a particularly strong swimmer, and his boots were filling
up and his coat becoming waterlogged, and he knew that he
had to find the grating soon.

He looked up as one of the big rollers swept under him and
lifted him out of the trough of the waves. The *Glasgow*, which
had looked so big from the deck of the *Ant*, now looked moun-
tainous as he stared up at her from the water. The two vessels
were so completely locked together that they appeared to have
been built that way, and now they were drifting fast downwind, drifting far faster than the men in the water.

Biddlecomb was breathing hard and treading water with
some difficulty, and he realized that he was still holding Lieutenant Shave's sword in his right hand. He considered dropping it, letting it sink unknown miles to the bottom, but he
could not bear to do that. He kicked harder as he reached over
with his left hand, found the lanyard on the pommel, and

looped it around his wrist, letting the sword dangle by his side as he resumed treading water.

The grating. He had to find it. He swiveled around and a swell lifted him again, and there it was, twenty feet away, three of the Americans already clinging to it.

He reached out and began flailing toward the makeshift raft, now visible, now hidden by the swells.

"Here, sir!" he heard Weatherspoon's voice, and as a wave lifted him, he could see that the midshipman had joined the other men already there. He stroked harder, trying, with little success, to keep the water out of his mouth as he worked his way through the sea.

He heard a splash to his right, a thrashing in the water, and his first horrible thought was "shark," but he assured himself that it was unlikely in those waters. He was in the valley between waves, water rising up all around him and blocking his view even of the British ships, and then the next swell lifted him and he saw Ferguson ten feet away, thrashing wildly. He moved his arms and legs as if he were trying to climb out of the sea, and it was clear to Biddlecomb that the man could not swim.

He turned and struck out for the sailor, catching glimpses of wild eyes bulging from his head. Ferguson caught sight of his captain and reached out his arms in terror until he started sinking, then thrashed at the water once more.

Biddlecomb approached to within five feet of the man and stopped. The sailor's eyes bulged out farther as he tried to grab at him. "Captain!" the sailor called in a strangled voice, water spilling from his mouth. "Help me! I can't swim!"

Really? Why didn't you tell me that before you jumped in the water, you stupid bastard, Biddlecomb thought as he said in a soothing tone, "Don't worry, Ferguson, I won't let you drown, don't worry."

Ferguson nodded, but his eyes were still big with fear. "Now listen, I want you to turn around and try to relax and I'll grab you." This was tricky; Biddlecomb had seen a man dragged down once by the person he was trying to save. "Okay, turn around."

Ferguson nodded and thrashed his way around until his back was to Biddlecomb. "I . . . I can't hold on much more, sir," he said, half-choking on salt water.

Neither can I, thought Biddlecomb. His boots were heavy with water, but not nearly as heavy as his coat. He thought about trying to slip out of the waterlogged garment, but doubted he could tread water long enough with just his feet. And he knew that trying to get boots off in the water was next to impossible.

He did not mention these things to Ferguson. "Relax, we're going to be fine, Ferguson," he said as he cautiously approached the man's back. "Just relax," he said, taking one last stroke and reaching out for the seaman's hair.

And then Ferguson spun around, his eyes wild with fear, and lashed out at Biddlecomb, trying to grab hold of something solid in that liquid environment. He flailed out as if intent on killing them both, which was just the thing he was about to achieve. He grabbed a fistful of Biddlecomb's coat, then threw an arm around his neck as he tried to climb up on him.

"Ferguson, God damn your eyes," Biddlecomb shouted, then was driven underwater by the frantic man. He clawed his way up to the surface again, gasping for breath, feeling his strength sapped by the cold water and the fight for air. Ferguson was on him again, clawing and pushing him down. He pushed the sailor away and kicked back to the surface. His right hand came out of the water, and now the sword was gripped in his fist. Ferguson lunged again, and Biddlecomb smashed the hand guard into the side of the terrified sailor's head, and Ferguson's body relaxed, like a baby going to sleep.

"Stupid bastard," he muttered as Ferguson's limp frame began to sink. He let the sword dangle from his wrist again and reached out for the man's head.

Like most veteran sailors' Ferguson's hair was tied in a long queue, tarred and clubbed, and it made an ideal towing bridle. Biddlecomb seized hold of the queue and turned toward the grating, stroking with one arm. The wind and swells were against him now, and each wave seemed to push him back farther than he was able to progress. He was nearing exhaustion.

He had stopped looking up, had stopped thinking at all, save for thinking that he was about done, when he felt strong hands on his shoulders. He felt himself pulled from the water, and someone was peeling his hand off Ferguson's queue. He gasped for breath and lay flat on the grating, desperately glad not to have to swim any longer.

At length he looked up. Every inch of the small grating was covered with men. Two of the Americans were ministering to Ferguson, bandaging his bleeding temple and forcing water from his lungs. The third was standing in the middle of the grating, looking around, and indeed there was little room for him to sit. Weatherspoon was kneeling beside him, his worried expression so maternal that Biddlecomb found it entirely annoying.

"Sir, can you hear me?" the midshipman asked.

"Oh, for God . . . yes, thank you, Mr. Weatherspoon, I'm quite well." Biddlecomb sat up. "Is anyone hurt?"

"Ferguson swallowed a lot of water," one of the seamen supplied, "and he got a gash on his head somehow, but he'll be all right once we sound his wells and pump him dry."

"Woodberry, what do you see?" Biddlecomb asked next. He considered standing himself, but he did not imagine that two men standing on that little platform would be a good idea.

"Them Brits is still locked together good, Captain. They got the sail off the sloop, but they're being set downwind fast." He swiveled carefully around until he was facing the other direction. "Convoy don't look so good, they ain't maintaining station anymore."

"What about the *Charlemagne?*" That was the most important consideration at that moment.

"Full and by, Captain. Looks like she's holding her course."

Damn. What was going on on board the brig? Biddlecomb

231

looked up and saw that everyone, save for Ferguson, who was vomiting over the edge of the grate, was staring at him.

"What's the plan now, Captain?" Weatherspoon asked.

"Well"—Biddlecomb looked over the faces of the men who had just, on his command, leapt off a perfectly good ship— "now we hope Rumstick takes the *Charlemagne* and comes to get us."

There was silence on the grating, and the sound of the water slapping on the wood and Ferguson's retching seemed unnaturally loud.

"That's the plan, sir?" Woodberry said at last.

"Yes, that's the plan. I hailed Rumstick just before we jumped and told him to take the brig," he said, a bit more peevishly than he had intended.

There was silence again and finally Woodberry said, "Well, I guess I didn't hear that," and turned his attention back to the vessels on either horizon.

Biddlecomb considered, as he was afraid every other man there was considering, what would happen if Rumstick did not take the *Charlemagne.* If they were picked up by the British, they would probably be hanged on the spot. If they were not picked up, they would go mad and die of thirst. Viewed in that light, hanging would seem preferable.

He stared around the grating, at the sullen faces of the men he had led off the *Ant,* and his guilt began to turn into resentment. Why should he feel bad? These men had not been dragged aboard the *Charlemagne* by some press gang. In fact, when they had thought that the *Charlemagne* would be privateering, they had all but begged to join his company.

Why should he take this on himself? He had never before felt the tiniest qualm about having men lowered over the side of a ship in a big sea to clear a fouled hawser, or sending them aloft at night to take in sail in the teeth of a howling storm or risk being swept away by a boarding sea. Why? Because he had done it himself, many times. He had spent hours aloft pounding ice from frozen canvas, bare-handed and bleeding, shortening down in a gale. He had stood at the helm for ten straight hours as the sea continuously broke over the deck, washing away all in its path. He had paced the *Icarus*'s quarter-deck as the *Rose* tore her to pieces, and he could just as easily have died as any of those who had. He had ordered men into the path of mortal danger, but it was a place that he had gone first.

He felt a sense of relief, like being pulled from the water again. These were grown men and they were fighting a war. He could either resign his commission or stop feeling afraid of leading them into danger.

And that was what he had done this time, and every time before. He had led them. Fitzgerald was right. Biddlecomb had always known that, but now he understood it. They were fighting for something important, and he was leading them. He had also jumped from the *Ant*, and he was also on the grating, floating in the open ocean. It was better to die on the anonymous sea than to be hanged before the mocking eyes of a crowd of British spectators. It was Biddlecomb's prerogative to decide for them the time and manner of their deaths. That was a part of commanding a man-of-war.

Woodberry did his shuffling turn and faced west again. Biddlecomb wanted to ask him about the *Charlemagne*, ask if she had reversed direction, ask if the British ensign was hauled down, but he remained silent. A part of him hoped that they would not be picked up, that they would drift on this grating until they died in madness. Then these men would know that his decisions were sacrosanct, that his orders were to be followed regardless of the outcome.

And then he realized that his thoughts were bordering on the insane. He hoped that the cold that was now making him shiver was not affecting his mental capacities.

"*Charlemagne*'s coming around, sir! She's . . . ," Woodberry shouted with a note of optimism that further annoyed Biddlecomb. "No, wait, she's in irons . . . no, there she goes, she's hauled her wind! She's around. Bloody sloppy, but she's around. She's falling off now."

Falling off. That meant she was turning around, heading

toward them. Biddlecomb could see smiles all around the raft. Even Ferguson, who was quite purged and lying on his back, managed a faint grin. Biddlecomb wondered if they all assumed Rumstick had taken the brig, or if they realized that it was just as likely to be the British lieutenant coming to help his stricken consorts.

If the latter was the case, then they would be prisoners again. But he had no way of knowing who was in command of the *Charlemagne*. If it was Rumstick, then he had to let the lieutenant know they were there. He had to take the chance. He slipped his hand out of the sword's lanyard and laid the weapon on the grating, then struggled out of his wet coat.

"Here, sir, you'll catch your death!" Weatherspoon protested.

"Oh, shut up, Mr. Weatherspoon," he said, then regretting his harsh words, added, "We need some sort of flag to signal the *Charlemagne*. I'll use my shirt."

Jacket off, Biddlecomb unbuttoned his shirt and pulled the tail from his breeches. The grating rose on the swell and the brisk breeze blew across his wet skin and made his teeth chatter again. He clamped his jaw shut and pulled his jacket back on. The cold, wet cloth on his naked flesh made him shiver uncontrollably, and he let his teeth go with abandon.

"Woodberry, sit down," he said when the chattering had subsided. "I'm going to stand and signal the brig."

Woodberry sat carefully in the small space that the others made for him, and just as carefully Biddlecomb rose to his feet, using his sword as a cane, then looked east.

The two British ships had drifted further downwind than he would have guessed, and from his current position, with a height of eye five foot eight inches above the water, their hulls were only visible when the grating crested the very top of the waves. He could see men swarming over the bows of both vessels as they worked to extricate one from the other. It would be a while before they did, and in any event they were not his immediate concern.

He turned carefully, and there, much closer than the British ships, was the *Charlemagne,* running large, heading to pass them about one hundred yards away. The sails were well trimmed and there seemed to be little activity on her deck, though that much was difficult to see. The British ensign, however, was not difficult to see, streaming forward from the peak of the gaff. Rumstick had failed to take the brig, or he had not even heard Isaac's hail.

Biddlecomb stabbed at his shirt with the point of the sword and raised the makeshift flag aloft. At least, he thought, he had for one last time cried havoc and let slip upon the British the dogs of war. As they were hanging him, he would remember the *Glasgow* crushing the *Ant,* and the look of surprise and agony on Shave's face when the lieutenant was run through with his own sword, and Isaac would smile. He hoped the others on the grating would feel so inclined.

He had not waved the shirt three times before he saw the *Charlemagne* alter course, wearing around, turning until the jibboom was pointing directly at the grating.

"She's coming for us, men," he said, unable to muster any enthusiasm, though he could see that his shipmates were more than pleased by the news. The *Charlemagne* came closer, plunging up and down in the sea. The foresail was hauled up and the topgallant yards clewed down. The brig was fifty yards away, and even she looked enormous to the men on the raft. Forty yards, thirty, twenty, the *Charlemagne* raced down on them. Biddlecomb was transfixed by the ensign flying from the gaff, a flag he had come to loathe.

And then the *Charlemagne* was up with them, turning into the wind, her main topsail coming aback as she hove to to pick up the men on the raft. Biddlecomb looked up at his old command and felt a sensation of relief, of unadulterated joy, that he had not felt in many, many years. He grinned a wide and idiotic grin.

Not a blue uniform coat was in sight, and the most familiar thing on that familiar vessel was Rumstick's hulking form, leaning on the quarterdeck bulwark and grinning back at him.

Ten minutes later the Americans were back aboard the brig,

and Sprout, with the frugality of a good boatswain, was seeing the grating hauled aboard. Biddlecomb was the last through the entry port, and his view of the *Charlemagne* was blocked by Rumstick's mass as his first officer crushed him in an unabashed bear hug.

"Isaac! By all that's holy I can't believe you're here!"

Biddlecomb pried himself from Rumstick's grasp and the two men grinned at each other like schoolboys. "You took the brig back, Ezra, I see."

"Aye. When the frigate hit the *Ant*, all hell broke loose on board here, them British sailors running around, not knowing which end was up, not knowing if they should stay with the convoy or go help. Most of us were on deck taking our air. We laid right into them, belaying pins and handspikes, swept 'em right aft and they surrendered. We have 'em locked in the bread room right now. There isn't above a dozen of them."

"So you heard my hail?"

"No. What hail was that?"

"I'll tell you later . . . Lieutenant. Right now I think it would be agreeable to put some longitude between us and them," Biddlecomb said, nodding toward the crippled men-of-war. "Those men that were with me need a dry shift of clothes, and send someone to my cabin to wrestle up whatever's there by way of a shirt and coat." It felt so natural, standing on that deck and issuing orders, like being in the shop in which one has worked all one's life. The brig seemed to overflow with excitement born of their blessed escape. The mood was infectious.

He stepped up to the quarterdeck, calling, "Hands to stations to get under way!" as he did. The men were at the running gear, ready to obey. The two lines of cannon, interspersed with pinrails, the fife rails, and the booms and gallows, made him feel at home again.

"On the mainmast! Let go and haul!" he called out, and the mainyards swung around and the topsail filled. "Mr. Rumstick, we'll have the topgallants back, and the foresail too, if you please!" He was grinning again, he could not help it.

"Aye, sir!" Rumstick was grinning as well.

Biddlecomb turned to the helmsmen. "Keep her falling off, there. We're going to run for it."

"Aye, sir," said the man on the weather side of the tiller. Biddlecomb looked forward, beyond the confines of the *Charlemagne*. The convoy was entirely in disarray. Some of the vessels were hanging back, waiting for their escorts, while others were charging ahead. Some were on starboard tack and some on larboard, and at least two that he could see had collided.

The men-of-war were about a mile away, almost directly downwind, and light was showing between them where the two hulls were being forced apart. The *Charlemagne* was swinging toward them as she turned; they would pass the British ships to leeward and about a quarter of a mile away.

"That's well," he said suddenly, turning to the helmsmen, "hold her there."

The helmsmen pushed the tiller amidships and the *Charlemagne* settled on the new course, the wind over the starboard quarter, on a course to pass just to windward of the stricken British men-of-war. Biddlecomb felt his stomach tighten and his soles tingle as the madness descended on him again. He realized he was grinning wider than before. He must look as mad as he felt.

"Mr. Rumstick, this is our course!" he called. "Clear for action! Mr. Jaeger, please see to your guns."

A hint of surprise was on Rumstick's face, but just a hint, and he turned to obey orders without a second's pause. "Hands to quarters! Clear for action! Clear for action!"

The Charlemagnes scattered, casting off gun tackles and running chain slings aloft and carrying out the myriad duties that ready a ship of war for a fight. The *Charlemagne* had halved the distance to the British men-of-war by the time Rumstick came aft to report the brig cleared for action.

"Listen up, you men!" Biddlecomb called down to the waist. "We're going to give these British sons of bitches the salute they deserve, then we'll leave them over the horizon. What do you say!"

His words were greeted with enthusiastic "Huzzah's" as he knew they would be. After weeks of fear and confinement and degradation, the men were ready to lash out.

"We'll engage on larboard side first! Stand ready!" Biddlecomb called, and the men ran to the larboard battery, peering over the bulwark and through the open gunports.

The British men-of-war were drifting helplessly. This would be as sporting as shooting a tethered animal, but Biddlecomb did not care. In a minute they would cross the frigate's bows, and there they were beyond the reach of her guns, even if there had not been a sloop impaled on her bowsprit.

The *Charlemagne* charged down on the two ships, now only a cable length away, and even without a glass Biddlecomb could see the panic on their decks. Men were scrambling out of the line of fire and someone was handing out muskets. On the *Ant*'s starboard side a gun crew was clearing away the sloop's four-pound guns. They would be a pitiful defense.

The small arms from the sloop began blazing away just as the *Charlemagne*'s jibboom came up with the *Ant*'s quarterdeck, and Biddlecomb could hear the occasional thud of a spent musket ball striking the brig's side. They were to windward of the *Ant* and nearly a hundred yards away. The enemy's muskets were next to useless at that distance, but one hundred yards was point-blank range for the *Charlemagne*'s six-pounders. He grinned a twisted grin in anticipation of the destruction his guns would do.

"Fire as you bear!" he shouted, and instantly the forwardmost gun on the larboard side went off, and then the next and the next. He watched the British ships through Weatherspoon's signal glass. The Charlemagnes were shooting well. The *Ant*'s bulwark was all but gone, and two of her guns had been overturned. Another gun went off and the *Glasgow*'s bowsprit cap shattered and fell to the *Ant*'s deck.

The *Ant* fired her two remaining guns, but both shots fell wide of the *Charlemagne*. Biddlecomb concentrated the glass on the quarterdeck. Yes, there was Shave, his arm in a sling, a huge brown bloodstain on his shirt. "A gift from the admiral's steward," he muttered as the aftermost of the *Charlemagne's* guns fired and the brig sailed past.

"Hands to wear ship!" he called next, and the sail trimmers ran to their stations for coming about. "Up helm!" he shouted, and the *Charlemagne* began her turn, swinging around toward the men-of-war, ready to pass them again, leaving them this time on the American's starboard side and much closer than before.

The *Charlemagne* turned and settled down on her new course, and the sail trimmers made fast the lines and the gun crews manned the starboard battery. "Fire as you bear," Biddlecomb called, but the revenge was out of him now. He had struck back and there was no more joy in battering the helpless enemy. The *Charlemagne* moved quickly past the British ships, inflicting more damage as she passed. "Aim for the frigate's bowsprit!" he shouted. "An extra tot for every gun crew that hits the bowsprit."

With the frigate now only forty yards away, the order cost him a fair amount of rum. Of the last five guns in the *Charlemagne's* battery three of them struck the bowsprit, doing considerable damage. But that would have been worth all of the rum on board, for with her bowsprit crippled the frigate lost nearly all ability to go to windward, and it would be many hours before she got it back.

"Full and by!" he said to the helmsmen, and the *Charlemagne* turned up into the wind, leaving the British ships in her wake. "Mr. Rumstick, lay aft, if you please."

Rumstick stepped up to the quarterdeck and saluted. He was grinning and his face glistened with sweat despite the cold wind. "Damn me, that was something!"

"Yes, it was, but I believe it's time to go."

"It is that. I think the lads were getting a little nervous hanging around as it is." Rumstick clearly did not share their sentiments, and Biddlecomb imagined he would have preferred to stay and batter the British ships until they sank. The sound of the guns and the wild activity on deck and the scream of metal flying overhead were like some vitalizing tonic to

Rumstick, and at that moment he seemed even bigger and more heroic than usual. Biddlecomb felt somewhat inadequate in his presence.

"The *Glasgow* and the sloop are almost disentangled, and it looked as if Maltby had another jibboom ready to run out. Of course now he has to repair the bowsprit as well."

Rumstick whistled. "They're working fast, and that's no lie. They didn't collide but an hour ago."

An hour ago. An hour ago Biddlecomb had been kneeling on the *Ant*'s quarterdeck, cleaning up after Lieutenant Shave, and now he was back in command of the *Charlemagne* with a bread room full of British prisoners. It had been quite an hour.

The *Ant* was all but clear of the frigate now, and Biddlecomb could see the stump of the *Glasgow*'s old jibboom splash into the water as it was cut free. But the men-of-war were already a quarter mile astern, and the distance between them and the *Charlemagne* was rapidly opening up.

He turned from them toward the convoy, sweeping his glass over the merchantmen, watching the confusion. He stopped, letting his sight rest on one particular ship. There was something familiar about it, some reason that it stood out from the rest. And then he realized. It was the *Sussex*.

He took the glass from his eye and looked around the deck, suddenly afraid that someone might guess what he was thinking. But no one was watching him, and he put the glass back to his eye. There was the *Sussex* again, still on starboard tack but sailing slowly under topsails alone. He watched her for half a minute more, then turned and again looked down into the waist.

The *Charlemagne* had an air of celebration as the men reveled in having escaped an unknown and doubtless horrible fate. They won't be so happy when they find out what we're doing next, he thought. He wondered if they would even be willing to do it.

No, damn that nonsense. They would do it, willing or otherwise. He was the captain. He would lead them down to hell if he wanted, as long as he was willing to lead. He stepped up to the break of the quarterdeck, ready to issue his orders in an unequivocal manner. He smiled as he thought of the reaction his words would receive. None of them, not even Rumstick, would have imagined he, the reluctant warrior, was capable of being this reckless.

CHAPTER
21

Stanton House

As he rode south over the frozen highway from Providence to Bristol, Major Fitzgerald once again sifted through his interview with Cooke, looking for any sign of treachery. He thought then of Stanton and Bowler and his plan for catching the one of the three who was a traitor. He turned those thoughts over in his mind, spinning them around like flotsam in the surf. The hardwoods had mostly lost their leaves, and framed against the gray sky, they gave a forlorn cast to the late-October day. When the road rose up on a hill, he could catch glimpses of Narragansett Bay. The water was a deep shade of blue, the same blue that his uniform had been when he first joined Washington's staff. The countryside was quiet and somber, in perfect keeping with his mood.

Over the fall of his horse's hooves Fitzgerald could make out the sound of another horseman far off to the south. He pulled back on the reins and his horse came to a stop. He could hear the other rider clearly now; he was perhaps a quarter of a mile away and pushing his horse hard.

He cocked his ear to the sound and his hand moved automatically to the butt of the big horse pistol slung on his saddle. His fingers curled around the grip and his thumb rested on the lock as he looked down the road.

The rider burst from the woods on his left, two hundred yards away, and charged across the cornfield that ran along the side of the road, twisting around the bundles of dry corn-stalks. He charged down on the stone wall that bordered the road, one hundred yards from where the major stood. Just when Fitzgerald thought that it might be too late, the rider jumped the horse and they sailed over the wall and came down on the road on the other side. The rider—he looked to be just a boy—wheeled the horse around, facing Fitzgerald, and then trotted toward him.

"Major Fitzgerald, as I live and breathe," the rider called. It was Virginia Stanton, and all of Fitzgerald's cultivated calm could not hide his surprise.

Virginia laughed out loud. "Really, Major, you look so scandalized." She reined her horse to a stop ten feet away. The horse's breath and the rider's were coming fast. "Surely your Southern women are given to riding?"

"Certainly, ma'am, but not nearly so well as yourself," he answered in complete candor. "I was impressed before by your knowledge of horses, but I had no idea you were so accomplished as a rider. I know men who have been hunting all their lives who couldn't ride as well as you."

"You flatter me, sir, but I don't mind. The fact is that the horse does the chief of the work."

Virginia's face had the ruddy look of cold air and a robust constitution. Several locks of her hair had fallen out from under her scarf, and she reached up with one hand and tucked them in again. Fitzgerald stared into her dark brown eyes. She was at least as beautiful as he remembered, and he yearned to see her again without her heavy riding cape and scarf. "Any good horse can run fast and jump high; it takes a good rider to make him do so the proper way," he said, not really thinking about the words.

"I don't imagine that you've come this way to critique my horsemanship."

"No. I've come about the letter that you received from Captain Biddlecomb."

"Rogers wasn't certain that you or the general took him seriously."

"We take all suggestions of treason seriously, Miss Stanton. I'm here to ferret out the traitor."

"Stanton House, I assure you, is not the hole to be looking down, Major Fitzgerald." He could see the temper flare in her eyes.

"I'm on my way to Newport, Miss Stanton, and I could hardly pass here without speaking to you or your father. No one at Stanton House is suspected, I assure you."

"I am very glad to hear that, sir." Her tone made it clear she was not convinced. "I hope that we can assist you. Captain Biddlecomb is much thought of in our home, and we are understandably eager to find his betrayer. Come, let's go back to the house. You must be quite frozen. And I know Father will want to speak with you and hear all about the goings-on in Boston." She wheeled her horse around and headed down the road.

The big house looked just as he had remembered, though it had been late summer when last he had seen it, and the house and grounds had had a more cheerful aspect then. The white clapboard seemed to pick up the gray color of the sky, giving it a funereal pallor, as if Biddlecomb's capture had cast a gloom over the place.

"Father!" Virginia called as she and Fitzgerald stepped into the warm foyer. The double doors to the drawing room swung open and William Stanton stepped out, just as Rogers emerged from the other direction.

"Major Fitzgerald," Rogers said in a tone that was as close as he was likely to get to feigned surprise. His face was immobile, expressionless. Fitzgerald thought he would not care to play cards with the man.

"Why, God in heaven, it's Major Fitzgerald!" Stanton said, and his delight and surprise seemed entirely genuine. "Major, how are you sir?" He grabbed Fitzgerald's hand and pumped it.

"I'm fine, sir, thank you. And General Washington sends his regards."

"Does he? Damned kind of him. I certainly hope to have

the honor of meeting him someday. Rogers, here, take the major's cloak," Stanton said, taking Fitzgerald's cloak himself. "Virginia, dear, pray see if the cook has anything hot. Major, would you care for some coffee? Or tea? Damned hard to come by these days, mind you." Then with an exaggerated wink he added, "But you know we Rhode Islanders have a rare knack for importing whatever we please."

"Indeed." The enthusiasm of Stanton's greeting was overwhelming, and Fitzgerald found himself wondering if it was genuine. This was the greeting he might expect from someone hoping to deflect suspicion.

"Here, Major, step into the drawing room. I've a prodigious great fire going here, let you warm up a bit." Stanton steered him into the drawing room where thick oak logs blazed away in the big fireplace. "Here, Major, please take a seat." He guided Fitzgerald into the heavy armchair near the fireplace, then sat in the smaller chair facing him. "Tell me, what drags you away from the siege at Boston?"

"It concerns Captain Biddlecomb, and his capture," Fitzgerald said in a businesslike tone. He stared into Stanton's face. The jovial smile was gone and he saw the pain pass across the old man's eyes.

"Your arrival here, sir, is a nice diversion from our grief. There's little else we've thought about, of late. I'm afraid that the news has affected us like we were at his funeral." Stanton smiled again, a weak smile. "We haven't buried him yet, mind you, we still have hope as long as he's alive, and we pray he still is. Isaac's gotten out of tight ones before."

"You cared a great deal for Captain Biddlecomb?" Fitzgerald's tone was softer this time.

"I did. I do, I should say." Stanton shook his head at his mistake. "Isaac was with his father aboard my ship back in '59 with Wolfe in Quebec. When his father was killed, he stayed on as an apprentice seaman. His mother had died the year before, you see. Most promising lad I've ever seen. It wasn't long before he was staying with us here at Stanton House between voyages, working for me as mate, then captain.

Best seaman on Narragansett Bay, and I'd hold him up to the best in all America. I built the stables and tack room from the money he made me on one voyage alone. He's as much a part of this family as any of us, Major.''

Fitzgerald stared into the fire and considered this. Could Stanton be the traitor among them? Would he betray this man he professed to love in order to deprive the Americans of gunpowder and the services of an active and intelligent sailor? Nothing in his record suggested Stanton was anything less than a loyal patriot, but of course that was true of all the suspects. Or did he feel that Biddlecomb had betrayed his trust by pursuing his daughter? If Biddlecomb was making him as much money as he claimed, then he had sacrificed more than one small ship. "What did you make of that letter that he sent?''

"Humph. It was damned odd, damned odd. This stuff about loving Virginia, and marrying her. It never occurred to me that there might be something there. Of course Virginia was as surprised as any of us. In truth, my greatest fear is that Isaac has become a bit unhinged. The letter made no sense really, that I could fathom.''

Fitzgerald stared at the old man, his white hair and deep-lined face, a face that one could see had stood a deck in all weather imaginable, and for many years. The comfort in which he now lived, the comfort he had earned in those long years, had not erased the marks that the sea had left. There was nothing perfidious about that face. "You don't think he was trying to communicate something?''

"Oh, Virginia had some notion of that, but it was beyond me. Something about Shakespeare. I love Shakespeare, mind you, and Isaac and Virginia and I used to spend hours reading his plays aloud. Virginia said something about it, then dropped it. I don't know what she thought, but I reckon she decided she was mistaken.''

Fitzgerald was about to go on, about to tell the old man the tale of Biddlecomb's further adventures, the tale he had conjured up from thin air, when Virginia stepped into the drawing room, holding a silver coffeepot and porcelain cups, and behind her Rogers with a tray of roast beef and bread and mustard.

"Ah, wonderful! set it down here," said Stanton, scooping a pile of books off the small table beside Fitzgerald's chair. Fitzgerald noticed several familiar titles: Humphrey Bland's *A Treatise of Military Discipline*, Field Marshal Count Saxe's *Reveries on Memories Upon the Art of War*, and Guillaume's *A Treatise of Artillery*, the last two of which he owned himself.

"You seem to be making quite a study of the art of warfare, Captain."

"Of course, we all must," said Stanton, piling the books on top of another already substantial pile on the floor. "And please, call me William. I've been leading the militia for five years now, and I've had a hand in some action, but I don't really know much about warfare, real warfare. I was at sea during most of the last war, didn't get the chance to see any action like Ward and Putnam and some of you other fellows up there in Boston. I've got some catching up to do, to learn about land fighting like experienced men such as yourself."

Fitzgerald nodded his head, acknowledging the compliment even as he felt himself flush. He knew about the few skirmishes that Stanton's militia had fought with the British, and while as far as battles went, they did not amount to much, they were still more in the way of combat than he himself had seen. The longer he held his commission, the longer he served as an officer without having been bloodied in battle, the more shameful it was to him.

"Oh, I've thought about joining you up there in Boston," Stanton continued, pouring steaming coffee into cups on the tray and distributing them to Fitzgerald and Virginia. "But I'm an old man, and all of the best and most active men from this colony are already gone. There needs someone left here in case the British reinforce that damned Wallace, so I read and prepare. There's a great deal to do, with the militia and our little navy. Still, I often wonder if I'm missing my duty not joining you."

"Father, you have no business going to Boston, and you know it," Virginia interrupted. "What should I do, alone and unprotected in this house, if you were to go?"

Stanton gave a short laugh. "My daughter, you see, tries to keep me from harm's way by playing at the helpless little creature, but I'll warrant she can take better care of herself than any dozen men I know."

Fitzgerald looked at Virginia and smiled and was rewarded with a smile in return, a flash of white teeth behind red lips. He wondered if all that Biddlecomb had written was a lie, a *ruse de guerre*, or if he did indeed have some claim on her heart. He could easily imagine himself falling in love with this woman. "If she can shoot anything like she can ride, then she needs no protecting I can think of."

Stanton turned to his daughter. "Virginia, have you been charging about these fields again like a madwoman? You promised me you'd stop that."

"Thank you for that, Major," said Virginia, but she was still smiling.

"You're no doubt a fine horseman yourself, Major? Please, help yourself to some of this roast beef," Stanton added, helping himself to some.

"Thank you . . . William." Fitzgerald piled roast beef onto a slice of bread and realized that he was very hungry. "As to horsemanship, I have been riding all my life, but I don't think I'd call myself a fine horseman."

"Nonsense, all you Southern gentlemen are fine horsemen. I've heard plenty about General Washington's abilities in that area. Did Virginia show you our stables?"

"No, sir," said Fitzgerald after he had managed to swallow an overly large bite.

"The stableboy took our horses, Father. I should imagine the major has seen stables before."

"Course he has, that's the point," said Stanton, standing up and reaching for Fitzgerald's riding cloak, which he had taken just a minute before. "Please come. I'd like to get your suggestions on how I could improve them. Greatest shipwrights and seamen in the world here in Rhode Island, but no one knows a damned thing about horses."

"Father, perhaps Major Fitzgerald would care to warm up a bit first."

"Nonsense," said Stanton, though the suggestion seemed agreeable to Fitzgerald. "The major is a soldier and a horseman, he'll want to see the stables."

A minute later Fitzgerald found himself walking back toward the stables, wolfing down the meat and bread he had managed to grab before Stanton escorted him out the door.

"I just expanded them to accommodate one hundred horses, though I don't have above seventeen now," Stanton was explaining as they walked. "A few of them are pretty long in the tooth. I bought them for studs and they've done well in that office."

Stanton swung the barn door open, and the two men stepped into the dark, warm stable. The smell of hay and horses and manure was familiar and comforting to Fitzgerald; it brought with it images of happier times on his father's estate.

"This seems quite a comfortable building, lots of room," he said, then noticing the fresh paint and straw and the rakes and shovels hanging in perfect rows like guns in a rack, added, "You certainly keep it clean enough."

"That's the sailor in me. Hard to break. On shipboard you get crazed about cleanliness and order. I drive the stable hands mad, but it's how I like things."

Fitzgerald and Stanton walked down the rows of stalls, and Fitzgerald cast his experienced eye over the horses there. They were good animals and well cared for, and he was happy to see that his own horse had been brushed and fed and housed in a clean stall with fresh bedding on the floor. It was hard for the major to suspect treason in a man who loved horses and treated them well, and he reminded himself of why he was there. It was time to tell Stanton Biddlecomb's story. He turned to the older man, and as he opened his mouth to speak, Stanton cut him off.

"Major, what do you think of cavalry?"

Fitzgerald stood with his mouth open and considered this surprising question. "Cavalry? Well, I recall the Philadelphia Light Horse escorted the general out of Philadelphia. They looked damn fine, to be certain," he said, flailing around for something more insightful to add.

"The Philadelphia Light Horse, yes. I've never seen them of course, but I like what they're doing. Though I have some concerns too, and I'd like your thoughts. For one thing, everyone in the Light Horse is rich, bloody rich. They have to be to outfit, and that's the problem; sooner or later a unit like that is going to decide that they don't have to take orders from anyone. Rich people are like that, you know."

"That's certainly a danger, sir, a real one. You're right on that point." Fitzgerald meant it, but he did not point out that both he and Stanton were themselves rich.

"So I'm collecting horses here," Stanton continued, taking Fitzgerald by the arm and leading him farther into the stable. "Trying to put enough together to start a cavalry unit myself. I provide the horses and the kit and the uniforms, so we can recruit people by merit, not by who can afford a horse and gear." He paused to straighten a hay rake that was hanging askew. "Dragoons, that's what we need for the fighting I see taking place in this war. Not heavy cavalry. Dragoons that can fight mounted or on foot, however they'll be most effective."

Fitzgerald was impressed. Not by the money that Stanton claimed he was spending—he could be lying about that—but by the thought that the man had put into waging war and his insights into that subject. "It's clear to me, sir, that you have an eye for horses, but I should have thought you would lean more toward the naval line."

"Of course, of course. We haven't forgotten that. We have a small navy already, but you knew that. *Charlemagne* was a part of that. She was my ship, a damn pretty one too." Fitzgerald saw Stanton's expression shift again, and the old man stared into the dark end of the stable. Fitzgerald felt a pang of guilt, as if he had reminded him of a child who had died.

"Do you think your navy can affect anything?" he asked quickly, hoping to draw Stanton back out.

"Oh, a bit, a bit. We can harry shipping, make the British use their assets to protect convoys, that type of thing. Drive up insurance rates, that'll make them howl back in London. Here, let's head back to the house." Stanton steered Fitzgerald back toward the door.

"You don't see Americans building a navy that could take on the British?" Fitzgerald asked, in part to keep the conversation going and in part out of genuine interest. Washington was convinced of the importance of sea power, and Fitzgerald knew nothing about it.

"That's a difficult question," Stanton said, shutting the barn door and heading back toward Stanton House. As the light faded in the west and the gray sky blackened, the big house looked inviting, with its promise of warmth and comfort. "We can build naval ships, the best ships in the world. But a man-of-war needs guns and powder. The *Rose* mounts twenty nine-pounder guns and carries almost seven tons of powder. Could the army spare the guns and powder to arm a similar vessel if we were to build one?"

"No, we could not."

"I thought not," said Stanton, stepping up onto the porch of his house. "And of course by Royal Navy standards the *Rose* doesn't amount to much at all. A sixth-rate, no more, can't even stand up in a real battle. No, for the time being we'll concentrate on smaller ships and do what we can, until guns and powder become more abundant. That's why I think the dragoons are more expedient right now." He pulled the big door open and stepped aside for Fitzgerald to enter. "Let's see about some supper, shall we, Major?"

Fitzgerald had already spent more time in Stanton House than he had intended, but the smells from the kitchen that greeted them as they stepped in from the cold were all the argument he needed to make him stay.

The meal that followed—rabbit fricassee and the last of the sweet corn, meat pies and potato pudding followed by bread and cheese—was the best that Fitzgerald had eaten since leaving Virginia, even though the food served at the general's headquarters was far from penitential. With the meal came wine from Stanton's wine cellar, well stocked during the days when Rhode Island was the continent's leader in illicit importations.

The conversation revolved around the growing fight with England, as most such conversations did, but Fitzgerald, after dining with the same officer corps for many months, was grateful for fresh company and fresh insights. Stanton was well informed and had put a great deal of thought into the situation, both military and political, and he brought to Fitzgerald's attention several points that the major had not before considered. Virginia debated in much the same manner as she rode; hard, passionately, and with expertise. Fitzgerald could see that she had been much influenced by the masculine character of the house, and the men in turn treated her like a fine and delicate work of art.

"You always eat like this, sir?" Fitzgerald asked, tossing his napkin on the table, unable even to consider taking another bite.

"Oh, no, mostly it's just Virginia and Rogers and I and we don't do anything fancy. It's nice to get some company and let the cook show it off a bit." Stanton walked over to the sideboard and pulled two cigars from a box there. "Smoke to go with that brandy, Major?"

"Well . . ." Fitzgerald hesitated. He glanced at Virginia and was met with a laugh.

"Really, Major," she said, "if I were to retire from the room whenever it is proper for a lady to do so, I should spend all my time alone."

"It's all right, Major," said Stanton, lighting his own cigar and drawing the smoke into his mouth. "I've quite failed in raising Virginia in a ladylike manner, and I despair of effecting that now."

Fitzgerald was curious about Virginia's mother, but after his faux pas in the stable he said nothing on that subject. Rather he said, "I think you've done a fine job, sir, raising as lovely a lady as a man could desire," meeting Virginia's eyes as he spoke. Virginia raised an eyebrow in mock surprise.

"It occurs to me, Major, that perhaps you can help me in my procurement of horses," said Stanton. "You must have some fine breeders, back where you're from."

"We do that, sir, the best in America. But I must say, this plan to outfit a company of dragoons will cost you a fortune."

Stanton laughed, a short, loud burst. "These hostilities have already cost me a fortune. My business is nearly ruined. I lost one ship, the *Judea*, because of all this, and now it seems they've taken the *Charlemagne* too. It's a lucky thing I have a fortune to spend."

"You'd spend all your money to help wage this war?"

Stanton considered the question. "No, I wouldn't spend all of it," he said at last. "Virginia needs to live, I won't have her dependent on some husband, and I wouldn't want to turn my people out of Stanton House. Other than that, yes, I'd spend every penny that's left.

"I see it this way, Major. If we lose this war, then the British will see I have nothing left but a jail cell, and if they're not interested in arresting me, then I reckon I've failed to do my duty. I'd rather spend my fortune fighting than have it taken away after we lose."

Fitzgerald looked into Stanton's face. "Sir, there is one thing that I have to tell you. It's about Captain Biddlecomb."

Fitzgerald saw the corners of Stanton's mouth turn down, heard Virginia's skirts rustle as she leaned closer to listen. "Go on, Major," she said.

"This concerns what happened to the captain after he wrote you the letter. We got this information from the captain of another American ship who met up with Biddlecomb a few weeks ago . . ."

The next morning brought no change in the weather, no relief from the cold and gray, somber sky. Fitzgerald stood outside the stable, his heavy cloak wrapped around him, stamping the ground in an attempt to keep warm as he waited for his horse. He pulled his watch from his pocket to check the time and in doing so was reminded again of the clothes that he was wearing. He frowned at his coat and breeches with a renewed disgust.

There was nothing inherently poor about his attire, quite the opposite; above the familiar black riding boots his breeches were tailored wool, and beneath the cloak was a silk shirt, embroidered waistcoat, and a coat that had been made by his tailor in London back when he was still doing business with that city. But they were civilian clothes, something that Fitzgerald had not worn in close to a year.

"Major, you look so handsome in your finery, why must you cover it up with that old cloak?" Virginia said, approaching him from behind. He turned to face her. She was dressed as she had been at their meeting on the road the day before, her face framed by her scarf, her fine figure wrapped in heavy clothes. He ran his eyes over her, savoring the memory of how she had looked at breakfast an hour before with her silk dress and tousled hair. Her father had been as expansive and indulgent as the night before, and Fitzgerald had enjoyed his company, but the main of his attention had gone to Virginia.

"And you, ma'am. You do yourself an injustice swaddled up like a milkmaid." He smiled and she smiled back, that alluring smile.

"My silk dress would do little to ward off the morning chill, Major. But perhaps you think women too delicate to wander far afield on so cold a morning?"

"Anything that you wear, ma'am, would seem dull compared to your smile."

"My goodness, you Southern gentlemen are a dangerous and flattering breed." Despite her feigned displeasure with the flattery Fitzgerald knew that she enjoyed it. He wondered if Biddlecomb ever spoke to her in that manner. He could not imagine a Yankee having the delicacy to charm such a lady.

"And why is it," Virginia asked, "that you have changed your spots, so to speak?"

"Newport, as I understand, is not so enthusiastic in their support of our cause, and as much as I dislike it, I think it would be best if I did not appear in the uniform of a Continental officer."

"Newport is the most Tory of cities in this colony, but I assure you that's not saying much," Virginia said, her tone defensive. "Rhode Island had joined the fight before most colonies knew that there was a fight at all." Then in a more conciliatory tone she added, "But you are right, sir, for your work to avoid unnecessary attention."

The stable door opened and the stableboy emerged from the gloom, leading Fitzgerald's horse with his left hand and Virginia's with his right. "I thought I would accompany you for a mile or so, Major, to make certain you're on the right road."

Fitzgerald wondered if that was meant literally or otherwise. "Please, call me Edward."

"All right, Edward. And you may call me Virginia."

"My pleasure, Virginia."

They took their horses from the stableboy and mounted. Fitzgerald had made his farewells to Stanton and Rogers, and now there was nothing to keep him in Bristol. "Please, Virginia, lead on."

She wheeled her horse around and headed down the gravel path away from Stanton House, and Fitzgerald fell in at her side.

They rode in silence, Fitzgerald lost in his consideration. He had only to speak to Bowler and that part of his plan was complete. But that was the simple part and would not of itself yield any results. Without the cooperation of Wallace's coxswain, Truax, he had no hope of catching his man, and he had no reason to believe that Truax could be induced to help. The thought of his potential failure was already causing him a great deal of anxiety.

"This is the edge of Father's property."

"It's a fine estate," he said, unable to think of anything more insightful.

"Thank you. Our land in New England is rocky and our soil is poor, compared to your Southern plantations. That's why we make most of our living from the sea."

"It's important for the country to have that diversity—"

Virginia interrupted, "Major . . . Edward . . . that story you told Father last night, about what happened to Captain Biddlecomb after his capture, that was a lie, was it not?"

"Yes, it was," Fitzgerald said, taken unawares by the abruptness of the remark.

"I imagine that you have your reasons for lying to my father," Virginia continued, her tone clipped. "And I further imagine that you won't tell me what they are."

"I can't. I'm sorry."

Virginia looked into his eyes. Her lips were pressed tight, and the animated, slightly mocking expression had deserted her. For once she looked as if she were at a loss for words. "Major," she said at last, "my father is not a traitor. Please believe that."

"I believe in your father's innocence. As much as I'll believe any man innocent until he is proven otherwise." He wished that he could give her some greater assurance, but he could not, and if he lied, she would know it.

"I was the one who initiated all this, at least after Isaac wrote that letter," Virginia said, "and I'll be happy to do anything that I can to help."

"Thank you," Fitzgerald said, half-listening to the words. Isaac, he thought. That's the third time she's called him Isaac. He considered how he might inquire into Virginia's relationship with Biddlecomb.

"Is there . . . anything?" Virginia asked.

"Pardon?"

"Is there anything I can do to help?"

"Oh, I don't . . ." She was so beautiful, he could not tear his eyes from her. Hers was the kind of beauty that gave a man a dull, ill-defined ache inside.

He was about to brush aside her offer of assistance when another thought began to take form. "Uh . . . ," he said to fill the silence as he turned this idea over in his head.

He was shocked that he would even think of such a thing, let alone consider doing it. But it could be the answer to his most pressing problem, and that made it worth risking. Anything was worth risking to run this traitor to earth. "Yes, actually," he said at last, "perhaps there is."

CHAPTER
22

Sussex

"LISTEN UP, YOU MEN!" BIDDLECOMB SHOUTED FROM THE BREAK OF the quarterdeck. The sound of fifty men working at their various tasks dropped off to silence, and all hands looked back at him. He glanced up at the convoy again. The *Sussex* was about a mile away, moving slowly under topsails alone, waiting, apparently, for her escorts to untangle themselves.

"We came out here for gunpowder," he continued, having decided to offer some justification for his decision. "If we don't return with gunpowder, then we fail, and the American army around Boston will be butchered." That was probably not true, he realized, but he hoped the point would be made. "That big merchantman over yonder is the *Sussex*. She's filled with powder. We're going to take her and bring her to Boston! We will fulfill our mission!"

He paused and looked over the faces that looked up at him. He had not expected cheers, but neither had he expected the expressions of shock and dismay that greeted him now. This was not the time to let them think.

"Mr. Jaeger, get some hands and break out the small arms, pistols and cutlasses and axes, then see the guns loaded and run out. Mr. Sprout, I believe we'll need grappling hooks aloft. Mr. Rumstick, you'll take command of the *Sussex*. Pick your hands; you can have twenty men. Pick twenty more to accompany us in the boarding party. Go!"

There was a second's pause, and then Rumstick began to bellow orders in a voice that would not admit question, and the men obeyed. Biddlecomb surveyed the scene, his face held grim despite his desire to smile like a lunatic. He was accustomed to the unquestioning observance of orders during the normal course of operations, but this was something else entirely. But they were doing it, they were obeying, despite the insanity of tarrying a moment longer in the presence of the British men-of-war.

And not just the men-of-war. The convoy itself was armed well enough that they could fight and even beat the *Charlemagne* if they could coordinate their efforts. Biddlecomb was betting on their not being able to do so, and judging from the wild disarray in which the convoy was now sailing, he knew it was a safe bet.

"Sail trimmers! To stations!" he called out. The *Sussex* was less than half a mile away now on the larboard bow, sailing close-hauled on the starboard tack while *Charlemagne,* on a larboard tack, was sailing at a ninety-degree angle away from her.

"Mr. Weatherspoon." He turned to the midshipman, who had already stationed himself on the quarterdeck, ready to do his captain's bidding. "Look around and see if that Continental flag is still aboard, the one with the pine tree."

"Aye, sir." Weatherspoon raced below to search for their proper flag, their American flag.

Biddlecomb looked astern. The *Ant* was free of the *Glasgow* now, though both vessels were still drifting as their crews raced to repair the rigging enough to carry sail. Between the collision and the *Charlemagne's* broadsides the *Ant* would be lucky just to stay afloat. He did not imagine she had any fight left in her.

But the *Glasgow* was far from finished. Her shattered bowsprit, attached to the end of a heavy tackle rigged from the foreyard, lifted from the bow and hung in midair, twisting slowly as the frigate rolled in the swell. The foreyard was braced around and the old bowsprit swung out over the water, then the tackle was released and the spar plunged with a great splash into the sea. The new bowsprit was lifted in place even before the old one had stopped bobbing.

They were repairing the damage with a speed that surprised even Biddlecomb, and he could imagine Captain Maltby, red-faced with anger and humiliation, driving his men to work faster, to get under way and seek their revenge. They would be able to set sail soon, sooner than Biddlecomb had thought. There was perhaps an hour before the *Glasgow* would again be able to work to weather. That meant he had an hour to capture the *Sussex* and flee, and not a minute more. There was no time to go chasing the merchantman around the ocean; he had to trap her somehow.

Weatherspoon appeared on deck again, empty-handed. "I can't find the ensign anywhere, sir."

Biddlecomb was not surprised. He had assumed that Maltby would take the ensign as a souvenir, and it pleased him to think how that souvenir would mock him now. "Look through that bunch of flags there and see if there's anything white."

The midshipman plunged into the bag of British signal flags, clawing around for something that would serve.

There appeared to be no alarm on board the *Sussex*, at least none that Biddlecomb could see. But that would change the moment he tacked the *Charlemagne*, the moment he made an aggressive move in their direction.

Just then another ship, astern of the *Sussex* and with a master apparently more skittish, dropped her courses and topgallant sails and sheeted them home. Her speed increased visibly, her wake deepening, and a moment later her jibboom was overlapping the *Sussex*'s transom as she passed to leeward of her powder-laden brethren.

Biddlecomb smiled to himself, the smile of a chess player watching his opponent make a fatal mistake. Just a few moments more.

"Here, sir," Weatherspoon said, unrolling the flag on the deck. It was the size of the British ensign but entirely white. "What's this for, sir?"

"I would guess it's either for the British to pretend to be French, or it's there if they want to surrender."

"Couldn't they just haul down their ensign if they want to surrender?"

"That was a joke, Mr. Weatherspoon. Part of your duty is to laugh at your captain's jokes, is that understood?"

"Yes, sir."

"Take that flag down to the boatswain's locker and see if you can find some green paint. There should be some that he uses for the figurehead, for Charlemagne's breastplate. Paint a pine tree on that, and the words 'An Appeal to Heaven.' "

Weatherspoon hesitated. "I ain't much of a hand as an artist, sir."

"It doesn't matter, we just need something, and we need it quick. You have four minutes. Now go." Weatherspoon grabbed up the flag and raced forward.

Even without the glass Biddlecomb could see the *Glasgow*'s new bowsprit swinging into place and he could just make out the swarm of men in her beakhead guiding the big spar into its step. It would be a jury rig, but once the forestays were set up, it would be enough to allow the frigate to run the *Charlemagne* to earth.

Rumstick stepped up to the quarterdeck and saluted. "I have my hands picked out, sir. I'd like to take Sprout, if I may."

"Certainly."

"Uh, Captain," Rumstick began in a lower voice, "are you sure this is such a good idea? Looks like they've already stepped a new bowsprit on the frigate. They'll be under way soon, and it'll go hard on us if we're caught."

"No, I don't think it's a good idea, but it has to be done." Biddlecomb was surprised by the madness that possessed him. He may have given the men patriotism as the reason for taking this risk, but that was not the demon driving him now. Biddlecomb wondered at his recklessness. "The *Sussex* is loaded to the gunwales with powder and small arms, and if we bring that in, then we can give the army around Boston a great advantage. It's worth the risk."

"Aye, sir," Rumstick grunted. Biddlecomb had to smile. How often in the past had Rumstick chided him for being too cautious, for having no dedication to the American cause? And now it was Rumstick who was equivocating. Biddlecomb knew that it had nothing to do with fear; as far as he knew, Rumstick had never experienced that sensation. He just thought that they were pushing their good fortune a bit too far, and it did nothing to ease Biddlecomb's fears to realize that Rumstick was probably right.

It took Fitzgerald half an hour to ride to Bristol Point, and an hour after that to find someone to ferry him across the half mile of water to Rhode Island. Another damned boat, he thought to himself as he stepped ashore on the opposite side, his horse in tow.

It was eight miles from the ferry landing to Newport, down roads so abysmal that they made it perfectly evident why the Yankees preferred to travel by sea. The afternoon was well advanced by the time Fitzgerald arrived in Newport.

On Spring Street he located a suitable inn with a small private room on the second floor. The diminutive window looked out over the harbor, where two dozen ships rode at anchor, many of them British men-of-war of various sizes. He imagined that some were frigates and some sloops and brigs and such, though he could not tell one from the other. Nor did it matter. One needed no knowledge of the sea to estimate the tactical advantage represented by the fleet riding at anchor.

He sat in a straight-backed chair, tilting it back with his stocking feet against the windowsill, and filled his glass from a bottle of mediocre wine sent up from the kitchen. He would talk to Bowler in the morning, and that would finish the first part of his plan. He felt an optimism that was more than just the wine. Things had gone well so far. But of course, he reminded himself, so far he had discovered nothing.

He considered the next part of his plan, the genuinely difficult part, and his optimism was snuffed out like a candle. Success or failure depended upon the cooperation of one man,

Truax, Wallace's messenger, a man who would not be in the least inclined to cooperate. And if he failed, then he would have to admit as much to Washington. Worse, a spy would remain on the loose, who would eat away at the American cause. He threw another log on the small fire and climbed into bed, considerably more depressed than he had been just five minutes before.

It was nine o'clock the next morning when Fitzgerald found the accounting house that Metcalf Bowler maintained, one block inland from the waterfront, from which he conducted his daily business. The office was like a library, filled with the musty smell of books and documents and a quiet broken only by the scratching of quills on paper.

"May I help you, sir?" one of the clerks asked as Fitzgerald stepped quietly through the door.

"Yes, I'm here to see Mr. Bowler. Is he in?" Fitzgerald asked in a hushed voice.

"Yes. Who may I say is calling?"

"Mr. Edward Fitzgerald, from Cambridge. Mr. Bowler will know my business."

"One moment, please." The clerk stepped through an open door to the right. "Sir?" Fitzgerald heard the clerk say.

"Yes, good God, what is it now?" came a voice in reply, and Fitzgerald remembered the grating, peevish tone in which Speaker of the House Bowler spoke.

"There's a Mr. Fitzgerald here to see you, sir. From Cambridge," the clerk said in an even tone.

"Well, what does he want?"

"He said you would know his business, sir."

"Well, I do not, do I?" Bowler snapped. "Who in all hell are these people?" Fitzgerald heard a chair scrape and steps from the office, then Metcalf Bowler appeared at the door, staring out at him. Bowler looked him up and down, as if he were a slave on the block, nothing but annoyance on the pinched countenance. Fitzgerald could not tell if Bowler even recognized him.

"You're Major Fitzgerald, from Washington's staff. Why

263

didn't you say as much?" The judge turned back into his office, calling, "Come in," over his shoulder.

Fitzgerald stepped into the office, brushing past the harried clerk and pulling his cloak off. Bowler was sitting at a desk against the wall, and he indicated with a wave of his hand that Fitzgerald should have a seat.

"Why are you not in uniform? You're still with Washington, aren't you?"

"Yes, sir. I just imagined it wouldn't be the best idea to parade around Newport in a Continental Army officer's uniform."

"No, I suppose not. What news have you?"

"Captain Biddlecomb was captured by the British while on the Bermuda expedition. We have no doubt that there was treachery involved."

Bowler stared into Fitzgerald's eyes, a penetrating stare. He was mean and unpleasant in the way of bitter, aging men, but he was also the second most powerful man in the colony, and, like Stanton and Cooke, part of the bedrock of the revolutionary movement here. But while Stanton was effusive in his hospitality, Bowler was shrewish. While Stanton was hard to suspect of treason because of his open nature, Bowler was hard to suspect because his unpleasant manner was not that of one hoping to ward off suspicion.

"And you suspect me?" Bowler asked at last, surprising Fitzgerald with his directness.

"Sir, I . . . we, I should say, General Washington and myself, suspect everyone. I think a man of the law such as yourself would appreciate that. I am here to ask you if you can think of who it might be? Is there anyone connected with the Bermuda venture that you think might have betrayed our cause?"

Bowler continued to stare silently into Fitzgerald's eyes, and the major wondered if he was mulling over the question. "Major," he said at last, "everyone that was involved in this thing . . . myself, Stanton, Cooke, we've been standing up for the rights of these colonies since you were running around fighting make-believe enemies with a popgun. No, I do not know who could have betrayed us."

"I understand. And of course you are right. I'll bid you good day." Fitzgerald made as if to leave, but hesitated, then sat down again. "Oh, incidentally, there is some good news. It concerns what happened to Captain Biddlecomb after he was captured. Quite extraordinary, actually." It was time to tell Metcalf Bowler a story.

Biddlecomb stepped up to the quarterdeck rail. "Mr. Sprout, Mr. Jaeger, Mr. Gardiner, step aft here, please."

A minute later the officers were assembled. "Here's what we'll do. I intend to come about and go right at them, throw them into a panic. We'll just lay the *Charlemagne* alongside. We'll tack, give them a broadside, then board them in the smoke." Biddlecomb paused. Board them in the smoke. He liked the sound of that, it had a military ring to it. "I'll lead the boarding party over the quarterdeck. Mr. Rumstick, you lead the men over the bow. And Jaeger, you lead your men in after us, wherever it looks like we need help. Mr. Gardiner, you'll have command of the *Charlemagne* while all this is going on. Rumstick'll have command of the prize once we take her, and we'll head for home waters. Any questions?"

He looked around at the faces of his officers. There were no questions. "This whole thing shouldn't take above ten minutes." He glanced back at the frigate. The bowsprit was settled into place and he could see men swarming out along it, and he imagined that they were passing gammoning turns and setting up the fore topmast stays. "If you have any doubts that this is worth the risk, put them aside."

The officers nodded slowly, and it was clear that they understood the importance of the coming action. "Good. You men go forward and make ready. I want boarding parties out of sight behind the bulwark now, and don't let them show themselves until we go over the side. Understood?"

The officers nodded and hurried forward, issuing orders as they went. The gang of armed men crouched down behind the larboard bulwark, cradling pistols and cutlasses and boarding axes in their arms. They looked to Biddlecomb to be as vicious a crew of pirates as ever plied the Spanish main, and he smiled to think of this grumbling, whining crowd as a murderous gang of desperate buccaneers.

Weatherspoon appeared on the deck, bearing the freshly painted flag as if it were a religious artifact. His hands were covered in green paint, and a wide swatch was on his left cheek. He spread the flag out over the bulwark and Biddlecomb ran an eye over it. Weatherspoon had not lied about his artistic ability.

"That's fine. Very good."

"I'm sorry, sir, the pine tree looks more like a green house."

And a most unique spelling of *appeal* as well, Biddlecomb thought. "It's fine, Mr. Weatherspoon. It'll answer famously."

"Aye, sir," the midshipman said with a look of relief.

The *Sussex* and the merchantman passing her to leeward were side by side now, and that meant that the *Sussex*'s master would not be able to turn away from the *Charlemagne* without slamming into the other ship.

"Ready about! Stations for stays! Ease down your helm! Helm's alee!" Biddlecomb shouted the orders in rapid succession and the *Charlemagne* spun on her heel, turning through the wind as her well-drilled crew put her about.

"Hold her there!" he said to the helmsmen as the brig's jibboom pointed straight at that of the *Sussex*, half a mile away. He felt the soles of his feet tingle with excitement, felt the concomitant tightening in his belly. Lieutenant Shave's sword, his sword now, hung at his side from a shoulder belt intended for a cutlass. He gripped the wire-bound handle tight and resisted the temptation to draw it, to feel the balanced weapon in his hand. He could imagine the consternation on the *Sussex*'s quarterdeck. In a moment he would turn that into panic.

He looked down into the *Charlemagne*'s waist. He could see the tension on the faces of the men as they readied themselves to follow Rumstick into the breach. Rumstick himself was standing near the bow, cutlass in hand. He of all of them seemed unconcerned, almost jovial, about the coming action, and Biddlecomb felt a twinge of envy at his friend's calm. After all these years he still did not know if Rumstick was genuinely unafraid or, like himself, just good at hiding it.

The *Sussex*'s foresail and mainsail tumbled off the yards as the merchantman cracked on more canvas, her master becoming at least suspicious, if not actually frightened.

"Mr. Weatherspoon, haul down the British ensign and send ours up in its stead. Larboard battery, fire!" Biddlecomb cried, and instantly the larboard guns roared out, flying inboard and slamming to a stop against their breech ropes. Biddlecomb could see the *Sussex*'s rigging jerk and wood splinters flying aloft. Most of the *Charlemagne*'s guns would not bear, but that did not matter. He intended to sail the *Sussex* away, he did not want to cripple her.

He put the glass to his eye and ran it over the merchantman's deck. Men were rushing fore and aft, hands were waving, lines were cast off. With the other ship alongside of them they could not turn and run from this new threat.

"Come on, put her about like a good boy," Biddlecomb muttered, still staring at the *Sussex*, and as if on his command, the merchantman flew up into the wind, coming around on the other tack. It was the only move that the merchant captain could make, the only one that could possibly keep him from the *Charlemagne*'s grasp, but it would not.

"Fall off a little there, meet her," he shouted to the helmsman, and the *Charlemagne* turned farther off the wind, keeping her sights solidly on the merchantman. "Lay her alongside!" He shouted the order, and his voice seemed to come from behind a wall. He was practically deaf from the broadside and he imagined that the helmsmen were too.

The *Sussex* was through the wind and filling away on the other tack, now presenting her larboard side to the *Charlemagne*, and the *Charlemagne* was all but on top of her.

"Hold her there!" he screamed to the helmsman, trying to

hear his own voice over the ringing in his ears. "Run the bowsprit just forward of the foremast!" The cloud of smoke from the *Charlemagne*'s broadside had rolled down on the merchantman, partially obscuring her.

The *Charlemagne*'s jibboom and bowsprit passed over the *Sussex*'s bulwark, and the brig's bow slammed into her side, sending a shudder through the vessel like the impact of a heavy broadside.

"Boarders away!" Biddlecomb shouted toward the bow.

Rumstick was standing on the bulwark, one foot on the caprail, the other on the cathead, and waving his cutlass in the air. He was a terrifying sight, like an enraged bear, and Biddlecomb thought that just the sight of Rumstick would make this enemy call for quarter.

"Charlemagnes, follow me!" Rumstick screamed, and with a leap he was on the *Sussex*'s deck. Behind him the boarding party screamed like the minions of hell as they leapt from the *Charlemagne*'s side into the merchantman's rigging and down onto her deck. Above the deck Sprout's handpicked topmen were laying out along the foreyard and clambering into the *Sussex*'s rigging, lashing the two vessels together.

The two ships were locked together at the bow, and now the *Charlemagne*'s stern was swinging toward the *Sussex*. Jaeger was standing on the caprail amidships and holding on to the main shrouds, waiting for the chance to lead his men across. Through the thinning cloud of smoke Biddlecomb caught glimpses of the boarding party. He could hear the sounds of yelling men and feet rushing along the length of the *Sussex*'s deck and the occasional clang of steel hitting steel.

The two vessels drifted closer, and with a yell and a wave of his cutlass Jaeger was over, disappearing into the smoke, his boarding party at his heels.

Biddlecomb looked down at the stretch of water between his quarterdeck and the merchantman's, and he knew that they would get no closer. He could not jump that distance, but neither could he remain on board the *Charlemagne* while his men fought aboard the *Sussex*. He was desperately anxious to join the battle.

"Mr. Gardiner, you have the *Charlemagne*. Boarding party, follow me!" he yelled, finally pulling his sword from the shoulder belt and waving it over his head. He led his boarders forward into the waist, forward to where the two vessels ground together. He leapt up on the *Charlemagne*'s bulwark and then flung himself across the narrow space that separated the two ships.

Biddlecomb hit the *Sussex*'s deck and crouched low, his sword held across his chest, waiting for an attack from the ship's defenders. The deck was still partially hidden by smoke; he could see as far aft as the break of the quarterdeck. Men landed to his right and left, similarly preparing for a rush of defenders, but none came. He straightened slowly, then a gust lifted the veil of smoke and he could see his own men on the merchantman's quarterdeck, clustered around the *Sussex*'s crew, who were in turn pressed against the bulwark, their hands in the air. He walked aft and the men stepped aside and let him through.

"You may put your hands down," he said, and the merchant sailors let their arms fall to their side. "You, sir." Biddlecomb pointed to the master he had watched through the glass only moments before, "step over here please." He felt rather silly now. Not above fifteen men were on the *Sussex*'s crew, and none of them armed, as compared to the forty well-armed men of the *Charlemagne*'s boarding party. He had gone about this as if he were boarding a first-rate ship of the line, and now he was embarrassed by the excess.

"Sir, I am Capt. Isaac Biddlecomb, of the United Colonies' ship *Charlemagne*. Your ship is now my prize." He could not think of anything else to say to the master, so he turned to the *Charlemagne*'s boatswain. "Mr. Sprout, get some hands and get their boat in the water, we'll set them off. They can reach another ship easily enough. Send some men back to the *Charlemagne* to roust up those British prisoners and set them in the boat as well. Mr. Rumstick, keep an eye on these prisoners.

You lot"—he pointed to a knot of Charlemagnes by the binnacle box—"follow me." He turned and marched forward to the main hatch.

The hatch was battened down, covered by a heavy tarp that was pinned to the combing by long, thin planks of wood, wedged in place. "Break that open," he said, and the Charlemagnes snatched up belaying pins and began hammering the wedges free.

Biddlecomb ran his eye over the hatch. The *Sussex* was a big ship and was built to carry a great deal. If only half of her spacious hull was filled with powder, it would be enough to keep the army supplied for some time. He felt a mounting excitement, like a child opening a gift, as the last of the wedges fell free and the heavy tarp was rolled back. He pictured the look on Fitzgerald's face as the major watched wagon after wagon of powder roll into camp, and he smiled at the image.

The Charlemagnes pulled off the hatch covers and threw them aside. The dull sunlight illuminated the tween decks below, crammed to the deckhead and as far fore and aft as Biddlecomb could see with boxy chests. A strong odor wafted up from below, a good smell, a familiar smell. Biddlecomb breathed deep until he realized what the fragrance was. His mouth hung open and he stared wide-eyed at the chests. It was tea. Pungent black China tea.

CHAPTER
23

Mayor of Plymouth

BIDDLECOMB LET OUT A CRY OF ANGER, A WILD CRY, A CRY THAT IN its primal rage surprised even him. He kicked the nearest chest over. It tumbled into the gangway between the cargo and broke open, and black tea poured out of the broken top and spilled over the deck. Then Biddlecomb turned and stormed aft.

The British crew was sitting on the quarterdeck, a dozen of the Charlemagnes standing over them with pistols on half-cock. Biddlecomb pushed the guards aside and pointed to the master. "You, sir! Stand up." His voice was low and menacing. The British master grabbed on to the pinrail and pulled himself to his feet.

"That's tea in your hold!" Biddlecomb said, his tone accusatory, but the master only looked confused.

"Yes, it is."

"You were supposed to be carrying gunpowder!"

"No, we was supposed to be carrying tea, and we are. I'm sorry to disappoint you."

Biddlecomb considered striking the master for his insolence. His arm jerked back and he realized that he was acting like a madman. Why had he thought that the *Sussex* was carrying powder? Because Shave had said so, and he had believed him, and that made him the biggest idiot of all. He turned away,

271

leaving the master leaning against the quarterdeck rail. It had been a long morning.

"Isaac," Rumstick said in a soft voice, "this here tea is worth a fortune, and it's a legitimate prize of war. Maybe we should just take what the Good Lord give us and go, not do anything crazy." He looked past Biddlecomb's shoulder toward the *Glasgow*, and Biddlecomb followed his glance. The frigate was a mile downwind and close to getting under way.

He turned and looked at the men assembled on the merchantman's deck and aboard the *Charlemagne* tied alongside. The two vessels were locked together, like dancers embracing as they spun slowly downwind, sails flogging overhead. The crews of both ships, and the British prisoners being hustled topside from the *Charlemagne*'s bread room, were all waiting for him to make a decision. He turned back to the master of the *Sussex*.

"Are you the owner of this vessel?"

"No," the master said, but Biddlecomb knew that he was lying. He always knew when a man was lying.

"Run down to the master's cabin," he instructed one of the men guarding the prisoners, "and bring up any papers in the master's desk." The man disappeared below and Biddlecomb turned back to the master. "We'll see."

"I'm partial owner," the master said grudgingly. "One-third owner."

One-third owner. If he was anything like most of the masters that Biddlecomb knew, himself included, then most of his money was tied up in his vessel. "You're probably not too keen on losing this ship and cargo, are you?"

The master was growing angry now, and he scowled at Biddlecomb. "No, I ain't."

"Which ship in this convoy is carrying powder and small arms?"

"What?"

"Which ship has the powder and small arms? That's what I want, not tea. I only have enough men to man one prize, so I'll take your ship unless I get the one I want."

"How in hell should I know who's shipping powder?"

"You know. You've been with the convoy long enough, and you certainly are going to know which ships could blow you to damnation. Which one is it?"

He stared into the eyes of the one-third owner of the *Sussex*, watching avarice do battle with patriotism, and knowing which would win. "Over yonder." The master nodded toward a ship half a mile off the larboard beam. "The *Nancy*, over there."

This was the master's last gambit, and Biddlecomb would not fall for it. "Understand I'll be using your ship to take the *Nancy*, and I won't hesitate to shoot you if you're lying, so for your sake I hope she is indeed carrying powder." He stared hard into the man's eyes, daring him to play out the hand, assuring him that he would loose.

"It's not the *Nancy*." Now Biddlecomb knew he was hearing the truth. "It's the *Mayor of Plymouth* back there." The master pointed over his shoulder at a cluster of ships half a mile astern. "The one standing clear from the others, with topgallants set."

Biddlecomb stared at the ship. It too was an unremarkable merchantman, around three hundred tons.

The seaman who had been dispatched to the master's cabin reappeared carrying various logbooks and papers, which he presented to Biddlecomb. Biddlecomb took up the lot and thumbed through them. They were what he expected: a bill of health, list of crew, general clearance, clearing manifest, invoice, bill of lading, logbook, the standard paperwork. He looked over the bill of lading and the invoice as he had done on many ships under his own command. The *Sussex* was shipping tea. There was other cargo as well—cloth, cookware, barrel hoops—but mostly it was tea.

"Captain," Rumstick said from his place across the deck, "maybe we should let it be. I don't think there's time for this. Maybe we best just take the tea."

Biddlecomb looked over at his friend, surprised and troubled by the note of uncertainty in Rumstick's voice. But then he saw it, the glint in the eye, the not quite entirely suppressed smile playing across Rumstick's lips as he ran his fingers along the blade of his cutlass. He was not backward in his courage, not for a second. Rather, he was giving his captain a chance to back away from this insane plan by pretending that he, Rumstick, had talked him out of it. That would allow the captain to save his hide and his dignity.

"I'm sorry, Boats—I mean, Lieutenant, it's beyond that now. We're taking the *Mayor of Plymouth*."

"Aye, sir," said Rumstick, and the trace of a smile spread into a full-blown grin. "Will you go aboard the *Charlemagne?*"

Biddlecomb looked to leeward at their prey. The *Mayor* was still close-hauled, actually sailing toward the *Charlemagne* and the *Sussex*. Perhaps her master thought the two ships had collided, that the *Charlemagne*'s broadside had been a desperate warning. Whatever the case, he was not yet fleeing for life.

"No." The *Glasgow* was more than half a mile downwind, but she had to be factored into the equation. From what he could see, fewer men were out on her bowsprit, which meant that they had completed the rigging of that spar. It would not be long now before she was under way. "We'll keep the men we have aboard the *Sussex* here and go after the *Mayor* with this ship. Get some hands aloft and cut the *Charlemagne* free."

Rumstick began to issue orders, and half a dozen men flung themselves into the shrouds and began to run aloft. Biddlecomb stepped across the deck and called to Gardiner on the *Charlemagne*'s quarterdeck, twenty feet away.

"Mr. Gardiner, we're going after that merchantman yonder. Once the *Charlemagne*'s clear, sail close-hauled until you see we've taken the other ship, then run down and join us. Do you understand?"

"Aye, sir! Close-hauled until you take the other, then join you!"

Biddlecomb looked aloft. The last of the lashings were cut away from the yards, and Rumstick was unhooking the grappling hooks and tossing them over the side. With a groan the

Charlemagne eased away from the *Sussex*'s side and the stretch of water between them widened.

The British prisoners taken from the *Charlemagne*'s bread room stood in a knot in the *Sussex*'s waist, glaring aft. Biddlecomb turned to the men guarding the *Sussex*'s crew. "Get these men down into the master's cabin, and those men from the *Charlemagne*. Lock them in and post guards around the door."

"Hands to the braces!" he called next, and his men ran to the merchantman's pinrails. Woodberry had already taken the wheel and stood ready for orders. "Fall off, three points. Let go and haul, square them up!" Overhead the yards swung around and the *Sussex* headed for the point on the ocean where Biddlecomb's sense told him their path and that of the *Mayor of Plymouth* would intersect. "That's well! Boarding parties, behind the bulwarks! Keep out of sight! We'll run this ship aboard the *Mayor* and board her, just like before!" The men made fast their lines and crouched down, waiting to storm their second ship of the day.

The *Mayor of Plymouth* had not altered course. Her master had no reason to panic; he would think that the *Charlemagne* was the enemy, not the *Sussex,* and the *Charlemagne* was sailing away from him. He would not know that most of the *Charlemagne*'s crew, armed to the teeth, were aboard the *Sussex* now, and closing fast with his ship.

The *Sussex* was sailing almost due west, sailing back over water they had just crossed, and now the *Glasgow* was over the bow rather than the stern. Biddlecomb looked at the man-of-war and felt his stomach tighten. It was foolish, idiotic, to give back distance he had gained from the frigate. Every second he was diminishing a solid lead. He was standing ten feet above a fortune in tea, a fortune that was his if he would just put the *Sussex* about and run for the horizon. But he had not come all this way for tea.

The *Glasgow* now had a fore topmast stay in place, and he could see figures wrestling a sail out along the new bowsprit. That was all they needed. When that sail was set, the frigate would once again be able to work to windward, would once again be able to come in pursuit, and that sail would be set within ten minutes.

The *Sussex* was just over a cable length from the *Mayor of Plymouth* and closing fast. Within ten minutes they would be able to take that ship and be gone, if their luck held and if the *Mayor*'s crew did not put up any great resistance.

There was a rush of activity aboard the *Mayor*, and hands were pointing toward them. It would be clear to the *Mayor*'s captain that the two ships were in danger of colliding if one or the other did not alter course. He has no idea of the danger, Biddlecomb thought.

The distance between the vessels had dropped to seventy yards when the *Mayor* flew up into the wind, her headsails flogging as she began to tack. It was a good move, the only move that might have avoided a collision, but as with the *Sussex* it would not save them. "Fall off some more, Woodberry. Meet her." The helmsman began to turn the wheel. "Slowly, don't let them see what you're about."

The *Mayor of Plymouth* was fifty yards ahead and pointing almost straight at them as she tacked, her main and mizzen yards bracing around, her foresails aback. She was well handled and her captain would have made a neat job of preventing an accident if the *Sussex* had maintained course. As it was, Biddlecomb could pick at leisure the spot where the vessels would collide.

"Careful of her bowsprit, Woodberry. Run our bow into her just aft of the fore-chains."

"Just aft of the fore-chains, aye."

The *Mayor* was helpless, caught halfway through her tack, like a man with his breeches around his knees. Biddlecomb had never, before that day, struck another vessel with a ship under his command, but already the novelty was gone.

The new headsail was fluttering up the *Glasgow*'s fore stay. It flogged in the breeze and then was sheeted flat, and the frigate fell off the wind, paused, seeming to hang motionless, then began to make headway, butting its bow into the waves. She was alive again, and she was in pursuit.

The *Mayor of Plymouth*'s crew was lining the merchantman's side, screaming and waving the *Sussex* off, even as the *Sussex*'s jibboom passed over their deck, just aft of the fore-chains. Biddlecomb started to order the foresail clewed up, but all that emerged from his mouth was a grunt as the *Sussex* hit the *Mayor of Plymouth* and he was flung to the deck like a discarded coat.

He propped himself up on his elbows. The yelling had increased in pitch and volume. He scrambled to his feet, yelling, "Boarders away!" as he did, and saw that Rumstick was already leading his boarding party over the side.

The Charlemagnes were swarming over the *Sussex*'s bow and onto the deck of the *Mayor of Plymouth* like the Visigoths descending on Rome. Biddlecomb pulled his sword from his shoulder belt and headed forward, calling for the men in the waist to join him. He could hear pistols banging out on the enemy's deck, and the clash of steel and men shouting. He jumped up onto the heel of the *Sussex*'s bowsprit and ran outboard, his eyes on the *Mayor*'s deck, now below him.

The *Mayor*'s crew had not been taken by surprise, not entirely, and someone had had the presence of mind to issue weapons. Biddlecomb saw cutlasses flailing and boarding pikes reaching out for his men. A pistol fired and two feet away one of the Charlemagnes dropped without a sound, the back of his head blown off.

Jaeger was pushed against the *Mayor*'s foremast fife rail, engaging two cutlass-wielding seamen at once, but the two together were no match for the Prussian's skill. Jaeger's generally tortured face looked calm now, even slightly amused, as he systematically fended off the attacks. One of the defenders lashed out. Jaeger knocked the man's cutlass aside, then with a continuity of motion brought his own blade across and slashed the other man's throat. Biddlecomb saw the man's eyes go wide and blood spurt from the gash in his neck, spraying

Jaeger, but the Prussian took no notice as he turned on the first defender.

Rumstick was further aft than the others, wielding his cutlass like a machete, cleaving his way through the *Mayor*'s crew. The Charlemagnes were not being beaten back, not yet, but neither were they winning.

Biddlecomb turned to the dozen men still on the *Sussex*'s deck. "Follow me, men, and yell like the host of hell!" he cried, then turned toward the *Mayor*, let his sword dangle from his wrist, and with a scream flung himself into the *Mayor*'s fore shrouds.

His left hand felt a shroud, then his right, and he grabbed on, kicking with his feet for a ratline. His toe caught one, and he stepped down, and then his shoe slipped and he was hanging from his hands. There was shouting all around him; the last of the boarders were pouring onto the *Mayor*'s deck, screaming like things possessed.

He kicked again with his feet, and something pushed against his side. He felt heat, searing heat, and then pain. He saw one of the *Mayor*'s crew on the deck below him, at one end of a boarding pike, and he was surprised to see the other end of the pike stuck into his side.

"Son of a bitch!" he shouted. The sailor's eyes were wild and his hair was sticking up at crazy angles. He pulled the pike back, tearing it free from Biddlecomb's side, and Biddlecomb could do nothing but cling to the shrouds and scream in agony and watch as the man drew back and prepared to run him through.

And then Jaeger was there, looming up behind the man. He raised his cutlass like an ax and brought it down on the sailor's skull, splitting it like cordwood and driving the man down to the deck, killing him before he hit the planks. Biddlecomb swung inboard and dropped to the deck. He doubled over and cried out again.

"Press down directly on the wound," he heard Jaeger say, and then the Prussian was gone, flinging himself back into the fight. He looked down again at the wound, at the blood flowing through his fingers. It looked bad, but the pike had gone into his side, and though it hurt like the torment of the damned, it had not hit anything important.

He stood as best he could and snatched up his sword, then pushed aft behind the wall of his men.

Rumstick had made it to the quarterdeck. Biddlecomb could see his big frame rising above the others, and he was fighting like an enraged bull. But they could not tarry long. The *Glasgow* was under way.

"Strike! Strike! Throw down your arms!" Biddlecomb began to bellow, shouting to be heard over the sounds of combat. "Throw down your arms!" he called again, and one, then another, of the defenders threw their cutlasses and axes to the deck. The spirit of the surrender swept aft, quicker even than the Charlemagnes, and soon all of the *Mayor of Plymouth*'s crew was unarmed, their hands in the air.

"Get them aft! Get them . . . stop that, you stupid bastard!" Biddlecomb knocked aside an ax held by one of his men, who in his madness was still attacking the *Mayor*'s defenders. "Get these men aft!"

A moment later the entire company was aft, crowded around the taffrail, glaring at the Americans, who glared back. Biddlecomb held his arms above his head, his coat and shirt hanging open, as Jaeger bound his wounded side. The cloth that Jaeger used was a flag, he noticed, one of the *Mayor*'s signal flags, and he wondered idly what it meant when it was not being used as a bandage.

"Hold them here for a moment, Ezra." He dropped his arms and stuck his sword back into the frog of the shoulder belt. He glanced over the stern, past the crowd of men. The *Glasgow* was under way and they were crowding on sail, heading for the *Charlemagne*. It was time to leave.

He dashed to the after scuttle, buttoning his shirt as he went. As he disappeared below, he heard Jaeger call out an admonition to be careful of his wound.

The master of the *Mayor of Plymouth* had furnished his cabin well, but Biddlecomb was interested only in the desk that was lashed to the starboard side. He pulled open the first drawer. The ship's papers were there. He pulled them out and rifled through them. On the first page of the ship's log was the crew list with the master's name, Gideon Wetherell, at the top.

He tossed the log aside, along with the sea letter and bill of health, and came at last to the invoice and the bill of lading. He ran his expert eye down the page, then down the next, and smiled broadly. The first item listed was gunpowder, then after that came gunpowder, gunpowder, two cases, small arms, gunpowder, gunpowder. He had found the right ship.

He made his way topside again, and stepping through the scuttle, he heard cannon fire, and not too distant. "Who the hell is shooting?"

"It's Gardiner, sir!" Rumstick said, pointing over the weather side. The *Charlemagne* was a half a mile away and racing down toward them, firing starboard and larboard at any vessel on which its guns would bear. The result was panic, pure panic, among the convoy, with ships scattering in every direction, colliding with each other, and firing wildly at the brig. One had even hove to and hauled down her colors, but Gardiner could not be bothered to acknowledge the surrender.

"Well done, Lieutenant Gardiner," Biddlecomb said. They would slip away in the chaos that Gardiner was creating.

"Get these men on board the *Sussex*, this is the ship we want," he ordered, and the Charlemagnes began to hustle the prisoners forward and over onto the former prize. "Rumstick, get that gig in the water. I'm going over to the *Charlemagne* when she gets down to us."

The first officer called out the orders, and a moment later the gig was in the water, the *Mayor of Plymouth*'s crew were ensconced aboard the *Sussex*, and the Charlemagnes were cutting the two ships apart, doing considerable damage to the *Sussex*'s rig in the process.

"Lieutenant, you have command here," Biddlecomb said as the *Sussex* began to fall away from the *Mayor*. "We'll make our escapes separate, run off close-hauled on opposite tacks.

We'll meet south of Cape Cod in two weeks' time, understood?"

"Um, sure, excepting that I don't know how to navigate, Captain," Rumstick said. "In fact, no one here does save you."

Of course he didn't. Biddlecomb shook his head at his own stupidity. "Very well." He cast an eye toward the *Charlemagne*, then toward the frigate. Maltby had laid a course to intercept the brig. "Head north, just keep going north until you're over the horizon, then heave to and wait for me if you're not being pursued. Understood?"

"Aye," said Rumstick, sounding doubtful. "And if I am being pursued?"

"Keep sailing north, or whatever you need to do to shake your pursuer. But I don't think you'll be chased too far, if at all. Maltby's first duty is to protect the convoy, and he won't want to make any more of a hash of the job than he has already."

The *Charlemagne* was up with them now and hove to, waiting for her captain. The convoy was a convoy no longer, just a random scattering of panicked vessels. Biddlecomb watched the *Sussex* as she drifted away. At any time she would have been worth a fortune; with the boycott of all English imports she was now worth several fortunes, perhaps more than he had ever earned in his lifetime. He wondered if the Isaac Biddlecomb of a year ago would have given her up in exchange for military stores that he intended to hand over for free. He wondered if the Isaac Biddlecomb of a year ago would have believed that he held in his breast the soul of his father. Fighting John Biddlecomb. Viking John. He did not think so.

The *Glasgow* was still half a mile downwind, limping up toward them. She would be no match for the *Charlemagne* in a race to weather.

The madness was gone, and Biddlecomb felt spent, exhausted, more exhausted than he had been in many years. He leaned against the bulwark, suddenly afraid that he might collapse. He wondered if he had lost too much blood from his wound, but there was nothing he could do if he had, and no time to worry. He pushed himself to his feet.

"You have your orders, Lieutenant," he said in an official tone. "We'll meet in about two days' time, if things go well." He stepped over to the entry port. The gig was bobbing in the water below—it seemed to him very far below—the crew waiting patiently for their captain. Biddlecomb looked at Rumstick, then past him to the *Glasgow*. "By God, I'll be glad to get out of here."

CHAPTER
24

Newport

CAPTAIN LILLIBRIDGE'S TAVERN ON THE PARADE WAS MUCH AS FITZgerald had imagined it would be. The ceiling was just high enough that an average-sized man could stand upright, which meant that he had to duck beneath the rough-hewn beams. It was dark inside, and the copious smoke from the patron's pipes made little halos around the candles scattered among the wooden tables. The floor was strewn with sawdust, which in the more trafficked areas has been trampled into a muddy paste.

He stepped through the door and stood aside, in the shadows, waiting for his eyes to adjust to the dim light. Of the many objectionable qualities that the tavern boasted, its clientele seemed to him to be the most objectionable of all. Red coats were much in evidence, with white cross bands and the shining black shoes of the marines. Naval officers were there as well, from older midshipmen to young lieutenants and at least one uniform that Fitzgerald thought to be of a post captain. He felt like Daniel in the den of lions, but thankfully enough civilians, men and women, were among the military crowd that his entrance caused not the least stir. Indeed, no one even looked up at him as he stood there surveying the scene.

True to Lieutenant Trevett's prediction, Truax was not hard to spot. He sat in a far corner, half-hidden by shadows, a tankard in front of him. The strange and flickering light only served to accentuate the gnarled quality of his face, the seemingly permanent scowl, and the underslung, bulldog jaw. He was the only man in the place dressed as a foremast jack, though his blue jacket, white trousers, and black tarpaulin hat were immaculate, the dress of a captain's coxswain, a captain who cared very much for appearances. Truax took a long pull from his tankard and set it down again, his eyes never leaving the spot on the table upon which they were fixed.

Fitzgerald stepped around the tables at which military men and civilians played all fours, whist, and loo, the various stacks of money indicating who had been lucky that night and who had not. He approached the bar and caught the publican's eye. "Give me two of whatever Mr. Truax in the corner over there is drinking." The publican poured the drinks, all the time regarding Fitzgerald with a suspicious eye, and not until the major laid a shilling on the bar and made no request for change did the man's dour expression lighten.

Fitzgerald pushed his way across the crowded room, sloshing the ale from the tankards, and came at last to Truax's private corner. "A word with you, Mr. Truax?"

The coxswain looked up at him with the air of a man who was well used to people trying to curry favor, a man who would give nothing away. "Who the fuck are you, then?"

"No one of any import." Fitzgerald slid into the seat opposite Truax and pushed one of the tankards across the table. "I bought you a tankard."

"Oh, well, I'm most bleeding taken with your generosity, your honor, and I am much in your debt." Despite the sarcasm Truax took a long drink from the proffered cup. "What do you want?"

"I understand that anyone wishing to get word to Captain Wallace sends a message through you. Is that so?"

Truax stared at him, silent, and at last having apparently decided that that was not tipping his hand too far, said, "All right, but the post service ain't free. You got something you wants the captain to know?"

"Oh, no, no, no," Fitzgerald chuckled. "No, indeed. I want to know what others are telling the captain. You see, I'm a merchant here in Newport, fairly successful, and it is worth a great deal of money to me to know what my competition is telling Wallace. And it could be worth a great deal of money to you."

Truax snorted and took another drink. "I don't know what it is you want, mate, but it sounds like it might be worth me post as coxswain if I was caught, and there ain't anything worth that risk."

"Here is a list of men that have been sending letters to Captain Wallace." Fitzgerald withdrew a note from his waistcoat, unfolded it, and slid it over to Truax.

The coxswain picked it up and ran his eyes over the words and nodded. "All right," he said in a doubtful tone, satisfying one of Fitzgerald's questions. Truax could not read. He took the note out of the man's hands.

"I'm not one of these damned rebels, and my interest is in money, not politics. Now, one or two of the men that are sending letters through you are from my competitors, and the information their letters contain would be most valuable to me."

"I don't know who sends these notes. I gets them from . . . from someone, none of your business who."

"It doesn't matter to me if you know or not. I'll know. I have no desire to interfere with your postal service, I want simply to read any note before you give it to Wallace for the next, say, ten days?"

"And what's in it for me, then?"

"Shall we say . . . five pounds for every letter?"

It was a large sum, about a month's pay for one of the *Rose*'s lieutenants, and by Fitzgerald's calculation large enough to entice Truax without making him overly suspicious. And judging from the emotions playing across his ugly face, it was working. "Letters is worth that much to you, eh?"

"Yes, that much. And not a penny more."

"If you does something on account of what you read in

them letters, someone might figure out that I was showin' 'em to you," Truax hypothesized, surprising Fitzgerald with his logic. "I don't know if I like them odds."

"There is one other thing I can give you," Fitzgerald said slowly, hesitating. "But now I'm not certain it's worth it."

"What?" The sailor's curiosity was engaged now.

Fitzgerald did not reply. Rather he turned slowly on the bench, turned to look back toward the front door. If something had happened, if she had changed her mind, which would be perfectly understandable, then his whole plan would fall apart.

But she had not. Virginia Stanton stood just beside the door in a circle of light cast by a clump of candles on the bar, looking as out of place there as one of the whores in the tavern would have looked in the halls of Stanton House.

Fitzgerald had not told her why he wanted her there; he could not bring himself to; just that he did, and she had agreed with no more information than that. It occurred to him then that he could genuinely love that woman.

She slipped her cloak off and draped it over her hands, revealing her slim figure in a low-cut, silk dress, her breasts pushed up and together in a tantalizing display of cleavage. Her eyes met Fitzgerald's. She smiled and gave him a little wave. Then she turned and stepped out of the tavern.

Fitzgerald turned back to Truax. His eyes were as big as the rims of their tankards, and the look of aching desire was so strong on his face that Fitzgerald nearly laughed out loud. "That's Nancy. She . . . works for me. You bring me your captain's letters for ten days and you can have her after that, for one whole night. But only on the condition that you leave off your rough ways. She's never . . . been with a man before."

Truax looked as if he would start clawing at the table. His eyes shone with lust and impatience. Fitzgerald had him, he knew it. "And the five pounds as well? Five pounds for each letter?" Fitzgerald nodded, impressed that the coxswain's libido had not entirely quashed his avarice.

"I'll come by this tavern every night for the next ten days. If you're here, and you have something for me, you just give me a nod of the head and I'll join you, like now. If not, shake your head and I'll have a glass and go. Then in ten days Nancy's yours." Fitzgerald stood and walked away before Truax could reply. He did not have to wait for an answer. The look in the sailor's eyes was answer enough.

George Truax, coxswain, Royal Navy, sat on the after settee in the great cabin of the HMS *Rose* and applied a chamois cloth to Captain Wallace's ceremonial sword, giving the weapon a mirror shine with a technique uniquely his own. It required no thought; he had shined that sword so many times that his hands went through the motions automatically, as if he were tying a bowline or tucking an eye splice. His mind, as it generally was, was occupied with thoughts of how to better his position.

Nothing, absolutely nothing, put him in better stead with the captain than providing him with some valuable intelligence. Unfortunately, he did not know how valuable it would be to tell Wallace of his deal with the rich merchant whose name he did not know. Of course, Wallace would want to know about their arrangement, but was it worth it to Truax to tell him?

It was worth it, he decided. Many of the *Rose*'s officers frequented Captain Lillibridge's, and any of them might mention his meetings to the captain. If Wallace got word of his clandestine dealings from any source but himself, then there would be the devil to pay and no pitch hot. He came to that conclusion just as he heard the captain's distinctive step beyond the great cabin door.

"Truax, I'll need the barge tonight, and the barge crew rigged out in their best," Wallace said, stepping into the cabin and tossing his cocked hat on the desk. "And I believe it's time to caulk and paint the gig. I want you to do it this time, not that fool of a carpenter and his gang of incompetents."

"Aye, sir." Truax hesitated, wavering at the last minute, then committed himself. "Sir, there's something I thinks you should know." He paused, trying to decide how much to give away.

"Yes?" Wallace said with no attempt to mask his impatience.

"Well, sir, this gentleman come up to me the other day, in the tavern, sir, and he offered me money to see any letters what them Yankees gives me to take to you."

"Indeed? And what did you tell him?"

"Well, sir, I didn't make no promises, but I reckoned it would be best to play along, see what was acting, maybe see what this cove was up to, so I told him we'd talk some more. But then I told you right off, didn't I, sir?"

Wallace stared out the window, apparently pondering this news. "Have you any idea why he wanted to see my correspondence?"

"He said business reasons, sir, but I don't know as I believe him. A lying bunch of bastards, these Yankees, sir, beg your pardon. Even the ones that style themselves gentlemen, like this one."

"Indeed. And when will you see him again?"

Truax hesitated, pretending to search his memory. Here was the tricky part; he had no intention of giving up five pounds per letter, and he certainly had no intention at all of losing his night with the girl. "He said he'll be back in town in a fortnight, sir. A fortnight, he said, and I was to show him any letters I got in that time."

Wallace met his eyes and held them and Truax tried not to squirm under the captain's gaze. He knew that the stare did not necessarily mean that Wallace thought him to be lying; he stared the same way when deciding what he would have for dinner; but still it never failed to make Truax uncomfortable. "Fortnight, eh?" Wallace said at last. "Very well, keep me informed." With that he sat down at his desk and pulled his ledger books toward him, the discussion closed.

Wallace spent the next three hours updating the ship's ledgers—casks of beef open, powder and shot expended, cordage and sailcloth used or condemned—while all the time keeping track of the workings of his ship from the sounds that came through the open skylight in the great cabin. While accounting the bread bags come aboard, he decided that Mr. Midshipman

Landon, standing on the quarterdeck above and laughing his simian-like laugh, was in fact not ready to take command of the maintop. Halfway through the master's deck log, listening to the groan and thud of the rudder as the ship rocked in the moderate swell coming into the harbor, he decided to have the tiller ropes replaced.

Just as he was opening the gunner's log, he heard the barge lift off the booms, the squeal of blocks, the stamp of feet, and the expectant murmur of the men getting a run ashore. He waited until he heard "Cast off the boat falls!" before calling to the marine sentry to pass the word for Lieutenant Saunders. Four minutes later Saunders, commanding officer of the *Rose*'s division of marines, was announced, and Wallace called for him to enter the great cabin.

"Lieutenant Saunders," Wallace said, running an eye over the marine's uniform, looking to find some imperfection in the red and white and black ensemble and knowing that he would not. "Please, have a seat. A glass of wine with you?"

He poured the wine even as Saunders said, "That would be marvelous, sir," and handed him the glass.

"You frequent Captain Lillibridge's establishment, do you not?"

"I have been there, sir, sure, but I don't know as I would say 'frequent.' "

"In any event, you have seen my coxswain, Truax, there?"

"I have, yes, sir."

"Have you ever taken note of who he talks with?"

"In my experience, sir, he generally sits alone. Not the most social fellow, you know, not exactly framed to invite companionship. Sometimes I see him sitting with others, none that I know. Usually of the lower sort."

Wallace thought about that, staring silently into Saunders's eyes. Saunders was one of the few people who did not fidget when he did that. Rather, he held Wallace's gaze and waited with seemingly endless patience.

"All right, Lieutenant, here is the situation. Truax tells me that a man has come to him asking to see all of my correspondence for the next fortnight, says he'll meet Truax again after that time. He told Truax he was a merchant, but that's nonsense. He must be involved with these traitors, no doubt trying to find out who in Newport are still loyal to the king so they can tar and feather them, or worse."

"If he was kind enough to tell Truax when and where they would meet, it should be easy enough to pick him up, sir."

"It should be. However, Truax is lying. Not about the man, or what he wants, I don't suspect, but I'm willing to bet he's lying about when the man will meet him. A fortnight? It makes no sense. Does he think Truax will hoard my correspondence until then? No, Truax and his type are always trying to play both ends against the middle, and they're rarely very clever at it. I think he wants to curry favor with me by reporting this and still get whatever it is that this man has promised him."

Saunders nodded as he listened.

"I want you to get a squadron together, about five marines should do. Station them out of sight around the tavern. Be careful, don't let Truax see them, he'll know something is up. He's a clever bastard, he'll smell a trap ten leagues away. You yourself can go into the tavern without making him suspicious, but none of the marines. The man we are looking for is a merchant, apparently quite wealthy. Anyone who matches that description who talks to Truax, I want him arrested."

"Arrested, yes, sir. And Truax too?"

"No, leave Truax be. He's a rogue but he does bring me useful information, and I don't want to queer him on that. This'll scare him enough to keep him on the straight and narrow. For a while."

"Very well, sir. And this Yankee, shall I bring him back to the ship?"

"Certainly, if he is cooperative, though I doubt he will be." Wallace considered the situation. The man was no doubt some kind of rebel spy. With Truax's testimony there was enough evidence to arrest him, and Truax would say whatever he was told to say. But what if the man genuinely was a wealthy merchant? He had arrested John Brown, the wealthy merchant from Providence, on as much evidence, and with as much reason, and that had become an embarrassing nightmare for him and the navy. "Yes, take him if you can, though if he's the one we're looking for, I would imagine he'll put up a fight. I would not, however, think it amiss if he was shot while resisting lawful arrest. If you take my meaning."

CHAPTER
25

Homeward Bound

IT WAS THREE DAYS BEFORE THE *CHARLEMAGNE* WAS REUNITED WITH
her prize. Rumstick, in perfect obeyance of orders, had laid
the *Mayor of Plymouth* close-hauled with her larboard tacks
aboard, sailing away due north. Biddlecomb had ordered the
Charlemagne put on starboard tack the moment he gained her
deck, and with all the sail she would carry, they had run away
on a taut bowline, weaving a course through the shattered
convoy.

William Maltby could hardly have missed the fact that the
Mayor of Plymouth was in enemy hands, that much was obvious, and it was equally obvious that he cared only about cap-
turing the *Charlemagne*. The *Glasgow's* bow had turned
unwaveringly toward the brig, and very inch of canvas she
would bear was stretched out aloft as she came in pursuit. But
it was a hopeless gesture; the frigate, with her battered rig,
could never hope to catch the nimble *Charlemagne*, and the
chase caused not the least bit of consternation aboard the
American ship.

Nor did Maltby have the luxury of chasing the Americans
to the far ends of the earth; his first duty was to the convoy,
to try to gather the scattered vessels together and bring them
into Boston with no further mishap. The *Glasgow* had pursued
the *Charlemagne* for less than two miles before Maltby hauled
his wind and turned his back on the Americans.

Three hours after that, Biddlecomb stood on the *Charle-magne*'s quarterdeck and watched the last of the convoy disappear from sight. The sun, just visible through the dense overcast, hung inches above the western horizon. He did not know how long this conflict would last, but he fervently hoped that as long as it did, he would never see William Maltby again.

It was another two days before the *Charlemagne*'s lookout reported a sail to the north, and five hours after that that the sail revealed itself to be the *Mayor of Plymouth*.

She was hove to, as Biddlecomb had instructed, and pretty much where he had expected to find her, though her drift had been faster than Biddlecomb's estimate. The *Charlemagne* ran down on the merchantman, rounding up fifty yards to windward of her and heaving to as well.

Twenty minutes later the *Mayor*'s boat was alongside with Rumstick sitting in the stern sheets, stately as an admiral, save for the idiotic grin on his face. He bounded up the boarding steps with an agility that always surprised Biddlecomb and grabbed Biddlecomb's hand in his, pumping it up and down like the bilge pump brake on a sinking ship.

"Damn me to hell, it's good to see you again, sir."

"You sound as if you had your doubts. But here, let's go below and have a wet and you can tell me what you've been about."

By the time the cabin steward had fetched the wine and poured out two glasses, Rumstick had finished his narrative. There was little to tell; they had sailed north, out of the convoy, and no one had tried to stop them. He had watched the convoy disappear to the south, had continued on for half the night, then had hove to and waited.

"The men behaved themselves?"

"Passing well," Rumstick said, draining his glass of wine, a fifteen-year-old Bordeaux, in one swallow and reaching again for the bottle. "There was rum aboard, which I didn't know about, and no surprise that no one told me. Some of the lads got into it the second night."

"Mr. Jaeger, I imagine, was leading that boarding party as well?"

"No, not at all," Rumstick said to Biddlecomb's surprise. "Jaeger caught them and ran them up on deck. He don't drink anymore."

"Jaeger doesn't drink anymore? What makes you so certain? What happened?"

"It was the damnedest thing, really." Rumstick slathered a biscuit with butter and shoved it in his mouth. "I went and had a talk with him, you know," he said as he chewed, spraying crumbs across his shirt, "about his drinking. He never seemed a proper drunk to me. You know about predestination, the way them Calvinists think on it?"

"No, not much."

"They figure that God determines at birth if a fellow goes to heaven or hell, and nothing for it. Course, most of them people figure they're predestined to go to heaven, but it seems Jaeger got it in his head he was predestined for hell, and nothing he could do to change it. I ain't ever seen the like."

Biddlecomb considered this. "That could make a man a bit desperate."

"Desperate ain't in it. So Jaeger starts drinking, and then he figures he's really damned for sure, so he drinks some more to try and forget, and on like that."

"But how'd you get him to stop?"

"I showed him the Gospel, right there in Luke, and in First Corinthians, where God says in plain English that anyone's got a chance at salvation."

"You astonish me, Ezra. Wherever did you learn so much about religion?"

"I have a mother, you know," Rumstick said with a defensive tone, "and she ain't backward in her duty."

"Well, I'm heartily glad to hear about Jaeger. He was a big part of our success the other day, and we may need more of the same. Not to mention that he saved my life." Biddlecomb thought of the boarding pike thrust into his side, and the grisly sight of Jaeger splitting his attacker's skull, and became aware again of the dull ache under the bandage around his waist. He shifted uncomfortably in his chair, bringing some relief to the wound. "We still have to get back to the Colonies and get this powder to the army outside Boston." He refilled his glass and Rumstick's as well. "Any thoughts?"

"We sure as hell can't go into Boston."

"Not Boston, no. We'll let the army move the powder overland, we've taken risk enough."

They had indeed, by his reckoning, taken risk enough already. No reasonable man could have thought him a coward, but superstition lurks in the heart of every person who uses the sea, and Biddlecomb was not above believing his luck was all but used up.

He looked over at the forward bulkhead. The sword that he had taken from Lieutenant Shave was hanging there, encased in a shining black scabbard, a gift from the crew of the *Charlemagne*, crafted out of leather from the boatswain's stores by some skilled and anonymous hand and adorned with worked brass fittings.

"No, we can't go into Boston," Biddlecomb said again, "or anywhere too close to Boston." He considered the question for a moment and then, coming to a decision, said, "We'll make for Cape Ann. Gloucester. That's close enough and still out of the navy's area of patrol." Cape Ann would keep them out from under the guns of any British cruisers around Boston and give them a good place to land their powder. They would have to be very unlucky indeed to be captured there.

"So it's the same damned thing all over again, eh? Sneaking into our own damned country like we're the enemy?"

"The same damned thing." Biddlecomb had already realized it, and the realization made him angry, that his own home was for him still the least safe place on earth. "I made up a few signals," he said, handing a sheet to Rumstick, deliberately changing the subject before he became angry again. "Just simple ones: tack, wear, engage the enemy—which, pray God, we won't need."

Rumstick looked over the sheet. " 'To cut cable and get

under way,' " he read, " 'loosen fore topsail and sheet home and fire a gun to windward.' "

"That's another one that, God willing, we won't need."

Rumstick looked over the rest of the sheet. "This should answer."

"Good. Then we had best be under way. Just keep astern of me. I'll burn a taffrail lantern at night and flash a second one twice at every turn of the glass so you'll know it's me. Will that answer?"

"Fine, Isaac, I'm full with you. And if we still happen to get separated?"

"Just lay a course anywhere between south southwest and north northeast and you're bound to hit something. It worked famously for Columbus."

For two days the wind graced Biddlecomb's little squadron, remaining steady and strong enough to drive the two vessels nearly three hundred miles to the southwest. The sea too, while far from flat, presented them with no more than long rollers and a short chop, which their round bows tossed aside in magnificent showers.

Not a sail was sighted and not a hint of the convoy was seen in all the two days that they made southing. Both mornings the *Charlemagne* greeted the dawn at quarters, both mornings the sun illuminated a slate gray sky and, spreading the light to each horizon, revealed an empty sea.

At local noon on the third day, with half of the Charlemagnes below eating dinner, Biddlecomb shot the sun with his quadrant. With that and the information noted on the slate, he marked their position on the chart spread out on the great cabin table. "Mr. Weatherspoon," he called to the midshipman once he had regained the deck. "Make a signal to the *Mayor of Plymouth*: 'tack in succession.' "

Five minutes later Biddlecomb watched the blue and white flag break out at the *Mayor of Plymouth*'s foremast head. "Acknowledge!" Weatherspoon sang out after looking the signal up on one of the three pages that constituted their signal book.

Biddlecomb turned and faced forward. "Rise tacks and

sheets!" he called, and the foresail was clewed up to the yard. "Ready about! Let go the headsails! Ease down your helm! Helm's alee!" he called next, and the *Charlemagne* came up into the wind, turning, coming about for the first time in three days.

Ten minutes later the two ships were again sailing in line ahead, *Charlemagne* in the van, nothing changed, save for the fact that the wind was over the larboard bow now, rather than the starboard, and the two ships were on a heading to fetch Cape Ann.

Biddlecomb felt a little thrill, a little stir of anticipation in his breast, and he indulged himself in the sensation. In the next two or three days he would deliver to General Washington an entire shipload of gunpowder. He would report to Major Fitzgerald that, while the plan that he, Fitzgerald, had endorsed had been a failure and a trap, Biddlecomb had nonetheless managed to bring back powder. Far more powder, in fact, than they had initially hoped for. That would certainly do much to annul the major's supercilious attitude. And if Virginia would not love him unless he fought for the American cause, then this should prove to her how dedicated and capable he was.

Virginia. He would see her again, in just a few days, a week at the latest, and this time he would not be a hesitant, stuttering fool. He watched idly as the last of the braces was coiled and hung. Two or three more days. His luck only needed to hold for two or three more days. He thought of the last time he had needed only a few days to sneak into a safe harbor. That had been the death of the *Icarus*. And then the thrill was gone from his breast, and he tried to ignore the anxious feeling growing in his guts.

Major Fitzgerald was becoming something of a regular at Captain Lillibridge's Tavern, a circumstance that was not at all to his liking. For three days he had taken his horse for long rides across the countryside, to exercise the animal and to clear his head, then arrived at the tavern at eight o'clock. Each night he made his way to the far end of the bar, ordered a tankard of the nasty, bitter ale that the good captain served, and as casually as he could manage, turned and glanced at Truax.

The coxswain, for his part was as clandestine as one could ask. He never met Fitzgerald's eye, never acknowledged his presence, and only after a minute or so of staring at the table, swilling his ale, and staring blankly into the smoke that engulfed the room would he give a barely discernible shake of his head. This night, so far, was no different.

Doubt like gangrene was starting to eat away at Fitzgerald. His plan had worked so perfectly up until that point: his access to the men involved in the Bermuda venture, his discussion with Whipple. Lieutenant Trevett had been a godsend, what more could he have hoped for? He told himself that the plan was as sound as it ever had been, that he could not expect some unknown traitor to work to his schedule. But still the doubt was there, and above all else, the fear of having to report a failure to General Washington.

His eyes were still fixed on Truax as the sailor went through his histrionics. He searched the tavern with more than his usual diligence, then turned toward Fitzgerald, met his eye for just a second, and gave a quick nod of the head.

Fitzgerald was so surprised by this, having been so prepared for another disappointment, that he did not at first know what to do. Then reason reasserted itself. He turned to the publican and ordered two more drinks, then made his way to Truax's table and slipped onto the bench facing the coxswain.

"Good evening, Truax," he said in a low and conspiratorial tone as he pushed the tankard across the table.

"Uh," Truax grunted, taking up the tankard and half-draining it with one swig. Fitzgerald waited, suppressing his excitement and his irritation, letting the coxswain do this at his own pace.

"Where's the girl? How come you don't bring that little bitch around?"

There was suspicion in Truax's eyes, as well as the gnawing desire on which Fitzgerald was counting. "She's around," he lied. In fact she had gone directly back to Stanton House after her one brief appearance. "She just doesn't belong in a place like this. I said she'll be yours when this is over and I meant it."

Truax grunted again, then set the tankard down and reached over for his tarpaulin hat, which was lying on the table. He paused and looked past Fitzgerald's shoulder with a startled, alert look, like a deer hearing a twig snap in the woods. Then he turned away, a less than believable look of innocence on his face. An officer walked past the table, a lieutenant of marines, and stepped out the back door.

"What was that about?"

"Nothing, just a bloody bullock officer," Truax mumbled. He tilted the hat back without looking down.

Lying beneath it was a letter. Fitzgerald could make out few details in the dark room, under the shadow of the hat, but he could see a wax seal and fine linen paper, as he might expect from a wealthy man. A wealthy man such as Stanton or Bowler or Cooke. He reached out his hand, but Truax slammed the hat down again.

"You got something for me, first, ain't ya?"

Truax did not miss a trick. If he had been born a gentleman, Fitzgerald thought, he would no doubt be one of London's most successful lawyers. The major reached into his breast pocket and pulled out a five-pound note, held it up just long enough to show Truax that it was the genuine article, then put it back in his pocket. "I see the letter first." He could not allow the sailor complete control.

Truax stared into his eyes, anger and greed playing across his face. Then he grunted and lifted the hat again and Fitzgerald picked up the note.

It was fine paper indeed, and Fitzgerald hoped he would be able to make out the watermark in the dim light of the tavern. Nothing was written on the outside. He stared at the wax seal. It was just a wafer, no imprint, but he had not imagined that there would be. He was considering the problem of how to break the seal when Truax slammed his tankard down on the table with a sharp intake of breath. Fitzgerald looked up, startled, and Truax snatched the letter from his hands.

"Get the hell out of here!" he hissed.

"What? What is it?"

"It's a fucking trap, that bastard Saunders must have his bloody bullocks outside! Get out of here, you stupid bastard!"

"Give me the letter!"

"Shut up, you motherless arsehole." Truax stood quickly and snatched up his hat. He turned, half-falling over the bench, and stumbled for the back door of the tavern. He pushed the door open and was gone, and with him went the letter.

Fitzgerald sat dumbfounded, staring at the door through which the coxswain had gone. Who in hell was Saunders? That letter was the one he had been waiting for, he was certain of it, and now Truax had carried it off.

He swiveled around on the bench and looked in the direction the sailor had been facing. The officer, the one who had passed them going out the back door, was standing at the bar, staring at Fitzgerald with a face disturbing in its lack of expression. Saunders. A bloody bullock officer. A trap.

Had Truax sold him out? He certainly did not appear to be acting when he had fled in terror; this trap, if such it was, seemed to be as much of a surprise to the coxswain as it was to Fitzgerald.

Not that it mattered. Saunders was there and Fitzgerald had no doubt that a force of marines was surrounding the tavern. He was trapped.

He held the marine's gaze, gave him back the passive stare, and with his right hand he fingered the big horse pistol that he carried in a pocket inside his cape. The marines would most likely be on foot, but he had a horse tied up just outside the tavern. He needed only a minute to get to the horse and he was gone. But first he had to buy that minute, and it would not come cheap.

He stood and walked over to the marine officer and stood next to him at the bar. "Evening, Lieutenant."

Saunders nodded and picked up his glass of brandy from the bar and gulped the last of it.

"I don't know your name, sir, but I would be grateful if you would step out with me. My commanding officer would very much like a word with you."

"I should think that he would," said Fitzgerald, staring at the obscene painting on the wall opposite them. He did not have much time, and he could think of only one way to get his minute.

He turned and faced the marine, taking a step closer, until less than a foot separated the two men. He reached under his cloak and pulled the pistol from its pocket, discreetly, so that no one in the tavern took any notice, save for Saunders. He pointed the big gun at Saunders's belly and gently, quietly, pulled back the lock. "Perhaps it would be better if *you* were to step out with *me* and see that your marines behave themselves."

Saunders stared into his eyes, and much to Fitzgerald's surprise, he smiled. "Come now, sir, do you really expect me to be a cooperative hostage?" His voice was loud, intentionally so, and Fitzgerald glanced quickly around, but no one in the tavern was paying them any attention. "This is a noble effort, really, but a useless one."

"I said, sir, perhaps you should step out with me. I shall not ask again."

"And then what? You'll shoot me down? Leaving you with no hostage, your gun unloaded, surrounded by British officers, and you having just shot one of their own? Not an enviable position. No, sir, you appear to be a gentleman, and I do not believe that you will kill me, an unarmed man, in cold blood."

And he was right. It was not the distaste of killing a man in cold blood that bothered him—Fitzgerald was a soldier and the lieutenant was his enemy—it was that if the lieutenant would not cooperate, then killing him would do no good at all. Fitzgerald lowered the horse pistol and let it dangle at his side. Saunders smiled, a victorious and gloating smile. Then Fitzgerald pointed the gun at Saunders's gleaming black shoe and pulled the trigger.

CHAPTER
26

Newport Road

THE FLASH AND BANG OF THE PISTOL SEEMED MUCH MAGNIFIED IN the close, dark tavern room. The crowd fell silent, but Fitzgerald's ears were filled with a ringing sound, and the report of the gun seemed to reverberate off the walls. He took a step back, screaming, "Oh, my God! Oh, my God!" as if he were as startled as the others by the gunfire.

Then the room was filled with noise. A woman screamed. Men began to shout and push, some toward Saunders, others pushing for the door. Saunders was screaming as well, a loud, piercing, agonizing scream, the sound taking up where the gun had left off. If he had been shot with an ordinary pistol, then he might have remained more in control, coherent enough to gesture at his assailant, but the .72-caliber balls of Fitzgerald's double-shot pistol had turned his foot into bloody wreckage.

The crowd pressed around the two men, uncertain of what had happened. "Did he shoot himself in the foot?" Fitzgerald heard someone ask.

Saunders was doubled over, but now he was craning his neck up, looking for Fitzgerald and screaming, "You bastard! You bastard!" The major took a step back into the crowd, then another, as people pressed around him, eager to see the wounded man.

The back door flew open and two marines ran in, muskets

held before them, bayonets fixed. Fitzgerald stepped around the crowd, away from the marines as they roughly pushed the tavern's patrons aside to get at their officer.

This was the moment. Fitzgerald took a step toward the front door, still facing the crowd. A confrontation was building between one of the marine privates and a drunken horse of a man who did not care to be shoved about in that manner. No one was looking at him. He turned and stepped through the door and collided head-on with another marine coming through the front.

"Where the bloody hell have you been!" Fitzgerald said in a loud voice, edged with hysteria. "Your lieutenant's been shot!" He pointed toward the dark interior of the tavern and the marine plunged through the door. Another appeared from wherever he had been lying in ambush and followed the first, followed Fitzgerald's pointing finger into the tavern. Fitzgerald marveled to see that the marines' much vaunted stupidity was no exaggeration.

He turned toward his horse and found himself facing yet another marine, but this one was not running. Rather he was standing stock-still, waving the bayonet at the end of his musket an inch from Fitzgerald's face, the cold, black, lifeless eye of the gun staring impassively. "In a hurry, are we?"

"Yes, damn it! Your officer has been shot, marine, and I expect you to go help him!"

The marine did not move, his eyes did not waver. He was older than the other two, thirty at least, and he would not take suggestion as easily as they had.

"I said your officer has been shot!"

"So I heard. Back inside with you." The bayonet moved back and forth under Fitzgerald's nose.

Fitzgerald took a step back, back toward the door, and the marine followed. His eyes moved from the soldier's face down to the bayonet and the musket below. The marine's thumb was resting on the lock, but the gun was not cocked. It would take the marine an additional half second to cock the weapon and fire; it was not much but it was something.

He stepped back again, then again, and the marine followed, step for step, the bayonet never more than an inch from the major's face. The doorframe, with its weathered wood and peeling paint, came into sight at the edge of his vision.

"Come on then, about-face and march, you Yankee bastard!"

Fitzgerald swept his arm up and knocked the bayonet aside. He lunged out and grabbed the barrel of the musket, the steel cold under his hands, then twisted around and with all of his considerable strength of arm stabbed the bayonet into the wooden doorframe. He saw the blade sink inches deep into the wood. The marine shouted something that Fitzgerald did not hear as he twisted the gun to free the bayonet, but it was stuck fast.

Fitzgerald reached into his cloak and pulled out the horse pistol, holding it by the barrel, then the marine fired his musket. Fitzgerald felt the hot flash and the sting of wood slivers hitting his hands and face as the gun blew a hole in the frame, jolting the bayonet free. The marine tried to step back, back far enough to use the bayonet, but it was too late. Fitzgerald swung the horse pistol like a club, striking the marine with the brass-bound butt just at the temple. His cocked hat slewed sideways at a comical angle and the soldier crumpled to the ground.

Fitzgerald leapt over the supine body and ran for his horse, fifteen feet away. He did not think the gunshot would go unnoticed, and he was right. The tavern's front door burst open and two more marines ran out, stopping short at the sight of their fallen fellow.

Fitzgerald spun the reins off the hitching post and reached for the saddle. "You there! Stop!" one of the marines shouted, but Fitzgerald did not stop. He grabbed ahold of the saddle and placed his boot in the stirrup just as the marine fired.

Fitzgerald felt a blow on his side that spun him half around, as if he had been punched, and then a burning sensation and knew he was shot. He stepped up into the stirrup, and the tavern and the marines spun around before his eyes as the pain engulfed him. He thought he might pass out, then realized how fortunate it was that he and not the horse had taken the bullet. He jerked the reins over as his right foot found the other stirrup, as natural a movement for him as walking, and his heels dug into the horse's flanks.

The horse, a good, spirited stallion, bolted forward. Fitzgerald could hear shouts and many voices as people poured out of the tavern, then the sound was lost in the report of a musket as the other marine fired. He felt the punch and the burn of a musket ball tearing through the flesh of his right arm, just below the shoulder. He fell forward in the saddle, the arm, now useless, hanging at his side, while his legs from long practice held him balanced in the stirrups, half-crouched against the horse's full gallop.

Another gun fired, but Fitzgerald did not know where the ball went. The dark road was flying past him now, the line of dead and ghostly trees whipping by in a blur. The horse was barely in control, running as much from fear as from Fitzgerald's urging. Don't shoot the horse, don't shoot the horse, Fitzgerald thought to himself, over and over as the agony in his arm and his side grew worse with each of the animal's footfalls.

Another gun fired, and another and another, and Fitzgerald realized that quite a number of marines had been waiting for him. There was the sound of running feet as well, and shouting men, but even as he heard them, they were growing faint in the blackness behind him. Of the marines, Saunders was the only one likely to have a horse, and he would not be riding anything for some time to come. Despite the pain Fitzgerald found himself grinning at the memory of the haughty marine lieutenant doubled over and grabbing at his shattered foot.

Soon the only sound he could hear was the hoofbeats of his own horse. He ran on for what he guessed to be another five minutes, though in his condition it seemed an hour. He slowed the animal to a trot and the jarring motion doubled the agony in his wounded body, so he slowed again to a walk. It was quiet around him on the road, no sound of pursuit, no sound at all save for those made by himself and his horse. He guessed that he had ridden half a mile in his frenzied gallop. Only one other horse had been at the tavern, and its owner was apparently not interested in pursuing him.

He felt a warm sensation inside his shirt and on his arm, and he knew that he was bleeding profusely. He reined the horse to a stop and struggled out of his cloak, the motion causing his arm to throb with pulsing agony. He remained on the horse for fear that he would not be able to remount if he got down. Awkwardly, with his left hand, he pulled a knife from a sheath on his saddle and cut strips of bandage from the cloak and wrapped them around his wounds. They would be of dubious benefit at best, but perhaps they would staunch the flow of blood long enough for him to get . . . where? Where could he go?

He looked along the road, stretching north as far as he could see on that dark night. He struggled back into his cloak and wrapped it tightly around him just as he began to shake with the cold. Going back to his room in Newport was out of the question. He could think of only one other place that he could reach in a reasonable time. He did not want to go there, did not even know if he would make it, but he did not see as he had any choice. He tapped his heels on his horse's flank and the animal headed off again, north along the frozen road.

It was twelve miles from Newport to Stanton House, twelve agonizing miles, and when Fitzgerald arrived there three hours later, he knew that he was not doing well at all. He sat slumped forward in the saddle—that seemed to ease the pain somewhat—and the sensation from his wounds was no longer sharp and burning but a deep, profound ache that was not localized at the wounds themselves but had spread through his body. His head lolled from side to side with each step the horse took, and the road and the countryside seemed to swim before him on those occasions when he looked up. He did not know if the bleeding had stopped, but he could feel his shirt, soaked with blood, cold and wet against his skin, and it added yet another element to his discomfort.

He pulled his horse to a stop, across the frozen manicured

lawn from Stanton House. It was the first pause since the Bristol ferry, where he had convinced the ferryman, at the end of his horse pistol, to make an exception to his rule of quitting at sunset. He had paid the man two shillings and had thus parted with him on good terms, but the look on the man's face gave Fitzgerald some indication of how frightening his appearance was. From there he had ridden nonstop through the dark town of Bristol to where he stood now, in the shadow of the woods.

He sat stock-still and tried to focus his mind as well as his eyes. He did not want to do this—William Stanton was as much of a suspect as the others—but if he did not, then he would die by sunrise. If there was only a way, he thought, to get ahold of Virginia without alerting her father. She would help him. He trusted her.

A light caught his eye, a light like a window, but bigger, and growing, and he realized that someone was opening the door to the well-lit stable. The stable was about fifty yards away from where he stood, and there, framed in the light, unmistakable even in her bulky riding clothes, was Virginia.

She was like a vision to Fitzgerald, and one last time he dug his heels in the horse's flank and walked it across the lawn toward the light and the warmth that it promised.

He was twenty yards away when Virginia heard his approach. She spun around and peered at him, but he could see that she was blind in the dark after the brightly lit stable. She took a step back and Fitzgerald's horse stepped into the light. Through the gathering fog in his head Fitzgerald could see her expression of recognition and delight.

"Maj—Edward! Whatever are you doing here?" Then he saw her expression change again and he was not surprised. He was slumped forward and to one side in the saddle. He did not know how bad he looked, but from Virginia's reaction he imagined that it was pretty bad.

"Are you injured?" Virginia said in an entirely different tone. She stepped toward him, taking the reins from his hands and leading the horse by the bridle into the warm barn. Her voice was so tender, her look of concern so genuine, that Fitzgerald wanted to weep at his salvation, wanted to collapse in her arms. He felt the warm air envelop him and he began to tremble again.

"What in the world has happened? My God, have you been shot? Here, let me help you down." Virginia stepped around and slipped his boot from the stirrup. Her grip was strong and sure, her actions without equivocation. She helped him swing his leg over the saddle and step down onto the hay-strewn floor. He felt his head swimming and clung to the saddle horn with one hand and Virginia's shoulder with the other.

"I ran into some trouble in Newport." Fitzgerald gasped the words. "Might I stay here the night?" The question sounded absurd, but a lifetime of decorum would not permit him to take hospitality for granted. Virginia smiled. She found the question genuinely amusing.

"I think we might find a room for you. Here, let's sit you down." She eased him away from the horse and toward a stack of hay bales against the wall of the stable. He leaned heavily on her and was afraid that her thin frame would not bear his weight, but he could hardly feel his legs and had not the least hope of supporting himself. Virginia seemed untroubled by the burden.

She eased him to a sitting position on a bale and wrapped a horse blanket around him, then knelt by his side. Her eyes were so kindly, so concerned, he again felt the urge to wrap his arms around her, to cry into her hair. "Wait here, Edward, while I fetch my father and Rogers. I don't believe I can get you to the house by myself."

He did not want William Stanton to know of his presence, he wanted to object, but his head was swimming and as in a dream he was not able to speak. She wrapped the blanket tighter around his shoulders and then she was gone.

Well past noon the next day he awoke. He lay still for some moments, his eyes closed, reconstructing the events that had led him there. He remembered the tavern, and the escape; the dull pulsing pain in his side and his arm would not allow him to forget that; he recalled the bitter-cold, agonizing ride north to Bristol and Virginia and the stable. And that was all. He did not know where he was or how he got there.

He could hear the sound of someone moving around, but it was from another room. He was aware of a delicious smell, like flowers of some description, and he heard a rustling of silk. He opened his eyes slowly and turned his head, and as he had hoped, Virginia was there, sitting by his bed. She smiled and he smiled back, as best he could, but he knew it was a weak effort.

"How do you feel, Edward?"

"Better. Hungry."

Virginia brushed the hair off his forehead. "We have a cure for that," she said, smiling, then stood and left the room.

He was in the guest room, he realized, the same airy, well-appointed room in which he had stayed the last time he visited that house. A fire was burning in the fireplace, filling the room with glorious warmth. The curtains were pulled aside and the first brilliant sunlight in days poured in through the window, illuminating even the fine dust that floated in the air.

He propped himself up on his arm and winced in pain, then eased himself into a more comfortable position. The makeshift dressing on his arm was gone, and in its place was a white cotton bandage, expertly wrapped, and bound, he was amused to see, in the same way one would bind a horse's ankle.

A moment later Virginia was back with a tray of steaming beef stew, bread, butter, and coffee, her father hard on her heels. She set the tray down and Fitzgerald tore into the food. It was very good, but Fitzgerald knew that anything, even the food that they served to sailors, would have been appetizing at that point.

"You were fortunate in your wounds, Edward, at least as fortunate as one can be who has been shot," Virginia spoke as Fitzgerald consumed his dinner. "The bullet in your side passed right through—I take it it was fired at close range—and the one in your arm just tore the flesh up. It didn't break the bone or lodge there. You lost quite a bit of blood, but beyond that I think you'll mend very well."

Fitzgerald nodded and continued to eat.

"What in the world happened to you, Major?" Stanton asked, pulling a chair up beside the bed.

"Apparently someone in Newport didn't care to have an American army officer poking around, asking questions."

"Do you not know who shot you?" Stanton asked.

"I do not. You probably noticed from my wounds that I was shot from behind."

"Yes, that was clear when we were dressing them," said Stanton, and Fitzgerald was struck with the thought that Virginia might have seen him naked.

"They shot me as I was mounting my horse," he continued quickly, before he became more disquieted by that last thought. "I managed to get away, obviously. There are not many horses that can outrun mine."

"Major, please, eat if you wish," Virginia said, much to Fitzgerald's relief. "Never mind us, we don't stand on manners at such a time."

Fitzgerald dug into his food once again as William Stanton railed against the Tories in Newport, the cowardly British, shooting a man in the back, and Rhode Island horses that could not outrun those from Virginia.

"Well, sir, I shall leave you for now," he said at last, standing and putting the chair back against the wall. "You are in good hands with my daughter. Virginia, pray, give the major a chance to rest."

"Thank you for your kindness, sir."

"Bah. Kindness would be to march my men down to Newport and drive them damned Tories into the sea. And I would if I could." And with that he left.

Fitzgerald lay back in the bed and looked at Virginia. She was so beautiful, so competent and kind. She had played her part in the tavern boldly, and to perfection. He felt his affection welling up, an affection that was something beyond the camaraderie he had so far enjoyed with her. "I owe you an explanation. Perhaps one a little more complete than the one I gave your father."

"You don't owe me a thing, Edward. But if you care to tell me, I will admit to a fairly ravenous curiosity."

He tore off a piece of bread and began to tell the tale, or parts of it at least, starting with Lieutenant Trevett, moving through the letter that Truax had showed him, that crucial letter that he had held for just a brief moment, and ending at the Stanton's stable. He omitted the details of how he had laid his trap, and how he had baited her father. And the part that Virginia had played. He was embarrassed by the shameful way in which he had used her and wished not to bring it up. He hoped that she would not ask.

"And the letter?" Virginia asked. "Do you think he's given it to Wallace, or might he still have it?"

Fitzgerald had already considered that question, the answer being of the utmost importance to him. "Truax will know that I escaped. He might hang on to the letter for that reason, hope to meet up with me again. He never got his money, and he seemed pretty anxious for it."

"And I flatter myself he was anxious for the . . . shall we say . . . carnal knowledge you promised him? Of me? I am right in guessing that such was my function in the tavern?"

Fitzgerald felt his face flush, felt his wounds throbbing with renewed vigor. But of course she had figured it out. She was not stupid, far from it. He could not recall a more humiliating moment in his life. What kind of an absolute swine was he? "God, Virginia, I don't know . . . ," he stammered.

"Never mind," Virginia said not unkindly. "If it was of some help in discovering our traitor, then I am proud to be of service. I assume that you did not intend to carry through with your promise?"

"My God, no, Virginia." She was just tormenting him now, making him pay for services rendered.

"Let's forget about it," she said. "If Truax still has the letter, he won't keep it for long. Someone must go to Newport tonight to see if a meeting can be arranged. Obviously that someone cannot be you."

"No, I fear not, though that meal has set me up quite well. Is there someone you can trust?'

"Yes, I . . . ," Virginia began, then paused. "I can send Rogers. He's trustworthy. Completely. We'll send him with another horse, see if he can get this Truax to come with him to Bristol Landing. You can meet him there. Do you think you'll be able to ride that far?'

"Yes. Yes, I do. I'm feeling remarkably better." He had always had an amazing power of recovery, and the sleep and the food had had a great restorative effect on him. "Tell Rogers to look for Truax at the boat landing first. I don't imagine he'll care to go back to the tavern for a while."

"The boat landing. Very well. I'll go and see Rogers and get him on his way. And you should get some more sleep. Let's say five hours from now we'll get you under way for Bristol Landing? And with any luck we'll get Truax there as well."

Fitzgerald nodded and fell back on his pillow, suddenly embarrassed to be lying in bed, nearly naked, with Virginia there at his side. "Yes, that's fine." Then he sat upright again as an alarm sounded in his head. "Virginia. You *are* sending Rogers, right?"

"Of course I'm sending Rogers. Who else would I send?"

He looked closely at her face, but it revealed nothing, like that of a gambler who might be holding a trump card or might be holding nothing at all. He settled back on his pillow. "Very good then . . ."

Half an hour later Fitzgerald heard voices in the yard below, and ten minutes after that he heard the two horses trotting away to the south, as Rogers headed off to his meeting with Truax.

Three hours later, as he drifted in and out of sleep, dreaming glorious dreams, he heard a voice shouting instructions across the lawn to an unseen stableboy. He sat up and cocked his head toward the sound, listening to the voice, then lay back down on the pillow. He closed his eyes and cursed softly, cursed himself for his stupidity. The man yelling instructions was Rogers, and if Rogers had not gone to Newport to meet Truax, then he knew full well who had.

For two solid days Biddlecomb's luck held steady, as steady as the wind that blew cold and strong from the south southwest. For those two days the *Charlemagne* plunged along, reaching northwest by north, her bow pointing toward Cape Cod as the wind and current set her north to fetch Cape Ann.

Not a sail was seen in that time, save for the *Mayor of Plymouth,* always two miles astern. Rumstick maintained his station so exactly that one might have thought that the *Charlemagne* was towing the *Mayor* on a two-mile hawser.

They were in soundings now, by Biddlecomb's dead reckoning. The wind, which had been brisk up until that morning, had dropped off to no more than a moist breath, and the sea rolled under them in long, oily swells. It was an hour past dawn, and the *Charlemagne* was hove to, a line of men standing along the larboard side, each holding a coil of the deep-sea lead. Woodberry stood in the fore-chains, swinging the heavy lead cone in every increasing arcs, then let it go.

The lead sailed fifteen feet to leeward of the brig, then dropped into the sea, sending little circles of water across the smooth surface of the swell, and the deep-sea lead line began to spin out of the first man's hand. In five seconds the first coil was gone and the line began to spin off the coil held by the second man, then the third, fourth, and fifth, then at last the sixth leadsman felt the line go slack and called out, "Bottom! Bottom at sixty fathoms!"

"Excellent," said Biddlecomb. "Haul it aboard and bring the lead aft." Hand over hand the dripping line was hauled aboard. At the bitter end was the thirty-pound deep-sea lead, pulled from the water like a fish on a line. Biddlecomb examined the tallow smeared on the bottom. Just clean sand stuck there, no shells, and no mud. They were south of Cape Ann, and not too far south at that. By nightfall they would be swinging at anchor in Gloucester's small harbor.

Biddlecomb turned and looked over the taffrail. For the first time in two days the *Mayor of Plymouth* was less than two miles away, Rumstick having not hove to when the *Charlemagne* had. The *Mayor* was carrying all plain sail and ghosting along at about three knots, the most one could hope to get from the slab-sided merchantman in that light air. A mile and a half now separated the two vessels, and that distance was slowly closing.

Biddlecomb thought of the *Mayor*'s hold, stuffed to the deck beams with barrels of gunpowder, beautiful black gunpowder, and his lips turned up in a smile. It felt like old times, like sneaking into Narragansett Bay with a hold full of smuggled molasses that would be sold for more than most men could make in a lifetime, and it had been too long since he had done that.

Gloucester. Biddlecomb knew better than to count his barrels before they were landed. He picked up his glass and stepped to the starboard rail. If his dead reckoning was right, then he might be able to see Cape Ann on the horizon. He raised his glass to his eye and looked north, and in that instant he knew that his fortune was about to change.

"Oh, damn it to hell," he said, low enough that he could not be heard. It was the end of his perfect luck, and it was rolling down on him like the legions of Rome, solid and unstoppable.

Fog, blotting out everything north of west in one long white wall, and moving down on them faster than they could move away. Biddlecomb lowered the glass. Fog was so deceptive, so easy to miss until it was on top of you, but now that he had seen it, it was obvious. There was no horizon to the north, and the sea and the sky just faded away into whiteness and the fog gobbled up more and more of it as it moved down on them.

Not that there was anything in the least unusual about fog in that part of the ocean, Biddlecomb reminded himself, at that or any other time of the year. Nor was it necessarily the ruination of his plans. In fact, if he was not so anxious to keep in company with the *Mayor of Plymouth*, he would put the *Charle-*

314

magne under way and feel his way through the gray night, taking his chances on the dangerous shoals around the Cape. But he was not in the mood to take chances, he had done enough of that. They would heave to and wait until the bank of fog burned off or rolled over them.

"Mr. Weatherspoon," Biddlecomb said. "Signal to the *Mayor of Plymouth:* 'Heave to.' "

" 'Heave to,' aye," Weatherspoon said, consulting his sheet of signals.

"The signal for 'Heave to' is clew up the main topsail to weather and hoist the ensign with a weft," Biddlecomb prompted, unwilling to wait for the midshipman to find it on the page. "Here, you attend to the ensign, I'll see to the topsail."

He stepped up to the quarterdeck rail, leaving Weatherspoon to fumble through the canvas flag locker. The first wisps of damp, white mist were reaching across the deck, swirling and moving on, leaving drops of water on the brightwork. The hands were still at their sail-trimming stations, ready to put the *Charlemagne* under way. "Clew up the main topsail, weather side only," he called, and a man at the fife rail cast off the sheet and three more hauled away on the clewline in obeyance to the strange order.

He turned his eyes from the fogbank, now less than a quarter mile away, to the *Mayor of Plymouth.* The prize was still under way; Rumstick had not yet received the signal as Weatherspoon, having just completed tying the ensign in a weft, was that moment bending it to the halyard. But even when the signal was complete, it was possible that Rumstick would not notice it in time.

Biddlecomb fidgeted with impatience as Weatherspoon hauled the ensign up. It had not occurred to him to create signals for fog, and all of his night signals involved using lights. He cursed himself for the oversight and vowed that when he had the time, he would create a comprehensive system of signals, recalling, to his further irritation, how he had mocked Whipple for doing just that.

315

"*Mayor of Plymouth*'s not acknowledged yet, sir," Weatherspoon said, the signal glass against his eye.

"Mr. Gardiner," Biddlecomb called to the acting first officer. "Fire a signal gun on the weather side, no shot . . . ," he began, and then the fog was on them. One second Gardiner was plainly seen at the far end of the deck, and then he was gone and everything forward of the mainmast was lost in a milky white nothing.

"I lost the prize, sir," Weatherspoon reported, still peering through his useless telescope. "I don't know if they saw the signal."

"Very good, Mr. Weatherspoon." Biddlecomb heard Gardiner's men running the gun out, though if he had not known that they were on the foredeck, he would not have known from which direction the sound was coming, so disorienting was the fog. The gun fired and a part of the gray mist flashed white, and even the loud bark of the gun seemed subdued.

He could just see the mainmast forward, and over the taffrail the world disappeared into whiteness. Even the sea below was gone. Visibility was closed down to ten feet at best. The *Charlemagne* was hove to now and would remain thus. He hoped that the *Mayor* was hove to as well, though he thought it likely that Rumstick would want to close the distance between them before doing so, increasing the chance of the two vessels' being in sight of each other when the fog lifted. He looked around again and felt the frustration of being deprived of sight.

There were footsteps on the quarterdeck ladder and a shape appeared, ghostly and vague, then materialized into Ferguson, feeling his way aft. "Mr. Gardiner's compliments, sir, and should he continue to fire the gun?"

"Yes, tell Mr. Gardiner I'll thank him to fire one shot every two minutes. There's a spare half-minute glass in the binnacle." If Rumstick was still under way, then there was a chance, however slight, that they would collide, and though it was almost impossible in fog to tell the direction from which a sound was coming, the relative loudness of the gun might give Rumstick an idea of the *Charlemagne*'s position.

"Aye, sir," said Ferguson, saluting and feeling his way aft to the binnacle.

They were in purgatory, a white purgatory, where they could see nothing farther than ten feet from their faces and they could do nothing to change their circumstance. Water dripped from the sails and rigging, soaking men and clothes and ship alike until it looked as if they had just emerged from a fierce thunderstorm. It was cold as well, even colder than before, a cold that seemed to find its way through cloaks and coats and down to the men's bones. People moved about quietly and spoke in hushed voices for no logical reason and strained their ears listening for any sound that might emerge from the fog. And every two minutes the gun fired, and the fog was lit with its brilliant flash and the quiet shattered, and then it all settled down again.

Biddlecomb soon lost all sense of how long they had been in the fog, but it seemed to him as if it had been a long time. It seemed as if he could not remember a time when the gun had not fired every two minutes, or a time when he had been able to see as far as the bowsprit and beyond.

The gun fired again, its lonely sound, and he listened to the familiar echo as the noise quickly subsided, lost, like everything else, in the impenetrable fog.

"Sir?" Weatherspoon was at his side with a question.

"Yes?" Biddlecomb turned to him, and just as Weatherspoon began to speak, he heard it. He held up his hand, cutting the midshipman off, and listened. It was a sound, not, he believed, from the *Charlemagne* but from out in the fog. He did not know what it was; a hatch cover dropped perhaps, or the crack of a pistol or a spar carrying away, but it was a sharp sound and he had heard it.

"Did you hear that?" he asked softly.

"No, sir."

"There was some kind of noise, like a cracking sound. Go forward and ask Mr. Gardiner if someone dropped something or broke something. And ask him to please discontinue the gun."

"Aye, sir," said Weatherspoon, hurrying forward.

And then Biddlecomb was alone in his white world and the closest thing he had to companionship was the specter of the helmsman, dimly seen aft. He cocked his head outboard and listened. He sifted out the creaking sounds made by the *Charlemagne* as she rolled and the slap of her sails and running rigging and listened.

It was a mistake. He had not really heard a thing. The more he listened the more he became convinced of it. He had heard a phantom noise the way one often sees a phantom light at night, a common occurrence in dense fog. He straightened and was about to turn away when he heard another sound.

This time it was a voice. He could not make out the words, but he heard the distinct tone and cadence of a human voice, and it sounded as if it had come from astern. He turned aft, not expecting to see anything but hoping at least to focus his hearing. Could it be the *Mayor of Plymouth,* Rumstick having come up with them? That made the most sense. Biddlecomb stepped aft, past the helmsman, who materialized into a flesh-and-blood person, and grabbled the speaking trumpet. He raised it to his lips, ready to hail Rumstick, when he heard the voice again, loud and eerie.

"Sixty fathom! Sixty fathom!" the voice called, and now it sounded as if it came from over the larboard side. Biddlecomb spun around. There was nothing there but swirling mist, and no more sound. Biddlecomb glanced at the helmsman, suddenly afraid that he was the only one who had heard the voice, but the helmsman's eyes were wide and he was looking from side to side and glancing over his shoulder.

"That sounded fucking close, sir."

It did sound close, but Biddlecomb could not even guess at the direction from which it had come.

A bosun's call pierced the fog, as if the man blowing it were standing on the *Charlemagne*'s deck, and Biddlecomb spun around again, looking over the starboard side. He heard the stamp of feet. He could see the water now; the visibility had lifted to twenty feet at least.

Something moved overhead, a small, dark object slowly breaking from the fog. Biddlecomb's first thought was that it was a bird, and he puzzled at how a bird could move so slowly and deliberately. But the object continued to come out of the mist, long and dark like a serpent with tendrils spreading out behind it and disappearing into the fog.

It was a jibboom, too high and too large to belong to the *Mayor*, and the long trails were a ship's rigging. Biddlecomb wondered how he could ever have mistaken it for a bird. And in that same instant he knew that the ship attached to the jibboom, a very big ship, was about to run them down.

CHAPTER
27

Cape Ann

HIS FIRST THOUGHT WAS TO ORDER THE MAINYARDS BRACED AROUND, but he did not. It was too late. The tip of the jibboom was directly over his head, thirty feet over his head, and now the bowsprit and spritsail yard were coming out of the fog.

"Fenders aft here!" Biddlecomb shouted. "Get some fenders aft!" Nothing on earth could stop them from colliding now; his only hope was to soften the impact.

The end of the bowsprit soared over the deck, and the ghost ship's spritsail yard struck the *Charlemagne*'s mainmast. Four hands appeared on the quarterdeck dragging a heavy rope fender. "Right there, put it over right there." He pointed to the spot on the *Charlemagne*'s hull that the strange ship's cutwater would strike, and the men hefted the fender over the side.

The other ship was moving very slowly, no faster than two knots, and Biddlecomb realized with a sense of relief that the impact would be slight. He could feel the *Charlemagne* being pushed sideways. The ship's jibboom guys were now hopelessly entangled in the *Charlemagne*'s mainsail gaff and mainyard. The tip of the jibboom had passed clear over the *Charlemagne*, and directly above his head the ship and his brig were locked together in a tangle of cordage that would take hours to pull apart.

He ran his eyes down along the jibboom above, along the

320

great bowsprit, and down to the ship itself. The fog was breaking up; the white gauze of mist tore apart, and behind it, at
eye level, was the ship's figurehead, the colors on the heraldic
shield and the lion rampant still muted by the vapors.

There was a great deal of shouting, but it was not coming
from the *Charlemagne*. Biddlecomb looked down into the waist
of his own command. He could see the full length of the deck
now and halfway out the bowsprit. His men were silent, standing motionless and staring up at the apparition that had appeared out of the fog and entangled itself in their main rigging.

"You there! Who in all hell are you? What are you about?"
someone was shouting from above his head. He looked up.
The person shouting wore white breeches and a blue coat. A
cocked hat was perched on his head. Biddlecomb knew the
uniform, knew it better than he cared to; it was the uniform
of a lieutenant in the Royal Navy.

"I should ask the same of you, sir!" he shouted back. He
had no idea of what he would do, but bluster was always an
effective way to buy time. "Making way through the fog, no
bells sounding, what were you thinking!"

The lieutenant shouted something back, and Biddlecomb
was aware of an indignant tone in the voice, but he did not
pay attention to the words. Instead he ran his eyes along the
strange ship's hull, as far as he could see around her bluff
bow. She was yellowish in color, with two decks of guns. The
headrails that formed her beakhead, the catheads and channels,
all seemed massive and unyielding. This was not a lithe frigate,
it was a two-decker, one of the most powerful warships to be
found in American waters, and they were tangled in her rigging like a fly in a web.

His next thought was for Rumstick. The *Mayor* was out there
somewhere in the fog, and the fog was rapidly burning off.
With any luck it would be gone entirely before the *Charlemagne*
was untangled from the strange ship's headrig. Then Rumstick
would see what had happened and make his escape. With
any luck.

The lieutenant had stopped talking and it was time for Biddlecomb to say something, to explain his presence aboard what was undeniably an armed brig of American registry. He cast around for something to say, something to do. He felt like a fox in a tree, bayed about, terrified and angry and desperately seeking some escape. He could disappear into the fog if his rig were not locked to the other. He could try to bluff his way out, but he needed a story and he could think of none, none that would hold up in light of the fourteen guns that lined the *Charlemagne*'s side.

He opened his mouth to say something, whatever would come out, when he was suddenly aware of more shouting from above. He saw the lieutenant cock his head, then turn as the shouting grew in volume. Biddlecomb stepped aft to the *Charlemagne*'s taffrail. From there he could see down the length of the two-decker's hull, rising like a cliff above his head, to where it disappeared into the fog seventy feet away. He could not see who was shouting, or why.

Twenty seconds later he knew. The *Mayor of Plymouth*, lost to sight from the *Charlemagne*'s quarterdeck, was apparently visible to those on the two-decker. The merchantman came ghosting out of the fog, her bow pointing toward the man-of-war's waist. She was turning, trying to avoid a collision.

Rumstick must have put his helm up the second he caught sight of the man-of-war in the fog. The *Mayor*'s jibboom described a wide arc as the ship swung slowly around. If Rumstick could turn and disappear back into the fog, then he could escape. Biddlecomb realized he was holding his breath.

And then the *Mayor of Plymouth* struck the two-decker. Biddlecomb saw the *Mayor*'s jibboom hit the man-of-war's main shrouds and check the ship in her swing, and then they came together, broadside to broadside, as softly as if the merchantman were warping alongside the bigger ship. The swell lifted them and they ground against each other, and then the prize was motionless, lying along the man-of-war's side.

Biddlecomb turned away from the two-decker, hiding his face from the lieutenant, and laughed. There was nothing else for it. It was absurd. On all the great ocean, in a dense fog, they had both managed to entangle themselves in the rigging of a powerful enemy. He doubled over, laughing hard and silent, unconcerned that his men might think he had lost his mind.

The laughter was a release, a purging of anxiety and anger, and when he straightened up again, his mind felt clear, like the blue skies after a storm, like waking up from a deep sleep. Now he was ready to look for his escape.

They could not fight their way out, not against so wildly superior a force, and with their rigs entangled they could not run. That much was sufficiently clear that Biddlecomb did not even consider those options. Only one route of escape was possible, if they could escape at all, which was far less than likely, and that was through trickery and fast talk. Fortunately, trickery and fast talk were Biddlecomb's strong suit, and he knew that he had to start talking fast and soon. He had to plant his story before someone guessed at the truth.

"You there, Lieutenant!" he shouted up to the man-of-war's deck, and the lieutenant tore his eyes from the *Mayor* and looked down at him. "I demand to see your captain at once, do you hear? This is an outrage, sir, an outrage! I shall collect my papers and come aboard this instant."

"I've no doubt, sir, that Captain LeCras will wish to speak to you as well," the lieutenant replied coldly. "I'll send a boat around."

"Oh, damn the hellish boat! Just lower a pilot ladder off your headrail there. We may as well take some advantage from the fact that you've run us down." With that he disappeared down the scuttle, calling, "I'll be back in a moment," over his shoulder.

He half-ran across the gunroom and flung open the door to the great cabin. He did not know exactly what he would say to Captain LeCras when he went aboard the man-of-war, and various possibilities ran through his head as he rummaged through the papers on his desk. He sorted them into two piles, the *Charlemagne*'s papers, what few were left or rewritten since

Bermuda, and the *Mayor of Plymouth*'s, then he snatched up the *Charlemagne*'s papers and stepped over to the gallery window and prepared to toss them into the sea.

Then he stopped as an idea began to germinate in his head. He stood there, his arms back, ready to fling the papers into the water, and ran through the various permutations of the plan. It was not a good one, but he could think of nothing better. He stepped back into the great cabin, the *Charlemagne*'s papers still in his hand. He pulled a haversack from under the desk and stuffed the papers into it. He grabbed the *Mayor of Plymouth*'s papers and flipped through them to the muster book and ran his eyes over the crew list, then stuffed them into the haversack as well. He slung the haversack over his shoulder and raced back to the deck.

A pilot ladder had been lowered from the beakhead of the man-of-war, and the lowest rung hung a foot above the *Charlemagne*'s quarterdeck. The fog was thinning rapidly now. He could see clear up to the man-of-war's main truck and aft to her quarter galleries. "Mr. Gardiner," he said to the acting first officer. "I'm going aboard the British ship. You're in command until I return. No one aboard the *Charlemagne* is to say anything to anyone aboard the man-of-war, understood?"

"Aye, sir." Gardiner made no attempt to hide his concern.

"And try to not hit anything else while I'm gone," Biddlecomb added with a smile, then stepped onto the pilot ladder and climbed up and over the man-of-war's headrail. He stepped down into the beakhead, steadying himself against the massive bowsprit, as big around as the *Charlemagne*'s mainmast. To his left were the seats of ease, three holes cut into a well-worn plank, and beyond the seats a door that lead through the bulkhead into the dark forecastle. He stepped across the beakhead and through the door.

The forecastle smelled of tar and hemp and men. Biddlecomb paused, standing still in the comforting darkness, and thought his plan through once again. It was as good as he was going to devise in these circumstances. But if he hesitated in his story, if he equivocated, then he was lost. He took a deep breath and let it out, then like a confident actor taking the stage stepped through the door and slammed into the lieutenant with whom he had spoken.

"Ah, here you are, Captain," the lieutenant said with a strained civility as he stepped back. "Welcome aboard the HMS *Somerset*. Come this way, please." With that he turned and walked aft, not looking to see if Biddlecomb was following.

The *Somerset* was huge, one of the largest ships that Biddlecomb had ever been aboard, though he knew that to people in the Royal Navy who were accustomed to such things, she was a mere third-rate, just able to hold her own in the line of battle. Still, to one used to the size of the *Charlemagne* and her gear, the man-of-war seemed more like a castle than a ship.

He followed the lieutenant aft along the starboard gangway, past the massive longboat perched above the waist, the ship's smaller boats stacked inside. The *Somerset*'s beam was close to forty-five feet, half of the *Charlemagne*'s entire length. He looked up, over the stack of boats. The *Mayor of Plymouth*'s jibboom was still hooked in the main shrouds, and her masts and yards, weak and spindly looking beside the man-of-war's, were visible overhead. He wanted desperately to see the *Mayor*'s deck, to know if the British were aboard her, to know if they had already discovered the truth, but the merchantman's deck was well below that of the *Somerset*'s and hidden to his sight.

Men were everywhere along the man-of-war's decks, literally hundreds of men, more than twice as many as had been aboard the *Glasgow*, and it had seemed to Biddlecomb that the frigate's company was enormous. He and the lieutenant moved past a knot of men straining to haul up the big main topsail, then up a ladder to the quarterdeck.

The quarterdeck, a seeming endless expanse of open space, was at least as densely populated as the waist. But rather than ragged seamen in tar-stained, slop-chest-issue shirts and trousers, the crowd here consisted of officers in their blue coats, gold trimmed, and black cocked hats, arranged along the starboard side. There was a smattering of civilians as well, including two women standing by the break of the poop.

There was little doubt as to which of the officers was Captain LeCras. He stood at the larboard rail, alone save for the clerk and two midshipmen who stood to the side and behind him, attending to his needs. He was older than the rest. His face was lined, his hair the color of the fog.

"Mr. Scott," the captain said, and the lieutenant stopped short and saluted.

"Sir, this is the captain of the brig," said Lieutenant Scott. Biddlecomb stole a glance over the starboard side, down at the *Mayor of Plymouth*'s quarterdeck. With any luck LeCras had not spoken to Rumstick or anyone else aboard the *Mayor*.

"I am Captain LeCras, His Majesty's Ship *Somerset*. And who might you be, sir?"

Biddlecomb looked into the captain's light blue eyes and swallowed. "I'm Capt. Gideon Wetherell, and I'm master and part owner of that ship there." He pointed down toward the *Mayor*. "She's the *Mayor of Plymouth*, on charter to the government for a transport." He opened the haversack and drew out the *Mayor*'s papers. "Here's all of the paperwork, sir, for your inspection."

Biddlecomb adopted an expression of patience mixed with a hint of anger, as if he had been done a great wrong and his explanation of himself needed no further clarification. He waited for a reply. Captain LeCras took the proffered papers, thumbed through them, then handed them to the clerk. He glanced at Lieutenant Scott and then back at Biddlecomb. "Captain of *that* ship?" he asked slowly, nodding toward the *Mayor*. "You were aboard the brig, were you not?"

"Yes, sir," Biddlecomb continued in the same patient tone. "That's . . ." He glanced down into the waist. Another of the seemingly dozens of lieutenants was standing by the gangway, stiffly welcoming Rumstick aboard and leading him aft.

"Oh, Captain, this, ah . . ." Biddlecomb stalled, waiting for Rumstick to step up to the quarterdeck in order that he might hear the story. "This here's my first mate"—he pictured the crew list in his mind—"Mr. Joshua Clutter. Mr. Clutter, this here is Captain LeCras."

"You are captain of that ship?" LeCras asked Rumstick, nodding again toward the *Mayor.*

"First mate, sir, like the captain here said," Rumstick replied with not the slightest hesitation, picking up the thread of the story as quickly as Biddlecomb had known he would.

"Like I was saying, sir," Biddlecomb continued, "the brig is the *Charlemagne,* an American privateer. She's my prize, sir."

"Your prize?" LeCras said, a little louder and more incredulous this time. "How do you happen to have a prize?"

"It's quite a story, sir, really. We was in convoy from England with about fifty sail. The frigate *Glasgow* and the *Fly* sloop were our escort, when this *Charlemagne* and another Yankee, ship-rigged, they work in pairs is how they do it, sir, came down on us. So while the navy was fighting off the other, this *Charlemagne* tries to board us. But we're armed, sir, four-pounders and plenty of small arms and a fair-sized crew, and we beat 'em off, and then I says to the lads, 'Come on, let's take the rascals!' and we boarded the brig and took her instead."

"Hot work, sir," Rumstick supplied. "Lost four of our own men, and two wounded that I don't think'll make it. You can see our rigging's pretty cut up."

LeCras frowned and nodded his head as he considered the story. "Most impressive, Captain," he said at length. "How is it you're not with the convoy now?"

"Like Mr. Clutter says, we was cut up pretty bad aloft, and all the prisoners to deal with, so we fell behind," Biddlecomb explained. "I think that the captain of the *Glasgow* thought we was taken and left us, the son of a whore, beg your pardon. Anyway, by the time we could get under way, the convoy was gone. And good riddance, I say. I don't care to share my prize money."

"You have the prisoners on board?" LeCras asked.

"No, sir," said the ersatz Captain Wetherell. "There was too many of them, too much chance they'd retake the brig. We seat 'em adrift and I reckon they was picked up by the other ship. That's why there's no boats on the brig there."

LeCras was quiet now for a long moment. He stared into Biddlecomb's eyes and Biddlecomb stared back, knowing that the man was considering whether to believe the story or not. He was no fool, Biddlecomb could see that, and he imagined that one could not be a fool and command a ship of the line. But Rumstick had played his part beautifully, and their story, if not entirely believable, was at the very least plausible.

"Why were you aboard the brig and not your own ship?" LeCras asked, finally breaking the silence. "I should think you would make Mr. . . . ?"

"Clutter, sir," said Rumstick, "Joshua Clutter."

". . . Mr. Clutter here prize-master."

Biddlecomb shrugged his shoulders. He did not want to sound too rehearsed. "I dunno, I like the brig."

"You're an American, are you not?"

"Yes, sir," said Biddlecomb, his tone defensive this time. "Not all of us is traitors."

LeCras nodded, and Biddlecomb was beginning to understand that the gesture was more habit than an acknowledgment of understanding. "Do you have a letter of marque, Captain Wetherell?"

"Uh, no, sir. No, I do not."

"Then you cannot legally take a prize. You know that, don't you?"

"Yes, sir, but what was I supposed to do, under the circumstances?"

LeCras looked forward and frowned, and Biddlecomb could see that he was done discussing the matter. "There are others, I think, who are better suited than I for straightening this whole thing out. Where were you bound, before you ran foul of us?"

And that was the question. Biddlecomb knew that it would be asked, and he knew only one answer would be consistent with the tale he had told. He glanced over the *Somerset*'s long taffrail. The fog was gone now, leaving in its wake a robin's egg blue sky. Off on the horizon, low and green, just as Biddlecomb had imagined it would be, was Cape Ann.

He turned back to Captain LeCras. "We was bound for Boston, sir," he said.

CHAPTER
28

Bristol Ferry

It was dark along Newport's waterfront, and the cobblestone streets and the brick buildings and wooden piers, wet with melting snow and the fine mist that was falling, gleamed with light reflected from open tavern doors and bright-lit windows above.

Virginia led the two horses down the road, walled on one side by the three-story buildings and on the other by the masts of ships tied to the quays, like walking through an ancient, burned-out forest. She fingered the small pistol she carried in the pocket of her riding cloak, but that did little to mitigate her fear. Men walked past, shadowy, imprecise figures, and stared long as they did, careless of any sense of decency, as if trying to decide whether or not to molest her.

It would have been frightening in any circumstance, even without the prospect of meeting Truax and luring him up a dark road toward Bristol Landing. But she had no choice in the matter. Fitzgerald suspected her father, as much as any of the others, of treason. She knew that he did, despite the major's assurances to the contrary.

Truax alone had the evidence that would trap the real traitor, and with one blow her father would be cleared and Isaac would be avenged. But first Truax had to be convinced to travel to Bristol Landing, and Virginia felt quite certain that she was the only bait that could lure him there.

A block away, Virginia could see a cluster of sailors milling about on the quay, a ship's barge tied alongside. They were not the tag-and-rag lot that one was accustomed to seeing, at least not as far as their dress was concerned. Rather they were tricked out in matching blue jackets and gleaming tarpaulin hats with ribbons trailing behind and bright white pants. They could only be the crew of a captain's barge, and she hoped that that captain was Wallace, and that Truax was still with them. The thought of entering that dark tavern was even less inviting than the waterfront street.

She walked closer, her hand now curled around the butt of her gun. She was twenty feet away when the sailors finally noticed her.

"Here now, what's this?" one asked in a voice that could be heard a block away. "You looking for me, then, my dear?"

"Her horse is looking for you, Jackson, you ugly whore's son," said another. "This here sweet thing's for me, ain't that right, love?"

The men began to move toward her, en masse, and as they stepped away from the boat, she could see Truax, leaning against a piling and picking his teeth.

Their eyes met, and Truax stood bolt upright in surprise as he recognized her. He took three long steps and his arm lashed out like a snake and he caught Jackson, who was leading the charge toward Virginia, by the collar. "Get back to the boat, fucking arse, all of you!" he said, and without as much as a sound the men stopped and stepped back to where they had been standing, glancing over their shoulders at Virginia.

Virginia stopped and waited as Truax approached. The surly arrogance in his stride seemed to dissipate with each step he took, until at last he stood in front of her and glanced around uncertainly.

"What do you want?" he asked at last.

"More to the point, what do you want? We both know what was promised you. Do you want it? Me?"

Truax's eyes glinted like the wet cobblestone and he ran his eyes over her body. She had seen desire in men's eyes before, not infrequently, but nothing as consuming and primal as this. His hungry look alone made her feel violated and dirty. If he or the entire boat crew decided to have their way with her, she realized, there was no one to stop them. Certainly not anyone who might be found along that dark street. She had only the one pistol, she could only kill one of them.

"Do you still have the letter?" she asked, interrupting what lewd thoughts the coxswain might be entertaining.

"Maybe. That bastard stupid enough to show his face around here?"

"No. You'll have to come with me to meet him. It's about ten miles. I brought a horse for you."

Truax looked over at the horse with some uncertainty. "Ten miles? What the fuck is this, then? This some trap?"

"Do you have the letter? Show me."

Truax's eyes never left her face. He reached into his blue jacket and pulled out a letter, bent and wrinkled, but made of the same paper and carrying the seal that Fitzgerald had described.

"My master believes that that letter is the one he wants. If it is, and if he sees it tonight, he'll pay you double. And you can have . . . the other thing. Tonight."

Truax stared into her eyes, and as he considered this, he slowly licked his lips. Virginia was afraid she would be sick and clamped her teeth together until the feeling passed. She wondered if anything short of intractable lust could induce a man such as Truax to do something that was, on its surface, as stupid as what she was asking him to do. She doubted it.

"Why should I trust you?" Truax asked, squinting at her as if to get a better look into her heart. "Ten miles up some sodding road? It don't sound too square to me."

"Very well, if you're afraid, bring along one of your men. Or two, we can double up on the horses. Unless you think the three of you not enough to deal with some trap I've set." The last she said with enough of a sneer to show contempt without actually making Truax angry.

Truax glared at her for long seconds, then said, "Wait here."

He stepped back to the boat crew, gave some instructions that Virginia strained to hear but could not. She felt the sinking feeling inside that comes with realizing that one has made a fatal mistake, and with conscious effort she held her fear in check.

She had assumed that her quick offer to allow Truax to bring more men would allay his fears. She had further guessed that he would not want any witnesses to his illicit dealings. But perhaps she had guessed wrong. If he brought two of the boat crew, she would not have the option of bolting away if things got out of hand; Truax would be on the horse with her.

The coxswain said something to his men, and though Virginia still could not hear the words, they had a tone of finality. Then he turned and walked back to her, alone, thankfully alone.

"Come on, then, let's hurry this up," he said.

Virginia led the second horse around and handed him the reins. The arrogance and self-assurance that had marked his demeanor thus far fell away as he reached a tentative hand up to the horse's snout. The horse was as benign a creature as ever lived; Virginia had chosen him for that reason; but Truax did not look at all comforted by its docility. He placed a foot in the stirrup, grabbed ahold of the saddle horn, and awkwardly pulled himself up into the saddle.

Virginia watched this operation with some amusement, then swung herself up into the saddle of her own horse. She felt suddenly safe, as if a great danger had passed, and the feeling made her giddy. And indeed she was safe, mounted as she was on her fast mare, and able with one kick of her heels to race away from Truax with an agility the sailor could never match. She turned and smiled at him, her biggest smile, and for that second she saw him forget his discomfiture. "Let's go," she said, nudging her heels into her horse's flanks, and with that they were under way.

It took them two hours to cover the distance to Bristol Ferry, two hours of near silence as Truax concentrated on keeping on his horse. The only conversation was the coxswain's occasional bursts of profanity and the sweet encouragement that Virginia gave him, promising and promising again the fine things that would come his way if he did not become discouraged, constantly stoking his greed and ardor to keep them burning hot.

At last the few houses that constituted Bristol Ferry hove into view a mile down the road, and beyond that was the black void that marked where the brackish water of Narragansett Bay separated Rhode Island from the Providence Plantations. Behind her, Virginia heard Truax cursing again, and she was just considering where she might find Fitzgerald when two figures stepped out of the woods bordering the road, twenty yards ahead, and stood directly in their path. She could see pinpoints of light leaking out around the door of a shuttered lantern.

Just as Virginia felt relieved that Fitzgerald had found her, it occurred to her that it might not be Fitzgerald at all. She reached for her gun and wrapped her fingers around the butt as one of the men called out, "Virginia?" She recognized Rogers's voice.

"What in hell?" Truax nearly shouted, apparently startled by the voice in the dark.

"Yes, Mr. Fitzgerald," Virginia called, then turning in her saddle said to Truax, "We're here." She slid out of her saddle and stood on the frozen road, and Truax, with much more difficulty, did likewise. The coxswain cursed with renewed vigor as he hobbled toward the others.

Fitzgerald opened the lantern door partway, throwing a pool of yellow light on the ground and lighting up his and Rogers's faces from below, giving them a macabre aspect. The flame glinted off silver buttons and illuminated the buff trim on Fitzgerald's coat, that part that was visible through his open cloak. The major was wearing his uniform once again. "Virginia, I'm pleased to see you. I asked Rogers to accompany me, since as it happens he was unoccupied. I had thought he might be away, perhaps to Newport?"

"Good evening, Rogers," said Virginia, ignoring the major's sarcasm.

"Good evening, Miss Stanton." Rogers had a musket held loosely in his hands, his thumb on the lock.

"Come on, we got business here and I'd like to . . . get on with it," Truax said, staggering into the light.

"You have the letter?" Fitzgerald asked.

"I do. You got the money for me? I want it first this time, you miserable bastard."

Fitzgerald reached into his coat pocket and pulled out a five-pound note and handed it to Truax. Truax took the note without so much as looking at it and stuffed it in his pocket. "That little bitch said something about paying double if that's the letter you want."

"I will. If it's the one I want. If not, our deal still stands."

"And if it is, I get her. Tonight."

Virginia looked at Fitzgerald and their eyes met and she watched with some amusement the major's discomfort. "Yes," he said, "now let's see the letter."

Truax pulled the letter from his jacket, slowly, and handed it over to Fitzgerald. "You can't break that seal or the captain'll know it's been opened."

Fitzgerald dropped the letter on the ground and stepped on it.

"Hey!" Truax yelled.

"Looks like someone dropped it and stepped on it by accident. Perhaps running from a tavern," Fitzgerald said, stooping and picking it up again. Virginia could see that his wounds and his bandages did not allow him to move with his usual grace.

He flipped the letter open and unfolded it, then handed the lantern to Virginia, who held it above the paper. She watched his face as he read through the cramped handwriting. His mouth was set and fixed in a frown that grew more pronounced as he read the note. He shook his head slowly. He seemed to read the letter again, and then a third time, and at last he looked up and met Virginia's eyes. "This is the one."

"All right then, pay up and let's get on with this," Truax said.

"Quite right," Fitzgerald said, reaching into his cloak again and pulling out his horse pistol, which he leveled at Truax's head. "I'll pay you just what you deserve, you treacherous bastard," he said in a voice just above a whisper.

Virginia stepped back, shocked, wondering if the major would blow the man away, but Truax was too outraged to show any fear. "You lying Yankee sod, we had a deal, you son of a whore!" The coxswain took a step toward Fitzgerald. The lock on the major's pistol and on Rogers's musket snapped into the firing position. Truax stopped where he stood.

"You're five pounds richer," Fitzgerald said. "You can go now, or I can kill you and take the money back."

"Give me that letter."

"I'm sorry. I can't do that."

"What're you going do with it?"

"Show it to the man who wrote it, and then kill him."

Truax had the look of a trapped and wounded animal. He glanced around at the shadowy figures in the lantern light. "They'll know I done this."

"Most likely. You could warn the man, if you knew who he was. Care to read the note?" Fitzgerald asked, holding the letter up for Truax's inspection.

"Sod off, you son of a bitch."

"Very well. Sergeant"—Fitzgerald turned to Rogers—"shoot this man."

Rogers stepped past Fitzgerald and aimed the musket at Truax's head, the barrel inches from his nose. "God damn you!" Truax shouted, twisting and flinging himself to the ground. He scrambled down the road on his hands and knees, then pushed himself to his feet and half-running and half-stumbling disappeared into the dark.

"You wouldn't have shot him, would you, Rogers?" Virginia asked.

"If he hadn't run away like a good lad, I suspect I would have, yes."

Fitzgerald stepped off into the woods beside the road and came back a moment later, leading two horses, one of which was his. "Thank you, Virginia. I've used you horribly, I know, and you cannot guess at my shame. But you have done us a great service."

"You are quite forgiven, Major. But how are you feeling?" She was genuinely concerned, and looking up at him, his tall, muscular frame, his dark and serious features, she felt something else as well.

"I'm fine, just fine. And I have to go now." He put his foot in the stirrup and stepped up into the saddle, not as effortlessly as Virginia had seen him do before, but easily enough.

"What are you going to do?"

Fitzgerald pulled the reins to one side and his horse stepped into the middle of the road. "Just what I told Truax I was going to do."

CHAPTER
29

Boston Harbor

DEER ISLAND WAS TO THE NORTH OF THEM, AND TO THE SOUTH WAS Long Island, and now Biddlecomb could see all of Boston Harbor opening up before him. Boston Harbor, the one place on earth that he least wanted to be. He put his glass to his eye and swept the area ahead of them. The harbor was familiar, almost as familiar as Narragansett Bay, and he began to mentally check off the various islands, necks, shallows, and mud flats that made Boston Harbor such a chore to navigate.

The *Charlemagne*'s bow was heading for a point midway between Governor's Island and Castle Island. Five miles distant, and half-hidden by Governor's Island, Biddlecomb could see the blue-green hill on which sat the city of Boston, and anchored off the Long Wharf on the east side of the city was the Royal Navy's North American squadron.

"Bloody good harbor, this. It'll be damn good to see some shipping going through here again," observed Lieutenant Sotherby, the *Somerset*'s fourth officer, who had been sent aboard the *Charlemagne* to see that all of Captain LeCras's orders were complied with. Captain LeCras had not quite believed Biddlecomb's story. He had not been dubious to the point of taking possession of the two ships, just to the point of insisting that the *Charlemagne* and the *Mayor of Plymouth* accompany him into Boston, where higher authorities could look into the matter.

Sotherby was standing on the quarterdeck at Biddlecomb's side, slapping his arms together to keep warm and enjoying the scene. The lieutenant had been aboard the *Charlemagne* for just over twenty-four hours, since they had begun extracting themselves from the *Somerset*'s headrig. He was competent in matters of seamanship, at once polite and droll, and despite himself, Biddlecomb found that he liked the man. Sotherby was the first naval officer about whom he could say that since he had been dragged into this conflict nearly a year ago. Under different circumstances they might have been friends, but as it was, he had other things weighing on his mind.

It had taken the better part of the previous day for the three vessels to untangle themselves and get under way. With the clearing skies had come a renewed wind, and the ships, in grudging company, had covered the twenty miles to the entrance of Boston Harbor just before sunset. But faced with an ebbing tide and the unpleasant thought of navigating through the tricky shoals at night, LeCras had ordered his little squadron to anchor at Lynn Bay.

The moon rose, full and bright, an hour after sunset, killing any hope that Biddlecomb had entertained of slipping the cable and escaping in the night. The moonlight illuminated the narrow stretch of water between the vessels, and he could see the officers of the watch on the *Somerset*'s deck and their constant surveillance of the *Charlemagne* and the *Mayor*. The least suspicious activity on the part of the Americans and the two rows of gunports would swing open and the *Charlemagne* and the *Mayor of Plymouth* would be blown away. By his estimate the *Somerset* fired a broadside of over seven hundred pounds, compared to his own forty-two. He had slept little that night.

It was just past noon, and they had been under way for less than an hour, having waited all morning for the capricious wind and tide to turn in their favor. The *Mayor of Plymouth* was once again astern of them, now only a cable length away. Biddlecomb looked to weather of his and Rumstick's position. The *Somerset*, with her two long rows of heavy guns and her crew of more than five hundred men, was plowing along under all plain sail, a great bear keeping an eye on her recalcitrant cubs.

Over the taffrail he could see His Majesty's Ship *Mercury* and the sloop *Otter* patrolling Broad Sound and the Main Channel, tacking back and forth, keeping an eye on all inbound and outbound ships, while the navy's smaller vessels worked like ferrets in the lesser channels. He and Rumstick had entered the house of the Royal Navy, and the door was closed behind them.

How long, he wondered, could he continue pretending to be Capt. Gideon Wetherell? Not above five minutes under any careful scrutiny, and it was only a matter of time before someone figured out who he was. He slammed his fist down on the caprail in frustration. After all of the nonsense he had just endured, he was no better off now than he had been aboard the *Ant*. In fact, probably worse.

"God, bloody hell, look at that!" Sotherby said. Biddlecomb turned to see what had attracted the lieutenant's attention. Sotherby had his telescope out and was training it forward, toward the town of Boston. "Bloody convoy must have arrived. Look at all those bloody ships. One might think one was in Portsmouth."

"Mr. Weatherspoon, the signal glass," Biddlecomb said, and the midshipman put the telescope in his hand.

"Say, that must be your convoy, isn't it, the one you were separated from? I imagine you've a thing or two to say to old Maltby of the *Glasgow*, leaving you to the mercy of those bloody Yankees. Oh, no offense, sir."

Biddlecomb twisted the tube and the field came into focus. "None taken," he said absently. In the lens of the bigger glass he could make out the startling number of masts clustered in the port of Boston. He slammed his fist down again.

"You know, Captain, I've been meaning to say, about this prize money, I should tell you honestly there isn't much chance of your getting it," Sotherby said, breaking the news with the utmost discretion. "You being without a letter of marque. Smacks of piracy, what?"

"I fear you're right," Biddlecomb said, not entirely certain of what he was agreeing with. He was not listening to Sotherby now, consumed as he was with how to save his and Rumstick's bacon.

They could not turn and run. The *Somerset* would pound them to kindling before they cleared Boston Harbor, and the blockading squadron was there to pick off anything that was left. They had to continue on as they were, but once they were in among the convoy, there was a good chance that they would be recognized. Biddlecomb did not imagine that the captain of the *Sussex* would soon forget him, nor the real Gideon Wetherell, who was no doubt aboard one of those ships. Still, there was a chance that they would not be noticed, particularly if they were made to anchor among the men-of-war. In that case only one other thing would mean certain and immediate disaster.

"Oh, look at this. The very man with whom you wish to speak," Sotherby said, sweeping the horizon with his glass. "Just beyond *Preston* there, there's the *Glasgow*. Good Lord, what's happened to her?"

Biddlecomb nodded his head. That was the one other thing.

As the *Charlemagne* had swung at her anchor in Lynn Bay, and Biddlecomb had sat in his tiny great cabin staring out the windows into the black night, Maj. Edward Fitzgerald had ridden his horse down the empty streets of Newport, sixty miles away.

He was going to avenge Captain Biddlecomb. That was not, of course, his primary objective. His primary objective was the eradication of a traitor, but as he considered his next move, it pleased him to think that vengeance for the death of an American officer was a part of it as well.

He assumed that Biddlecomb was dead, or on his way to England for trial, which for the captain was the same thing. He could do nothing to stop that, and he was sorry for it. In their brief time together he had come to like the man. He could, however, see that it did not happen to anyone else, and that he would most certainly do.

Somewhere in the city a bell rang out midnight, and from the fleet at anchor in Newport Harbor came the higher-pitched chime of ship's bells, ringing eight times each, four sets of two.

He felt his sword thump against his thigh and the silver buttons of his coat polishing themselves against his cloak. It felt good to be in uniform again, it felt honest, and that night's work was not the kind to be done in civilian dress. He turned his horse off Thames Street and began the uphill ride to Newport's more affluent neighborhoods, an area he had thoroughly scouted out during the long afternoons he had waited to see Truax.

Fitzgerald stopped his horse and dismounted two blocks from the Bowler home. He led the animal into a clump of trees and hitched the reins around a sapling, then walked the balance of the way, stepping from shadow to shadow. He took one last glance around before plunging into the alley beside the house, running his hand along the ivy-covered wall until he reached a wrought-iron gate. He lifted the latch and swung it open, just enough for him to step through, and thankfully it did not squeak.

A light was burning in a back room. Fitzgerald stepped up to the hedges around the back door and peered through the window and into the kitchen. The housekeeper was still awake, bustling around, straightening away the last of the day's work and preparing for the next. He watched her for a moment. She would scream bloody murder if he startled her, and that he did not need.

He stood for a moment in the darkness, then rapped gently on the back door. He heard the housekeeper stop. It was quiet. He knocked again.

"Who is it?" the housekeeper hissed through the door.

"Message for Mr. Bowler. From the Committee of Safety."

There was a pause, then, "The judge is asleep. Come back in the morning."

"This is urgent. The British are landing in Providence."

At that the latch to the door was lifted and the door swung open. Fitzgerald stepped into the warm, fragrant kitchen. "I don't want to disturb Mrs. Bowler, or the others."

"No others, sir. Mrs. Bowler and the girls is gone to New York and it's just me and the judge here now."

Now that's convenient, Fitzgerald thought. "Step over here a moment, please. I need a word with you first." He took the housekeeper by the arm and led her over to the open pantry door. "I need you to go in there for the time being."

"What?" was all the housekeeper had time to say before Fitzgerald pushed her into the pantry and slammed the door, dropping the latch in place.

After a moment's pause the door rattled as the housekeeper tried to open it. "Hallo," he heard her call, her voice muffled by the heavy wooden door. "Hallo!" she called again, louder this time. She began pounding on the door, and her cry of "Hallo!" turned to "Help!" Fitzgerald hoped she would not wake Bowler. He wanted some time before then.

He took the lantern that illuminated the kitchen and stepped through the door, closing it behind him. The housekeeper's frantic cries and pounding could scarcely be heard even in the next room.

He held the lantern above his head as he moved through the house. The dim light fell on beautiful hardwoods and rich upholstery, portraits and several ship models, but the major did not yet see what he was searching for. He stepped into the foyer. A wide staircase led up to the second floor where he imagined that Bowler was sleeping peacefully, untroubled by his own treacherous ways.

He moved past the staircase and through the door on the other side, leading, he discovered, to a library. The lantern illuminated a book-lined wall. At the far end of the room, dimly seen, was a fireplace, and above that the portrait of a stern-faced man peered out of the shadows. He seemed to be glaring at Fitzgerald, angry at the intrusion. Fitzgerald ran his eyes over the furniture placed around the room. A desk was pushed up against the wall opposite the bookshelves, its surface nearly lost under a pile of papers. That, he hoped, was it.

He crossed the room and set the lantern on the desk, and the swaying circle of light came to a rest. He grabbed a handful of papers and shuffled through them, but they contained nothing of interest. Bills of lading, manifests, business correspondence, all meaningless to one such as himself who was ignorant of the ways of commerce.

He pulled open the top drawer and rifled through the papers there. Again there was nothing beyond the routine paperwork of a prosperous businessman. The same was true of the second drawer. He tried the third, but it would not open. He picked up the lantern and held it near the face of the drawer. There was a keyhole, and the drawer was locked.

Fitzgerald crossed over to the fireplace and took the poker from the rack. He worked the tip of the poker in around the drawer, forcing it down until it had good purchase, then wrenched the drawer open. The still room was filled with the sound of splintering wood, and the front of the drawer was torn in two. Now, Fitzgerald thought, we'll see how sound the Honorable Judge Bowler's conscience allows him to sleep.

He set the lantern near the edge of the desk where it cast its yellow light into the now open drawer. More papers were in there, as well as various sticks of sealing wax and a heavy seal with a wooden handle. He snatched up the papers. They were letters mostly. There were no names, of course, or seals or any marks of identification. Fitzgerald read quickly, holding the papers up to the lantern. Requests for information concerning the workings of Rhode Island's Committee of Safety, requests for lists of those disloyal to the crown, official acknowledgment that the bearer has been of service to the crown, references to payments made. He wondered why Bowler had not burned these letters. Proof of his loyalty, perhaps, to be brought out after the British had won the war and those who had served on Committees of Safety were rounded up.

The stairs beyond the door creaked, a tiny noise that would

have been missed had the house not been as quiet as a tomb. Fitzgerald cocked his head and listened. There was nothing else, but he had heard enough. He dropped the papers and moved swiftly across the room. He pressed his back against the wall three feet from the door and waited.

The doorknob rattled, just a hint of a sound, as someone on the other side laid his hand on it, and then the door flew open, crashed against the wall, and bounced away, obscuring Fitzgerald's view of whoever was on the other side. He heard a gasp, a sharp intake of breath, as Bowler, it had to be Bowler, saw the lantern perched on the desk and the once-locked drawer now broken and hanging open.

Fitzgerald felt his muscles tense. The wounds in his side and his arm throbbed and ached. He was two feet from his enemy with the heavy door between them. He heard a step, soft and tentative, and then another. Around the edge of the door, glinting in the dim lantern light, he saw a cocked pistol. Fitzgerald stepped forward and brought his hand down on the gun, grabbing it between the flint and the pan and jerking it out of the gnarled hand that held it.

He stepped around the door and looked into Metcalf Bowler's startled eyes. His left hand shot out and grabbed Bowler by the collar of his robe and yanked him away from the door. He kicked the door closed with his foot as he spun Bowler around and shoved him into the middle of the room. The Speaker of the Rhode Island House of Representatives flailed around in the air, fighting to maintain his balance, then collapsed in a heap on the floor.

"Good evening, Judge Bowler." Fitzgerald eased the pistol's lock down and tossed the gun aside. "Stand up, please."

Bowler glared up at him as he scrambled to his feet, surprisingly lithe for a man of his years. "It's you. Fitzgerald. What in all hell do you think you're about? What are you doing?" The Speaker's anger and indignation were genuine and mounting rapidly. "You had better have a damn good explanation, God help you! General Washington will hear about this!"

"He most certainly will. I was going through your papers there. An interesting correspondence you keep."

"Correspondence I intercept, you calf! That is material of the most sensitive nature. I was this far from catching the traitor! The one who betrayed the Bermuda mission!" Bowler fairly yelled, holding up his thumb and forefinger to demonstrate the distance.

Fitzgerald could not help but smile. "I'll bet you were."

"How dare you come in here, destroy my desk—"

"This correspondence is yours, sir. Correspondence between you and the ministerial butcher to whom you are betraying your country. This letter here, is it from this Captain Wallace I hear about?"

"Get out of here at once, you whore's son! I'll have you arrested!" Bowler was shouting, no fear in his voice, just indignation. Fitzgerald was impressed. He stepped over to Bowler and again grabbed him by the collar, then shoved him against the wall by the desk.

"Stanton is the traitor, you idiot!" Bowler shouted. "Stanton and Rogers and that little whore daughter of his! I am on the verge of proving it!"

Fitzgerald pulled his sword from its scabbard, gritting his teeth at the pain that the sudden movement caused his wound, and touched the stiletto point to Bowler's neck. He took a step forward, cocking his arm, holding the metal to Bowler's throat. The old man's eyes danced in the lantern light, but defiance was still in them, pure defiance and hatred. Fitzgerald wanted to kill him then, but he could not. Bowler had to see one more thing. With his left hand he pulled Truax's letter from his coat pocket.

"Do you recognize this, sir? It looks like your hand, and the paper's the same as that in your desk. It was to be given to Captain Wallace. I took it from his coxswain."

"What is that? That's meaningless, nonsense! Any number of people have a hand like mine, how dare you? I am the Speaker of the Rhode Island House of Representatives, God

346

damn your eyes! You do not behave in this manner to me, you pup! You do not question my judgment!"

"This letter reports that Biddlecomb is bound for Charleston and suggests that Wallace send a ship to the port of Charleston to intercept him." Fitzgerald's voice took on a new tone as he worked to suppress his rage. "You were the only one, Mr. Speaker, who thought that. I told Governor Cooke that he was bound for France, and the Stantons that he was bound for Jamaica. You were the only one that thought that he was bound for Charleston. I made that up five minutes before we first spoke. Now, would you explain again that treasonous correspondence locked in your desk?"

Fitzgerald looked into Bowler's eyes, watched the gleam of reflected light as it danced across the wet surface. Bowler had the look now, the look of profound guilt, the look of desperation. His tongue flicked out and he licked his dry lips.

"I yield the floor to you, Mr. Speaker," Fitzgerald said softly. He was pressing his lips together hard, fighting down his revulsion. Bowler was a loathsome thing.

"You can't be my judge and jury." Bowler tried a new tack and his voice carried a hint of the old defiance. "I demand a trial, a jury trial. What are we fighting for? Justice, Major. Justice for all Americans."

"And we'll have that, Mr. Speaker," Fitzgerald said, his eyes locked into Bowler's. "After we win the war."

Fitzgerald straightened his arm and the needle point of his sword ripped through Bowler's throat. The Speaker's eyes bulged and his mouth opened as if to scream, but only a soft gurgling sound came out. Fitzgerald felt the point deflect off Bowler's spine and he drove the blade in farther. Blood pulsed from around the steel and ran thick from Bowler's mouth. Fitzgerald felt the sword give, then embed itself in the wall at Bowler's back.

Like a stuck pig, Fitzgerald thought, like a stuck pig. He watched Bowler flail in his final seconds of life, his mouth open, trying to scream through his torn throat, blood splat-

tering against the wall, and Fitzgerald thought of the old sim-
ile. That was exactly right. Like a stuck pig.

Fitzgerald tugged the blade free, twisted it, and cut sideways, tearing through Bowler's neck and jugular vein, sending
a fountain of dark blood over the desk and the wall. The
Speaker fell back and slumped to the floor, landing in a crumpled heap beside his desk. He did not move. He had died
while still on his feet.

Fitzgerald wiped his sword on the Honorable Judge Metcalf
Bowler's silk jacket and slid it back into its scabbard. He
snatched up the papers from the broken drawer and shoved
them into his coat, then picked up the lantern on the desk. He
now had only to let the poor housekeeper out of the pantry,
and his work in Rhode Island was done.

CHAPTER
30

The North American Squadron

VIRGINIA STARED OUT THE WINDOW OF HER FATHER'S STUDY, THE book she had gone in there to retrieve unopened in her hand, and watched Maj. Edward Fitzgerald riding slowly toward the house.

She could not make out his face—it was early and the sun would not show above the trees for another fifteen minutes—but his posture on horseback was unmistakable. This despite his being one hundred yards away, on the far side of the frozen lawn. She knew not three other men who looked as natural riding a horse as he did, even with his wounds.

She had been thinking about Major Fitzgerald, the tall, handsome equestrian, quite a bit of late. Wounded twice hunting down a traitor to his cause. And her cause. An officer on the staff of General Washington.

She was not one to flit mindlessly from one love to the next, out of control, letting her affections jerk her around like some marionette. She had loved no one but Isaac Biddlecomb since she was old enough to fall in love. And what good had it done her? Was her love requited?

This affection for the major was no idle flight of fancy. Edward was exciting. He was rich. He loved horses. He had involved her in his plans. She had relished her part in running the traitor to earth, even if her sense of decorum had forced

349

her to act scandalized at having been tricked into playing the whore. Yes, Edward excited her. As Isaac did.

But unlike Isaac, over whom she had been mooning for years, Edward was ready to show his affection, ready to profess his love for her. She could tell. She had seen it in his eyes when she attended him in his sickbed, and in the way he looked at her before riding off from Bristol Landing. She was not surprised to see him now. She had been anticipating this moment, when he would come back to her. And she was ready to accept his overtures.

She loved Isaac, no doubt always would, and she felt a twinge of guilt, thinking of another man while he was a prisoner of the British. Well, from now on she would love him as a brother. But as to the matter of a lover, she could not wait forever. She was getting no younger; she would be eighteen soon and she had to think of herself.

If Isaac had ever said that he loved her, had given her some assurance, then she knew she would never think of another, not even the wonderful Major Fitzgerald. But he had not. The closest he had ever come was the note from Bermuda, and that had been a sham.

With no real desire to do so, she ran through the letter in her mind. She had read the damn thing so many times she knew every word, every loathsome word.

" 'My beloved Virginia,' " she recited softly to herself in a mocking tone, " 'Before all else, I must tell you that I love you, as I have always said I love you, and' et cetera, et cetera, et cetera. What a pile of sodding rubbish. 'And feel your warm love against a cold night. I love you, please understand, despite. . . .' "

She stopped, and her eyes went wide and the book she was holding slipped out of her hands and fell to the floor. "Oh, my God," she whispered. She turned and fled from the drawing room as if something were chasing her, holding her skirts up as she ran, and raced up the stairs to the second floor.

"Virginia, are you all right?" she heard her father call.

"Yes, fine," she answered, flying down the hall and into her bedroom.

The letter was in her dresser; she had meant every day to burn it, but had never been able to bring herself to do so. She fished through her stockings until she found it and with trembling hands unfolded it and read it anew.

I know not when I will again hold you in my arms, and feel your warm love against a cold night. I love you, please understand, despite all that might seem madness, I truly love you.

Yours,

I. Biddlecomb

She smiled, and the smile turned into a laugh and the tears rolled with abandon down her face. " 'I love you, despite all that might seem madness, I truly love you,' " she said out loud. Why hadn't she seen it before? He *was* professing his love for her, assuring her that, as insane as the letter might sound, his love, at least, was genuine. More than just word of a traitor had been encrypted in that note.

So completely occupied was she with thoughts of Isaac that she said hardly a word at breakfast, despite the fact that Fitzgerald was there and had apparently completed the task for which he had come to Rhode Island. He deflected her father's questions with vague answers about reporting to Washington, but Virginia had a sense that the situation had been dealt with already, swiftly and mercilessly. And still she had a hard time thinking of anything but Isaac.

The morning was cold, too cold for snow. At Fitzgerald's request Virginia walked with him to the stables. They were alone, and she was in no doubt as to what the major had on his mind. It was the scene that she had anticipated with pleasure for the past day, right up until the moment she had smoked Isaac's hidden message, his other hidden message. How could she ever have doubted him, the love of her life?

She felt the sting on her cheeks and saw her breath come in

white clouds as Fitzgerald led his horse out of the stable. The major's gait was stiff, the wound in his side apparently aching.

"Are you in pain?" She felt suddenly awkward.

Fitzgerald stopped and turned to her. She stopped as well and he put a hand on her shoulder. She wondered if he might kiss her. She did not know what to say; she had no experience with this sort of thing.

"I've been better, to be sure, but I'm doing fine, after such tender ministrations. Seeing you is a big improvement."

She smiled and glanced away. "Perhaps you should spend the day here, recover your strength a bit before your ride."

"No, regrettably, I've been gone too long as it is. If I ride hard, I can be back in Cambridge early this afternoon. I'm anxious to get back to my duties."

"Well, I'm sorry." Virginia still enjoyed his company, his sense of humor, and his flattering remarks and attention. She was sorry that he was going away. But, she realized, not entirely.

"I'm sorry too, Virginia. Very sorry." He ran his hand down her back and pulled her close against his chest, then stroked her cheek, tilting her face up to his. He leaned toward her and she felt his cool lips on hers, kissing her with a gentleness that surprised her, and without thinking she kissed back. His hands were on her waist, drawing her close.

"I'm sorry, Edward." She pushed him back, pulling herself from his grasp. "You're wonderful, really, and I'm a fool, but . . ." No more words would come, so in their place she sighed.

Fitzgerald smiled, a brittle smile. "Is it Biddlecomb?"

Virginia smiled as well. With those three words Fitzgerald had released her from the difficulty of trying to explain. "Yes. I'm sorry."

"I understand." He smiled again, and then quite without warning he leaned forward and grabbed her around the waist with his left arm, pulling her close and kissing her again. She was startled, taken aback, but she returned his kiss, resting her hands on his broad shoulders, swept away by his passion. And then he released her.

"Good-bye, Virginia." This time his smile was raffish. "We'll meet again."

"You take great liberties, sir," Virginia said, but she was flustered and her tone did not convey the outrage that she had intended it to. Fitzgerald swung himself up onto his horse, still smiling, and with a kick of his spurs he wheeled around and rode off the way he had come.

She wrapped herself deeper in her cloak and watched him disappear as the road wound its way into the woods. He was handsome. He was charming and he was rich and he had devoted his life to a cause that was her cause as well, and she had sent him away.

She did not know when, if ever, she would see Biddlecomb again. She did not even know if he was still alive. But she had no other choice but to wait, not now, not with her love requited. If God granted her a second chance, she would not hold him at arm's length again, she would risk the last syllable of her dignity and tell him of the love that she had for him, the love she had always had for him. She turned and walked slowly back toward Stanton House.

Biddlecomb watched tiny Bird Island slip by to the north of them until it was hidden from his view by the great bulk of the HMS *Somerset*. It was the last piece of land, insignificant as it was, between the *Charlemagne* and the Royal Navy's North American Squadron moored in the port of Boston a little over a mile ahead. He put the signal glass to his eye and scanned the distant fleet, hoping something, anything, would suggest itself as a means of escape.

They were close enough now that the glass revealed all the details of activity in the port of Boston. The convoy was clustered around the Long Wharf. Some of the ships were tied up alongside, landing men and cargo. Others lay at anchor, their cargoes discharged and their empty hulls riding high in the water, revealing bands of white and green along their now exposed waterlines.

Biddlecomb turned the glass north to where the men-of-war lay. There was one big ship, a two-decker, and a frigate, the *Glasgow*. Her foremast was stripped bare of top-hamper and her jury-rigged bowsprit was gone, probably waiting for a permanent replacement, but still there was no mistaking that ship. He searched the other anchored vessels for some sign of the *Ant*, but he did not see the little sloop. No doubt she was in a dock somewhere, if she had made it back to Boston at all.

"We'd best get things laid along for anchoring, Wetherell," Sotherby said, but Biddlecomb heard only the sound of his voice, not the words. He was in the middle of the British fleet and there was no way out. If he could recognize the *Glasgow*, then it was a sure bet that anyone aboard the *Glasgow* would recognize the *Charlemagne*. It had been but eight days since they had parted from the convoy, and Biddlecomb knew William Maltby would not forget the *Charlemagne* in eight days or in eight years or eight decades, for that matter. His charade of being master of the *Mayor of Plymouth* was over before he even had an opportunity to play it out.

"Forgive me, Captain Wetherell," Sotherby said again, a bit louder this time, and Biddlecomb remembered that he was Wetherell and must remain so for as long as he could.

"What was that?"

"I say, we'd best lay things along for anchoring. We'll anchor up by the squadron. The two-decker's *Preston*, the flag, and I imagine Captain LeCras will want you anchored in her lee. You seem to have a bloody dearth of anchors here, what?"

"We had a bit of trouble in . . . Portsmouth," Biddlecomb said, then calling forward said, "Mr. Gardiner, pray ready the stream anchor for letting go."

What choice did he have but to anchor? If they tried to run for it, the *Somerset* would either pound them to death or drive them into the jaws of the blockading squadron. If he ran his ship into Long Wharf, there was a chance, a very slight chance, that they could escape. But most likely the British would hunt them down as they would have done in Bermuda, for like Bermuda, Boston was essentially an island, save for a narrow and heavily guarded strip of land. What was more, the British would have the *Charlemagne* and the *Mayor* with her cargo of powder. Washington would still be defenseless, and it would be only a matter of time before he was overrun. That thought was intolerable to Biddlecomb.

"Ahoy, *Charlemagne!*" a voice floated over the water from the Somerset's quarterdeck. "Anchor in our lee!"

Sotherby picked up the speaking trumpet. "Anchor in your lee, aye!"

Biddlecomb tried not to look as miserable as he felt. He heard the *Somerset*'s officer issue the same order to the *Mayor*. This was it. Once the anchors were planted on the bottom, then they were hooked like fish.

He looked around, feeling the desperation come over him like a rising tide. There was Boston, and beyond the town, brooding over all, were Breed's and Bunker Hills. Biddlecomb could see the scars in the ground where the American militia had dug in and fought on that June day almost five months before. The British were there now, occupying the redoubts that the Americans had dug, and the American troops had moved south, spread out along the Charles River and Back Bay. Plowed Hill and Cobble Hill were just visible beyond the city of Boston. Those two high points straddling the causeway leading to Charlestown formed the left flank of the American line, or so Biddlecomb had been led to believe.

And then a thought struck him, struck him like the concussion of cannon fire. Why should he try to sail out of Boston Harbor? He wanted to bring this powder to General Washington, and there he was, just three miles away, along with fifty thousand armed Americans. Well, perhaps not fifty thousand, but enough in any case to hold the British at bay.

He looked around, considering what had to be done, afraid that it was already too late. The *Somerset* might still pound them to kindling, but if the thing was timed to perfection, she would not get the chance. The *Glasgow* was going nowhere for a while, and the *Preston* had the look of a ship long on its mooring, and it took such a ship hours, not minutes, to get under way.

"Pass the word for Mr. Gardiner. Hurry," Biddlecomb said to Weatherspoon. In the twenty seconds that it took for Gardiner to come aft, Biddlecomb had made a decision.

"Mr. Gardiner, load number three gun, no shot, and tell the gun crew to stand ready to fire on my command. We're going to signal to the *Mayor*." The orders began to tumble out of Biddlecomb's mouth as the vacuous idea began to take solid form in his mind. "I want the best man with an ax standing by to cut the cable. Is that clear?"

"Aye, sir," said Gardiner, smiling with anticipation of he knew not what as he walked forward, quietly issuing orders.

"Excuse me, Captain, but what are you about?" Sotherby asked.

"Oh." In the flush of pending action Biddlecomb had forgotten about Sotherby. "I'm going to effect an escape, as it happens."

"You're . . . what?"

"Going to effect an escape. I'm sorry, truly, but I'll have to confine you below for the duration."

Sotherby did not reply, indeed he did not seem capable of speech, but rather stood there with his mouth hanging open.

"You two," Biddlecomb called out to two rather large members of the afterguard standing at the main topsail halyard. "Please take Mr. Sotherby below and confine him in the bread room, as . . . uh . . . politely as you can."

"Aye, sir," the afterguards said, stepping up behind Sotherby and seizing him by the shoulders.

"Are you mad?" the lieutenant shouted, finding his voice again.

"I'm sorry about this, but I really can't have you running around while I'm trying to do this thing. Go." This last was said to the afterguards, who in turn began to drag Sotherby forward, his heels striking black lines across the quarterdeck planking.

"You—," Southerby began to scream, then a hairy hand clapped over his mouth, cutting his pronouncement short.

"It's best if you was quiet now, sir," one of the seamen said as the lieutenant was pulled through the scuttle and disappeared below.

"Well, I reckon we'll never be friends now," Biddlecomb said to himself, then turning, continued, "Mr. Weatherspoon, do you recall the signal I devised for cutting the cable and running?"

"Ah, well, it's . . . ," the midshipman began to stammer.

"Loosen fore topsail and sheet home and fire a gun to weather. We're going to make that signal in a moment."

"Aye, sir."

They were in among the fleet now. The *Somerset*, still on the *Charlemagne*'s starboard side and one hundred yards away, was taking her place to windward of the flagship. Her courses and topgallants disappeared as the crowd of men along the yards fisted the canvas. Biddlecomb could see the best bower, over four tons of anchor, hanging from the larboard cathead. The two-decker began to round up into the wind, and Biddlecomb knew that the *Charlemagne* and *Mayor* were expected to round up with her, expected to anchor between the *Somerset* to windward and the *Preston* to leeward.

He heard the distant sound of shouting, of men cheering. The *Glasgow*'s sides and shrouds were crowded with her company and they were all yelling. Biddlecomb imagined that they were well pleased to see the *Charlemagne* again, caught between two ships of the line.

"Start rounding up, follow the *Somerset* around," he said to the *Charlemagne*'s helmsman, and the brig began to follow the two-decker up into the wind. Fifty yards astern Rumstick was following in their wake. "Clew up the topgallants and the foresail! Hands to the topsail gear!" he called forward.

The *Somerset*'s topsails began to ripple as the ship turned head to wind, and then the fore and main topsail halyards were let go and the yards came shooting down the topmasts, reducing the taut sails to gray, shapeless heaps of canvas tumbling over the tops. The mizzen topsail came aback and the great ship stopped in her wake, paused, and began to make sternway.

This was the moment, the critical moment, and Biddlecomb knew that his timing here would mean escape or death in the next hour. He saw a figure by the two-decker's cathead let the ring stopper fly, and then the best bower plunged into Boston Harbor, dragging the thick cable out of the hawsehole and down with it.

The *Charlemagne*'s topsails were beginning to flog as the brig came up into the wind. "Let go the sheets and clew up fore and main topsails! Clew them up! No, no, keep those halyards made fast! Take your hand off that halyard! Just clew the sails up to the yards!" It was not what the Charlemagnes expected; any competent captain would have let fly the fore topsail halyard and let the main topsail go aback. Biddlecomb hoped that Captain LeCras, watching from the *Somerset*, would dismiss what he was doing as stupidity. And he hoped that Rumstick was watching as well, because Rumstick would know that he was up to something.

The *Charlemagne*'s headway fell off until she too was stopped, hanging motionless between her forward momentum and the backward pressure of the wind. "Let go!" Biddlecomb called next, and the *Charlemagne*'s sheet anchor dropped from the cathead just as the brig began to make sternway.

He turned and looked over the taffrail at the *Mayor of Plymouth* astern. Rumstick had clewed down his fore and main topsails, and the *Mayor* was making sternway with a backed mizzen topsail. Her anchor would bite deep. That was the proper way to anchor if one was intending to stay put.

The men on the *Somerset*'s topsail yards were already putting the finishing touches on their elegant harbor furls, smooth bundles of canvas in the slings tapering out to fine white points at the yardarms. The captain's gig was lifting out of the stack of boats in the waist, and the marines were forming up at the gangway to see LeCras over the side. The *Somerset*'s anchor had not been on the bottom for five minutes, and already the ship was snugged down as if she had been there a month. This was the efficiency and elegance of a navy that had the advantage of over two hundred years of tradition and practice. Now Biddlecomb was going to show them the advantage of being a tag-and-rag upstart of whom little was expected.

"Sheet home the fore topsail! Number three gun, fire! Cut the cable! Cut it away!" he called at the top of his lungs. There was no need for stealth now. Number three gun went off with a roar and Gardiner's ax fell on the cable, rose and fell again, hacking quickly through the stiff hemp. The fore topsail was hauled down, the men at the sheets fighting with the sail now held aback by the wind.

Biddlecomb turned and looked at the *Mayor*. The merchantman's mizzen topsail collapsed like a piece of paper crumpled in a fist as the halyard was let fly, and the fore and main topsails were sheeted home. He saw the fore topmast staysail jerking up its stay where it would help turn the *Mayor* off the wind and get her under way again. He could picture Sprout hacking away at the anchor cable. Rumstick understood what they were doing, and he had reacted as if they had been planning it for a week.

Biddlecomb felt the *Charlemagne* slewing to larboard. He looked forward in time to see one end of the severed anchor cable disappear out of the hawsehole while the other end lay limp on the deck. The brig's fore topmast staysail was going up as well, and three men held it aback as the wind on the canvas pushed the *Charlemagne*'s head around.

"Hands to braces! Sharp starboard tack!" he called, and the fore topsail filled with wind. "Sheet home the main topsail! Sheet home the topgallants! Sheet home the foresail! Hands aloft to set stu'n's'ls!" He felt wild, reckless, and exhilarated.

"*Mayor*'s acknowledging the signal, sir," Weatherspoon shouted. Rumstick would not ignore a naval formality, unnecessary though it might be.

The *Somerset*'s deck was swarming with men and the air around the ship was filled with shouting and the shrill scream of bosun's calls. It looked and sounded like bedlam, like utter confusion, but Biddlecomb was not fooled by the appearance. The two-decker had a well-trained and disciplined crew, and he knew that his perfect timing had bought him at best a few minutes and a couple of hundred yards.

The larboard and starboard shrouds of the big man-of-war were black with men swarming aloft to loosen sail, and in the beakhead he could see a gang of men buoying the cable in preparation to slip. Behind her wooden walls he knew that hundreds more were clearing away the main batteries. In ten minutes at most they would be ready to fire, three-quarters of a ton of metal ready to tear his brig apart. If he allowed the *Charlemagne* or the *Mayor of Plymouth* to get under those guns, then they would be swept from the face of the earth in one broadside. He had caught LeCras with his breeches down, but it was only a matter of minutes before he would have them up again.

The wind was northeasterly and brisk. They would be sailing large clear to the American lines, and that was as good as Biddlecomb could hope for. The *Preston* seemed to sweep past the bow as the *Charlemagne* turned, and then the *Mayor of Plymouth* came into view. The merchantman's fore, main, and mizzen topsails were sheeted home, and hands were tailing onto the halyards, the sails spreading flat as they were hoisted. The *Charlemagne* would pass between the *Mayor* to larboard and the stern of the *Preston* to starboard, and the *Preston* would shield them, for the time being, from the *Somerset*'s guns. Then, with the *Mayor* in their wake, they would run northwest around Boston and south through the Charles River to Cambridge. Simple.

Biddlecomb smiled to himself, as much a grimace as a smile. He had enough naval experience by now to know the difference between such theory and practice.

The *Mayor of Plymouth* was sailing parallel to them and crowding on sail. The *Somerset* had slipped her cable, and already the fore topsail was set aback and the huge man-of-war was making her ponderous turn, ready to fly in pursuit. With all of her plain sail set she would be much faster than any inconsequential brig or tubby merchantman. They had to distance themselves from the two-decker now, while they still could.

In the waist the Charlemagnes not engaged in setting studdingsails were starting to mill about, and Biddlecomb could see the worried looks on their faces. They had to be kept busy. He stepped up to the quarterdeck rail.

"Mr. Gardiner, get a party together and start the fresh water. I want every drop pumped overboard, save for the scuttle on deck. Woodberry, break open the hatch and start jettisoning the food, and all the carpenter's stores, bosun's stores, whatever can go over. Sail trimmers, remain at stations! Go!"

The men moved to comply with his orders. The work would keep them busy and it would make the *Charlemagne* faster and lighter, easier to maneuver over the shoals and mud that awaited them on the other side of the Boston peninsula.

And then the *Somerset* fired, unleasing a full broadside, something Biddlecomb had been certain she would not do. The sound of the screaming metal, the crash of wood, the horror wrought by the twenty-four- and thirty-two-pound guns was many times worse than any broadside he had ever experienced. Eight feet of bulwark by the foremast collapsed like a sand castle, and two guns were tossed to the deck.

Biddlecomb looked to larboard at the *Mayor*. Her mizzen gaff was hanging like a broken wing, and a section of her bulwark was crushed. One unlucky shot among all that powder and she would go up in an awesome display of fireworks.

He looked back at his own command. Half-leaning against the fore fife rail was the day's first fatality, a young man in the starboard watch. Just the day before Biddlecomb had been discussing with him the charms of his native Gloucester. Now his shirt and slop trousers were wet with blood and a long oak splinter jutted from his chest. His lifeless eyes were open and staring aloft. And this was only the first broadside.

Biddlecomb had thought that LeCras would not have the nerve to fire with the *Charlemagne* right under the flagship's stern. Obviously he had underestimated LeCras's nerve. But now the two-decker was turning, taking up the chase, and her main battery would not bear. A bow chaser went off, the thunder of the long gun seeming insignificant in the wake of the broadside. Biddlecomb saw a hole appear in his main topsail.

"Come starboard," he said to the helmsman. "Make your head to pass around the north end of the town."

The *Charlemagne* ducked under the *Preston*'s stern, and now the flagship served as a floating wall between the brig and the *Somerset*'s terrible broadsides. To larboard the *Mayor* was following them around, and in a second she too was shielded from the two-decker.

"Mr. Weatherspoon, do you still have that ensign, the pine tree with AN APPEAL TO HEAVEN?"

"Oh, yes, sir," Weatherspoon said, smiling.

"Good. Run it up to the gaff, if you would."

As Weatherspoon dug into the sack of flags, Biddlecomb looked west over the larboard side. They were three miles from the American lines, and to get there they had simply to outrun the *Somerset*, dodge the North Battery at the end of the Boston peninsula, and run through the plunging artillery fire from the British positions on Breed's Hill. Then they would be safe, if there was not another man-of-war in the Charles River on the west side of the city. He reminded himself that he had formulated this entire plan over the span of thirty seconds. Three miles. It would be a long three miles indeed.

CHAPTER
31

Back Bay

SOMETHING WAS HAPPENING, SOME EXCITEMENT, AND MAJOR FITZ-gerald was suddenly afraid that after months of inactivity he had been absent for the first real action on the Continental line. He passed through the fortifications around Prospect Hill and approached the great sail tents under which the 21st Massachusetts Regiment from Marblehead lived at the base of the recently fortified Cobble Hill. The camp was deserted; not even a sentry remained to question his passage, and the tools with which the men had been improving the redoubts had been left discarded on the fresh mounds of turned earth.

He pulled his horse to a stop. He was tired and his wounds ached terribly. It was two o'clock in the afternoon, and he had been awake since eleven o'clock the night before. Not that that in itself would have worn him down, but as it happened, he had undertaken an inordinate amount of activity in that time and had just lost a fair amount of blood.

He had left Bristol an hour after dawn and rode the sixty miles back to Cambridge. Bowler was dead. He had thrashed out his life on the end of Fitzgerald's sword. It did not make Fitzgerald feel good or relieved or particularly heroic. He had not fought Bowler, he had murdered him, but he had no moral qualms about murder for a higher good. One more obstacle in the way of American independence was gone, like smoothing out a lump in a bedspread. He did not know how to categorize his feelings; satisfied, perhaps, but that was not quite it.

He turned his horse off the main road and headed up toward the redoubt at the summit of Cobble Hill. He had been making his way to the American left flank, seeking out General Washington, when he found the Twenty-first's deserted camp.

Not until he actually entered the redoubt did he see the Twenty-first, all two hundred or so men, looking more like a man-of-war's crew on a run ashore than like a regiment of infantry. They stood along the top of the earthen wall, looking out toward Boston Harbor, their loose white trousers flapping in the breeze, their tarred queues hanging down their backs. Scattered among them were the artillerymen who maintained the eighteen-pound guns on Cobble Hill, a heterogeneous band assembled from the many units along the line.

He reined to a halt and slid down from his horse, but still no one noticed his coming, so engrossed were they in the spectacle beyond. He stepped up on the mound of earth, his much abused body protesting every move, and shouldered the men aside.

"Hey, watch your sodding arse, Jack," a private said, then noticing Fitzgerald's uniform, muttered, "Oh, beg pardon, sir."

Fitzgerald did not expect a salute, and the man's grudging apology was more than he could have hoped for three months ago in the way of respect, so he let it go and instead asked, "Where is Colonel Glover?"

"Off to headquarters, or somewhere. Sir," the man said with a shrug.

"Beg pardon, Major." Someone had pushed his way up to the redoubt behind Fitzgerald, and the major turned to see who was addressing him. The man who spoke was wearing a long brown homespun coat and white breeches. A red cockade was on his cocked hat. "I'm Captain Carlisle, Twenty-first Massachusetts, I'm senior officer here. Uh, I apologize for not seeing you arrive, sir."

The captain was in his late twenties perhaps and seemed to display more military bearing than his men, though, indeed, it would be hard to do otherwise. "Your sentries didn't see me either, Captain, as they're not at their posts. Nor for that matter is anyone else."

"Sorry, sir. We've had a bit of excitement up here, in the naval line, sir, and as most of the men in the Twenty-first use the sea, it's a bit of a distraction."

Fitzgerald wanted to order the men down from the redoubt, but his own curiosity stood firmly in the way. "Show me, Captain."

Carlisle led Fitzgerald to the top of the earthworks, ordering his men aside in a loud voice calculated to demonstrate his command of the situation. The vista that lay before Fitzgerald was a familiar one, one that he had seen almost every day for the past four months, but one that he was used to seeing from Prospect Hill, half a mile behind him. By taking and fortifying Cobble Hill the Americans had pushed their lines closer to the Charles River and Boston and brought both within range of their big guns. He looked past marshy Lechmere Point below them and over the far-flung harbor beyond, trying to see what had caused this great excitement, but all looked as tranquil as it always did.

"There, sir, you see the Royal Navy squadron, just off Hancock's Wharf?" Carlisle pointed toward the east side of the town of Boston, two miles away. Fitzgerald followed his finger. He could see a great many ships there, but none that he could identify as those of the Royal Navy.

"Uh, yes, I suppose," he equivocated.

"There, sir, see that bloody big one, setting sail as fast as ever she can?"

This time Fitzgerald could see which ship Carlisle meant. It was one of the few that had sails set, and it was far bigger than most. "Yes, I see it now."

"Here, sir." Carlisle offered Fitzgerald a telescope, which the major took and held to his eye, twisting the tube until the distant ships were in focus. He could see the big one now, the yellow and black sides, the square holes out which the guns were run, the huge white ensign with its red cross streaming from the staff mounted at the back.

"That's the *Somerset*, sir, sixty-eight guns. After the *Boyne*, she's the biggest ship in North America," Carlisle continued his patient explanation. "She just came to anchor, with that little brig and the other ship in her lee, then they all got under way again, and the bloody *Somerset* fired a full broadside, at the other two, I reckon. I've never seen the like."

"What other two, Captain?" Fitzgerald asked, still squinting through the glass.

"Just move the glass to the left a bit, sir. See them now?"

Fitzgerald did as he was told. He saw another ship, almost as big as the *Somerset*, but that one was not moving. And then he saw the two that Carlisle meant. They were diminutive in comparison to the *Somerset*; one in fact had but two masts. A brig, if he recalled the nomenclature, or a snow. Only seamen such as those of the Twenty-first would have noticed this tiny drama.

The two smaller ships were also carrying a lot of sail, or so it seemed to Fitzgerald. He considered how to pose the question without sounding as ignorant as he was. "They have quite a bit of sail set, do they not?"

"All they have, sir. Stu'n's'ls aloft and alow," Carlisle noted, which did nothing to clarify the situation for Fitzgerald.

"What're they about, Captain?" Fitzgerald asked, taking the glass from his eye. "I confess I don't have a tolerable idea what's going on."

"Nor do I, sir. The brig and that little ship are running like smoke and oakum and the *Somerset*'s blasting away right in the middle of the anchored fleet, so she must want to stop them something fierce. All I can think is the brig and the ship were prizes, and now they're running for it."

"Indeed," said Fitzgerald, his interest mounting as he began to better understand the situation. He put the glass back to his eye and surveyed the smaller vessels. A flag was going up on the brig. He could not make out with certainty any details; the flag was more often than not streaming straight at him, and

366

at that distance it was but a smudge of color in the glass; but he could make out vaguely the flag's pattern. It was a white field, and in the center was a dark spot and a bold line above that. Perhaps a line, or perhaps a series of words. Perhaps the words AN APPEAL TO HEAVEN above a pine-tree motif. And suddenly the distant, silent chase was very interesting indeed.

Biddlecomb heard the *Somerset*'s bow chaser go off. The main topsail jerked and another charred hole appeared in the bunt. He had fought temptation long enough; he turned and looked at the man-of-war in his wake.

She was less than a quarter mile astern and closing. Her great mountain of canvas sails loomed over them, her topgallants and their attendant studdingsails nearly two hundred feet above her deck. Her bow was breasting the green water of Boston Harbor and flinging it aside in a white, frothy wave as she bore down on her insolent offender. He had pushed his luck too far this time. This time he would die, and he would take the companies of two ships with him.

But he would not hang. He had learned that much aboard the *Ant*; he would not be a prisoner again. If he was going to take these men to their death, it would be a fighting death, not the slow spectacle of a public execution, calculated to be an example to others. Biddlecomb could not put the fear down, not entirely, but the remorse was gone. The men on the *Charlemagne* and the men on the *Mayor of Plymouth* would follow him, if need be to a violent death, because he was leading them there.

He turned his back on the *Somerset* and looked forward, past the *Charlemagne*'s bow to the north end of Boston. One quarter mile more and they would turn that corner and be shielded, for a few moments anyway, from the *Somerset*'s guns.

He heard another gun go off, not from the two-decker, but away to the west and closer. He looked over the larboard side, past the *Mayor of Plymouth*, which was directly abeam and fifty yards away, toward Boston. Another gun fired, the blast of gray smoke marking the position of the North Battery, the first obstacle in the gauntlet through which they were being chased. The officer in command of the battery would see that a British ship was in a running fight with two other vessels and deduce that the two vessels were enemies to be stopped.

The fine curve of the *Mayor*'s mainsail was gone in a flash, and in its place was flogging canvas blowing down to leeward; a lucky shot from the North Battery had shot out the *Mayor*'s main tack. The prize crew flung themselves to sheets and clew garnets and hauled the sail up to the yard.

Rumstick stood on the *Mayor*'s quarterdeck, beside the helmsman. He waved and Biddlecomb waved back, as if they were on a yachting holiday, and the friendly gesture made their situation seem that much more unreal.

The guns of the North Battery roared out again, like the voice of an angry God. The *Charlemagne* shuddered as the heavy shot, four in all, crashed into her side. "Larboard guns, fire as you bear!" Biddlecomb called out. The gunners, well trained under Jaeger's tutelage, took careful aim, sighting along the nine-foot barrels, working the quoins in and out before bringing the match down on the touchholes. Biddlecomb saw clouds of dust kicked up from the North Battery as the six-pound shot struck home.

The Battery fired again, the distant guns silently belching smoke. Biddlecomb heard the scream of the shot and the sound of cracking wood, like a dry twig snapping, then trailing behind the iron came the dull sound of the gunfire.

He looked forward, past the deep belly of the foresail. The jibboom was shot halfway through. It lifted up, pulled by the strain of the jib, distorted like a broken nose, and then the last tenacious fibers of wood and rope parted and the spar fell away, disappearing from his sight below the bow. "Mr. Gardiner, send some men forward and cut that wreckage away!" he shouted.

The *Somerset* fired her bow chaser, as if to remind them that she was still there. She was firing on the *Mayor of Plymouth* now, but Biddlecomb could not see any damage that she might have done. The *Charlemagne*'s larboard battery began again with their ragged broadside, each gun firing as fast as its crew could load and run out. They could not hurt the Battery on-shore, but perhaps the gunners there would not aim with as much aplomb if they themselves were under fire.

The men at number two gun ran the weapon out, the gun captain squinted down the line of the barrel, then stepped back and shook his head. They were past the North Battery, past where the big guns could reach them. They had sailed through the first circle of hell and suffered only a smashed jibboom, which would slow them down some, but not stop them. He looked over at the *Mayor* and she too seemed intact. And they were half a mile closer to safety.

Fitzgerald watched, transfixed like the men of the Twenty-first, as the distant battle played itself out. The fight was silent, save for the faint sound of the guns that was carried on the wind long after the shots had been fired. It all seemed to hap-pen with an agonizing slowness, though he imagined it did not seem that way to the men on the ships.

"What do you make of this now?" he asked Captain Carlisle, still standing beside him.

"Like I figured before, sir. Those two, the brig and the mer-chantman, they're running from the *Somerset*, and I reckon they're trying to get to the American lines. Trying to get to the Charles River and maybe up to Cambridge would be my best guess."

"Will they make it?"

"No. The *Somerset*'ll most likely overhaul them, but even if she doesn't, the frigate'll stop them."

"What frigate is that?"

"There, sir." Carlisle pointed down and to their right. At the base of Cobble Hill, past the marshy area of Lechmere Point, the mouth of the Charles River was a wide expanse of water, bordered on one side by the peninsula of Boston, and on the other by the series of hills occupied by the American line. Halfway between Boston and the Army of the United Colonies, sailing slowly north, was yet another man-of-war, smaller than the *Somerset,* but big enough.

"Frigate's always there, sir, to make certain we don't attack Boston over the water."

Fitzgerald knew that, and he silently admonished himself for forgetting. It had been so long since they had considered an offensive against the city that it had slipped his mind.

"But don't they see the frigate?" Fitzgerald heard snickers along the redoubt and men nudged each other, and he knew he had asked a particularly stupid question.

"No, sir, the city's in the way. They won't see the frigate until they round Barton's Point, the northwest point there of the city. By the look of it, they'll run smack into her when they come around."

Fitzgerald looked over the scene below. It was obvious, now that he had been told, that the two smaller ships were ignorant of the frigate's existence. And when they came around the point, the frigate would be right there in front of them, with the other man-of-war right on their heels. They were trapped, and they did not yet know it.

And suddenly Fitzgerald felt anxious that they should not be trapped, that they should get away. Whoever they were on those two ships, they were enemies of the British, and that meant they were friends of his. They had fought valiantly so far against heavy odds, running through the North Battery's cannonade, trying desperately to outsail the two-decker. He could not let them be trapped by that arrogant frigate that flaunted Britain's naval superiority, patrolling the Charles River as if the Continental line posed not the slightest threat.

Fitzgerald felt himself growing angry and frustrated to be stuck onshore with no chance to help, and he began to understand the sentiments that were passing among the men of the Twenty-first, men of the sea. But they were not without any ability to help, not entirely.

"That frigate will have to pass less than a mile from us, will she not?"

"She will," Carlisle agreed. "More like half a mile, or maybe a little more."

"What's to prevent us from firing on her?"

Carlisle looked at Fitzgerald, and it was clear from his expression that firing on the frigate had not occurred to him. "We've had orders to hold our fire, sir. We're not to shoot the great guns."

Then they would ask permission of the ranking officer, Fitzgerald thought, then he realized, with a start, that he was the ranking officer. No one was there to whom he could defer; any action taken would be on his authority, any consequences his to bear. It would be easy enough, of course, to locate someone of higher authority, and Fitzgerald knew that he should, but he told himself there was no time. And even as he came to that conclusion, he knew that he was kidding himself, and he did not care. He wanted to act, and he would. He would not risk the chance of someone of higher authority saying no. He felt a surge of apprehension, and a surge of elation. He could not equivocate now.

"We'll shoot the great guns, on my authority," Fitzgerald said, committing himself entirely. "Send a company over to Prospect Hill with a wagon and fetch more powder, enough for ten more rounds per gun. My compliments to Captain Bosworth of the Twelfth New Hampshire, and tell him to form up his battalion and stand ready. Get the artillerymen to their stations and form up the Twenty-first by company. We have a great deal to do." Fitzgerald looked out over the harbor as Carlisle began to bark orders. If the British are going to win another victory here, he thought, then they will pay for it, as they paid for it on Bunker Hill.

Biddlecomb felt an uneasy satisfaction as he looked around him. Once clear of the North Battery's guns, he had turned the *Charlemagne* northwest to skirt the Boston waterfront as close as he could, sailing, as the expression went, with one foot on the beach. Now they passing Greenough's Wharf and Verin's Wharf at the northeast end of the city with less than twenty feet of water between the *Charlemagne* and the docks. The *Mayor of Plymouth* was in their wake, thirty feet astern, and the *Somerset* three hundred yards behind her.

The North Battery, far from being a threat, now stood between them and the *Somerset,* and they would not be under the two-decker's guns until she had cleared that obstacle. Even then the *Charlemagne* and the *Mayor* could continue to duck out of the big ship's line of fire as they rounded the top of the city. Biddlecomb felt his stomach untwist a quarter turn. They might make it after all. There was a chance.

The *Charlemagne* flew past Hudson's Point and into the wide-open water above the Mill Pond at the north end of Boston, the *Mayor* still in her wake. He looked over the starboard side, north toward Charlestown. There were batteries on Breed's Hill, looming over that city, just half a mile away. They could, if they so chose, subject the *Charlemagne* and the *Mayor* to a devastating cannonade, plunging fire. He swept the redoubts with his glass but could see no sign of activity there. Perhaps they had not seen the distant fight or did not want to risk dropping round shot on the town of Boston where their commander in chief made his home.

The bang of a twenty-four pounder, the high-pitched shriek of flying metal, told him that the *Somerset* had broken out into open water. He turned to look. She was clear of Hudson's Point, clear of the land, and pursuing them over the mouth of the Mill Pond where she enjoyed the advantage of greater speed. She fired again and the *Mayor*'s starboard main topmast studdingsail was torn to rags.

He turned his back on the two-decker. Barton's Point was straight ahead, only seven hundred yards away. They could round it close, and once again the land would shelter them from the *Somerset*'s guns. What was more, mud flats extended out five hundred feet from the point. If LeCras knew about the mud, then he would give the point a wide berth and fall farther behind. If he did not, then he would run aground. Even with the tide as high as it was, there would not be enough water for the two-decker to pass close to the point, while the

Charlemagne and the *Mayor*, with their shallower drafts, would just make it. Or so he hoped.

The *Somerset* fired again, the sound followed by a prolonged, sickening crack aloft. The *Charlemagne*'s main topgallant mast leaned to starboard, farther and farther, then collapsed, tearing a gash in the main topsail as it flailed about at the end of the remaining shrouds.

"Damn! Damn it to hell!" Biddlecomb shouted. He had been envisioning their escape, like a fool, instead of considering what to do in a case such as this. Men were already scrambling aloft, axes stuck in their belts, to cut the wreckage away. This was real damage and it would slow them down. But in their favor were the shallows around Barton's Point and the mud flats all the way to Cambridge, mud flats that he knew and could play to his advantage. It would be a close thing.

The *Somerset* fired twice more and missed both times before the *Charlemagne* reached Barton's Point. The loss of the topgallant sail slowed the brig; Rumstick had had to alter course to avoid running them down, but the *Somerset* had turned north to avoid the shallows and the gap between the foxes and the hound grew wider.

Biddlecomb watched Barton's Point slip by, fifty feet off the larboard beam. He held his breath, staring over the side, waiting for the telltale jerk as the flying brig ran aground. He felt a nudge, just the slightest catch as the keel hit mud, and then they were past, around the point and in deep water again, the *Mayor* still with them.

Beyond the larboard bow was the wide Charles River, the last stretch to the American lines and safety. Lechmere Point was straight ahead, across the mouth of the Back Bay, and more and more of the distant shore became visible as they rounded the point. He smiled, and then he saw the frigate.

He froze in his place, staring, and felt his stomach twist up again. She was the size of the *Glasgow* at least and less than five hundred yards away, sailing straight for them. Suddenly the entire situation was altered, and what tiny advantage he had wrung out of shaving Barton's Point was more than lost. They were caught between two men-of-war.

A spout of water shot up between the *Charlemagne* and the frigate, and Biddlecomb heard the muffled sound of heavy guns firing from some distance. He glanced up at the shoreline. A long cloud of smoke was lifting off a distant hill where a line of artillery had just fired. He had thought that the American lines extended as far as Lechmere Point, but obviously they did not. The *Charlemagne* and the *Mayor* were trapped not just between two men-of-war, but between the ships and the British battery onshore, whose long guns were already reaching out toward them.

The *Somerset* had turned more northerly, skirting the shallows. She was five hundred yards away, her two decks of guns loaded and run out.

"Oh, no" was all he had a chance to say before the *Somerset* fired her full broadside, thirty-four guns going off at once. The *Mayor of Plymouth*'s fore topgallant mast was swept away like a twig casually brushed aside. The *Charlemagne* shook beneath his feet as the shot struck home, his ears filled with the crush of wood and the screams of men and flying metal. The starboard cathead and a four-foot section of bulwark were gone, and lying among the torn wreckage was a crushed and bleeding shape that a second before had been a living man. The mainmast had a scar five inches deep, jagged shards of wood sticking out at odd angles. The mast would not survive another hit like that.

This was as far as they went, the *Charlemagne* and the *Mayor of Plymouth.* They would not surrender, never again. They would try to sail out of this trap, and failing that they would make their stand here; they would fight it out on this piece of water on the Back Bay, and here they would die. Biddlecomb could see no other conceivable option.

CHAPTER
32

The Continental Line

"GOOD, TWO AT LEAST STRUCK HOME," FITZGERALD SAID, STARING at the frigate through Carlisle's glass. He knew he was talking loud, but it was difficult to hear even his own voice after the deafening sound of the entire Cobble Hill battery going off at once. The artillerymen, augmented by the Twenty-first Massachusetts, were already running their guns up to the redoubt for the next shot. The men's grim faces were punctuated here and there with smiles as they worked the artillery. Their former sense of helplessness, like Fitzgerald's, was replaced now with the satisfaction of fighting back.

"Careful with the aim! Take your time!" Fitzgerald called down the line. "It does us no good to hit the water!" He watched the captain of each gun sight down his barrel and call for adjustments to the gun's lie. He was grateful for the care they were taking. His neck was firmly on the block for this waste of gunpowder; if nothing was gained by it, then the ax would undoubtedly fall.

One gun fired, red flames shooting from the muzzle as it leapt back on the big wheels of the field carriage, then another and another and then the entire battery. Fitzgerald watched the frigate just beyond Lechmere Point, three-quarters of a mile away. It was a long shot, but far from impossible, certainly not when firing from the high ground of Cobble Hill. He saw

375

flashes of white marking where the iron shot fell into the Charles River.

And then he saw that something was different about the frigate, her profile was altered somehow. As he turned to mention it to Carlisle, he heard a man cheer, and the yell was quickly taken up along the entire redoubt until the cheering seemed as loud as the gunfire.

"Knocked her main topgallant mast off, sir!" Carlisle explained as the cheering died out and the men turned to reloading the guns.

"Will that stop her?"

"No, but it'll slow her down. And now she knows we're here."

"Good." Fitzgerald reached out for the glass. He wanted them to know that the American line was there. They no longer held dominion, the arrogant bastards, over all that they surveyed.

"Fire!" Biddlecomb shouted, and the larboard battery unleased its pitiful broadside against the frigate, flailing out even as they faced their destruction. The frigate's spritsail yard was cut in two and Biddlecomb saw a ball plow through the stack of boats in her waist. In the distance, like muted thunder, he heard the British battery on Cobble Hill fire down on them.

The *Mayor* was twenty yards astern, and Lechmere Point was less than a quarter mile off the starboard beam as the two vessels sailed line ahead, sailing southwest toward where the Charles River turned and ran up to Cambridge. The *Somerset* was four hundred yards astern, just working her way around the mud flats off Barton's Point.

Then, to Biddlecomb's great surprise, the frigate's main topgallant mast began to topple over. He put his glass to his eye and surveyed the damage. The doubling where the topmast met the topgallant was shattered, torn apart, and one by one the topgallant shrouds parted and the long mast fell, tearing braces and stays as it went. Both masts were destroyed, and that destruction had not been wrought by the *Charlemagne's* pathetic six-pounders.

He looked up toward Cobble Hill, a round green hump looming over Lechmere Point. A cloud of smoke was rising from the earthworks there, revealing the brown redoubts on the ridge, and he understood. They were not shooting at the *Charlemagne* at all, they were shooting at the frigate. That was not a British battery on the crest, it was the American line.

The *Somerset* fired again, her full broadside tearing up the water around the *Charlemagne* and crushing the transom below Biddlecomb's feet. He looked over at the *Mayor*, now between the *Charlemagne* and the *Somerset*. The merchantman had taken the worst of that broadside. Her mizzen topmast was gone, snapped in two, and it had dragged the main topgallant mast down with it. Her fore topgallant had been cut away ten minutes before. She did not have much left.

The *Somerset* cleared the mud flats and turned south, pointing her wide bow toward the *Charlemagne* and the *Mayor*, running down on them, coming to finish them off. Biddlecomb clenched his teeth and grabbed the caprail with both hands. LeCras thought he had them trapped, but LeCras was wrong. Now they had a place to go.

He would let the *Somerset* run down on them; as long as she was chasing them, she could not bring her broadside to bear. Then the *Charlemagne* and the *Mayor* would tack together and pass down the *Somerset's* side, and if they endured that one point-blank broadside, they would run the two ships aground at the base of Cobble Hill, as if laying an offering at the feet of the American army.

"Mr. Weatherspoon," he said. "Make this signal to the *Mayor of Plymouth:* 'Tack in succession.' "

"Beg your pardon, sir," Carlisle spoke, and Fitzgerald tore his eyes from the battle at his feet.

"Yes, Captain?"

"Sir, I reckon the frigate's pretty well knocked about and I

377

think the *Somerset,* the big one there, is more of a threat to those two. And she should be in range now."

Fitzgerald looked to his left. The big ship, the *Somerset,* had turned south and was closing in on the two smaller ships, closing the trap that the men on Cobble Hill had seen set thirty minutes before. She was in range, and she was a larger target. He hoped they could knock her to pieces. "Very good, Captain, shift your target to the *Somerset.*"

Carlisle called the order down the line of artillery. "Fire at will!" he sang out, and instantly half of the guns went off, followed, one after another, by the rest of the battery. Fitzgerald put the glass to his eye and stared at the *Somerset.* A part of the bulwark was smashed and there appeared to be a jagged hole in the deck just behind the foremast. The activity on deck, coupled with the distance, made the big man-of-war look very much like an anthill freshly kicked apart.

Biddlecomb now knew with certainty that he had friends on Cobble Hill, friends who understood the fight in which he was engaged. They had turned their big guns on the *Somerset* as she bore down on the *Charlemagne* and the *Mayor* and were firing with some effect. Biddlecomb was certain that at least two of the shots had struck home, plunging fire from overhead that struck the *Somerset* not on her thick sides but on her relatively fragile deck. He hoped that this new assault would send them into some disarray.

The *Somerset* was now three hundred yards away and coming down fast, quickly overhauling the damaged Americans. They had to come about. Another two minutes on their present heading would place them under the frigate's broadside.

"Hands to the braces! We're going to tack!" Biddlecomb shouted, and the sail trimmers left the guns where they had been assisting and took up their bowlines and braces. The *Mayor of Plymouth* was twenty yards astern, a red pennant at the main topmast head.

"*Mayor* acknowledges the signal, sir," Weatherspoon said.

Biddlecomb drew a long breath, held it, then let it out, calling, "Helm's alee!" as he did.

The *Charlemagne* began to turn, swinging to larboard. The sound of flogging canvas came aft as the fore topmast staysail was let go. The *Mayor* was turning as well, her headsails also flogging as she rounded up into the wind. The *Somerset* was two hundred yards away, rolling down on them like an avalanche, her long guns jutting from her sides. Biddlecomb hoped that his sudden tack would take LeCras at least a bit by surprise.

"Mainsail, haul!" he called out as overhead the square sails began to luff. Even with her main topgallant mast gone, the *Charlemagne* was still nimble, and she turned fast through the wind. The *Mayor* was around as well, turning slowly with her much-battered rig.

The two ships were now on the starboard tack, sailing straight at the *Somerset* like jousting knights, their bowsprits and jibbooms lances held before them. Less than a hundred yards separated the Americans and the two-decker. They would pass within twenty feet of each other, and Biddlecomb knew that the *Somerset* would unleash a fury such as he had never seen. He clasped his hands behind his back and tried not to think of what was coming. If they lived through it, then there would be nothing but water between them and the base of Cobble Hill.

The *Somerset* was fifty yards away, the distance falling off, when the *Mayor of Plymouth*, directly ahead of the *Charlemagne*, began to turn, her bow pointing closer to the wind.

"Ezra, what the hell . . . ," Biddlecomb muttered to himself. On that heading the *Mayor* would cross the *Somerset*'s bow, assuming that Rumstick had turned in time.

And then he realized what Rumstick was about. He was going to pass down the *Somerset*'s larboard side while the *Charlemagne* passed down her starboard. There was no reason to let the two-decker have them in a neat row, one after the other. "Well done," Biddlecomb said out loud.

The *Somerset* was twenty yards ahead when she fired her

bow chasers, larboard and starboard, the sudden detonation making Biddlecomb jump. The ball passed over the deck and tore a four-foot gash in the mainsail as it disappeared astern. The Charlemagnes were manning the starboard battery now, the guns at their highest elevation, ready to blast away at the *Somerset* as the ships passed on opposite tacks. This was the classic ship-to-ship duel, though absurdly mismatched; the *Charlemagne*'s six six-pounders against the thirty-four heavy guns in the *Somerset*'s broadside.

The *Mayor of Plymouth* was up with the *Somerset*, their bowsprits overlapping as they converged, and the forwardmost guns in the *Somerset*'s broadside went off. Biddlecomb could see the *Mayor*'s fore topmast staysail blown apart, as much from the concussion of the gun's blast as from the impact of the ball. The *Somerset*'s bow passed the *Mayor*'s waist, and then the *Mayor* was lost to his sight, her hull blanketed by the huge two-decker, the *Somerset*'s guns going off in pairs as she and the *Mayor* passed each other.

And then it was their turn. Biddlecomb looked up as the two-decker came down on them, her gunwale nearly as high as the *Charlemagne*'s foretop, her black guns leering from the two cavernous gundecks. He grit his teeth and his hand reached for the hilt of his sword. He pulled the weapon out of the shining black scabbard and held it over his head.

The *Somerset*'s jibboom was abeam of them now, just forty feet away, and it was a matter of seconds before the two ships overlapped. He drew in a breath and held it. The turn of the *Somerset*'s bow was up with the bow of the *Charlemagne*, the muzzles of her lower tier of guns five feet above the *Charlemagne*'s bulwark. He was vaguely aware of a noise, a tremendous noise as the two-decker's larboard battery pounded away at the *Mayor of Plymouth*, but it seemed very far away.

The *Somerset*'s forwardmost guns fired, terrifying blasts that shot red flame out over the *Charlemagne*'s bowsprit. "Fire!" he shouted, slashing down with his sword. The *Charlemagne*'s number one gun went off, scarring the *Somerset*'s planking. The two vessels, the *Charlemagne* and the *Somerset*, were side by side, passing on opposite tacks. The *Charlemagne*'s guns were firing continuously now, but the two-decker was not returning their fire.

As Biddlecomb looked across the thirty feet of water that separated the ships, wondering why the two-decker's guns were silent, the *Somerset* let loose with her full broadside, thirty-four heavy guns firing at once.

All sound, all sight, was lost in the blast of the great guns. Thirty-four columns of flame lashed out, and the *Charlemagne* seemed to come apart beneath him. He heard the crush of wood and screaming and felt the sensation of the brig rolling over. He looked up at the rig over his head, confused, trying to get a sense for how the *Charlemagne* was sitting in the water.

He heard a series of faint thuds, like someone chopping firewood a long way off. His leg jerked and there was a burning sensation and he drew away, but the burning was still there. He was lying on the deck, he realized, lying flat on his back with his head jammed against the bulwark. He sat up and leaned on his elbow, then struggled to his feet.

The *Somerset* was still alongside, her quarterdeck looming overhead, her guns running out once more and firing one at a time, but the *Charlemagne* was swinging away from her. He looked aft. One of the helmsmen was jammed up against the bulwark as he himself had been, the other was draped over the tiller. The *Somerset* had fired over their heads; the ships were too close for her great guns to hit the *Charlemagne*'s low deck, but the concussion from those guns had swept away everyone on the raised quarterdeck like the hand of God.

It was painful to walk, but Biddlecomb staggered aft, moving faster as his head cleared. He grabbed the helmsman, unconscious or dead he could not tell, and dropped him to the deck, then pushed the helm over to starboard, bringing the *Charlemagne* back on her old heading.

He heard the sound again, the chopping sound. He looked up at the *Somerset*, looming clifflike beside them. Her bulwark was lined with red-coated men, marines, firing down on the *Charlemagne*. The brig's waist was littered with men, some squirming in agony, others lying still. Blood was everywhere, more blood then he could have imagined, dried brown patches and bright red.

But still the Charlemagnes were running their six-pounder guns in and out, blasting round shot into the great behemoth now thirty feet away. Those not working the guns had taken up small arms, and Biddlecomb could see that they were firing into the open gunports on the *Somerset*'s lower gundeck, firing with some effect judging by the lack of return fire from those ports.

The deck was slick under his foot. He looked down at the planking. It was covered with blood, running over his shoe and soaking into the grain of the wood. His stocking was covered with blood as well, and he was aware of a dull ache in his thigh. The leg of his breeches was torn, and though he could not see it, he knew that a bullet had ripped a gash in his flesh. Now that he was aware of it, it ached terribly, but at that moment he could do nothing.

He looked over the starboard side, up at the *Somerset*'s quarter gallery. They had passed the two-decker, run the gauntlet of her broadside. They had been beat half to death, but yet they lived. The two-decker passed by, revealing behind it what was left of the *Mayor of Plymouth*.

She was fifty yards ahead and still making way. Nothing was left of her mizzenmast, not even wreckage, but of course she had lost the mizzen topmast twenty minutes before. The mainmast was gone now as well, save for a six-foot stump that stuck up from the deck like the remnants of a tree struck by lightning. The rest of the mast, yards, and sails were hanging over the larboard side and trailing in the water, a great tangle of wreckage that blanketed most of the hull from the midships aft.

Only the foremast and fore topmast remained, and the foresail and the fore topsail, shredded though they were, were still set and drawing, dragging the shattered merchantman through the water like a dying man crawling for safety. Biddlecomb wondered if Rumstick was alive, if anyone was left alive in that slaughterhouse.

Yes, people were still alive, he saw, people still struggling to live. Axes rose and fell on the tangle of rigging and the mainmast fell away in jerks, slipping farther and farther toward the water.

And Rumstick was one of those still alive. Biddlecomb saw him step up onto the bulwark, flailing with an ax at the main shrouds. The ax was a blur as it moved up and down, hacking away at the rigging. The heavy shrouds parted one after another, whipping away as they were severed and the strain released. Watching Rumstick, he was reminded of a bas-relief he had seen once in a cathedral, of Samson slaying the Philistines. Rumstick seemed indestructible, looming over the battered ship, and seeing him there, like the Colossus of Rhodes, gave Biddlecomb the first glimmer of hope he had felt in some time.

The wrecked mainmast slipped farther and farther toward the water. And then the last tenuous shroud parted and the entire thing plunged over the side, disappearing under the brown water, then bobbing up again. The *Mayor* ceased her slewing to larboard and straightened on her course, making way under the pull of her two remaining sails, her jibboom pointing toward Lechmere Point.

"Here, sir, let me take that." Biddlecomb pulled his eyes from the *Mayor of Plymouth*. Woodberry was standing in front of him, gesturing at the tiller.

"Yes, of course. Thank you." He relinquished the helm and limped over to the weather rail. "Just keep us on this heading."

The *Charlemagne*'s gun crews had abandoned their charges, now that they had no target that would bear, and they were dragging their dead and wounded mates out of the way, a dozen men at least. Biddlecomb watched Ferguson and Gardiner drag a dead gun captain onto the main hatch, his body leaving a wide swath of blood along the deck, like a red path on the white planking.

He heard a groaning of wood on wood, slow and lugubrious, like a vessel sounds when it's coming apart, and he saw the mainmast, which he had thought to be largely intact, leaning to larboard. The mainsail and the main topsail were set and drawing, and the *Charlemagne* was making way, five knots at least, but Biddlecomb now saw that the mainmast was shot clean through, save for a six-inch section of wood that still held. A puff of wind heeled the brig. The mast protested anew, and the shrouds drew up tight with the popping sound of line under extreme pressure, but they did not break and the mast did not fall. If the *Somerset* had not shot their main topgallant mast away, relieving the shrouds of that additional pressure, then the *Charlemagne*'s mainmast would already be over the side.

Lechmere Point was on their larboard beam and the *Mayor* was to starboard, and a quarter mile ahead was the marshy land at the base of Cobble Hill. That was as far as they had to go; then they could swim or float or wade ashore and walk up to the American lines.

The *Somerset* was firing again, her guns going off one by one as she turned to continue her pursuit, but Biddlecomb neither saw nor cared where the shot landed. He leaned over and picked up his sword, which he had dropped in the concussion of the *Somerset*'s guns. It felt good in his hand. His eyes were fixed on the land at the base of Cobble Hill. There they would be safe in the bosom of the American army. But first they would get the gunpowder ashore.

"Damn me, damn me, damn me, this'll be a close son of a bitch!" Captain Carlisle was practically dancing with excitement as he stood on the redoubt and looked through his glass at the ships below. Major Fitzgerald at his side showed more restraint, as was befitting an officer, but he ached to snatch the glass from Carlisle's hand and survey the damage.

The guns on Cobble Hill had been silent as the two smaller ships ran past the *Somerset*'s broadsides; there was as much chance of hitting them as there was of hitting the British two-decker; and the men of the Twenty-first Massachusetts, as well as Major Fitzgerald, had all but held their breath as they witnessed the slaughter below. The three-masted ship was a one-masted ship now, and though he could not tell for certain, it looked as if the mainmast on the smaller vessel was leaning a bit to one side. They had passed Lechmere Point and were heading for the marshy shore at the foot of Cobble Hill. Fitzgerald felt the warmth of triumph and safety spread through him like a draft of strong liquor, as if a dear friend, or as if he himself, had been aboard one of the ships below.

"*Somerset*'s coming around," someone on the line observed, and Fitzgerald could see it was true. The big two-decker had turned and was sailing in pursuit of the two damaged vessels, but that action gave him not the least anxiety. The guns on Cobble Hill were warm and the gunners had proved themselves to be competent beyond his hope. The detached company had returned with more powder from Prospect Hill, and the sergeant reported that the Twelfth New Hampshire was forming up. They had inflicted damage on the frigate three-quarters of a mile away; the *Somerset* was a bigger target and she was only a half mile distant and closing. Fitzgerald smiled at the thought of what he was about to unleash on the man-of-war.

"Listen up, you men!" he shouted down the line. "You see your target, the *Somerset!* Let's blow her to hell before she does the same to our friends down there!"

The gun captains were careful with their aim and it took three minutes for the entire battery to fire, but in that three minutes Fitzgerald saw visible damage done to the two-decker. Something was broken, hanging down at an odd angle. He heard the term *main topsail yard* passing around the men of the Twenty-first and he assumed that that was the thing they had hit. He turned to ask Carlisle when a man called out, "She's hauling her wind!" and that yell was taken up along the line until the words degenerated into random cheering.

He looked down at the stretch of water below. *Hauling her wind* he assumed meant the same as turning around, for that was what the *Somerset* had done. She had broken off the chase and turned her back on the battery on Cobble Hill, as had the frigate. The omnipotent Royal Navy had been turned away. He wanted to cheer as well, but he contented himself with a smile and a congratulations to Captain Carlisle.

At the base of Cobble Hill the ship with only one mast remaining had run itself up on the mud, twenty feet from dry land, and the other ship, the two-masted one, was closing. Fitzgerald looked down the line at the men of the Twenty-first. He would assemble two companies and march down to the edge of the water to see who it was they had saved and to offer any assistance that they could provide.

He looked across the stretch of water to Breed's Hill, just over a mile away. The British troops in the redoubts there would have had a view of the battle almost as good as his own. He wondered what they were thinking as they watched their vaunted navy driven back and the two enemy ships now safe at the Americans' feet. He smiled at the thought of the British officers watching the action in impotent frustration.

He shifted his gaze toward Bunker Hill, their immediate neighbor only half a mile away, and the smile froze on his face and vanished. A causeway linked Bunker Hill with the land at the base of Cobble Hill, a causeway that had become a no-man's-land with British and American artillery trained on it, ready to decimate any troops that tried to cross. But now all of the American artillery was pointed out to sea, and across the causeway, two men deep and one hundred long, their red coats brilliant in the afternoon sun, their feet and arms moving in perfect syncopation, came a full regiment of British troops. There were over two hundred men—battalion companies, grenadiers, and light infantry—and they were already as close to the two vessels as the men on Cobble Hill.

"Son of a bitch," Fitzgerald said, louder than he had intended. He had to do something. He knew that. After driving the *Somerset* away and saving those two ships, they could not let the British army march up and take them away. But the troops below, in their long scarlet line, were the most well-trained, disciplined, and tested troops in the world. They had

386

fought nearly every army in Europe, and they had beaten them all. And the men of the Twenty-first Massachusetts had never once marched into a formal battle.

Nor had he. Fitzgerald realized, and it surprised him to realize, that the moment for which he had longed, the moment he had dreaded, was on him. The humiliation of being a major without having ever been in combat would be over in an hour, and he would either redeem himself or he would be dead. But whatever the outcome it would not be the result of recklessness or stupidity on his part.

"Captain Carlisle," he began, issuing orders, "form up your men by company, double file, we're going over the redoubt to meet the enemy head-on."

"Yes, sir." Carlisle saluted and began to call out instructions to sergeants, who in turn shouted the men into order.

"Sergeant." Fitzgerald grabbed the first artilleryman of any rank that he could find. "Get some guns around on the causeway again, stop any reinforcements from coming across." Fitzgerald looked at the scene at his feet. They would have to attack soon, before the British reached the two vessels. He wondered where Washington was. The general must have heard the cannonade, in which case he must be making for Cobble Hill. Fitzgerald hoped that he would not arrive before they went into battle, and it did not bother him that he felt that way. This fight was his.

Biddlecomb was surprised at how close to shore the *Mayor of Plymouth* reached before easing her bow gently into the mud, though of course the loss of several tons of masts, spars, and rigging had done much to reduce her draft.

The merchantman was twenty feet from dry land when she stopped. Biddlecomb turned to Woodberry at the *Charlemagne*'s helm. "Ease her alongside. Just run us into their starboard side."

"Aye, sir," said Woodberry, turning the brig more northerly.

"Mr. Gardiner," Biddlecomb called down into the waist. "Clew up the main topsail, please. Mr. Weatherspoon." He looked down at the midshipman, who was tying, a bit too snug, a bandage around the torn flesh on Biddlecomb's leg. "Ease away the peak halyard there, if you would." He disengaged himself from Weatherspoon's grip and took the main gaff's throat halyard off its belaying pin. Together they eased the big sail down until it lay in a heap across the quarterdeck.

With the loss of the mainsails the *Charlemagne*'s speed dropped off to a knot at most, and when she hit the *Mayor of Plymouth*'s side, it was as gentle as two lovers coming together. The mainmast leaned farther, the wood and rigging groaning loud, but it did not fall.

Biddlecomb stepped up onto the quarterdeck bulwark. "All hands, abandon ship! All hands, onto the *Mayor of Plymouth!*" He turned and stepped over the gap between the ships, onto the *Mayor*'s quarterdeck, and took hold of Rumstick's outstretched hand. "Welcome to . . . wherever we are. Cambridge? Somewhere in Massachusetts."

"Welcome indeed," said Rumstick, "and damn glad to be here."

"I want to start unloading this powder, we can float it ashore. The people manning that battery on the hill can help us get it up there. I imagine they'll be happy to see it."

"Sir? Beg your pardon," Biddlecomb heard Jaeger's voice behind him.

"Yes, Jaeger?" He was delighted to see the Prussian, though after living through the *Somerset*'s attack he realized that there was little that did not delight him.

"There is a British column approaching, sir, regiment strength or close."

Biddlecomb and Rumstick stared at him in silence for what seemed a long time before Biddlecomb asked, "What was that?"

"Here, sir." Jaeger led them to the larboard side, the landward side of the *Mayor*'s quarterdeck. Biddlecomb looked along the shoreline in the direction that Jaeger was pointing. A column of men was marching toward them, less than a quarter mile away, and the marshy ground did not alter the perfect rhythm of their steps. He did not know what a regiment consisted of, but there appeared to be a couple hundred men. There was no mistaking the precision and the scarlet coats.

"No! Son of a bitch, no!" Biddlecomb shouted. It was impossible. They had taken the high odds and they had won, they had reached the American lines. This could not be happening, it was too much.

"There's American troops up on the hill," Rumstick said. "We can abandon the ships now and make it to the American lines before they get here."

"We're not leaving the powder. We did not come this far to give this damnable powder back to the British, we're not leaving it."

"Sir, if I may?" Jaeger interrupted. "Let me take the men we have, the ones that are good with the musket, and form a skirmish line. I think we can hold them off, for a while, anyway."

Biddlecomb considered this suggestion. He did not know what a skirmish line was any more than he knew what a regiment was. It was madness, it was all madness, but he would not give the powder back to the British. He pushed past Jaeger and stepped up to the *Mayor's* helm.

"All hands, listen to me!" he shouted, and the many and loud conversations stopped and every eye was turned toward the captain. "The bosun and his mates and you"—he pointed toward a knot of men by the stump of the mainmast—"remain on board. The rest of you get muskets and go with Jaeger! Go!"

Three minutes passed before the first of the skirmishers had crossed the crude bridge of hatch boards and spare planks that the bosun's party had made from the *Mayor* to the marshy shore. The stay tackle, rigged from the foremast to the stump of the mainmast, was already in motion, swaying barrels of the precious powder out of the hold and dumping them in the water alongside. The men worked furiously, hauling away, emptying the hold of powder.

Biddlecomb moved past the working parties toward the

bow, his beautiful sword in his hand. He jumped up on the heel of the bowsprit and looked toward the shore, where Jaeger was deploying the sparse and ragged troops.

He had split the men into pairs and had them spread across the wet field between the ships and the British troops in what Biddlecomb assumed was a skirmish line. It seemed an odd sort of defense, but Biddlecomb was quite willing to concede that he knew nothing about such things. He hoped that Jaeger could hold back the British infantry, hold them for another twenty minutes at least. He turned and looked at the growing number of powder barrels floating alongside, then up to the redoubt on Cobble Hill. If they did not get help soon, then their efforts would be wasted.

"They're forming a skirmish line," Fitzgerald said to Carlisle with undisguised surprise in his voice. The skirmishers were paired off and flung out in a wide arc before the advancing troops, and while they did not move with the assurance of experienced troops, still their tactics were more sophisticated than he would have expected from sailors.

The British light infantry stopped in their march and formed up into their ranks for firing, hoping to sweep away the annoying skirmishers like a man swatting flies. Their muskets went off in sheets of flame and smoke, but with little effect. Firing by ranks was intended to decimate a close-packed group of enemy soldiers, not to pick off individuals in a sparse skirmish line, and as far as Fitzgerald could see, not one of the sailors had been hit. What was more, they had just given Fitzgerald the two minutes more that he needed to organize his attack.

He heard the pop pop of the skirmishers' muskets, and the forwardmost men in the thin line began to fall back. The British troops stood and formed into columns once more and continued their unflinching march into the face of the skirmishers' guns. As well they might. There were not above sixty skirmishers to the two hundred or more well-trained men of the British regiment of foot.

Fitzgerald pulled his sword from its sheath and held it over his head. He had already picked his words—"Twenty-first Massachusetts, quick step, follow me!"—but before he could say them a new thought came to him.

He had as many men as the British, but the British troops were experienced in combat, and they could fire faster and more accurately than any troops in the world. If he flung the Twenty-first Massachusetts headlong at them, then the Americans would be slaughtered and the British would take the ships anyway. It was a heroic tactic, but a stupid one, and not the way to win a fight. There was a smarter way to do this.

"Captain Carlisle! Take charge here! Lead your men on the double time down the hill and slow the enemy advance as best you can. Make your stand about there." Fitzgerald pointed with his sword.

"Yes, sir. You're not coming, sir?" Carlisle asked, his tone confused and a bit angry.

"I'll be there, Captain, fear not. Now go."

Carlisle stood up on the redoubt and drew his sword, as Fitzgerald had, and turning to his troops, yelled, "You men of Marblehead, on the quick step, follow me!" He turned and jumped down on the far side of the redoubt, stumbled, recovered, and raced down the hill, two hundred yelling seamen at his back.

The men at the stay tackle paused at the sound and looked up toward the top of Cobble Hill, up toward the glorious sight of American troops pouring out of the redoubt and down the hill.

Jaeger's skirmishers were falling back. The British troops were fifty yards from the *Mayor of Plymouth* and still advancing, though Biddlecomb could see scarlet-clad men lying on the wet grass, left behind by their comrades, some thrashing about, some lying still. The skirmishers had held the light infantry back, forcing them to stop and fire, long enough for the troops from Cobble Hill to advance.

Now the British were stopped again and again forming up

into three ranks, kneeling and standing, as the American troops came tearing down the hill like a pack of wolves. Jaeger detached himself from the skirmish line and ran toward the advancing Americans, waving his arms and gesturing for them to spread out, but the Americans appeared to be crazed as they rushed at the British.

One hundred yards away, seventy-five, they ran toward the triple line of red. Fifty yards away and Biddlecomb heard, as clear as a ship's bell on a still morning, the order "Fire!" and the Americans ran into the wall of flying lead. They staggered, those in the lead falling dead and those behind tripping over their bodies. The charge was done. Some men staggered forward, some just stood still, dazed by the noise and the slaughter.

"Form up! In a line! In a line!" Jaeger was yelling, pushing men here and there, trying to establish a line of defense. The men were taking steps backward, one step back, then another and another, and Biddlecomb could see they were on the verge of running. "Form up! Form up! You there, kneel and load!" Jaeger was shouting, oblivious to the British muskets at his back. Slowly the men obeyed, spreading out and forming a rude facsimile of the British line. The *Charlemagne*'s skirmishers fell back and melted into their ranks.

The British were moving again, advancing toward the Americans, now thirty yards from the *Mayor*. An officer on the American line raised his sword and yelled, "Fire!" and the Americans' guns went off in a ragged volley. British infantrymen dropped, some screaming, some dead, but the scarlet ranks closed up and the infantry marched on.

"Ezra!" Biddlecomb called aft along the deck.

"Aye?"

"Get ready to put the ships to the torch. Combustibles around the mast on the main deck should do with the powder still on board. The British infantry will be all over us in five minutes; I want both ships burning well by then. And let Sotherby out of the bread room."

There was pause, just a second's catch in Rumstick's throat, before he replied, "Aye!" and began to issue orders for powder barrels to be broken open and straw and wood and oil to be scattered around the mainmast. Biddlecomb turned back to the fight onshore. He did not watch the preparations being made to burn the vessels. He could not stand it.

The British infantry had stopped again, and again they fired on the wavering American line. The men from Cobble Hill stepped back, leaving dead and wounded comrades in their wake. Biddlecomb could hear the American officer and Jaeger calling for the men to hold fast. Their admonishments seemed to be the only thing holding the American line in place, and those would not hold them for long.

It was the most horrible thing that Fitzgerald had seen, and the most wonderful. The Twenty-first had run right into the British fire and had been driven back. But they had not broken and they had not run, and the dead men, redcoats and Americans, that littered the ground were testament to that steadfastness. Now the British would really pay for the hurt they had thus far inflicted.

Cobble Hill rose to Fitzgerald's right, hiding from the British the one hundred and fifty men of the Twelfth New Hampshire marching behind him. The British regiment of foot was formed up fifty yards in front of him, and they did not yet see him, they did not know he was there. He was staring at their wholly exposed and unprotected flank, and in a second he would roll up that flank like a hurricane.

He smiled as he raised the sword in his right hand over his head and took a firmer grip of the horse pistol in his left. This day, this moment, was his. He picked up his pace to a quick step. In his excitement he had all but forgotten his exhaustion and the ache of his wounds. He heard at his back the men of the Twelfth New Hampshire keeping pace with him. Now the bastards would pay.

The American line and the British infantry fired at the same instant, like two miniature broadsides, and when the smoke cleared, another dozen men lay wounded or dead. Biddlecomb heard the order "Fix bayonets!" and all along the British line blades flashed out, and were fixed to the ends of the muskets, three rows of needle-sharp steel advancing on the American troops.

"Isaac, we're ready to fire the ships." Biddlecomb turned and looked at his friend Rumstick, whose eyes were in turn fixed on the battle just beyond the *Mayor*'s bow.

"Do it. Let's do it and go. The Americans will be in a full run in a minute, and we'll be lucky if the British let us get up to the top of the hill."

"I'm sorry, Isaac."

"So am I." Biddlecomb turned to watch the end of the Americans' campaign.

The Americans fired again, their volley ragged as some men loaded faster than others. British troops fell all along the line, but the advance did not slow, not one step. There was something mechanical and inhuman in the way the infantry moved, every man seemingly oblivious to the death around him as they pressed on, not to be stopped.

Biddlecomb heard the crackling of flames as the *Mayor* was fired. A waft of smoke, the smell of burning paint and dry wood, reached out to him, and he knew he had to go. The hold was still half full of gunpowder, and it would not be long before it went up. He hoped the ship was full of British troops when it did.

He was consumed by the feeling of loss, as he had been the night the British forced him to drive the *Judea,* his beloved *Judea,* up on the rocks. But this way at least the British would not get their powder back, and they would not lay their filthy hands on his *Charlemagne.* As he turned to go aft, something caught his eye, some movement beyond the British line.

Soldiers. More soldiers. They were coming around the base of Cobble Hill, coming fast and yelling, not the perfectly matched uniforms of the British but the eclectic dress of American troops. The British advance faltered as men in the regiment of foot turned to look, as surprised as Biddlecomb by this sudden assault.

"Form square! Spread out! Flank companies!" the British officer yelled as he waved his sword over his head. A group of soldiers stepped aside and began to form up in a line to face the new assault, but it was too late. The newly arrived Americans fired, a withering fire, and the British line toppled as the Americans came up. Biddlecomb swung around and looked aft. "Rumstick!" he shouted. "Put out the fire! For God's sake put out the fire!"

Fitzgerald saw the British light infantry fall like wheat under a scythe as the Twelfth New Hampshire, himself at their head, rolled down on the British flank. The enemy had responded well, but too slowly, and now they would die.

A British officer was waving his sword, rallying his men. His eyes met Fitzgerald's, fifteen feet away, and Fitzgerald leveled his horse pistol and fired. The top of the officer's head exploded; Fitzgerald saw the man behind him wince as he was splattered with blood and bone and the officer was flung back, dead before he hit the wet earth.

Fitzgerald flipped the pistol around in his hand, gripping the warm barrel and holding it like a club as he ran the last ten feet to the British line. He could see the men step back, wavering, leaderless.

And then Fitzgerald was on them. A bayonet thrust out at him but he knocked it aside with his pistol and drove his sword into the attacker's belly, twisted it, and wrenched it out. A musket was swinging at his head and there was no time to duck. He raised his arm, his right arm, and the heavy butt smashed into him, knocking him sideways. He staggered, gasping in pain. He could feel blood running under his sleeve where his wound had opened up again. He clenched his teeth against the pain and slashed out with his sword, felt the blade bite flesh, heard a scream, and the musket fell to the ground.

He straightened and looked around for another enemy, another man whom he could kill—he did not want to stop killing—but only Americans were around him now. The attack had swept past him, the British regiment of foot was pushed beyond his reach, pushed back to the water's edge. He ran after them, working his way through the American troops, wanting to get at the frightened enemy.

More yelling came from his right, and he saw that the Twenty-first Massachusetts had rallied again and flung themselves at the enemy's disorderly ranks. The British infantry shrank from this assault as well, backing away from both lines of attack. And then, as synchronized as if following an order in a marching drill, they turned and fled.

Muskets and hats and cartridge boxes were thrown aside as the British regiment of foot ran for the causeway and Bunker Hill beyond, their order and precision lost in a fog of panic. They ran, each man as fast as he could, the Twelfth New Hampshire and the Twenty-first Massachusetts at their heels.

"Stop! Stop! Form up!" Fitzgerald shouted. The Americans would run all the way to the British lines if he let them. They slowed and stopped, satisfying themselves with flinging insults at the infantry's backs. Fitzgerald looked at the untidy soldiers under his command. They had fought well that day. He turned and looked at the two ships that they had come here to defend. They were safe now. He could see smoke rising from the larger one and he wondered at the cause of it.

Biddlecomb grabbed a capstan bar and ran aft. Someone in the hold below had flung a burning mattress up through the gray smoke that rolled out of the tween decks. Biddlecomb speared it with the bar and lifted it up and ran with it to the side of the ship. The heat from the burning straw was searing, and flaming bits fell on the deck. He reached it out over the side and realized he was about to drop it onto four dozen barrels of powder bobbing in the water.

"Son of a—!" he shouted as he raced across the deck and dropped it hissing into the river off the starboard side.

He heard the clanging of the wash-deck pump, that welcome sound, as it was got up. Rumstick and two others were working the pump brake up and down, the two men trying to keep pace with their first officer.

More burning material, oil-soaked rags, pieces of wood, and buckets of paint were flung up from below, and Biddlecomb wondered how the men could remain down there in the heat and smoke. He knew they were not thinking about the fireball that the *Mayor* would make when she blew, just as he was not thinking about it. If they thought about it, they would all run for their lives.

The canvas hose attached to the pump jerked and straightened as if coming to life. Biddlecomb snatched it up as the first jet of water shot out of the end, and he ran with the hose to the hatch. In the hold was a square of light where the pale sun came in through the few missing hatch boards, and the rest was smoke and darkness. Aft by the mainmast he could see a yellow and flickering glow through the fog as the fire consumed the combustibles there.

He jumped down and his feet hit the top tier of barrels on the deck below. He staggered and fell and stood again. His eyes were streaming tears and his throat burned with the first breath. In his hand was the hose, water shooting out of the end and spraying in all directions. He dragged it aft, toward the flames that were licking around the mast, illuminating the hold with their weird light and dancing over the barrels, row upon row, stacked fore and aft and filled with gunpowder.

He pointed the hose at the flames and steam welled up from the base of the mast and mixed with the swirling smoke. Around the flames men glistening with sweat appeared and disappeared through the smoke as they pulled the stacked flammables apart, reaching in and jerking back like savages dancing around a fire.

Biddlecomb swept the space with the stream of water, dousing each flaming element that was pulled away. Overhead he heard the stamp of feet, many feet on deck. He directed the stream at a flaring pile of rags and they went out with a hiss, and suddenly the hold was dark again. That was the last of the fire and it was out. The smoke moved and lifted as a draft of fresh air moved through the tween decks, and Biddlecomb found himself wrapped in the comforting dark.

The water continued to course through the hose and he wetted down the deck as far as the stream would reach. He turned to a dark shape beside him. "Go tell Rumstick that the fire's out and he can secure the hose."

"Aye, sir," the other said, and disappeared, and Biddlecomb was alone in the dark, warm space.

He heard voices on the deck above, heard Rumstick say something about "Captain Biddlecomb's in command here." Another voice, an American voice, familiar, though he could not place it, and incredulous, was saying, "This is Captain Biddlecomb's ship? Isaac Biddlecomb of Bristol . . . ," but he did not catch the rest. He stared into the dark.

Relief, that was what he felt. Warm, delicious relief, like finally lying down in one's own bed after an exhausting and arduous journey. Then with a groan he turned and climbed up on the tier of barrels and pulled himself through the hatch, blinking in the watery daylight.

"Captain Biddlecomb?" It was the voice he had heard below. He rubbed the tears from his smoke-filled eyes. It was Major Fitzgerald, and the major was looking at him with an expression of the most profound surprise, with not a little bit of shock mixed in.

Fitzgerald stepped up to him, the former shock now replaced with a huge grin, his hand extended. Biddlecomb took the hand and shook it; his own, he could see, was black with soot and he imagined his face was as well, where the tears had not cut paths in the grime. No wonder the major, in his immaculate uniform, looked so surprised.

"Congratulations, Captain," Fitzgerald said. "I . . ."

"Thank you, Major." What more to say? There was so much. "I brought you your gunpowder." It was all Biddlecomb could think of, and it was wholly inadequate.

"Gunpowder? My God, we . . . well, we thought you were

dead, to be honest." Fitzgerald was still shaking his hand and clapping him on the shoulder. "Virginia will be delighted."

"Virginia? You've spoken with Virginia?"

"Just this morning. She misses you very much."

And he missed her, and he would go and see her, and this time he would not be a backward, stuttering fool. He had earned a leave. He had, after all, brought powder to Washington, had laid a whole shipload of it right at the general's feet. The fight was over for him.

And then he smiled at the absurdity of such a thought. Whom was he hoping to fool? Himself?

"Shall we go aboard the"—Biddlecomb looked over at his beloved, much battered *Charlemagne,* her decks dark with dried blood, her mainmast leaning heavily to one side—"aboard the United Colonies brig-of-war *Charlemagne,* Major? We'll have a glass and I'll relate the circumstances that have led us here. If there's anything left of my cabin. Would you join us, Lieutenant Rumstick?"

He gestured with his arm and the major stepped carefully across to the *Charlemagne,* followed by Rumstick. Then Biddlecomb stepped across as well, across to his own quarterdeck, the quarterdeck of a man-of-war. The fight was not over for him. It was now just fully joined.

Historical Note

Fighting between the American colonists and the British authorities began long before anyone ever considered waging a war for American independence.

Nowhere was this more true than in the colony of Rhode Island and Providence Plantations. Most of the people in that colony made their living from the sea, directly or indirectly. Many of them had made fortunes through "importing" goods such as molasses and ignoring the official duties, which were, in any case, rarely enforced. So lucrative was this illicit business that, in those few instances when the British authorities did attempt to collect duties, the people of Rhode Island resisted bitterly, and often with force.

In 1764, Rhode Islanders fired on the British schooner *St. John,* and in 1769, angered by further attempts on the part of the British to curb smuggling, they burned the revenue sloop *Liberty.* On the ninth of June 1772, over a year and a half before the Boston Tea Party, Rhode Islanders in open boats attacked the stranded revenue schooner *Gaspee.* Led by John Brown and Capt. Abraham Whipple, they burned her to the waterline and shot her commanding officer, Lieutenant Dudingston. The next two years, during which time the British did not attempt to replace the *Gaspee,* were relatively peaceful and prosperous on Narragansett Bay.

Then, in November 1774, Admiral Graves in Boston dispatched the twenty-gun frigate HMS *Rose*, under the efficient command of Capt. James Wallace, to take the *Gaspee*'s place. For Rhode Island and Providence Plantations the arrival of the *Rose* marked the end of any peace the colony would enjoy until the close of the American Revolution.

Wallace and the *Rose* proved terribly effective in stopping the illegal traffic on Narragansett Bay and Long Island Sound, but the people of Rhode Island were not inclined to stoically accept their fate. In June of 1775 the General Assembly voted to create a Rhode Island navy, the first official naval force in America. Half of that two-vessel navy consisted of the armed sloop *Katy* (later renamed *Providence*) under the command of Capt. Abraham Whipple. *Katy* removed cattle from the various islands around the bay, depriving Wallace of fresh meat, and with another vessel attacked and took back the sloop *Diana*, which Wallace had earlier taken from her American owner and armed for his own use.

In August of that year the General Assembly instructed its delegates to the Continental Congress to "use their whole influence, at the ensuing Congress, for building, at the Continental expense, a Fleet of sufficient force for the protection of these Colonies," thus laying the groundwork for what would eventually become the United States Navy.

In July of 1775, while the *Rose* and *Katy* were chasing each other around Narragansett Bay, Gen. George Washington took command of the various New England militias, sixteen thousand men strong, that encircled Boston. Under siege in that peninsular city was the British army, called by the Americans the "ministerial army" in the mistaken belief that it was parliament alone, and not King George, that harbored hostile feelings toward the colonies. A myriad of problems confronted the new commander in chief, ranging from a lack of housing and uniforms for the troops to an almost subversive disregard for his general orders. But the worst of his problems would not reveal itself for another month.

Washington had been led to believe the army had three hundred and eight barrels of gunpowder on hand; not an enormous supply, but adequate. On August 2 he discovered that an inexperienced quartermaster had reported not the amount that was available but the total amount that the army had ever received, much of which had already been used. In fact, there were only thirty-six barrels of powder for all troops and artillery, a critical situation indeed.

Washington undertook various means to rectify this problem, including a failed mission to Bermuda to liberate the store of gunpowder that the British maintained on the island. Though that effort proved unsuccessful, the situation was somewhat ameliorated in November of 1775. In that month the schooner *Lee*, a vessel commissioned by Washington to cruise against the British, captured the ordnance brig *Nancy*, loaded with military stores. By early 1776, Washington was able to amass enough gunpowder to avoid a disaster by coercing it from the colonies and using his small fleet to capture British ships transporting it for the use of the British army.

Metcalf Bowler, Speaker of the House of Representatives in Rhode Island, signer of the Rhode Island Declaration of Independence, and all-around patriot was indeed a British informer. His nefarious acts came to light during an extensive cataloging of Sir Henry Clinton's papers beginning in the late 1920s. Bowler's correspondence reveals a man who was at once anxious to please the British authorities and obsessed with the danger to which he was subjecting himself, as well as being desirous of pecuniary help from the Royal government he served.

The *Charlemagne*, the *Ant*, and the ships in the British convoy are the only vessels in this work that are figments of the author's imagination. The others are real ships in more or less their correct historical locations.

My thanks to Peter Wolverton at Pocket Books for his editorial work, and to Stephanie Nelson and Richard Bailey for the same. Thank you to Thomas Page for his invaluable help with the horses. It is no coincidence that both Isaac Biddlecomb and the author are shamelessly ignorant on that subject, and any mistakes herein are my own.

Glossary

Note: See diagram of brig for names and illustrations of all sails and spars.

abaft: nearer the back of the ship, farther aft, behind.

aback: said of a sail when the wind is striking it on the wrong side and, in the case of a square sail, pressing it back against the mast.

abeam: at right angles to the ship's centerline.

aft: toward the stern of the ship, as opposed to fore.

afterguard: men stationed aft to work the aftermost sails.

backstay: long ropes leading from the topmast and topgallant mastheads down to the channels. Backstays work with shrouds to support the masts from behind.

beakhead: a small deck forward of the forecastle that overhangs the bow. The crew's latrine was located there, hence in current usage the term *head* for a marine toilet.

beam reach: sailing with the wind abeam.

belay: to make a rope fast to a belaying pin, cleat, or other such device. Also used as a general command to stop or cancel, e.g., "Belay that last order!"

belaying pin: a wooden pin, later made of metal, generally about twenty inches in length to which lines were made fast, or "belayed." They were arranged in pinrails along the inside of the bulwark and in fife rails around the masts.

bells: method by which time was marked on shipboard. Each

405

day was generally divided into five four-hour "watches" and two two-hour "dogwatches." After the first half hour of a watch one bell was rung, then another for each additional half hour until eight bells and the change of watch, when the process was begun again.

binnacle: large wooden box, just forward of the helm, housing the compass, half-hour glass for timing the watches, and candles to light the compass at night.

bitts: heavy timber frame near the bow to which the end of the anchor cable is made fast, hence the term *bitter end.*

block: nautical term for a pulley.

boatswain (bosun): warrant officer in charge of boats, sails, and rigging. Also responsible for relaying orders and seeing them carried out, not unlike a sergeant in the army.

boatswain's call: small, unusually shaped whistle with a high, piercing sound with which the boatswain relayed orders by playing any of a number of recognizable tunes. Also played as a salute.

boatswain's chair: a wooden seat with a rope sling attached. Used for hoisting men aloft or over the side for work.

boom: the spar to which the lower edge of a fore-and-aft sail is attached. Special studdingsail booms are used for those sails.

booms: spare spars, generally stowed amidships on raised gallows upon which the boats were often stored.

bow: the rounded, forwardmost part of a ship or boat.

bow chaser: a cannon situated near the bow to fire as directly forward as possible.

bower: one of two primary anchors stored near the bow, designated best bower and small bower.

bowline: line attached to a bridle that is in turn attached to the perpendicular edge of a square sail. The bowline is hauled taut when sailing close-hauled to keep the edge of the sail tight and prevent shivering. Also, a common knot used to put a loop in the end of a rope.

brace: lines attached to the ends of the yards, which, when hauled upon, turn the yards horizontally to present the sails at the most favorable angle to the wind. Also, to perform the action of bracing the yards.

brake: the handle of a ship's pump.

break: the edge of a raised deck closest to the center of the ship.

breeching: rope used to secure a cannon to the side of a ship and prevent it from recoiling too far.

brig: a two-masted vessel, square-rigged on fore and main with a large fore-and-aft mainsail supported by boom and gaff and made fast to the after side of the mainmast.

bulwark: wall-like structure, generally of waist height or higher, built around the outer edge of the weather decks.

bumboat: privately owned boat used to carry vegetables, liquor, and other items for sale out to anchored vessels.

buntlines: lines running from the lower edge of a square sail to the yard above and used to haul the bunt, or body of the sail, up to the yard, generally in preparation for furling.

cable: large, strong rope. As a unit of measure, 120 fathoms or 240 yards, generally the length of a cable.

cable tier: a section of the lowest deck in a ship in which the cables are stored.

cap: a heavy wooden block through which an upper mast passes, designed to hold the upper mast in place against the mast below it. Forms the upper part of the DOUBLING.

caprail: wooden rail that is fastened to the top edge of the bulwark.

capstan: a heavy wooden cylinder, pierced with holes to accept wooden bars. The capstan is turned by pushing on the bars and is thus used to raise the anchor or move other heavy objects.

cascabel: the knob at the end of a cannon opposite the muzzle to which the breeching is fastened.

cathead: short, strong wooden beam that projects out over the bow, one on either side of the ship, used to suspend the anchor clear of the ship when hauling it up or letting it go.

cat-o'-nine-tails (cat): a whip with a rope handle around an inch in diameter and two feet in length to which was attached nine tails, also around two feet in length. "Flogging" with the cat was the most common punishment meted out in the navy.

ceiling: the inside planking or "inner wall" of a ship.

chains: strong links or iron plates used to fasten the deadeyes to the hull. The lower parts of the chains are bolted to the hull, the upper ends are fastened to the chainwale, or CHANNEL. They are generally referred to as forechains, mainchains, and mizzenchains for those respective masts.

channel: corruption of *chainwale.* Broad, thick planks extending like platforms from both sides of the ship at the base of each mast to which the shrouds are attached.

clear for action: the process by which a ship is prepared for an engagement. Also the order that is given to prepare the ship.

clew: either of the two lower corners of a square sail or the lower aft corner of a fore-and-aft sail. To "clew up" is to haul the corners of the sail up to the yard by means of the clewlines.

clewline: (pronounced *clew-lin*) lines running from the clews of a square sail to the yard above and used to haul the clews up, generally in preparation for furling. On lower, or course, sails the clewlines are called clew garnets.

close-hauled: said of a vessel that is sailing as nearly into the wind as she is able, and her sails are hauled as close to her centerline as they can go.

conn: to direct the helmsman in the steering of the ship.

course: the largest sails, in the case of square sails, those hung from the lowest, or course, yards and loose footed. The foresail and mainsail are courses.

crosstrees: horizontal wooden bars, situated at right angles to the ship's centerline and located at the junction of lower and upper masts. Between the lower and the topmasts they support the TOP; between the topmast and the topgallant mast they stand alone to spread the shrouds and provide a perch for the lookout.

deadeye: a round, flattish wooden block pierced with three holes through which a LANYARD is rove. Deadeyes and lanyards are used to secure and adjust standing rigging, most commonly the SHROUDS.

dead reckoning: from *deduced reckoning*. Calculating a vessel's position through an estimate of speed and drift.

dirk: a small sword, more like a large dagger, worn by junior officers.

dogwatch: two-hour watches from 4 to 6 P.M. (first dogwatch) and 6 to 8 P.M. (second dogwatch).

doubling: the section where two masts overlap, such as the lower mast and the topmast just above the top.

driver: a temporary sail, much like a studdingsail, hoisted to the gaff on the aftermost fore-and-aft sail.

fall: the loose end of a system of blocks and tackle, the part upon which one pulls.

fathom: six feet.

fife rail: wooden rails, found generally at the base of the masts and pierced with holes to accept belaying pins.

first rate: the largest class of naval ship, carrying one hundred or more guns. Ships were rated from first to sixth rates depending on the number of guns. Sloops, brigs, schooners, and other small vessels were not rated.

fish: long sections of wood bound around a weak or broken SPAR to reinforce it, much like a splint on a broken limb. Also, the process of affixing fishes to the spar.

flemish: to coil a rope neatly down in concentric circles with the end being in the middle of the coil.

fore and aft: parallel to the centerline of the ship. In reference to sails, those that are set parallel to the centerline and are not attached to yards. Also used to mean the entire deck encompassed, e.g., "Silence, fore and aft!"

forecastle: pronounced *fo'c'sle*. The forward part of the upper deck, forward of the foremast, in some vessels raised above the upper deck. Also, the space enclosed by this deck. In the merchant service the forecastle was the living quarters for the seamen.

forestay: standing rigging primarily responsible for preventing the foremast from falling back when the foresails are ABACK. Runs from under the fore top to the bowsprit.

forward: pronounced *for'ed*. toward the bow, or front of the ship. To send an officer forward implied disrating, sending him from the officer's quarters aft to the sailors' quarters forward.

fother: to attempt to stop a leak in a vessel by means of placing a sail or other material on the outside of the ship over the leaking area. The sail is held in place by the pressure of the incoming water.

frigate: vessels of the fifth or sixth rate, generally fast and well armed for their size, carrying between twenty and thirty-six guns.

furl: to bundle a sail tightly against the YARD, stay, or mast to which it is attached and lash it in place with GASKETS.

futtock shrouds: short, heavy pieces of standing rigging connected on one end to the topmast shrouds at the outer edge of the TOP and on the other to the lower shrouds, designed to bear the pressure on the topmast shrouds. When fitted with RATLINES, they allow men going aloft to climb around the outside of the top, though doing so requires them to hang backward at as much as a forty-five-degree angle.

gammoning: heavy lines used to lash the bowsprit down and counteract the pull of the STAYS.

gangway: the part of the ship's side from which people come aboard or leave, provided with an opening in the bulwark and steps on the vessel's side.

gantline: pronounced *gant-lin.* A line run from the deck to a block aloft and back to the deck, used for hauling articles such as rigging aloft. Thus, when the rig is "sent down to a gantline," it has been entirely disassembled save for the gantline, which will be used to haul it up again.

garboard: the first set of planks, next to the keel, on a ship's or boat's bottom.

gasket: a short, braided piece of rope attached to the yard and used to secure the furled sail.

gig: a small boat generally rowed with six or fewer oars.

glim: a small candle.

grapeshot: a cluster of round, iron shot, generally nine in all, wrapped in canvas. Upon firing, the grapeshot would spread out for a shotgun effect. Used against men and light hulls.

grating: hatch covers composed of perpendicular, interlocking wood pieces, much like a heavy wood screen. They allowed light and air below while still providing cover for the hatch. Gratings were covered with tarpaulins in rough or wet weather.

gudgeon: one-half of the hinge mechanism for a rudder. The gudgeon is fixed to the sternpost and has a rounded opening that accepts the PINTLE on the rudder.

gunwale: pronounced *gun-el.* The upper edge of a ship's side.

halyard: any line used to raise a sail or a yard or gaff to which a sail is attached.

headsails: those sails set forward of the foremast.

heaver: a device like a wooden mallet used as a lever for tightening small lines.

heave to: to adjust the sails in such a way that some are full and some aback so that the vessel is stopped in the water.

hogshead: a large cask, twice the size of a standard barrel. Capacity varied but was generally around one hundred gallons.

holystone: a flat stone used for cleaning a ship's decks.

hoy: a small vessel, chiefly used near the coast, to transport passengers or supplies to another vessel.

hull down: said of a ship when her hull is still hidden below the horizon and only her masts or superstructure is visible.

jolly boat: a small workboat.

lanyard: line run through the holes in the DEADEYES to secure and adjust the SHROUDS. Also any short line used to secure or adjust an item on shipboard.

larboard: until the nineteenth century the term designating the left side of a vessel when facing forward. The term *port* is now used.

leech: the side edges of a square sail or the after edge of a fore-and-aft sail.

leeward: pronounced *loo-ard.* Downwind.

letter of marque: a commission given to private citizens in times of war to take and make prizes of enemy vessels. Also, any vessel that holds such a commission.

lifts: ropes running from the ends of the yards to the mast, used to support the yard when lowered or when men are employed thereon.

limber holes: holes cut through the lower timbers in a ship's hull allowing otherwise trapped water to run through to the pumps.

line: term used for a rope that has been put to a specific use.

log: device used to measure a vessel's speed.

longboat: the largest boat carried on shipboard.

lugsail: a small square sail used on a boat.

mainstay: standing rigging primarily responsible for preventing the mainmast from falling back when the mainsails are aback. Runs from under the maintop to the bow.

make and mend: time allotted to the seamen to make new clothing or mend their existing ones.

marlinespike: an iron spike used in knotting and splicing rope.

mizzen: large fore-and-aft sail, hung from a gaff abaft the mizzenmast.

mizzenmast: the aftermost mast on a three-masted ship.

painter: a rope in the bow of a boat used to tie the boat in place.

parceling: strips of canvas wrapped around standing rigging prior to SERVING.

partners: heavy wooden frames surrounding the holes in the deck through which the masts and CAPSTAN pass.

pawls: wooden or iron bars that prevent a windlass or capstan from rotating backward.

pintles: pins attached to the rudder that fit in the GUDGEONS and form the hinge on which the rudder pivots.

post: in the Royal Navy, to be given official rank of captain, often called a post captain, and thereby qualified to command a ship of twenty guns or larger.

privateer: vessel built or fitted out expressly to operate under a LETTER OF MARQUE.

quadrant: instrument used to take the altitude of the sun or other celestial bodies in order to determine the latitude of a place. Forerunner to the modern sextant.

quarter: the area of the ship, larboard or starboard, that runs from the main shrouds aft.

quarterdeck: a raised deck running from the stern of the vessel as far forward, approximately, as the mainmast. The primary duty station of the ship's officers, comparable to the bridge on a modern ship.

quarter gallery: a small enclosed balcony with windows located on either side of the great cabin aft and projecting out slightly from the side of the ship.

quoin: a wedge under the breech of a cannon used when aiming to elevate or depress the muzzle.

ratline: pronounced *ratlin.* Small lines tied between the shrouds, parallel to the deck, forming a sort of rope ladder on which the men can climb aloft.

reef: to reduce the area of sail by pulling a section of the sail up to the yard and tying it in place.

reef point: small lines threaded through eyes in the sail for the purpose of tying the reef in the sail.

rigging: any of the many lines used aboard the ship. *Standing rigging* holds the masts in place and is only occasionally adjusted. *Running rigging* manipulates the sails and is frequently adjusted, as needed.

ringbolt: an iron bolt through which is fitted an iron ring.

ring stopper: short line on the CATHEAD used to hold the anchor prior to letting it go.

ringtail: a type of studdingsail rigged from the mainsail gaff and down along the after edge of the mainsail.

round seizing: a type of lashing used to bind two larger lines together.

run: to sail with the wind coming over the stern, or nearly over the stern, of the vessel.

running rigging: see RIGGING.

sailing master: warrant officer responsible for charts and navigation, among other duties.

GLOSSARY

scantlings: the dimensions of any piece of timber used in ship-building with regard to its breadth and thickness.

schooner: (eighteenth-century usage) a small, two-masted vessel with fore-and-aft sails on the foremast and mainmast and occasionally one or more square sails on the foremast.

scuppers: small holes pierced through the bulwark at the level of the deck to allow water to run overboard.

scuttle: any small, generally covered hatchway through a ship's deck.

service: a tight wrapping of spunyarn put around standing rigging to protect it from the elements.

serving mallet: a tool shaped like a long-handled mallet used to apply SERVICE to rigging.

sheet: lines attached to the CLEWS of a square sail to pull the sail down and hold it in place when the sail is set. On a fore-and-aft sail the sheet is attached to the BOOM or the sail itself and is used to trim the sail closer or farther away from the ship's centerline to achieve the best angle to the wind.

ship: a vessel of three masts, square-rigged on all masts. Also, used generally to mean any sea-going vessel. *To ship* is to put something in place, thus shipping capstan bars means to put them in their slots in the capstan.

short peak: indicates that the vessel is above the anchor and the anchor is ready to be pulled from the bottom.

shrouds: heavy ropes leading from a masthead aft and down to support the masts when the wind is from abeam or farther aft.

slack water: period at the turn of the tide when there is no tidal current.

slings: the middle section of a yard.

sloop: a small vessel with one mast.

sloop of war: small man-of-war, generally ship rigged and commanded by a lieutenant.

slops: ready-made clothing carried on shipboard and sold to the crew, the price of which was deducted from their wages.

snatch block: a block with a hinged side that can be opened to admit a rope.

spar: general term for all masts, yards, booms, gaffs, etc.

spring: a line passed from the stern of a vessel and made fast to the anchor cable. When the spring is hauled upon, the vessel turns.

spring stay: a smaller stay used as a backup to a larger one.

spritsail topsail: a light sail set outboard of the spritsail.

spunyarn: small line used primarily for SERVICE or seizings.

standing rigging: see RIGGING.

starboard: the right side of the vessel when facing forward.

stay: standing rigging used to support the mast on the forward part and prevent it from falling back, especially when the sails are ABACK. Also, to *stay a vessel* means to tack, thus *missing stays* means failing to get the bow through the wind.

stay tackle: system of blocks generally rigged from the MAIN-STAY and used for hoisting boats or items stored in the hold.

stem: the heavy timber in the bow of the ship into which the planking at the bow terminates.

step: to put a mast in place. Also, a block of wood fixed to the bottom of a ship to accept the base or heel of the mast.

stern chasers: cannons directed aft to fire on a pursuing vessel.

stern sheets: the area of a boat between the stern and the aftermost of the rowers' seats, generally fitted with benches to accommodate passengers.

sternway: the motion of a ship going backward through the water, the opposite of *headway.*

stow: as relates to sails, the same as FURL.

swifter: a rope tied to the ends of the capstan bars to hold them in place when shipped.

tack: to turn a vessel onto a new course in such a way that her bow passes through the wind. Also used to indicate relation of ship to wind, e.g., a ship on a "starboard tack" has the wind coming over the starboard side.

taffrail: the upper part of a ship's stern.

tarpaulin hat: wide, flat-brimmed canvas hat, coated in tar for waterproofing, favored by sailors.

tender: small vessel that operates in conjunction with a larger man-of-war.

tholes: pins driven into the upper edge of a boat's side to hold the oars in place when rowing.

thwart: seat or bench in a boat on which the rowers sit.

tiller: the bar attached to the rudder and used to turn the rudder in steering.

top: a platform at the junction of the lower mast and the topmast.

top-hamper: general term for all of the spars, rigging, and sails; all the equipment above the level of the deck.

train tackle: arrangement of BLOCKS and tackle attached to the back end of a gun carriage and used to haul the gun inboard.

truck: a round button of wood that serves as a cap on the highest point of a mast.

trunnions: short, round arms that project from either side of a cannon and upon which the cannon rests and tilts.

truss: heavy rope used to hold a yard against a mast or bowsprit.

tween decks: (corruption of *between decks*) the deck between the uppermost and the lowermost decks.

waist: the area of the ship between the quarterdeck and the forecastle.

waister: man stationed in the waist of the vessel for sail evolutions. Generally inexperienced, old, or just plain dumb seamen were designated waisters.

warp: a small rope used to move a vessel by hauling it through the water. Also, to move a vessel by means of warps.

water sail: a light-air sail set under a boom.

wear: to turn the vessel from one TACK to another by turning the stern through the wind. Slower but safer than tacking.

weather: the same as *windward*, thus "a ship to weather" is the same as "a ship to windward." Also describes the side of the ship from which the wind is blowing.

weather deck: upper deck, one that is exposed to the weather.

weft: used to mean a flag, generally the ensign, tied in a long roll and hoisted for the purpose of signaling.

whip: a tackle formed by a rope run through a single fixed block.

wooding: laying in stores of wood for cooking fuel.

woolding: a tight winding of rope around a mast or yard.

worming: small pieces of rope laid between the strands of a larger rope to strengthen it and allow it to better withstand chaffing. Also, putting worming in place.

yard: long, horizontal spars suspended from the masts and from which the sails are spread.

yardarm: the extreme ends of a yard.